Masquerade

Books by
Nancy Moser

Mozart's Sister

Just Jane

Washington's Lady

How Do I Love Thee?

Masquerade

Nancy Moser

MASQUERADE

BETHANYHOUSE

Minneapolis, Minnesota

Published by Bethany House Publishers
11400 Hampshire Avenue South
Bloomington, Minnesota 55438

Bethany House Publishers is a division of
Baker Publishing Group, Grand Rapids, Michigan.

Printed in the United States of America

Library of Congress Cataloging-in-Publication Data

Moser, Nancy.
    Masquerade / Nancy Moser.
       p. cm.
    ISBN 978-0-7642-0751-8 (pbk.)
    1. Heiresses—Fiction. 2. Household employees—Fiction. 3. British—United States—Fiction 4. New York (N.Y.)—19th century—Fiction. I. Title.
    PS3563.O88417M37   2010
    813'.54—dc22

                                         2010007457

To Emily, Laurel, and Mallory

For the wonderful women you are—and will come to be

NANCY MOSER is the author of three inspirational humor books and twenty-one novels, including *Mozart's Sister, Just Jane,* and *Time Lottery,* a Christy Award winner. She is an inspirational speaker, giving seminars around the country. She has earned a degree in architecture; run a business with her husband; traveled extensively in Europe; and performed in various theaters, symphonies, and choirs. She and her husband have three grown children and make their home in the Midwest. Read more about her books at *www.nancymoser.com.*

Chapter One

"I've told you, Father, I won't marry him."

Thomas Gleason held a matchstick to the bowl of his pipe and puffed repeatedly, luring the tobacco to ignite. "It's a good match, daughter. Everyone has heard of the Tremaines, even here in England."

Heard of their money, perhaps . . .

Lottie remembered the whispered rumors about the Tremaines. She knew her parents hated gossip—or pretended to for propriety's sake—but now was not the time for her to be timid. "Some say the Tremaines are *nouveau riche*. The elder Mr. Tremaine is but one generation away from those who peddled their goods on the streets of New York City."

Her father pointed his pipe at her. "Perhaps. But Tremaine's Dry Goods has grown to encompass a five-story building, taking up an entire city block."

Mother shook her head and said beneath her breath, "A glorified shopkeeper."

Father shot her a glance.

Mother nodded to the maid, Dora, to pour the tea. "We are the ones doing the Tremaines the favor. You are Sir Thomas Gleason," she said. "The Gleasons have ties to Richard the Second. Our name is listed in *Debrett's*."

A puff of smoke billowed in front of Father's face. "Now, now, Hester. By seeking a goodly match for our daughter, we're not negating our own roots. It's a blessing the Tremaines have shown interest in our Charlotte, especially since they've never met any of us. And considering—"

Lottie interrupted. "You act as if meeting me might cause them to change their minds. I may not be a ravishing beauty, Father, but I've been complimented many times regarding my appearance."

"No, no," he said. "Don't take offense. You're a lovely girl. I was merely pointing out the odd circumstances of . . . our situation."

Hester coughed and put her ever-present handkerchief to her mouth.

Lottie tried unsuccessfully to squelch her annoyance at her mother's cough. Hack, hack, hack. Perhaps if Mother spent more time outside, walking the grounds of their Wiltshire estate, her health would improve. But Mother prided herself on indoor pursuits, namely her needlepoint chair cushions. Best in the county, she bragged. Lottie didn't care for such nonsense. To go to so much work only to have someone sit upon it was absurd.

As was this conversation.

Lottie set her teacup down, rose from her chair, and moved to the windows that overlooked the front lawn. "I don't see why we have to talk about this now." *Or ever.* "It's my birthday and my friends will be arriving for my party soon and . . ." She turned to her mother directly. "Speaking of my party, why aren't you bustling about? A dozen of my friends will arrive in just a few hours, yet if I didn't know better, I'd think the party was next Tuesday rather than today."

The handkerchief rose once again. "You said you didn't want an extravagant soiree, dear, just a light repast with cakes and sweets for your friends. Mrs. Movery is quite busy with the food preparations,

I'm sure." She glanced at Dora. "In fact, toward that end . . . Dora, why don't you go see how things are coming along in the kitchen."

Dora said, "Yes, ma'am," and left them.

Lottie wished she would have stayed. Dora was her lady's maid and her best friend in the entire world. But lately her parents had started asking Dora to do other tasks, even helping out in the kitchen, which was unthinkable. Lottie *had* noticed a few of the housemaids and parlormaids were no longer in service with the family, but that didn't mean Dora should suffer. "I don't understand why Dora is suddenly being asked to expand her duties. She's *my* maid. I assure you I keep her very busy."

"I'm sure you do, daughter," her father said. "But . . . well . . ."

Mother continued the thought. "With the preparations for your party this afternoon . . ."

Something wasn't being said. Lottie wished her parents would tell her what was going on. She had a good mind. She could practically recite the novels of Jane Austen and the Brontë sisters by heart. Didn't that prove she had an intellect worth utilizing? Sometimes Lottie thought she would scream for lack of purpose. To sit in the house all day, reading or doing needlework, waiting for someone of consequence to call, was silly. She would happily trade two women of means for one person who could offer amusement or witty conversation. Odd how those attributes were sorely lacking in polite society, among people who were far too polite to be of interest.

But now, looking out upon the front drive and the vista of the green that carpeted the house to the road, she abandoned her worries for the anticipation of seeing carriage after carriage arriving for her party. Guests laden with presents—for her. Perhaps purpose was overrated. In all her nineteen years she'd found it quite acceptable—pleasant, really—to let the world beyond their country home dip and spin without her. What did she care of labor acts or problems in Ireland or whether Queen Victoria became Empress of Burma? Where in the world was Burma?

Lottie preferred experiencing life through novels where the characters were always enjoying a lovely ball or romp through the countryside that would lead them to their one true love. Her copies of *Pride and Prejudice, Sense and Sensibility,* and *Little Women* were threadbare. Lottie especially enjoyed stories about sisters—perhaps because she had none. Conversely, she did not enjoy the books of Elizabeth Gaskell or Charles Dickens with the same zeal, finding their stories too driven by social inequities. She didn't want to read about the world's problems. She wanted romance, diversion, passion, and a happy ending—in her books *and* in real life.

And yet, she also wanted to feel of *use*. There was a stirring inside that niggled like an empty stomach demanding *something* of her. From her. When she felt such discontent she usually sought the outdoors, where the movement of her body and the addition of fresh air were a good counter to her restlessness. Until she could pinpoint the answer to this inner unrest, she planned on marrying well and setting up her own home in a nearby estate. Surely true love would be the key to unlocking her purpose. But marrying an American as her parents suggested? There could be no key in that. Even if he was rich, he would never understand her inner need, and she'd be held in bondage, far from family and friends and the dream she had of becoming . . .

Something. Someone.

Her mother interrupted her thoughts. "Conrad Tremaine seems to be a very nice young man."

In this context, *nice* was a lethal word, one that was used when better words like *dashing, handsome,* and *debonair* did not apply. Judging from the letters Lottie had received from the *nice* Mr. Tremaine, along with the small photograph . . . She'd read the letters many times and had dissected the photograph with her father's magnifying glass, but no matter how hard she looked at his representation in either word or countenance, Mr. Tremaine was no Mr. Darcy. Or Willoughby. Or even Heathcliff. He came off sounding stumbling in the first and looking bumbling in the latter.

And pudgy. With a weakish chin. And a hairline that promised to recede into nothingness sooner rather than later.

Apparently not knowing what else to say, her father repeated his mantra: "It's a good match, daughter."

Lottie suffered a shiver of disgust. Her parents had endured an arranged marriage—with emphasis on the word *endured*—and now they expected her to do the same? Although they put up a good front, Lottie recognized her mother's stern and pinched appearance to be the consequence of enduring rather than enjoying her life. Lottie had become cognizant of it a few years previous when she'd looked more closely at her parents' wedding photograph. She'd been shocked to find little resemblance between the sweet expectation upon her mother's face and the dour mask that existed now. Did expectation of *any* sort remain behind that mask? Or had it been extinguished through a union that was false in all aspects but the law?

And her father . . . his countenance had not changed, nor had his premarriage behavior. He was unfaithful. His longtime mistress, Mrs. Lancashire, lived in Bath, just thirteen short miles away. Certainly Mother knew, for she had long ago refused to go to that city, even though the medicinal benefits of its spas might have helped her chronic health issues.

Lottie had seen this mistress once, at age twelve, when she'd accompanied her father to Bath. Lottie had known nothing of his weaknesses before the trip. But as a young person just awakening to the world of adult desires, her eyes and ears were aware of lingering looks and hushed rumors about her father and "another woman." When Lottie finally saw her, she found Mrs. Lancashire to be a pretty thing, yet rather mindless in that she laughed too much and too loudly. At the gathering, Mrs. Lancashire had been accompanied by her husband, which had been confusing, considering the rumors. Nanny had tried to explain to Lottie the truth of things as best she could. It was the first time Lottie had ever heard the word *adultery*—the seventh commandment come to life.

After she returned from that trip, Lottie had vowed she would never, ever marry without love. And she would never, ever place herself in a situation where she would have to be the understanding wife to her husband's indiscretions. She would never, ever—

The butler entered the room with several letters on a silver tray, and Mother perked up at the diversion. "Oh, lovely. The post has arrived." She extended the top letter toward Lottie. "I recognize this handwriting. Conrad's ears must have been burning."

Lottie abandoned the vista of the window, retrieved the letter, and opened it.

"Come now, daughter. Show some enthusiasm. What does Conrad have to say?" her father asked.

Lottie scanned the lines to find something of interest, but the words merged into inane dribble and drabble. "He extends his greetings and those of his parents."

"How very nice." Hester nodded to her husband. "We ask that you extend the same to his family in your next correspondence."

Bland niceties sent across the sea. As passionless and unappealing as milk toast.

Or tea. Lottie returned to her chair and took a sip. She'd never liked tea much. And after reading the American novel *Little Women*, she'd tried coffee and had liked both the beverage and the book very much. Those working-class American girls were always drinking coffee, having adventures, and feeling free and loved. Oh, to have three sisters, three confidantes. Lottie had a handful of female friends here in Wiltshire, but none in whom she could fully confide. The only friend she could count on was her lady's maid, Dora. But it wasn't the same as having a true sister.

Lottie had never found the courage to ask her mother why she had no siblings. Such subjects were private and beyond mention. But she couldn't help wondering if her mother's melancholy countenance was partly the result of this deficit. More children might have changed much.

The March family in *Little Women* was not nearly as wealthy as Lottie's family, yet the members possessed something the Gleasons lacked with an utter completeness: vitality and *joie de vivre*.

Lottie had spent too many teatimes in her parents' company where no more than a dozen words had been exchanged while her father read some newspaper and her mother created another seated masterpiece. Why gather only to share silence? When the families in her novels got together, there was exuberance and laughter. Sometimes she longed to blurt out something outrageous, just to witness its effect.

Today might be a good time to do such a thing as a means to veer the subject away from this annoying talk of marriage. But what should she yell out? *Tea no more! Down with bustles!*

She noticed her mother opening a small note, which caused a furrow to form upon her mother's forehead.

"Bad news?" Father asked.

Mother shook her head, slipped the note in the space between her skirt and the chair, perused the others in the pile, and offered them the same fate—unopened.

"Aren't you going to read them?" Lottie asked.

"Later," Mother said. With one letter remaining, she offered a smile that removed all facial lines. "See here? It's our turn. For yours is not the only letter from the Tremaines." She handed it to her husband.

He set his pipe aside, broke open the envelope, adjusted his spectacles, and read to himself, mumbling the words in a totally unintelligible manner.

"Thomas! Read it aloud. Lottie and I would like to hear it too."

"Yes, yes, of course." He cleared his throat and began. "'Dear Sir Thomas and Lady Gleason. Greetings from New York City. My wife and I are duly pleased at the connection that has formed between our two children. In order that it might proceed in a suitable manner, we believe it would profit all involved if Miss Charlotte and you, Lady Gleason, sailed to America for a visit as our guests.'" Her father read a few more lines to himself, then removed his reading glasses. "They send greetings and request a quick passage before the winter comes in order that Charlotte be there for the start of their social season in mid-November."

Mother clapped her hands together. "America! And the wedding preparations! The dress, the wedding supper, the flowers, the—"

"I'm afraid you are not well enough to travel, my dear," Father interrupted.

Her countenance fell. "But I must. Going to America would be a way for me to . . ." She did not finish the sentence.

Lottie felt a dash of compassion for her mother's plight, yet in the end, it was not about her, it was about Lottie. And so she stood, unable to tolerate the notion of this marriage a second longer. "All of you are making plans without me. I must have some say in the matter!"

Her parents gave her their respective versions of disapproval. She had to calm herself.

"Forgive me, but from what little I've come to know of Mr. Tremaine, I find it hard to imagine . . . Well, he's just not . . ." How could she assemble her thoughts into a tangible defense? Her reasons were as ungraspable as mist upon the air.

Her mother rose and moved the unopened letters to a drawer of her desk nearby. Then she stood behind her husband's chair, a soft cough accompanying her. "No young couple truly knows one another before marriage," she said. "It's not possible."

Would years of marriage alleviate that issue? Did her parents truly know each other now?

"At any rate, young people don't know what's best for them," her father said. "Marriage is . . ." He looked to his wife.

She hesitated, and Lottie was truly interested in what she would say.

"Yes, Mother? Marriage is . . . ?"

Her mother attempted to hide her blush behind the handkerchief at her mouth. "Marriage is a serious responsibility. It is—"

"A measure of a woman's success," Father said. "'Tis the only way for a woman to advance her position." He glanced toward the door, then added, "Women who are independent are incomplete and unfinished. Spinsterhood is failure."

Lottie realized he had lowered his voice in case Aunt Agatha had returned from her errands in the village. At age thirty-eight, never married, with all prospects long ago extinguished, her mother's sister had no recourse but to live on the charity of her family.

Mother continued her definition. "Above all, marriage is an act of faith in order to perpetuate, to propagate . . ."

"Yes, well," Father harrumphed. "We know where that goes."

Actually, Lottie knew nothing about where that went, or how it was accomplished. She'd been taught to be pretty and alluring but had little knowledge of what to do once she was successful. She'd certainly received no clues from her mother. Her childhood had been best accomplished under the charge of her beloved nanny, Eliza Hathaway. Except for her formal education under the tutelage of a stern governess whom Lottie had detested, she had looked to Nanny to provide all of her personal needs until Lottie grew too old and Dora came along and filled the bill as companion and overseer. Lottie rarely saw her mother for more than meals or an outing into society. And she never confided in her. Dora was the one who was privy to all her he-said-she-said anecdotes. In fact, Dora was the one who had explained the facts of womanhood when Lottie's body had traversed from childhood to adolescence. And now that her mother wanted her to marry . . . Lottie wished to know the private issues marriage involved but would never dream of asking her mother. And certainly not her father, who knew far too much.

Would Dora know of such things?

Lottie found her voice. "If I were to marry this man and have a family with him, I must love him." She thought of something to strengthen her stand. "Even the Bible says we are to love one another. If there is no love, there should be no marriage."

Her father's eyebrows rose. "Where does the Bible say that? About marriage specifically?"

She was suddenly confused. "I'm sure it does. Somewhere."

Mother returned to her chair. "Of course we wish for love to be present, Lottie. But how can love blossom between you and Conrad if you don't even meet him?"

Lottie could not imagine traveling to America and being beholden to a strange family that would scrutinize her every ruffle and flaw. She liked her life here in Wiltshire. She was quite willing to stay here in the loving arms of . . .

"Ralph Smythe has continued to show interest in me," she said.

Her father adjusted himself in his chair, making grunting sounds—caused by his posture or Lottie's comment? "I'm afraid you don't understand, daughter. And perhaps I've been remiss in not telling you more about what has occurred."

"Then tell me," she said. "If I'm old enough to travel to America, if I'm old enough to marry a stranger, then I'm old enough to know why all this is being thrust upon me."

Her father retrieved his pocket watch, snapped open its gold cover, then stood. "I must go check on the horses. A mare is due to foal."

She rushed to his side, putting a hand upon his arm. "Please, Father. Tell me why you're so keen on my marrying this American."

He didn't meet her eyes. "Do as you're told, girl."

As soon as he was gone, Lottie turned to her mother. "Why won't he tell me?"

Mother's voice was soft. "Why won't he tell *me*?"

It had never occurred to Lottie that her mother was unaware of the details of their life. If she knew about Father's mistress, certainly she knew about other, less delicate matters.

But instead of an explanation, Mother stood and went to the mantel. "I wish your father had not had to leave, but I know he wanted you to have this birthday gift from the two of us."

All thoughts of Conrad Tremaine were forgotten as Lottie took the velvet box. The shape divulged the contents as jewelry, Lottie's favorite gift in the world.

She untied the pink satin ribbon and opened the hinged case. Inside was a ruby necklace.

"It was my mother's."

"I know." *I know, I know, I know.* Lottie had seen her mother wear the necklace a hundred times and had always thought it an old-fashioned, vulgar thing. It was fitting for a woman turned ninety, not nineteen. Her parents knew her taste flowed toward more modern stylings. They'd always done well with their previous choices, even having pieces custom-made.

"Don't you like it?"

Lottie forced herself to at least feign pleasure. "It's quite . . . nice."

"You don't like it."

If only she had a less-transparent face. Unfortunately, every emotion felt was heralded for all to see. In order to avoid her mother's gaze, Lottie kissed her cheek. "Thank you for thinking of me, Mother."

"It's from your father too."

She snapped the box shut. "I'll be sure to thank him. Now I'd better get ready for my friends' arrival."

Lottie was greatly glad her party was not a formal affair where her mother might insist she wear the ruby eyesore.

Surely her friends would have better taste in gifts.

***

"Lottie! If you want to change your hair, let *me* take the pins out." Dora gently slapped Lottie's hands away. Her mistress had no talent whatsoever in the art of hairdressing—or undressing.

And no patience either.

"I'm sorry to make you redo it, Dora, but I want my hair to look more sophisticated for the party. I'm not a girl anymore; I'm nineteen. I want to look like a woman and be treated as such."

Dora smiled. She was only a year older than her charge, but Dora felt a decade ahead in maturity. Although Dora had always found Lottie's naïveté charming, she knew Lottie would have a hard time being seen as an adult by anyone who knew her. She had an able mind, but the girl possessed limited savvy when it came to real life. And her willful nature often reminded Dora of a child, insistent about getting her way. To Lottie, life revolved around pretty gowns, jewels, seven-course meals, and dancing until two. Yet she was not a snob. Lottie treated Dora well and was never demanding in a mistress-servant sort of way. Dora had never heard her speak sharply to anyone in service and doubted there was a mean bone in her body. She was simply a young aristocrat who knew nothing beyond her tightly wound sphere.

Lottie was alarmingly ignorant of the world at large. Did she know the Marquess of Salisbury had become the prime minister for the second time last summer, or that the president of the United States was Grover Cleveland?

Dora was proud *she* knew such things and gave credit to her habit of snitching Mr. Gleason's newspaper when he was through with it. One time she'd tried talking to Lottie about an article she'd read regarding a workers strike, but Lottie had covered her ears with her hands. "Please don't, Dora. It's not that I don't care what's going on, but since I have no say in it . . ." She'd looked at Dora with her innocent eyes. "Is it wrong to erect a dome around myself? I'm happy and I strive not to make others unhappy, so is it so wrong to not know about such things?"

Dora had assured her it was not wrong to be as she was. Childish, perhaps, but as far as Dora knew, ignorance was not a sin. In a way, Dora didn't want Lottie tainted by the harshness of the world. She was a perfect rose to be admired. Dora feared if Lottie were accosted with the baser realities, she would wilt and fade and die.

But today was her birthday and *now* she suddenly wanted to blossom into a woman? "Perhaps you *should* wear the rubies," Dora said. "You yourself admit they reveal a more mature taste. With your hair all swept upward . . ." She took the hair that fell upon Lottie's shoulders and wound it into a hank that could be pinned.

Lottie studied her reflection. "That does make me look older, doesn't it?"

"Just old enough, I'd say."

"Then let's try that. Maybe a new hairstyle will spur Ralph toward a proposal."

Dora was surprised by the statement. "He's that close?"

"A hairsbreadth away, if I can read men."

Dora wasn't sure Lottie *could* read men. Or women. She seemed in a perpetual state of self-absorption—not in a bad way necessarily, but in the way in which the boundaries of a child's world were drawn close and she didn't have enough experience to realize what she was missing beyond its borders.

As far as Dora could determine, Lottie had no knowledge that her family had suffered any financial setbacks. It was the talk of the village, and the servant grapevine between the country manors vibrated with rumors and gossip. Dora had resisted the talk and had even defended her master and mistress—until Mr. Gleason ordered the north wing of the house closed up and cut the staff in half. Dora wasn't used to serving at meals or doing other downstairs work, but in the past month all the remaining servants had been called into more extended service.

Dora had been with the family since she was thirteen, when Lottie was only twelve. She'd started as a housemaid, but had soon been asked to help out with Lottie. Although she'd not been called a lady's maid—nor had she been paid as much until Lottie had turned sixteen—she'd had the advantage of the work being less grueling than the constant scrubbing and polishing of a housemaid. Of course the preferential treatment had caused issues with the other servants. In their eyes she was not truly one of them. Not quite a full-fledged friend to Lottie, and not quite a full-fledged servant, Dora often felt lonely, as if she lived in a no-man's-land between two worlds.

Service was all she knew. Her mother had been in service, as had her grandmother and her aunt. Not that this was their first choice of occupation, but there were few options for poor, widowed women.

Actually, her mother had always wanted to own a little shop, selling candies or cakes. But such a dream was impossible. Once a maid, always a maid.

As for Dora's situation, if circumstances worsened, she was certain she could obtain good character references from the Gleasons. But the thought of finding another position was harrowing. Besides, she knew everything there was to know about Lottie. Since neither one of them had sisters, they'd naturally fashioned a bond that was closer than that of mistress-servant.

Sitting at her dressing table, Lottie held a handful of hairpins in her hand, palm up. "All this talk of my marrying an American. It's absurd. There are plenty of men around here who eat out of my hand. I have only to fall in love with one, to choose *one*."

Dora took a hairpin and put it in place. "Didn't you tell me Gilbert Collins asked you to dance more than his fair share at the last ball?"

Lottie shuddered. "He asked, but I put his name on my dance card but twice. He has deplorable breath."

"Rodney Barrister is a handsome—"

"Engaged."

"To whom?"

"Octavia Morris."

"Oh."

"Exactly."

"How about Reginald Thurber?" Dora asked. "I hear his father is sick and doing poorly and he's due to inherit—"

"Reggie is a philandering pig. I wouldn't trust him in church." Lottie sighed. "No indeed, although could I have my choice, I'd choose Ralph. He's the one love of my life."

Dora tried not to make a face. It was hard for her to imagine a man named Ralph being the one true love of anyone. And his surname was not much better. Smythe? Charlotte Smythe? Atrocious. Yet since it was apparent Lottie had set her sights on him . . . "Do you love him?"

"I could love him. If he asks me to marry him I *will* love him." She closed her hand upon the hairpins and gazed at Dora in the mirror. "I wish to marry for love. Is that too much to ask?"

"Not too much, but . . ."

Lottie sighed with the full drama of an actress. "There's someone out there just for me. I believe that man is Ralph, for other than him . . . the men I've met say all the right things, do all the right things, but they don't make me swoon."

"Swoon?"

Lottie nodded in the dressing table's mirror. "Swoon, Dora. Every woman deserves to swoon over the love of her life."

Dora shook her head. "*Deserves* and *gets* are two different things." She motioned for more hairpins.

Lottie opened her hand to the cache, and Dora finished the upsweep. "There. All grown up."

Lottie studied her reflection. "I look years older, don't you think?"

"Years."

Months.

※

Lottie went to the window a third time. Or was it her fourth? Dora had lost count.

"Where are they?"

Dora repeated the answer she'd given before. "I'm certain they'll be here soon." She diverted to the buffet and rechecked the serving utensils that were ready for the dishes Mrs. Movery had prepared for the birthday celebration.

"Where's Mother?" Lottie asked.

"I don't know." Again, it was a repeated answer. Even Dora found it odd Mrs. Gleason was elsewhere. As the mistress of Dornby Manor, shouldn't she be fluttering about, making sure everything was in perfect order? Dora had been happy to don a black maid's uniform in order to assist—for it would give her firsthand knowledge of who said what

21

and what gift was received—but as the hour passed into the quarter, then the half, then the three-quarter . . .

Lottie needed her mother's reassurance. And so, Dora took matters into her own hands. "I'll go find her for you."

"Thank you. I—" Lottie ran from the window toward the door. "A carriage!"

Dora raced into the foyer after her, hoping Lottie didn't wrench open the door before the guests even had a chance to knock.

Davies, the butler, intercepted Lottie before she did just that. And with a stolid look he implied she would not interfere with *his* duty of greeting all comers.

Dora gently tugged Lottie back into the drawing room. "Be here to greet them. Don't look too eager. Remember you're a grown lady now."

Lottie's blink told her she *had* forgotten her goal. She moved a few feet inside the room, her hands assaulting the bottom button of her bodice.

As Dora feared for the button's safety there was a knock on the door. Lottie bounced upon her toes. Dora pressed the air with her hands. *Calm now. Calm.* Then she moved to the fireplace wall, making herself inconspicuous.

There was a voice in the hall and then Miss Suzanna Weaver entered. Lottie smiled, but her eyes moved past her friend into the foyer, clearly expecting to see others.

"Dearest Lottie." Miss Weaver set a small package on a table, then took Lottie's hands in her own and kissed her cheeks. "The happiest of birthdays."

"Thank you," Lottie said. "Please have a seat. I'm sure the others will be here presently, but until then I'd love to hear all the latest—"

Miss Weaver looked to the floor, her one hand finding comfort in its mate. "I'm sorry, I'm afraid I can't stay."

"Can't stay? What—?"

"My parents don't even know I'm here, and they'd be ever so upset if they . . . But I had to come to wish you the best, and . . ." She backed toward the door.

Lottie rushed toward her, taking her arm. "Suzanna, do tell me what's going on."

Suzanna did a double take when she spotted Dora, but Dora merely dropped her gaze to the floor. She was not about to leave until Lottie told her to do so.

Suzanna moved toward Lottie in confidence. "I can't be the one to tell you, Lottie. It's not my place."

"But it is. We're friends. Friends tell each other everything."

Suzanna's head shook no, making it appear she was denying both her position to tell the truth as well as her friendship with Lottie. She was *not* one of Dora's favorites—nor Lottie's either. Suzanna Weaver was far too full of herself and put on airs beyond her due. Lottie had told Dora an anecdote about a party when Suzanna had directed where everyone would sit and stand, to the extent that the entire affair had seemed like an audience before a queen.

"Fine. Don't tell me," Lottie said. "I'll just wait until Ralph arrives. He'll tell me whatever I want to know."

"Ralph isn't coming either. And . . ." Suzanna's face changed from one full of regret and sorrow to one steeped with smug self-satisfaction. "No one is coming to your party, Lottie. Not a one."

Lottie stood mute, and Dora saw her jaw tighten.

"Did you hear me?"

Lottie found her voice. "Hear you? Yes. Understand you? Not at all."

But Dora understood. The rumors about the Gleasons' financial difficulties must have reached every ear in Wiltshire.

Every ear except Lottie's. Dora wished she could step forward and order Miss Snobby Suzanna to leave this very minute. Some friend.

Suzanna moved toward the door on her own accord. "I really must go. Do try to have a pleasant birthday, Lottie."

And she was gone.

Dora held her breath, waiting to see what Lottie would do. She still didn't know the truth—only the truth's consequences, and Dora certainly didn't want to be the one to tell her. *Please don't ask me.*

Lottie's eyes blazed and flitted from the door to Dora and back again.

Then suddenly she said, "Come with me."

"Come—? Where are we going?"

Lottie beat Mr. Davies to the door and burst outside, striding down the steps to the drive. Dora ran after her and had trouble keeping up with her gait. "Lottie, I'm so sorry."

"You have no idea."

"But where are we going?"

Instead of answering, Lottie veered toward the stables. She called after the stableboy. "Hitch up the cabriolet, Derek. Now."

"You want to go somewhere, Miss Charlotte? I'll take you."

"Dora will go with me. Now go!"

Although his face revealed a hundred questions, Derek did as he was told. Dora had her own questions, but the stony mask on Lottie's face revealed it was a time to be silent and follow.

And perhaps pray for the best.

⁂

Lottie whipped the reins on the horse, making him fly down the road. She would have liked him to go even faster. If she had her way, and if such things were possible, she would instantaneously be at the Smythe house so as not to waste another second. How dare Ralph not come to her party! What had Suzanna said to him? What lies?

She'd take care of Suzanna Weaver later; that was for certain.

"Lottie, please. Slow down."

"Never."

With a glance, Lottie saw that Dora held on for her life, one hand on the edge of the seat and the other on her mobcap. For some reason

24

the sight of that stupid cap incensed her. Dora, all dressed up in the formal uniform of a parlormaid, for a party that was not to be . . .

Lottie called above the sound of hooves on the road, "Take that thing off. And your apron too. You're my lady's maid, not a parlormaid."

Dora pulled the cap free and stuck it in the space between them. Then—using but one hand—she untied the apron in the back and pulled its bib over her head. She began to fold it as best she could without letting go of the seat.

The act fueled Lottie's fury, and she grabbed the apron and threw it into the air behind them.

"What are you—?"

Lottie added the cap to the wind.

"What are you doing? I'll be charged for those," Dora said.

Don't be ridiculous.

Lottie slowed in order to turn into the Smythes' drive. And slowed more as they approached the house. Whatever would she say to Ralph? She'd come to chastise him for his absence but also to find answers for whatever Suzanna had been unwilling to tell her. She hoped he would take her in his arms and comfort her. *I'm so sorry, Lottie. I should have come. I love you and despise that I've upset you. Can you ever forgive me?*

When the house came into view, Lottie handed the reins to Dora.

"I don't know anything about driving."

"Nothing to know. Just pull on the reins to get them to stop."

"But—"

"Shh!" Lottie realized she'd left the house without a bonnet, and the hair that Dora had so skillfully arranged for the party had escaped its bonds with stray pieces hanging this way and that.

"Help me fix my hair," she said.

Dora shook her head. "I can't drive *and* fix your hair."

A true point. Sometimes Lottie regretted her impulsive nature. She should have taken the time to put on a bonnet, should have let Derek drive her, and . . . and what had she been thinking throwing away Dora's cap and apron?

"Whoa . . ." Dora said.

The horse complied, and a stableboy ran forward to take it by the bit while a footman stepped forward to help the ladies out.

Lady. Just Lottie. Belatedly, Lottie realized the awkward situation she'd created by bringing Dora along. Dora had no reason to enter the Smythe home.

"I'll wait here," Dora said. "You won't be long, will you?"

"Hopefully not."

It was awkward leaving Dora in the carriage, but the girl couldn't very well step down and sit upon the front step.

The butler greeted Lottie at the door. She tried to tuck in the most offending strands of hair and said, "Good afternoon, Walters. I'd like to see Mr. Smythe, please."

"I . . ."

"Please, Walters. Is he available?"

Ralph walked out of the drawing room. "Miss Gleason. Please come in."

Miss Gleason? They were a hairsbreadth away from being engaged. They'd even shared a clandestine kiss.

Lottie entered the drawing room and was surprised when Ralph closed the double doors behind them. Yet she was glad for it, because her anger had returned.

"Where were you?"

"I beg your pardon?"

She wagged a finger at him. "Don't start with me, Ralph. Suzanna showed up long enough to inform me that no one was coming to my party. Not even you."

He moved to a safe place behind a chair. "I . . . I couldn't come, Lottie."

At least he didn't call me Miss Gleason.

She sat on the settee where their one and only kiss had occurred and folded her hands in her lap. "I'm waiting."

His fingers pulled across the carving at the top of the chair. "Father wouldn't let me come."

"Since when do you do what your father says?"

"I'm the heir, Lottie. I have a responsibility to listen to the dictates of my parents."

"Again I ask, 'Since when?' And beyond that, I have no idea what you're talking about."

A furrow formed on his brow. He hesitated, then with a burst of movement went to a drawer in a bureau. He removed a book that had a ribbon tied around it. "Birthday greetings, Lottie."

It was a copy of *An Old-Fashioned Girl*.

"It's by Louisa May Alcott. It's about a country girl who goes to the city and—"

Lottie liked the gift very much, and yet . . . "Why didn't you bring it yourself? And why didn't you send word you weren't coming? Why did I hear it from—?"

"I did send word. I sent a note of regret."

"It was never received."

His face revealed an inner conflict that seemed so genuine she knew he *had* sent a note.

Suddenly an image from that morning came to her. That of a stack of letters in her mother's possession, her mother opening a single note and dismissing the rest. Had others sent their regrets as well?

"You know why I couldn't come, Lottie. Don't make me say it."

But I don't know! She felt like throwing the book at him. Instead, she set the book beside her on the settee and laid a hand upon it, staking claim. "I'm afraid you have no choice, Ralph. I'm not leaving until I hear the truth, whatever it may be."

He retreated to his place behind the chair. "For one, your family's financial situation has become an issue."

She was shocked for but a moment. Snippets said by her parents that very morning—and before—came back to her, hints and innuendos about something amiss. Whatever the "situation" was, Ralph wasn't making it up. "Tell me what you mean."

He looked confused. "Surely you know as much as I do."

"I know nothing! Just tell me. Now."

His face revealed his reluctance—which gave her some comfort. At least he wasn't taking pleasure in it. "My parents and the other families in the county have heard talk of fiscal impropriety on your father's part. I don't know the details, but the fact remains that society will not condone such indiscretions."

What has Father done? "I have nothing to do with the financial interests of the estate, nor do I have any knowledge of them," she said.

"I know you share no guilt, Lottie."

She suddenly remembered something else Ralph had said. "What do you mean by 'for *one*'? Is there some other sin you're holding against me?"

Ralph blushed, and with this involuntary act, Lottie guessed the essence of the other sin. If people around Wiltshire knew of Mrs. Lancashire . . .

But even so . . . Lottie had heard gossip about more than one of the gentry set. Although she found such indiscretions repulsive, it should not be the cause of—

"Your father is being named in a divorce suit."

"Named?"

"By the husband of the adulterous wife."

"I . . ." She didn't know what to say, how to respond.

"People have their dalliances, but to be named is a scandal, and that, added to the financial issues . . ." His face softened. "I am surprised your parents haven't told you something about it, if for no other reason than to warn you of forthcoming repercussions. I feel bad you're the one having to suffer."

Her thoughts rushed from the unfathomable news to the intense desire to find comfort in his arms. "Then don't make me suffer a moment longer, Ralph." She stood and went to him. "I care for you, and you care for me. We—"

Suddenly, through the French doors, Lottie caught sight of a woman in the garden beside the house. Lottie rushed to the glass and pointed. "What is Edith Whitcomb doing in your garden?"

"She just stopped by and—"

Edith saw Lottie and scurried behind a rhododendron. Friends who just dropped by didn't scurry.

Lottie whipped open the doors and entered the garden. "Olly olly oxen free."

Edith stepped into the open, her eyes seeking Ralph's direction.

"Well, well, well. Who do we have here?" But even as Lottie said the words she wanted to retreat and unsay them all. She couldn't stand to hear more unpleasant truths. If only she'd never seen Edith, if only she'd pretended she hadn't seen Edith.

Edith's face revealed her panic, and she ran to the safety of Ralph's arms.

"There, there," he told her, stroking her hair.

And there it was. As painful as a slap to Lottie's face.

She felt the life drain out of her. With a simple breeze she would dissolve into a puddle of empty clothes. She didn't even have the strength to voice a question.

And perhaps there were no questions to voice. The situation was abundantly clear: on this day, on her birthday, her life had been forever changed.

She heard herself speak in barely a whisper. "I have to go now."

Ralph relinquished Edith to herself. "I'll see you out."

"No!" With a rush Lottie found herself again. "I don't need your help or your pity. Good day, Mr. Smythe. Miss Whitcomb."

She strode back into the drawing room, detoured to claim her book, then with great drama flung open the double doors. Walters had to scramble to open the front door for her.

She barely let the footman help her ascend the carriage, took her place beside Dora, and thrust the book into her care.

Lottie shook the reins and the carriage jerked into motion, taking them home.

Her parents had some heavy explaining to do.

Chapter Two

The journey home from the Smythes' was accomplished in silence. Dora had a thousand questions, but by the look on Lottie's face, now was not the time to ask—or offer condolences. Whatever had transpired with Ralph had not been good.

The return trip was made at the same speed as the trip away, but this time Lottie surrendered her hair to the wind and pulled it completely loose, letting it flow in odd hanks behind her. Dora had the feeling if Lottie could have removed all her clothing and flung the pieces to the wind, she would have. Whatever had happened had shut a door—and locked it.

When they reached the Gleasons' home, Lottie got out first and uttered her first words. "Meet me upstairs."

Mr. Davies helped Dora to the ground, but instead of asking after Lottie, he appraised Dora's attire. "Where is your cap and apron?"

An explanation would take too long and would not be understood. "Flung to the wind in a fit of freedom," she said.

"Excuse me?"

She strode to the door. "No, excuse me. Miss Charlotte is waiting."

Mr. Davies called after her. "You'll have to pay for those."

As Dora headed upstairs to Lottie's room she heard a commotion coming from the drawing room.

"I demand an explanation!" Lottie shouted.

Dora paused on the steps, wanting to hear. But when Lady Gleason closed the doors, Dora continued up the steps. She'd hear the details soon enough.

"Do calm yourself, daughter," her father said. "We shan't talk to you when you're in such a state."

"I'm in such a state because of you."

"Watch yourself . . ."

It was good advice. Lottie knew her parents and knew the way to handle them was through gentle persuasion, not outright confrontation. While moving to a chair, she caught sight of herself in the mirror above the fireplace. She looked like a crazed hag escaped from some asylum. She patted her hair for hairpins, but finding only one intact, secured just one hank of hair. It was a single bandage on a gaping wound.

She let the hair be and sat down. With great effort she calmed her breathing and the beating of her heart. "No one came to my party."

Her mother raised a finger. "Didn't Suzanna—?"

"Oh yes. Suzanna came—for a moment. I understand there were other regrets? Notes received?"

Her mother pulled at the lace on her handkerchief. "A few."

"Why didn't you tell me? Why did you continue with the preparations and let me anticipate and wait?"

"I . . ."

Her father took over. "Check your tone, daughter. Your mother meant well."

Mother nodded. "I hoped some would still come and—"

"And you didn't want to face the reason why they weren't coming," Lottie said.

"Fickle rumors," her father said.

A sliver of hope split open the rock of her worry. "So the rumors are false? My friends are mistaken?" she asked.

He walked to the fireplace and hit the bowl of his pipe against its stones, emptying it. "It's true we *have* suffered a series of financial setbacks."

"Ralph implied there was some . . ." How could she say it? *Should* she say it? "Some impropriety?"

Lottie watched her father's face redden. "I assure you I meant no harm. The deal seemed legitimate and . . ." He fiddled with his pipe, then retreated to his favorite chair.

He focused only on the financial. Was he choosing this lesser evil over the other, more lurid, sin? Yet Lottie couldn't bring it up in a blatant manner—for her mother's sake. "Ralph mentioned something else, another more personal issue."

Her father avoided her gaze—and that of his wife. "I don't know what to say. I—"

Her mother moved to her usual place behind her husband's chair. "Do you see why it's so important you marry well—marry Conrad Tremaine?"

How could Mother be so forgiving? Her husband's infidelity had been revealed for all the world to gawk at and whisper over. Where was her pride? Her dignity?

And yet, seeing her parents united in spite of everything . . . Suddenly the world fell into place and one plus one equaled two. If her parents could marry Lottie off to a rich American, it would give the appearance that the Gleasons were still a well-respected family. It would also help hide their financial difficulties.

"We didn't seek this arrangement for you, daughter," Father said. "But when this current downturn began, and then the murmurings of this other situation began to brew, it coincided with your uncle George's return from New York City after meeting the Tremaines. He was the one who brought forward the idea of uniting our two families. We appreciate the financial stability of the Tremaines' rising fortunes, and they are enamored with the thought of their son marrying the daughter of a knighted Englishman with a vast estate. It's quite puzzling, really. Even though the Americans are proud of their independence from the motherland, they still yearn for many of its accoutrements." He suffered a sigh. "All that being said, the timing is right. We need . . . we want you to find stability, for if things go badly, in the future there might not be the usual inher—".

Lottie finished the sentence for him. "The usual inheritance?"

Father slipped the pipe into the pocket of his tweed jacket, and Mother coughed into her handkerchief. "We currently have a dowry set aside for you, but circumstances may force us to dip into that income in order to . . ."

Survive? Fight a lawsuit? Pay your way out of the scandal?

Another notion came to her. "Why didn't you tell me what was going on?"

"You had no wish to know, dear," her mother said.

"Of course I wished to know. I am not a child."

"Perhaps not," Father said. "But you see the world as a child. As far as the financial issues, didn't you notice the closure of the north wing? Or how we've been forced to let half the staff go?"

Oh. That. "Of course I noticed."

"Didn't you ever once wonder why?"

Lottie felt the fool. How stupid to have the signs set before her, yet pass them off as inconsequential.

Lottie's mother relinquished her place, sat beside Lottie, and cupped her daughter's chin in her hand. "Now is not the time for delay, Charlotte. The Tremaines wish to meet you and me. We must accept their invitation in order to cement the match. For your sake. And our own."

Lottie had a realization. "The Tremaines are unaware of our troubles?"

Father cleared his throat. "What the Tremaines don't know won't hurt them."

Mother shook her head slightly. "The Tremaines are unaware—as yet. But again, dear, time . . ."

Time would wait for no man.

Or woman.

The clock was ticking.

※

Dora paced the floor in Lottie's bedroom from bed to window and back again. What was happening downstairs? What was taking so long? What had transpired between Lottie and Ralph?

Without warning the door opened and Lottie stormed into the room. Dora ran to her. "What happened? What did they say?"

Lottie flung herself on the bed. "It's over. My life is over."

Dora had witnessed other tantrums for reasons as inconsequential as not getting a new dress or Lottie having to finish her lessons before going riding. Yet she knew that this time, on this day, there was the potential for true torment.

She climbed upon the bed beside Lottie and moved the hair from her face. "Tell me. Perhaps I can help."

Lottie shook her head. "No one can help. Father is ruined; our family has no money. Ralph has shunned me for Edith Whitcomb, and I *have* to go to America and marry Conrad Tremaine before they find out I'm not an English heiress but a pauper—with a father who's being named in a divorce."

"What?" Dora knew about the financial situation, and Lottie had told her about Mrs. Lancashire, but she hadn't heard anything about a lawsuit. This was bad. Horrible.

Lottie stared at the ceiling. "Apparently a man can be unfaithful as much as he wants and society looks the other way. But when the woman's husband asks for a divorce and cites the guilty man by name, it's unacceptable and grounds for scandal."

The list of crises was nearly too much for Dora to grasp. Each one deserved its own tantrum, much less the swell of them together. "I don't know what to say."

Lottie attempted to sit up, but her bustle and the drapery of her birthday dress worked against her. Fully frustrated, she clambered to the floor, where the layers of her dress fell into place. "Help me out of this thing."

Between the two of them, Lottie's dress was relinquished and a dressing gown put on. Lottie sat at her vanity and, with a sigh that moved shoulders from up to down, gazed upon her reflection. "Just look at me. I fully look the part of a pauper. No wonder Ralph wants nothing more to do with me. I'll be fortunate if Conrad doesn't run from the pier at the first sight of me. If only I could run from *him*."

Dora smiled. "Hand me the brush and I'll change you from wind-swept to breathtaking again."

Lottie succumbed to the pull of the brush and closed her eyes. Dora could feel her tension dissolve. Lottie had always loved to have her hair brushed, and Dora was glad to oblige. It was such a little thing and brought Lottie such pleasure.

"How can my entire world change in a single day? And on my birthday too."

"Perhaps all at once is better than a little at a time," Dora said.

"Is that supposed to make me feel better?"

"Doesn't it? For surely tomorrow can't bring worse."

Lottie nodded. "Surely . . ." She retrieved a pair of sapphire earbobs she'd recently removed and played with them in her lap.

If Lottie's world had changed, so had Dora's. "So you and your mother are going to America, then?" Unasked was whether they planned on letting Dora go along.

"It's not America I object to," Lottie said. "I've always wanted to see it. But marrying a man I've never met, that I may find disagreeable, a man who doesn't excite me one whit through the few tidbits I've gathered in our courtship by the post . . ."

"You don't have to marry him," Dora said. "Do you?"

"My parents are depending on it. They imply it's my duty as a means of untarnishing the family name. And perhaps it will be my only chance to marry well at all." She paused, then began again. "But I suppose if we were not at all suited . . ."

Yet maybe that would *not* be a consideration. If the parents of Lottie and Conrad agreed to the match, there would be a match. Sometimes Dora was glad she belonged to a lower class. *She* could marry for love.

Or could she?

Barney Dougan. The butcher's deliveryman.

She was not in love with him. Not really. But she'd heard from Cook that it was a fine thing to have Barney's interest, because it saved Cook a trip in to Lacock to the butcher's. Barney would linger when he came to the Gleasons' with a side of lamb or a brace of pheasants, and made Cook call Dora down from her upstairs duties. Barney was a nice enough chap, and nice enough in looks too—burly and strong, with dimples that magically appeared when he smiled.

At her. Smiled at her. Dora knew Barney would propose. Soon, if she had any understanding of the current gist of his affection. And barring another man miraculously dropping into her life, she would probably say yes. She wanted children. She wanted her own home. And like Lottie, she too wanted love.

The trouble was, other than Barney there were few chances to find a mate. Dora worked sixteen hours a day and rarely left the house. Once there'd been a footman who'd caught her eye. He'd even shown interest in return, but Dora had called an end to it. Romance between servants was forbidden, and if they had been able to manage it—and had been caught—it would have been Dora who would have been dismissed. More proof that female servants were on the lowest rung of life's ladder.

And so, even though she bragged that she could marry for love, it was not totally true. She could choose someone to love with a little more freedom than Lottie had, but mere choosing did not ensure the emotion would follow.

Yet whether Lottie loved Conrad or not, Dora didn't think such an arrangement would be the end of the world. Being rich was the key. At least a rich woman could spend her days wearing lovely clothes and jewels, and go to balls where she could dance until the orchestra put away their instruments.

"I'm so confused," Lottie said. "I'm sure Mother will accept the Tremaines' invitation. And perhaps Conrad isn't as dreadful as I suspect. But not being dreadful is hardly what I look for in a husband."

Dora had been privy to Conrad Tremaine's letters when Lottie had read them aloud. She didn't find them nearly as mundane as her mistress did. And if his photo showed him to be a bit plump . . . wasn't plumpness a sign of wealth? Dora took no offense to it as long as the man was not overly so and was not slovenly about it. "If you don't want him, I'll take him," she said.

Lottie dropped the earrings on the dressing table and looked at Dora's reflection.

Dora felt embarrassed. "I was just joking."

Lottie rose and swept the train of her dressing gown to its proper place. "You joke about my life being ruined? You think it's funny?"

"No, of course not."

Lottie fell upon the bed a second time. "What's happening to me should not be the subject of a joke. All is lost. My family expects me to marry Conrad and so I'll be forced to marry Conrad."

Dora didn't know what to say. "I—"

"Oh, leave me be." Lottie turned on her side, showing Dora her back.

Dora quietly pulled Lottie's door shut, needing to escape to her own room. So much had happened. But not two steps down the hall she was intercepted by Lottie's Aunt Agatha. "Connors. I was looking for you."

She offered a slight curtsy. "Yes, Miss Agatha?" She noticed the woman was carrying an evening gown. Dora knew what would come next.

"This old dress needs some adjustment to make it more . . . usable. Take off the lace here and here."

There was no request for alterations; it was assumed. "I'll take care of it, miss."

At the end of the hallway Dora opened a door, lifted her skirt along with the heavy burden of the evening dress, and climbed the steps to the attic rooms. All the rooms were empty now but for her own bedroom and that belonging to Jean, the housemaid. Dora entered her small chamber amid the eaves and moved its chair toward the window to utilize the best light. But before she settled in to work, she sidestepped to her bureau and held Miss Agatha's lavender dress against herself, enjoying her reflection. It was amazing how a dress could change everything.

She'd joked about marrying Conrad. But wouldn't it be grand to marry a rich man and be a real lady of society?

A bird flew into the window, startling her from her dream.

Enough. Dora was not a fine lady; she was a maid. Pure and simple.

She gathered her needle and thread, sat down, and got to work.

Chapter Three

Lottie considered skipping breakfast, staying in her room, shunning her parents as her friends had shunned her.

But to do so would negate her chance and great ability to pout in their presence and make them suffer. If they wanted to sacrifice her life to the wolves of America and arrange a marriage-for-money . . .

Behold! The martyr.

"What are your plans for today?" her mother asked.

Lottie said nothing but waited for Dora to serve the eggs and stewed tomatoes. Dora moved on to Aunt Agatha.

Lottie's father picked up a scone and knife, perused the table, then said to Dora, "Preserves? Where are the preserves?"

"I'm sorry, sir. I'll go fetch some."

Unfortunately, Dora hurried out of the room. Lottie wanted her there as a witness so they could discuss the success of Lottie's revenge later.

Father sprinkled a pinch of salt over his eggs. "I'm going to ask Derek to get steamer trunks from the attic so you ladies can see the baggage space you'll have available for the trip. Is that agreeable?"

"That would be very helpful, Thomas," Mother said.

Lottie was confused. Her father had suggested her mother was too ill to travel. Had he given in to her desire out of guilt?

"Don't you think that's a good idea, Lottie?" her mother asked. "About the trunks?"

Lottie took advantage of yet another chance to kill them with her silence.

Father cleared his throat. "Yes. Well. That's that, then."

Aunt Agatha put her fork down with extra emphasis. "This is absurd. Lottie, you're acting like a five-year—"

Mr. Davies came in carrying a tray. "A special delivery, sir."

Lottie glanced up and saw fear flash across her father's face. Was he expecting bad news?

Apparently, for he let out a sigh steeped in relief when he saw whom it was from. "It's from the Tremaines. And it's quite thick."

Lottie gave her eggs her full attention. She had no interest in whatever the Tremaines might have to say—or so it must appear.

"Lottie, why don't you open it," her father asked.

She faced a conundrum. To refuse, she would have to do more than shake her head; she would have to speak. But by accepting, she would be showing interest. She settled on "Let Mother do it."

Mr. Davies brought Mrs. Gleason the packet, which was thicker than a letter but smaller than a package.

Mother opened the envelope and pulled out the contents. Her face beamed as she lifted for display—"Tickets! Two tickets!"

"My, my, that was quick," Father said. And timely. It was as though the Tremaines and her parents had orchestrated the entire thing.

Lottie's mother perused the tickets. "It's passage on the steamship *Etruria*. First class." She repeated the final two words for Lottie's benefit. "First class, Lottie!"

What did her mother expect? Steerage?

Father shook his head. "Again, I bring up the issue of your health, Hester. Such a long journey . . ."

"Nonsense, dear. The accommodations will surely be luxurious. It will be as if I were at home."

"But not at home."

Wasn't that the point?

Lottie's need to speak overrode her need to pout. "I didn't say I'd go. We haven't even responded to the Tremaines' invitation as yet."

"A bit presumptuous of them to be sure," her father said. "But also quite American. From my experience they have trouble taking no for an answer."

"But I haven't said yes," Lottie repeated.

Her aunt rolled her eyes. "Oh, don't be such a twit, girl. Your family found you an excellent match. It's your duty to embrace it. A woman may not get a second chance."

Lottie knew that in her youth Aunt Agatha had spurned a proposal. Lottie couldn't imagine any man being interested in her. She was as pinched and tasteless as a dried prune. Or was the latter the result of the former?

"I am not being a twit, Aunt. I am merely wanting some say in my future."

"And why do you think you deserve this *say*?"

"It's marriage. It's forever."

"My opinion stands."

Lottie's mother put the tickets back into the envelope for safe-keeping. "But, dear, now that you know the extent of our situation, I don't think we can wisely close the door on this opportunity."

Who wanted to be wise? When had Lottie ever been asked to own such a trait?

Apparently now.

Her father cleared his throat. "I know this entire situation is regret-table. I will go to my grave laboring over . . ." He did not elaborate. "But the truth of the matter is, Charlotte, you must go. You must meet this

Conrad. You must make every—*every*—attempt to find him amiable and acceptable, and you must marry him and be kept safe and happy and provided—" His voice broke and he stood. "If you'll excuse me."

At his departure, the silence that encompassed the room was far different from the silence Lottie had attempted to create with her moping. She'd never seen her father break down like that, never imagined he ever felt full of regret and despair. She was tempted to run after him and console him, but considering she had never done such a thing . . . it would be too awkward. Besides, did he *deserve* consoling?

The need to pout was set aside. "Is everything really so horrible, Mother? Is everything ruined?"

Her mother put a hand to her mouth, her eyes downcast. "The threat of ruination is horrible indeed, and the acts that brought it down upon us are . . ."

"Deplorable?" Lottie offered.

With a moment of hesitation Mother nodded, then looked at her daughter. "A woman's lot is to endure. It is only the extent of that endurance that varies between individuals of our sex."

Lottie had never considered being a female to be as awful as that. Yes, there were limitations and expectations that had occasionally colored Lottie's life, but in general, she'd been quite happy.

"Everything seems upside down," she said.

Her mother leveled her with a gaze. "Which is why you and I must do this thing, must get away from Wiltshire and find solace elsewhere."

Lottie had not thought much about how the arrangement could be to her mother's benefit. "You wish to get away?"

"I wish for peace—something I fear I will never be able to find here. Not with your father—" She commenced coughing, and it soon turned into a full-fledged fit. Lottie brought her a glass of water and stood by her side until the horrible hacking had passed. Mother handed Lottie the glass. "Help both of us, Lottie. Marry Conrad. Gain a good future before it's too late to do so."

Lottie's throat grew tight. Oddly, one of her favorite lines from

Sense and Sensibility came to mind. When Willoughby was asked why he disliked Colonel Brandon, he said, "He has threatened me with rain when I wanted it to be fine." His words were well suited, for Lottie disliked how the current situation threatened her life with rain when she wanted—and expected—it to be fine.

Aunt Agatha interrupted her thoughts. Lottie had forgotten she was even present. "See here, girl," Aunt said. "Don't you think it's about time you think of someone besides yourself? What little money is left they're giving to you in a dowry, to assure your future. Our world is collapsing around us. Escape while you can—and take your poor mother with you."

Lottie felt a swell of shame. Suddenly the concept of going to America enlarged its scope. It was not only about pounds and pennies; it was about protection and permanence—and survival.

Her mother extended a hand, and her fingers grazed Lottie's arm. "We love you, Lottie. I know we are lax in saying as much, but . . ."

Suddenly, in spite of their flaws and errors, Lottie knew this to be true. Her parents *did* love her. Although she'd known it in theory, she was now faced with their love revealed, exposed, and presented in a very tangible way. Love was not a word, nor even an emotion; it was an action, providing shelter and shield.

They loved her, but had she ever loved them in return? She'd used them, manipulated them, annoyed them, worried and ignored them. She'd made fun of them in private and had wasted their times together with selfish thoughts of what she could get out of the meeting.

Her mother glanced toward the door and rose. "I must go check on your father."

Lottie, left with the unpleasant prospect of being alone with Aunt Agatha, also said, "If you'll excuse me?"

"Sit down."

Lottie was stunned by her aunt's tone.

"Do as I say, girl. Sit your body down and listen to me."

Lottie returned to her chair, her nerves tingling.

44

"I really should check on my parents," she said.

Her aunt had something else in mind. "What you really should do, Charlotte Regina Gleason, is grow up. Immediately. You've been treated like queen of the castle far too long and to bad results."

"I beg your—"

Aunt stopped Lottie with a hand. "You can beg all you want, but I won't listen to a bit of it. Your father is a fool. He made decisions that will affect all of us badly. And though she is my sister, I must also call your mother a fool to put up with that man's philandering." She shook her head in disgust. "You haven't helped matters with your pouting and whining and acting never satisfied."

Lottie thought of her lukewarm reaction to her parents' birthday gift. Now she realized they'd given her an heirloom because they couldn't afford something new.

Aunt Agatha wasn't through with her yet. "But I forgive you all that because they encouraged your behavior and did nothing to stop it. A child will push until a parent pushes back."

Lottie would accept the scolding but didn't need a full lecture. It was best to apologize and be done with it. "I see now that I've not acted as I should."

Her aunt shook her head. "Feel bad on your own time. I don't care if you fall on your face, beg forgiveness, and give all your possessions to the poor. What I do care about is that you help this family in a tangible way by marrying Conrad Tremaine. Only with you and your mother off to America, attended to and established, can your father deal with the repercussions of his own folly."

"What repercussions?"

"You think he tells me?"

No. Even Lottie's mother didn't know the full details. But Lottie herself had already felt a good dose of the consequences of her father's mistakes. It could only get worse.

"Not that you've given me a thought, but I plan to find solace in London with a cousin."

Lottie was further shamed, for she had not considered her aunt's future for even a moment.

"The point is, girl, life is changing for all of us, and we don't need the distraction of Little Lottie whining about the loss of a friend or the absence of a new dress."

"I'm not *that* shallow," she said.

Aunt leveled her with a look. Then her face softened and she reached a hand toward Lottie, letting it fall upon the lace tablecloth between them. "You've been given a chance to help, girl. Take it. Go to America and take your mother away from the humiliation here. What you do once you get there is not my concern as long as my sister doesn't have to worry about you. Do you understand?"

"I do." Far too well. But oddly, although the news was bad, it felt good to *know*.

Her aunt sat back in her chair and nodded, obviously satisfied. "That's a good girl, then. So go on now. Attend to the preparations and act happy about it."

Lottie rose, then did something she'd never done in her entire life. She went to her aunt's side, leaned down, and kissed her on the cheek.

She left her aunt there, with a hand to that cheek, as stunned as Lottie herself.

"All these trunks?" Dora asked.

"Three for mother and three for me," Lottie said. She blew a coat of dust off the top of one.

"Don't do that. I'll wipe them off." Dora studied the stickers on the trunks. "These trunks have been all over Europe."

"Before I was born, my parents traveled extensively. I went with them a few times when I was little, but I don't remember any of it."

"Didn't you say Ralph was going on a grand tour next year?"

Lottie's head snapped in Dora's direction. "Don't ever say his name in my presence again."

"I'm sorry." Dora opened one of the trunks to check the space inside. If only the current fashion didn't require the bulky padding of various bustles. Yet they were infinitely better than the full hoops of the previous decades. "How many gowns are you going to need?"

Lottie bit her lip and thought a moment. "All of them? Or should I assume Mr. Tremaine will shower me with a new wardrobe?" Lottie moved to her armoire and examined her dresses, pulling out the skirt of a royal blue silk, then one of deep rust, then a burgundy. Dora loved the vibrant colors that were in fashion. "I've always liked the blue silk because it brings out the blue in my eyes," Lottie said.

"Did Ralph tell you that?" *Why did I say that?*

Lottie stopped all movement and glared at Dora. "I told you not to mention his name. What's wrong with you?"

Dora sank onto one of the trunks and shook her head. "I don't know. I'm never snappy like this."

Lottie sat beside her. "And you're never rude. I've always been able to depend on your constancy and patience."

With little trouble, Dora recognized what was bothering her. "You're leaving for America, but I'm not. I'll be left behind. Do I have a job here? Should I look for employment elsewhere? I've never worked for another family."

Lottie jerked her head to look at Dora. "We'll be separated. We've never been separated. We can't be separated."

"We don't have a choice. The Tremaines only sent two tickets."

Lottie stood. "Then I'll ask Father to buy another one for you. It wouldn't be first class, of course, but—"

"I doubt there's the money."

"Then I'll smuggle you in." Lottie opened a trunk. "Here, get inside and see if you fit."

Dora got up and closed the lid. "I can only imagine what the ship's captain would do with a stowaway. I have no wish to walk the plank."

"But we can't be separated."

"We have no choice."

Lottie opened the trunk again as if considering a way to make it work. Dora knew it was hopeless. No matter how much Lottie wanted Dora to go with her, it was not to be.

Then suddenly Lottie let the lid of the trunk fall, her face aglow with an idea. "As soon as I get there, I'll get Conrad to send for you. I'll tell him I can't live without you and—"

"And you'll bat your eyes and pout and smile and get your way."

"It is what I do best."

If anyone could get it done, it was Lottie. "So we'll not be apart terribly long, then," Dora said.

Lottie took Dora's hands and spun her around. "Before you know it, we'll both be in New York City. And your presence there will make the experience with the Tremaines far easier and bearable."

Dora felt better. *If* it ever came to pass . . .

⁂

Even though Lottie was out of breath she kept walking.

She'd made a good attempt at accepting the inevitable. She'd made peace with her mother and would do so with her father when he returned from work. She'd made peace with Dora and had vowed to find a way for them to be together in New York. And she'd even forced herself to be practical and go through her clothes and choose which ones would stay and which would go.

Go.

The notion of leaving the house and taking a long walk had grown into a necessity, so when Dora was called to other duties, Lottie fled into the sunshine and the wide hills that surrounded Dornby Manor.

The coolness of the day was a good counter to her exertion. Although Lottie held a thought in the back of her mind that she was leaving this place and might never return, she could not allow the thought full access. She would think about that later. Right now she needed to find the joy the country always provided.

September heralded her favorite time of year. She loved the changing leaves of autumn and the way they'd relinquish their perch to carpet the ground. At the moment, there was still competition between summer and fall as to which would win: green or orange, warm or cool, lush or lean.

Happy or sad, wealthy or poor, loved or rejected.

Lottie stopped beneath the canopy of a huge elm and sat upon an ancient bench. She chided herself for not bringing a book. She'd read many books in this spot and had traveled to many unknown worlds here.

Soon I truly will be traveling to an unknown world. America.

She'd looked at the United States of America on a map and had been shocked to see its size. England was the size of a single state instead of a separate country. A person could easily get lost in such an expanse of space.

She blinked and straightened her back as though straightening the thought. "I could get lost over there . . ."

Lost.

Run away.

Missing.

Never to be heard from again.

The notion was frightening, yet . . .

In its own way it brought her comfort. If the Tremaines were a disappointment—if Conrad proved to be a man she could *never* marry—she could simply run away. Turn right when her mother turned left.

But what then?

Perhaps it wouldn't matter. Once she was in New York and had adapted to the feel of things, she could go off on her own and start over.

And Dora could go with her!

She laughed at the thought. Two best friends exploring a new world? The possibility lessened the burden of her parents' plan. Since they supported the marriage with the goal of Lottie being secure and cared for, surely they also wanted her happiness. What did it matter if she found happiness in a different direction?

Lottie lifted her face to the sky, letting the sun dapple through the leaves and caress her face.

It was a plan. A secret plan.

The best kind.

※

Dora was roused from sleep by an unknown sound. She sat up in bed and listened.

Voices were coming from the floor below.

It was still dark, but moonlight revealed the time on her dresser clock. Two-fifteen. Who was up at this hour—and why?

The sound of a horse's gallop made her speed to the attic window. It appeared to be Derek, the stableboy, riding away as though a ghost were chasing him.

Someone had to be hurt or ill or . . .

Dora pulled a shawl over her nightgown and rushed downstairs. She didn't need directions to the source of the voices, as the hallway contained Mrs. Movery wearing a robe, Mr. Davies in his uniform—sans tie—Miss Agatha, and Lottie.

Where were the elder Gleasons?

Lottie spotted Dora and hurried to her side. "It's Mother. Her cough . . ."

Now that Dora's ears were tuned to it, she could indeed hear a horrible hacking coming from Mrs. Gleason's room. She heard Miss Agatha telling Mrs. Movery to make some tea.

Mrs. Gleason had suffered coughing fits before, but never one that sounded this severe. "What can I do to help?" Dora asked.

Lottie shook her head. "Mr. Davies sent Derek for Dr. Graham. Mother is coughing up blood."

That wasn't good.

"I don't know what to do," Lottie said.

Dora did a quick inventory and made an observation. "When your father comes out—"

"Father isn't here."

Dora was taken aback. "Not here? But it's the middle—" She stopped before she brought more attention to his absence. "If no one is with your mother, why don't you go to her?"

Lottie's face looked stricken. "I wouldn't know what to do. I've always made fun of her coughing, thinking she was exaggerating it for pity's sake. But this is real, and it's serious and—"

Dora gave her a little push. "Go to her. Let her know she's not alone."

Reluctantly, Lottie nodded and wove her way through the others until she disappeared inside her mother's bedroom.

Left alone, Dora stood ready in case someone needed something, and did the only thing she knew to do.

Please help Mrs. Gleason. Help them all.

Lottie entered the room with trepidation. A lone gas lamp on the bedside table cast odd shadows. Her mother lay against a multitude of pillows, nearly upright. Her eyes were closed, her arms limp by her sides, one hand gripping a handkerchief tinged with blood.

Is she . . . ?

Mother opened her eyes. "Lottie?"

Lottie rushed closer. "I'm here."

"Is the doctor . . . ?"

"Derek's riding to get him."

She offered a nod that was nearly imperceptible.

"What can I do?"

Another movement, this time in the negative. "Stay with me."

"Of course." Lottie felt completely awkward. What should she

51

say? What should she do—could she do? "I'm sorry for being annoyed at your coughing."

Her mother smiled. "I'm annoyed too."

Another fit caused her to thrust forward. She fumbled for a bowl amid the covers, and Lottie helped her hold it to her mouth. Sputum and blood . . .

Lottie's thoughts swirled with panic. *Help her! Please make my mother well!*

The realization that she'd prayed surprised her. Even though she went to church with her parents every Sunday, sitting in the pews and bowing her head like a good daughter, she never said anything to God. Until now she'd never felt the need.

Until now.

So why would God listen to *her* prayers? Lottie knew the importance society put on getting a proper introduction. It seemed wrong to introduce herself to God so abruptly, wanting something, demanding something, begging for something.

Yet wasn't that her forte? With few exceptions Lottie expected to get whatever she asked for. And up until the current financial trouble, her parents had been very generous. They'd never said no to—

One time they'd said no. A year ago Lottie had set her heart on getting a new wardrobe for their annual trip for the London season. But Father had restricted her to three new dresses and directed her to fill the gap with ones from her existing wardrobe. She remembered pouting about that.

She doubted her heavenly Father would condone pouting.

Mother moaned, a sound that ripped Lottie's soul. She sought her mother's hand and cringed to find it so frail and fragile. "Please tell me what to do," she asked.

Mother's eyes were closed, her body spent. She mouthed a word. "Pray."

Proper introduction or not, Lottie gave it her best attempt.

Chapter Four

～

"Lottie. Lottie . . ."

She opened her eyes and saw Dora standing over her.

"You fell asleep in the chair," she said.

The events of the night rushed back to her: *cough, Mother, doctor.* She last remembered sitting in a chair outside her Mother's bedroom, vowing to stay awake in case she was needed.

So much for that.

Lottie searched Dora's face for answers even before she asked the question. "How is she?"

"Resting. She wants to see you."

Within a few steps Lottie felt the consequences of her awkward night's sleep. But what did a few stiff muscles matter compared to her mother's ordeal?

The room was still barely lit, though Lottie could see a sliver of daylight through the draperies at the window. When had it turned to day?

Her mother was still propped up by a dozen pillows, her face pale, her eyes closed.

"Perhaps I should come back—"

Mother's eyes opened. "I'm awake. Please stay."

"Are you feeling better?"

"Much."

"What did the doctor say?"

"I'll live."

Mother held out her hand, and Lottie fell upon it as if it were a holy relic deserving her worship. "I'm so glad, so glad. Thank you, thank you."

Lottie felt foolish but would not retract her impulsive gratitude. God had heard her prayers and answered them well. It was a stunning victory, yet she felt oddly humbled rather than triumphant.

"Where is your father?" her mother asked.

"I . . ."

"He's with her, isn't he?"

Was he? Surely not. And yet . . . "I don't know."

Mother nodded slightly. "I do. Which is why you must listen to me very closely. You must go to America."

There was something in her mother's tone that spoke beyond her words. She'd said *you*, not *we*. In the span of one stressful night had everything changed? "You can't go with me, can you?"

Her mother shook her head. "The doctor will not allow it."

"But you need to get away too. The trip was for your sake as well as my own."

Her mother paused, as if the weight of this lost chance weighed heavily upon her. "It's not to be. I must remain here."

Lottie cringed at the disgrace her mother would have to endure in the coming months.

To endure. Such was a woman's lot.

With a determined breath that seemed to give her courage, Lottie's mother continued, her voice stronger than before. "I still want you to marry Conrad Tremaine. I want you taken care of by a family of standing—as you would have been here if things had not . . ."

She hated to see her falter. "I don't need to marry a rich man, Mother. Although I've certainly enjoyed the life of high society, it's not as important to me as marrying for love."

"You speak as a child who has no idea what a life outside our set is really like."

"I weary of saying it, but you're wrong. I'm no longer a child. Please give me some credit. I can adapt as well as anyone to whatever situation life affords me." She *hoped* what she said was true.

Lottie's mother extended a hand once more. "I am heartened by your attitude, but as it is . . . even though I cannot travel, you will not travel alone."

Lottie suffered the horrible thought that Aunt Agatha would act as her mother's surrogate. Lottie would rather travel with a woman off the streets than with her aunt. She shuddered at the thought of an entire voyage filled with her aunt's lectures addressing Lottie's short-comings.

Considering this alternative, and though the thought of traveling alone was daunting, she had to offer a show of confidence. "I *can* go alone. I don't need a chaperone. I know I could do it." But did she want to do it? Going to America still involved marrying Conrad. Lottie needed time to think, to figure out her best strategy. It was all happening too fast.

"I've come up with an alternative." Her mother coughed softly.

"Forgive me, but I don't want Aunt Agatha—"

"I agree," Mother said. "Frankly, the notion of my sister representing our family at the Tremaines' . . ." She shook her head. "God love her."

And keep her here.

Mother continued. "My alternative involves having Dora accompany you."

Lottie's legs turned to butter and she took hold of the bedside table for support. "Dora?"

"Is she not your friend as well as your maid?"

"She is," Lottie said.

"Which is why I want Dora to use the other first-class ticket and travel as your friend, not your servant. That way you'll have a companion during all segments of your voyage."

A laugh escaped and Lottie clapped a hand over her mouth.

"You find this amusing?" her mother asked.

"No, no," she said. "I find it perfect, beyond anything I could have planned myself. Will Father agree?"

"I will give him no choice."

Lottie had never heard her mother sound so determined. Had the time for "enduring" passed?

Mother offered some advice. "Although it's a blessing that Dora has already rid herself of the peculiar language mannerisms of her class, you *will* have to instruct her in numerous points of etiquette and loan her some of your clothes. Do you think they will fit?"

"We will make them fit." Lottie couldn't wait to see the look on Dora's face when she heard the news and when she tried on one of Lottie's gowns. On more than one occasion Lottie had offered to give Dora the experience, but Dora had shied away from it, saying it wouldn't be right.

Until now.

Mother closed her eyes, then opened them for one more bit of instruction. "I need you to go to America and find a good life, Lottie. Find a good man. Be happy—for me."

There was something slightly singular about this request. Absent was any mention of Conrad or the Tremaines. What was her mother really saying?

"Do you promise to be happy?"

"I do," Lottie said, even though she had no idea what that would entail.

Her mother studied her, as if seeking the truth behind Lottie's promise. Giving up her search, she said, "I need to sleep. Go on, now. Go share the news with Dora."

Dora hated kitchen duty. Not only was it well beneath her position as lady's maid, but the smell of raw food made her stomach threaten to do something nasty. It wasn't that Mrs. Movery was a bad cook; it was the preparation involved that turned her stomach.

But this morning she'd been called into kitchen service because Cook had decided the way to cure Mrs. Gleason's cough was to drown it with food. Under way were bread, stewed vegetables, baked apples, and two kinds of soup.

Cook looked up from stirring the steaming pots, her face perpetually flushed from the heat of the stove. "Chop those onions next, Dora, and don't give me no lip about hating to do it. I'm having to do with two hands what used to be done with six."

She looked to the bell on the wall that was marked *Charlotte*. Surely Lottie would ring for her as soon as she was free and remove her from this hell.

Until then, Dora peeled the skin from the first onion.

"Nice'n fine, now," Mrs. Movery said.

With the very first slice, Dora's eyes smarted and watered. And tears flowed.

As did her prayers for Mrs. Gleason. In many ways the woman was the only mother Dora knew—certainly the only mother figure she'd had since she was a girl. Dora hoped God would listen to her request—though He certainly had reason not to. Lately she'd grown lax in her prayers. She knew God hadn't moved away; she'd done the moving. And it wasn't that she hadn't experienced moments of heartfelt prayer. When her sister was born sickly, she'd prayed for her health.

The baby died a week later.

Two other siblings died young. . . . Dora barely remembered them, as if they'd been visitors, come and gone away.

When her father died after a cart of ice fell on him, she'd prayed that she and her mother would make their way without him.

Dora had been forced to go into service at age thirteen—starting out at the Gleasons' as a housemaid, spending endless hours polishing the silver and dusting. Her mother had gone to Canterbury when the family she'd been serving moved there. Dora hadn't seen her mother since; letters had sufficed.

Which was why Dora thought of Mrs. Gleason in a maternal fashion. She cared for the woman and often found more to like in her than Lottie did.

Perhaps that's the way it was with mothers and daughters—a delicate balance between love and hate that was as precarious as carrying an overfull cup of tea up an entire set of stairs. Dora hoped Mrs. Gleason's current bout with illness would bring mother and daughter closer. Usually good came from bad—if you looked for it.

Suddenly the door leading upstairs burst open and Lottie rushed in. "Dora! There you are."

Dora's heart sped to her toes. "Is your mother—?"

"No, no. She's better. Just come with me." But instead of leading Dora back upstairs, Lottie pulled her out the kitchen door, around the side of the house, and back toward the gardens.

"Lottie! Let go! You're going to make me fall."

Lottie let go of her hand, which enabled both of them to fully lift their skirts to move faster. "Come on!"

The girls ran into the formal gardens behind the house, weaving their way through the maze of pruned hedges, which were looking a bit ragged from lack of care. Lottie was first through a rose-covered arbor leading to a circle of benches.

"Sit!" she commanded.

"Gladly." Dora fell upon a bench. "Why the rush? What happened? Is your mother fully recovered? You seem so happy."

"I am happy beyond measure. And what's happened? The world has changed in our favor."

"What are you talking about?"

Lottie finally planted herself in front of Dora's bench. "Mother can't go to America with me."

"I'm not surprised. Does that mean you're staying?" That would be ideal.

"Not at all. I'm going without her."

"You're going alone? Your parents, who will not even let you take a walk in the village alone, will let you cross an ocean?"

She shook her head. "I will have a companion."

Dora's heart flipped and she began an inner argument, a defense against the new hope that had been suddenly born. . . . "And who would that be?"

"You!" Lottie pulled Dora to standing and spun her around in a circle. "We're going to America!"

"On a ship?"

Lottie stopped their circle and laughed. "Yes, on a ship. How else would we get there? Fly?"

Silly her.

But Lottie wasn't through. "Yet that's only half the news. Are you ready?"

More than ready. "Quit being so dramatic. Just tell me."

"You are not traveling as my maid but . . . as my companion. You will use the other first-class ticket and we will share accommodations like bosom friends!"

Dora sought the solidity of the bench. It was incomprehensible. "Your parents suggested this?"

"It was Mother's doing. She knows how close we are. And this way we can both go to the Tremaines', and you can help me with any wedding preparations in her stead."

"So now you want to marry Conrad?"

Lottie plucked a rose from the arbor and put it to her nose. "Of course not. But one thing at a time. I see how much it means to my parents to have me go. They have enough to worry about with Mother's health and all the other issues here. I don't want to burden them with more worries. Unnecessary worries."

Lottie thinking of her parents' feelings? This was a surprise.

Lottie tossed the rose into the garden. Then she ran through the arbor, where she stopped and taunted Dora. "Follow me! We have work to do."

Dora rose to follow. "Packing?"

"Lessons. Our first priority is teaching you how to be a proper lady."

The packing would be the easier task.

⁂

Lottie threw open the doors to her wardrobe and combed through the dresses. She pulled out a satin gown of yellow and brown. "Here," she said. "Try this on."

Out of habit, Dora shook her head. This was not the first time Lottie had offered Dora a chance to try on her clothes. Dora had always been tempted. The dresses were so luscious and pretty. But she'd never given in to the temptation, for if Mrs. Gleason or even Miss Agatha had come in, Dora would have been sacked for certain.

But now everything had changed. Now she had the blessing of the lady of the house.

"Come on, Dora. Put on the dress." Lottie held the two pieces toward her.

Permission or no, Dora still hesitated. Although she'd been guilty of holding one or two of Lottie's gowns against herself, she had never been brave enough to actually put one on. Being given permission to do so now—being directed to do the very thing she'd always forbidden herself to do . . .

"Dora, what's wrong with you? It's just a dress."

A dress that represented the ever-present chasm between them. Just as Lottie would never consider wearing a maid's uniform, Dora had never considered wearing—

Actually, she'd considered it, had even dreamt about it. What servant hadn't thought about what it would be like to be on the other side of the service?

Lottie sighed. "This is ridiculous. If you don't want to even try it on, I'll just put it away and tell Mother you refuse to travel as my companion and—"

"No!" Dora said. "Let me try it."

Dora unbuttoned her black blouse. Feeling a swell of modesty—for though she had seen Lottie in all manner of undress, the act had never been reciprocated—she turned away from Lottie to remove it. Then her skirt. She set the garments on Lottie's bed and took the gown, one she had seen Lottie wear on numerous occasions.

The skirt portion went on first. It had a long train and was as cumbersome to wear as it was to mend or press. But it was a beautiful dress. The top basque had a rounded bottom and three-quarter sleeves. Although Dora had touched such luscious fabric before, she had never felt it on her arms or shoulders. Caressing her arms and shoulders.

Lottie helped her with the front buttons. Looking at her mistress helping *her* . . . it was odd to have their roles reversed.

"It's such a pretty yellow color," Dora said. "And the lace at the arms and neck is beautiful."

"It's not just 'yellow,' Dora. You should learn the terminology. The bodice and train are an Isabelle yellow in a satin brocade. The draping across the front is a golden brown plush. And the lace you mention is white point duchesse." She finished the buttoning and pointed to the fringe at the bottom of the front drapery. "The fringe is made of amber beads and is set upon a crimpled silk edging." She went back to the wardrobe and brought out an armful of pleated muslin. "And once we attach this balayeuse under the train instead of a petticoat . . . I do love the way it swishes behind me when I walk, and how the pleated trim of the muslin shows."

Dora was unable to help with the attachment and had to allow Lottie to do the work. She knew there was no way for a woman of means to dress herself in such a gown. And now, to be dressed by another . . .

Lottie emerged from under the train, her hair falling this way and that across her face. "There," she said as she blew a strand away with a puff of air. "Now come to the mirror and behold the lady."

They moved to the full-length mirror in the corner. Dora gasped at the sight. "It's so lovely. I feel like a princess." Dora found it hard to take her eyes off her reflection and stood taller, her chin raised in a regal pose. She felt oddly important.

"Ah, but the look is not yet complete." Lottie rushed to her jewelry box and returned with a necklace. She clasped it around Dora's neck. "Citrine and Bohemian topaz. Father gave these to me on my seventeenth birthday."

"I know," Dora said. She touched the stones warily as if they were the crown jewels. "They are stun—" Dora noticed Lottie staring into space. "What's wrong?"

Lottie blinked. "You know."

"Pardon me?"

"You know about Father giving me the necklace on my seventeenth birthday."

Dora didn't understand. "Of course. I was there. As I was present for your thirteenth, your fourteenth, and fifteenth and—"

"Every birthday since I was twelve."

"Yes."

"And every Christmas."

"Yes."

"And Easter."

Dora didn't understand the direction of the questioning.

Lottie took her hands. "Don't you see? You know all about me. You've witnessed every moment of my life."

"Not every moment." Dora thought of the balls, the teas and parties—occasions where she'd been left at home.

"Everything that has occurred in our household has been under your scrutiny."

"I would not call it scrutiny, but yes, I've been here." Dora still didn't understand Lottie's point.

"So coming to America with me . . . it's perfect."

Once again Dora peered at her image in the mirror. The dress, the jewels . . . much of being a lady lay in the trappings.

But not all. Far from all.

"I *don't* know how to make conversation with your set. And though I've observed the etiquette, looking and doing aren't the same thing. The only education I've had is sitting in when your governess taught you and helping you with your lessons."

"You may be undereducated, but you are far from stupid, Dora. And your speech patterns reveal little of your roots."

Dora would agree. The advantage of living with the Gleasons from such an impressionable age is that in many ways she'd become one of them. And unlike Lottie, Dora could name all the counties in England and could list its monarchs back to William the Conqueror. Not that any of this information was useful, but she was proud just the same.

Lottie retrieved a cloisonné comb and tried to place it in Dora's hair. "With just a few lessons, I could teach you all you need to know about being a lady."

"Just like that?"

Lottie bit her lip—which meant the transition would not be "just like that."

"What you must remember," Lottie said, "is the first rule of being a lady."

"Which is?"

"You must be polite, prompt, pretty, and proper."

Dora could be polite and prompt, but the rest . . . "What if I make a fool of myself? What if people guess that I'm not really a lady but—"

"Remember the lady's second rule."

"What's that?"

"Smile. A smile is the best defense against offense."

Unfortunately, Dora feared her offenses would be too numerous to defend in any manner, smiling or not.

※

"Dora!" Barney's face lit up at the sight of her. He quickly wiped his hands upon a bloody apron. "You rarely come to the village. I ain't complaining, but—"

"I need to talk to you." She glanced at the others in the butcher shop and recognized a few. There would be talk, of that she could be certain. But she had no choice.

Barney conferred with the owner of the shop. With a wink, the owner nodded, setting Barney free.

He came round the counter, removing his awful apron along the way. "I'm so glad to see you. I missed you the last time I came deliverin'. Mrs. Movery wouldn't e'en call you down. That cow. I—"

She took his hand and pulled him out of the shop. On the street she let go but led him past a milliner's, to the covered stoop of a vacant shop. As soon as she stopped, he grinned and leaned closer, pushing her against the stone wall. "Oh, I get it. You wants to be alone."

She shoved him away. "Stop it! I need to talk to you."

He sighed and ran a hand through his hair. "Fine. Talk."

There was no good way to say it. "I'm going to America with Miss Charlotte."

He blinked. "America. Why America?"

"She's getting married."

"Ain't none of the dandies round here good 'nuf for 'er?"

"'Tisn't a question of good enough, 'tis—"

He nodded knowingly. "'Tis a question of money. And the sticky wicket Sir Thomas got himself into. I've 'eard the talk."

Dora ignored the infidelity issue. "It's always a question of money, Barney." Although she and Barney were not officially engaged, they had spoken about Barney's means of supporting her and the family that would surely follow.

He kicked a pebble out of the doorway. "So once she marries, you'll be comin' back, eh?"

Seeing him look so hopeful she nearly told him to forget everything she'd said. They'd known each other for years. He was a good man and a hard worker, and more than that, he had feelings for her—he'd said as much.

But did she love him? She cared about him, but love . . . She remembered Lottie's desire to find a man who would make her swoon. Did Barney—?

"Dora, you didn't answer me. You *are* comin' back, ain't ya?"

Was she? Even if Lottie decided not to marry Conrad, Dora couldn't imagine either of them coming back to Wiltshire. What was here for them? Disgrace? Shame? Complications?

Until this moment, Dora had never thought through the full implications of their trip abroad. Unless something changed drastically, it was a one-way journey.

She grabbed a fresh breath and looked at him straight on. He deserved that much. "No. I'm not coming back. I'm sorry, Barney."

He stepped away onto the sidewalk, nearly colliding with a man carrying a bushel of apples. His whole body, which usually brimmed with life and strength, seemed to deflate. "Yer leaving me?"

"I . . . I have to go with Lottie. With her mother sick and unable to go . . . she needs me." As soon as she said the words, she wanted to take them back.

Anger filled him up again and he stood tall, his chin strong. "And I don't?" At first it was a question, but then he repeated it as a declaration. "And I don't." He pointed a finger at her. "I don't need you, Dora Connors. There's plenty o' women who'd love to marry me."

What was she doing? What was she giving up? Dora was going to America to fulfill Lottie's future. But what about her own? "I know there are other women who admire you and consider you—"

"Why did I waste me bloomin' time waitin' for you, anyways? I shoulda known better. You and your fancy ways and proper talkin'. The Gleasons 'ave done you no favors making you think yourself better than the rest of us clods."

Dora was stung by his bitterness. She knew he would regret it, and she didn't want him burdened with wishing he could take it back. She would have enough regret for both of them. For within his bitterness lay the truth. Dora *had* thought of herself as a step above the other laborers in Lacock. She'd held few illusions that she would ever marry above her station, but she had taken satisfaction in educating herself, in being *more* than they.

She put a hand upon his arm, and though he tried to shake it away, she held strong. "The Gleasons have been good to me, Barney. I'm not being fancy or putting on airs by learning from them. Given the opportunity, I took it. And I care for you, I truly do. You are a good and able man, and I'm sorry matters are taking me away from you, from this town, from this country."

"Not that sorry," he said.

She drew him back into the entryway, and with him close again, she put both hands upon his. "I had no plans to hurt you, and it grieves me to do exactly that. But I have to take this chance in America, Barney. I must."

"Oh, I've 'eard it all right. Streets paved with gold. 'Tis just talk, Dora."

Was it? She'd heard amazing tales. "I go with my eyes open—as much as they can be. And truth be, I'm not just going for Lottie. I'm going for me."

"Leavin' me's more like it."

There was no way around it. She put a hand upon his cheek. "Leaving you is my one regret."

"Then don't—"

"I must. Until now I've risked little. I've never been given such an opportunity. That's why I go. To be brave and step forward on faith."

He put his own hand over hers and looked deep into her eyes.

"You'll write to me," he said. Asked.

She could only nod, even though she knew she would do no such thing.

He lifted her chin with a beefy finger. "I jus' want you safe and happy, Dora. Be that for me, eh?"

She leaned her head against his chest, closed her eyes, and tried to burn this moment into her memories. Was she making the biggest mistake of her life?

Unfortunately, by the time she knew, it would be too late.

Chapter Five

◦◡

Lottie gazed at her bedroom—the room she'd never see again.

The carriage waited outside. Her parents waited. Dora waited.

"What am I doing?" she whispered.

The room which had been privy to every private moment of her life offered no answers.

Everything was falling into place in a way that made Lottie think this trip to America was meant to be. Yet she resisted the notion. Although she was ecstatic about having Dora accompany her to New York, the events that were supposed to transpire once they arrived made her enthusiasm wane. But that was a worry for another day. Today she was leaving home—a home she loved. Lottie had never lived in a city, and her family's yearly treks to London for the social season always left her longing for the serenity of the Wiltshire countryside, where she could find solitude and escape into a good novel. She would miss this place horribly.

She wouldn't miss the people beyond her family. It surprised her how little regret she had in leaving Rodney Barrister, Gilbert Collins,

Suzanna Weaver, and the rest of their crowd. And yes, even the thought of never seeing Ralph Smythe and his evil Edith elicited no sorrow. Let them all rot in their cruel snobbery. If she had her way, their names would never cross her thoughts again.

Lottie looked out the window at the carriage below. Dora was overseeing the trunks being tied to the back.

Dora had proven to be an apt pupil. The fact that she'd lived with a family of society for so long had been of great benefit. There was no lower-class accent to overcome, and Dora had witnessed and absorbed most of the peculiarities of etiquette. She was also knowledgeable about a lady's attire and the proper time and place to wear each gown, each glove, each bonnet.

Dora had embraced her new ladyhood with aplomb. Lottie had been less successful in accepting the notion of her own situation and upcoming marriage to Conrad. Despite her desire to appease her mother—which had oddly lessened as her mother's health improved— she still wished to marry for love, not convenience. But was she judging Conrad Tremaine too harshly? Many men weren't eloquent in their letters. She had judged him solely by the pen.

I want to be free and independent.

She'd read a poem that offered the boast that America was the land of the free, the home of the brave. Lottie hoped some of its intrinsic courage would become hers once she landed.

Until then . . . she pulled a leather box to her chest. Her mother— away from her father's ears—had instructed Lottie to take along all her jewels as insurance against the unknown. If the worst imaginable happened and Conrad was a cad, Lottie could sell the jewels and buy a passage home.

She knew the notion was simpler than the act. In the past weeks of preparation Lottie had come to recognize her own naïveté. Her lack of knowledge about the world and even day-to-day living left her very glad for Dora's companionship. As far as selling the jewels? Lottie knew nothing about dollars and cents. If she did find an American jeweler willing to buy her offerings, she'd have no idea if they were cheating her. And how much did things cost in New York? A hotel room? Or a meal? Or transportation? Father had never given her more than a few shillings to carry in her purse. When she went shopping it wasn't proper to ask the price, and her father had accounts at all the dressmakers and sundry shops in the local village and in London. Life in America would be far different in that respect. Was an American penny worth the same as an English penny?

She'd asked Father to explain it to her, but had been assured there was no reason for her to know such a thing. "Conrad will take care of you."

The notion was a relief—and a burden. To be beholden to this stranger, to arrive totally dependent upon this family she didn't know, added another layer to her fear. And what about the Tremaines' morals? If her own father's character could be held in question, what of these Americans? She had always held the image of an American as being bold and brash. She was just a country girl. Would she be totally overwhelmed?

Fear had led Lottie to ask her father if they had any other acquaintances in New York City. They did not. At that point Dora had mentioned a third cousin who'd emigrated there five years previous. The connection was tenuous, yet any contact was better than none. At Lottie's urging Dora had sent the cousin a letter announcing their arrival.

They'd received a brief letter in return, with an open invitation toward contact if the need arose.

In spite of this, they had no idea whether the cousin was well-off or destitute, upright or dishonorable. Yet they received comfort knowing they had an alternative place to go.

With that thought Lottie opened her reticule to make sure the paper with the cousin's address was present. It was.

There was a rap on the door, and Dora stuck her head into the room. "Lottie?"

"I know," Lottie said. "I'm coming."

Perhaps she might best handle her good-byes by ignoring any hint of finality. Perhaps if she pretended . . .

Without another look around her room Lottie moved into the hall. "Come. It's time."

To take a leap of faith.

※

Dora sat in the carriage and watched as Lottie told her parents good-bye. Mr. Gleason's chin was stiff as though he was restraining his emotion, and Mrs. Gleason gripped her daughter's hand as if she might never see—

There was that possibility.

Dora adjusted the buttons on her gloves, then rested them on the black leather of the jewelry box Lottie had given her to hold. She had so many unanswered questions about the future. There was movement outside, and Dora watched as Lottie offered her mother a final embrace before walking to the carriage. Surprisingly, there were no tears.

Dora pulled her skirt aside so Lottie could sit, and the driver pulled away.

She waited for Lottie to speak first, but when nothing was said . . .

"Are you all right?"

Lottie averted her gaze and looked out the window. She shook her head, once.

Dora respected her silence and entered into some of her own.

As the roads of Wiltshire sped by, Dora knew she might never see them again, never see Barney. She was relieved to realize she felt little regret. Fear, yes, but no regret.

Yet.

※

Lottie handed the attendant their tickets. He looked them over and nodded. "Welcome aboard, Miss Gleason. Miss Connors. If there is anything the crew can do to make your journey more comfortable, please let us know."

Speaking of comfort . . . Dora's traveling suit felt stiff and confining. But her brimmed hat, complemented with some feathers dyed aubergine to match her costume, made her feel regal. To a girl used to the simple lines of a maid's uniform, the detail of her new clothes was both fascinating and daunting. The pleated skirt had drapery drawn across the front and into a bustle, and the jacket had long, tight sleeves and a high collar that was far more restrictive than anything she'd ever worn. But she'd get used to it—for the sake of fashion.

The two women ascended the gangway and were helped on board by more attendants. While the boarding continued they strolled arm in arm along the outer deck that ran around two huge smokestacks beneath three masts set with sails. It was a little confusing. Was the *Etruria* a steamship or a sailing vessel? Dora decided it really didn't matter as long as the ship got them to America.

As they walked around the promenade deck, gentlemen tipped their brims and smiled appreciatively—to the consternation of many a woman companion on their arm. Dora had never received such attention. Traversing the streets of Lacock or London in her maid's uniform or a simple dress had rendered her invisible to any man of means. "They're flirting with us," Dora whispered.

"They're appreciating us," Lottie said as she acknowledged another gentleman. "Get used to it, Dora. This is one of the best perks of society."

Dora couldn't argue with her. She'd never walked past a man and had him gaze at her with utter admiration. She'd received the occasional lustful scrutiny of a workingman on the street, but never this . . . never adulation. Never . . . awe.

When a gentleman with a dashing mustache tipped his hat and smiled directly at *her*, she felt herself blush. Then she did as Lottie had done and nodded back at him with just a hint of a smile upon her lips.

How luscious.

Lottie handed the stateroom key to Dora. "You may do the honors."

With a little wiggling, Dora turned the key in the lock and opened the door to what would be their home for the next eight days.

She gasped at the sight of it.

Lottie strode around the room, nodding. "My, my, this is more luxurious than I expected."

Dora didn't want to say so, but the stateroom was grander than the best room in the Gleasons' home. It was filled with ornately carved furniture, and the small windows were draped with heavy velvet curtains. Fancy bric-a-brac made the room feel more like a home than a ship's cabin.

"Ah," Lottie said, opening the door to one of the two armoires. "Our trunks have been delivered and unpacked."

"They do that for us?"

"They do if we ask them to, which I did."

Dora noticed Lottie still held the leather box of jewels. "What are you going to do with those while we're on board?" she asked.

"Mother instructed me that once we are under way, I should ring for the purser to put them in the ship's safe."

"Wouldn't it be better to keep them here, with us?"

Lottie shook her head. "I may trust my gowns to unknown servants coming and going, but never my jewels. Remember that, Dora." She opened a drawer beside a bed and placed the box inside, stuffing a shawl around it. "We aren't trying to impress anyone here, not to the extent of risking my jewels. I've brought along lesser pieces that will be sufficient adornment. No one will dare ask if they're real; they'll assume as much." She gave the shawl an extra tuck.

A long blast sounded. Then another.

"What's that?" Dora asked.

"I believe it's an all-ashore. The guests must leave now."

"Guests?"

"You didn't think the ship would be as crowded as it is now for the entire trip, did you? Father told me guests are allowed on board for the two hours before sailing."

"So your mother and father could have come to see us off?"

"They have enough to deal with at home. Besides, they wouldn't want to spend the train fare to Liverpool and back. And lodging."

"So what do we do now?" Dora asked.

"I suppose we go to the railing and wave our good-byes."

"To whom?"

Lottie thought a moment. "To England." She extended a hand toward the door. "Shall we, Miss Connors?"

❧

As the ship began to pull away, the dock swarmed with well-wishers, waving hats and handkerchiefs to the passengers lining the rails of the ship. Lottie marveled at how high she and Dora were from the ground, as if God had lifted them up to carry them across the sea.

"*Arrivederci,* Paolo!" came a voice from a lower deck.

Holding on to the railing, Lottie leaned forward to look at the decks below. There were at least two levels beneath the one for first-class passengers. The people waving from these decks were dressed in simple dark-colored clothing, the women with kerchiefs covering their hair and babies swaddled in shawls tied across their chests. They looked poor.

Dora must have seen the direction of her gaze. "There are ever so many, aren't there?"

"Who are they? And why are they going to America?"

Dora offered her an incredulous look. "Haven't you heard about the thousands of people emigrating to the United States from all over Europe?"

Why would she know such things? "Why do they go?"

"For different reasons. They flee poverty or persecution or politics. Or maybe they simply seek adventure."

The decks below were crowded compared to the spaciousness of the first-class deck. "I'm very glad they are down there and not up here with us."

Her statement brought another look from Dora, this one less gracious. "They'll not bite, you know."

Lottie felt herself redden. "I'm sorry if they make me uncomfortable. I can't help it if I've never been around such people. Mother and Father protected me from the baser elements."

"Perhaps they protected you too much."

It was a concession she might have to make. The world Lottie had known was tightly guarded, with high walls that prevented the entry of disparate persons. And yet they had also prevented Lottie from any knowledge of their existence. The village of Lacock, nearest her family's home, had provided her knowledge of people of lesser means, but not the mean issues of their existence.

Dora nodded at the crowd below. "I admire them."

"Admire?"

"It takes courage to flee the known and step toward the unknown." She looked at Lottie. "Sometimes I wonder what *we* are fleeing."

Fleeing? It was a strange word to contemplate. Unlike the emigrants, Lottie was not fleeing poverty, persecution, or politics. Her life in Wiltshire had been rife with advantage.

Had been rife.

The full consequences of her family's downfall were still unknown. Even if she'd stayed behind, her life would have changed. Her parents had mentioned they would be moving elsewhere to start again. Lottie shuddered at the notion. It was as if they were retreating in shame.

Shame. Was that what Lottie was fleeing? She'd experienced enough of that already. The memories of her party still smarted and elicited sadness and anger. From that day until this one, not a single friend had come calling to say their good-byes or express their regret. How odd it was to realize that a lifetime of friends had turned out to be nothing more than acquaintances. What a waste.

Her own inability to recognize the shallow nature of these friends disturbed her. Did Lottie own the ability to identify true friendship? And if she didn't know how to have a true friend, did she know how to *be* one?

She glanced at Dora, waving at the crowd on the docks below. They were traveling as friends. Although Lottie had always considered them as such, the truth was she'd always embraced an element of distance. Friends or no, Lottie had been the mistress and Dora the maid. But here on board the ship she was to treat Dora as an equal. Could she do that?

Dora interrupted her thoughts and looked at Lottie with a full smile upon her lips. "Seeing all these people . . . we must get it in our heads we are not fleeing *from* something but flying *to* something. Something better."

Lottie nodded and turned her gaze skyward. The sight of the clouds moving to the east as the ship moved west accentuated their departure.

God help me.

God help us.

Dora's stomach danced in a most uncomfortable manner as they neared the dining room for the evening meal. This was her first real test of being a lady.

"Don't hold on so tightly," Lottie whispered.

Dora eased her grip on Lottie's arm.

"Remember: polite, prompt, pretty, and proper."

Dora was more concerned about not tripping over her train, or spilling soup down her front, or saying something inane.

There was a parade of couples heading to the dining room, the men in tailcoats and bow ties and the women in elegant off-the-shoulder gowns, layered with drapery, lace, beading, and fringe.

The decorative layers fascinated Dora, but the layers beneath the gowns fascinated her even more. As a maid she'd worn a corset and a petticoat, but to wear the layers and weight of the undergarments that fine ladies endured was beyond cumbersome. It was ironic how women cinched in their waists to portray a thin silhouette when they could appear even slimmer if only they would remove some of the layers between skin and gown.

And the dresses themselves . . . Dora's was made of sky-blue satin and brocade, with an overlay of ecru lace ruffled at the bodice and floor. She had no idea how many yards of fabric were used to make the bustle, train, and drapery, or how many different beads or measures of trim decorated her dress, but the result was stunning.

And heavy. Dora felt as if she were dragging several sacks of flour or grain behind her, or perhaps a good-sized child had become a stowaway on board her train, taking a ride.

By her own right, Lottie looked stunning in her gown of sage green, and their chokers made of rhinestones still managed to glisten under the gaslights.

There it was. The dining room.

Two liveried footmen stood stoic beside the double doors as the wealthy and important passed by. Were any of these grand people a pretender like Dora?

If so, she wouldn't guess it. Everyone seemed to know what they were doing and what they should be saying, and they seemed to be confident in the effect they created by merely *being*.

The dining room itself made her gasp. It was two stories in height, with a balcony rimming the room. Columns edged in gold filigree held up a coffered ceiling that was crowned by a stained-glass dome.

"Where is our table?" she asked Lottie. She'd feel more at ease seated. She eyed the place settings, checking to make sure she knew the specified use of each fork and knife as Lottie had taught her.

"Table seven. We'll find it—eventually." Lottie offered soft greetings to those they passed. "The rich never hurry, Dora, nor let on that they are hungry, thirsty, or need to sit. Now is the time to see and be seen."

Upon further observation that was exactly what was happening. Diners stood about the room in small groups of four or six, making introductions and chatting with the ease of like acknowledging like. No one appeared out of place or nervous. All portrayed a confidence that was both reassuring and presumptuous. Absent was all hint of fear. Apparently that sentiment was Dora's alone.

A middle-aged gentleman with a woman on his arm approached, and Dora tried to restrain her urge to flee. Lottie took a step toward them, her face open and inviting.

"Good evening, ladies," said the man.

"Good evening," Lottie said. She dipped her head slightly, and Dora followed suit.

"Let me introduce myself. I am Lord Thorwald, and this is my wife."

Dora had heard of him. He was a baron. Would he recognize Lottie's family name? She hoped not. She didn't want Lottie to have to defend a scandal at sea.

"A pleasure to meet you, my lord, my lady. I am Miss Gleason and this is my friend, Miss Connors."

"Evening, sir," Dora said. "Ma'am."

Lottie flashed her the quickest of looks, and Dora realized she hadn't addressed the couple in the same manner Lottie had. She felt her face grow hot.

"Miss Connors, Miss Gleason . . ." The baroness looked to her husband. Dora feared the woman's next comment would be in regard to Sir Gleason's indiscretions. But the baroness had something else on her mind. "Didn't the captain mention these young ladies, telling us if we met them to take special care?"

Lord Thorwald eyed them with new interest. "I believe they are the ones. You are traveling alone, yes?"

"Yes," Lottie said. "My mother isn't well enough to accompany me."

"Are you traveling to America on holiday?" the baroness asked Dora.

Dora had no idea how to respond. They hadn't rehearsed such an answer.

Lottie stepped in. "We are, your ladyship. We've always wanted to see New York City, and since we were invited by friends . . ."

"Who are your friends? Perhaps we know them," the baron said.

Dora hoped not. She longed for anonymity.

"The Tremaines," Lottie said.

"Martin Tremaine? Of the Tremaine's Dry Goods Tremaines?"

"You know them?"

"Not at all. But we have heard of them. Who hasn't?"

It gave Dora pause to realize Lottie was set to marry into such a family. She hoped Lottie's opinion of Conrad would rise a bit at the complimentary mention.

Waiters began to make their way through the crowd, carrying glasses on large trays. A man in a fancy uniform stood on a dais and clinked a spoon against a glass. "Welcome, welcome, ladies and gentlemen. I am Captain McShane. Please gather a glass for a toast."

Lottie took two glasses and handed one to Dora. Dora was grateful for the liquid and started to take a sip, then noticed everyone else was waiting.

As soon as all had been served, the Captain raised his glass. "To a fine voyage, to health, and to prosperity."

Everyone clinked their glasses, and Dora forgot her nerves long enough to enjoy the sound of it, like a hundred prisms tinkling together. Encouraged, she turned to tap her glass against one held by a woman to her left and—

And missed.

And dropped her own glass to the floor.

Where it broke.

A thousand pieces scattered.

Liquid splattered on the floor.

And on the shoes of a gentleman.

"Oh! I'm so sorry! So sorry!" Dora knelt to the floor and began picking up the pieces, depositing them into her gloved palm. A waiter came to her side with a towel, and she took it from him and began mopping up the mess.

"Dora! Dora!" Lottie whispered. She pulled at her arm.

It was then Dora looked up and saw the spectacle she'd created. People were looking on, aghast.

Fine ladies didn't mop up messes or pick up shards of glass, even if the breakage was their fault.

Dora tried to get to her feet, but with one hand full of broken glass, she got entangled in her dress and toppled into the gentleman whose shoes she had wetted. He righted her, and she saw the surprise upon his face.

I have to leave! Now!

She rushed toward the entrance of the dining room, brushing into the rich and famous as she made her retreat.

Lottie called her name, but Dora didn't stop until she'd reached the safety of their stateroom. She tried to retrieve the key from her reticule, but only then realized she still held pieces of glass in her hand.

A steward approached. "May I help you, miss?"

She held out her open palm. "Please take these."

He hesitated, then held out his hand.

Just then Lottie strode down the corridor. "There you are." She removed her key and nodded to the steward. "Thank you."

"Can I offer more assis—?"

She opened the door. "No thank you. We're fine."

They entered the room and Lottie closed the door behind them. Then she pounced. "Whatever were you thinking?"

Dora sank to the bed. "I didn't mean to break it; it just slipped out—"

"I'm not talking about dropping the glass. Accidents happen. If you had simply laughed at yourself and taken another one, all would have been fine. But getting down on the floor and picking up the pieces, then mopping the spill with a towel . . ."

Humiliation washed over her. "It's habit. I felt so bad, and it had splashed upon a gentleman's shoe."

"At least you didn't start wiping *that* off."

At least.

"And then you called the baron and his wife *sir* and *ma'am*." Lottie paced the room, expertly flipping her train at every turn. "I used the correct terms of address. All you had to do was repeat them. You need to listen and observe or you're never going to fool anyone into thinking you're a lady."

Dora swiped away tears. "But I'm not a lady. I never have been and never will—"

Lottie stopped pacing and took a breath. "I don't mean to be harsh. I know this was your first outing. And take heart, after this voyage we'll never see these people again."

She could only hope.

"Perhaps your largest sin was not in trying to help clean the mess but in running away."

"I couldn't just stay there and—"

"Luckily, I know how to fix it." Lottie removed a handkerchief from the dressing table and dabbed at Dora's face. "Just a small refurbishment and we can go back—"

Dora pushed her hand away. "I can't go back to the dining room."

"You must."

"They'll stare at me. They'll talk about me."

"They have already done both. But if you return with your head held high and a hint of *Ç'est la vie*, they'll—"

"Sayla-what?"

"Such is life. Things happen but life goes on, Dora." She took her arm. "And so do we. Besides, I'm famished."

At least Dora would go down with a full stomach.

≈

Dinner was under way. Lottie had secretly wished it were not so, for now they had to enter the room as the only ones standing. They would be noticed.

She paused at the door and said to a footman, "Table seven, please."

They snaked their way through the tables to the far side of the room. Lottie smiled and nodded. Her arm ached from the clench of Dora's grip.

To their credit, some diners barely gave them notice, but others leaned head to head and whispered.

Just a little farther . . .

With only a few steps to go, Lottie felt Dora let go of her arm and, to her horror, saw her detour to the left. Lottie nearly called after her, but simply stopped instead.

And waited.

And watched.

Dora approached a table of eight, and those present halted their eating and conversation.

Where is she going?

Dora moved halfway around the table and stopped beside a gentleman with long sideburns. He looked up at her expectantly—but also with a bit of trepidation. "Yes, Miss . . . ?"

"Connors." She handed him her lace-edged handkerchief. "For your shoes."

He took the handkerchief and studied it a moment. He ran a finger along the monogram: *DC.* Then he let out a laugh. "Good show. Yes, yes, good show."

Dora offered a small bow, then returned to Lottie. Her smile was perfect—self-composed, amused, and above all, in control.

She took Lottie's arm and said, "Shall we dine, Miss Gleason?"

"Absolutely."

Bravo, Dora.

❦

"Are you asleep?"

"No," Lottie answered.

"I *can* do this, you know. Be a lady."

"I know."

Dora turned on her side and adjusted the pillow against her cheek. The rest of the dinner had gone well. She'd followed Lottie's advice about listening and observing, and had even joined the conversation on more than one occasion.

Yet the highlight of her evening, her biggest triumph, had been when she'd made the gentleman laugh.

During that one moment she knew she'd found the key to getting by in society.

Chapter Six

Dora moved her parasol aside to let the sunlight bathe her face. "'Tis a grand day."

Lottie fiddled with the buttons on her gloves as they strolled around the first-class deck. "I'm glad you're not content to sit under the awnings. Those ladies there, afraid of a little sun. I know it can wreak havoc on the complexion and Mother always warned me it would make me look common, but to sit in the shade all one's life . . . what a waste."

Dora loved the sun. The awnings set up for shade made her feel as if she were sitting in a tent, far removed from the world.

Which is exactly what they were. Under way for the second day, beyond sight of land, the sea and the sky stretched endlessly. It was invigorating, yet also a bit frightening.

"I do think we should keep track of the number of times we make a go round this deck," Lottie said. "I believe this is number four?"

Dora wouldn't have objected to it being number forty-four. This was the first time she had experienced the sky from horizon to horizon, to horizon, to horizon. It was as if God had inverted a lovely blue bowl over the ocean, which, in turn, gratefully reflected its blueness. And the air . . . although she was used to the clear country air of Wiltshire, this air seemed bitingly fresh.

She gazed over the white-capped sea looking for the sea gulls that had seen them on their way, dipping low on the water before rising into the sky. Their freedom to soar had made her feel as if the world were hers.

But the birds were gone. Was the ship too far out to sea for their comfort? Had they instinctively returned to the safety of land rather than taking a chance on this contraption moving through the water? The ship was so large. How did it ever float at all? And if everyone suddenly moved to one side of the ship, would it capsize? The depth of the water was beyond Dora's comprehension, other than to know there would be no way to survive in it.

She studied the people around her. No one else looked worried. She was being silly and had tainted her delight of the lovely day.

She heard children's laughter and was drawn to a railing that overlooked a lower deck. Boys were throwing someone's shoe into the air, teasing the younger one by keeping it just out of reach.

"Come away," Lottie said, pulling on her arm. "We shouldn't watch—"

Dora knew the emigrants made Lottie uneasy, but *she* was fascinated with them. The first-class deck was spotted with proper ladies and gentlemen taking a stroll or sitting upon deck chairs, reading a book or sharing refined conversation. But the lower decks—she'd heard their accommodations called *steerage*—teemed with families dressed in dark colors and drab, functional clothes. Mothers rocked babies, and men gathered in groups, nursing their pipes amid animated conversation. And children ran and played, finding joy within their constrained space.

A woman looked up at her. Dora began to wave, then thought better of it. The emigrants wouldn't look upon her kindly. She was a *have* and they were definitely *have-nots*. Yet the knowledge that they were traveling to America to find a new beginning did cause her to admire them.

"Dora, away." Lottie's voice was softly urgent.

When Dora turned back to the first-class deck, she found more than Lottie's eyes upon her. Apparently looking down upon the lower classes was only acceptable in less literal ways.

She took Lottie's arm and returned to their circuit.

The children's laughter faded.

*

"This isn't fair," Lottie said. "You look as if that dress were meant for you—as if all my dresses were made for you."

Dora stopped adjusting the floral trim that diagonally bisected the lace bodice and culminated beneath two silken bows upon her shoulders. "You're very kind, Lottie. But I will never forget these are your dresses. And this one would look lovely on anyone."

Lottie appreciated her effort to appease but knew Dora's statement was not true. The peach-colored gown of silk with layers of ivory lace looked far different on the present Dora than it had on the maid Dora, who'd first tried it on in Lottie's bedroom. At first, trying on the possible gowns for the trip had overwhelmed the maid, but now *she* wore the dresses; they did not wear her. Dora was truly taking on the persona of a lady.

She put on earrings—also borrowed from Lottie. "I certainly hope I don't tread upon anyone's toes at the ball tonight. You've been a patient teacher, but I fear I will forget every lesson once the music begins."

Lottie was more concerned that no one would invite Dora to dance. Her first-night faux pas still rumbled through the occasional overheard conversation. There was not an official shunning afoot, but neither was there acceptance. Tonight would be a true test as to how the rest of the sailing would go.

"This train . . ." Dora said, taking a few steps. "Its weight, coupled with the fact that it will be in the way . . ."

"Use its weight," Lottie advised. "There is nothing like the swing of a train as you sail across the floor."

"What if I trip?"

Lottie didn't want either of them to think of that.

They left their cabin and headed to dinner—and the ball.

❧

The ballroom was more intimate than Dora expected, but considering it was aboard a ship . . . it still glittered with light, jewels, and beaded gowns.

She fanned herself in order to have something to do and noticed a few sideways glances from other attendees, a few whispers behind ornamental fans. Were they still holding last night's gaffe against her? Her confidence waned. Maybe she should return to the cabin and let Lottie attend alone.

Just then a man with long sideburns approached—her man with the wetted shoes. Had his laughter last night been reconsidered?

But when he smiled, relief washed over her.

"Good evening," he said with a bow.

"Good evening."

"Forgive me for not introducing myself last evening. The name is Edmund Greenfield." He clicked his heels together and nodded.

She offered a small curtsy. "Dora Connors." She now had reason to use the fan. He was a handsome man, a bit swarthy, and definitely intriguing.

He removed something from his pocket and unfurled it into the air between them. "I believe this is yours?"

It was her handkerchief. "Yes, thank you," she said. But on a whim she returned it to him. "The night is young, Mr. Greenfield. Perhaps you should keep it. Who knows what I might spill."

He laughed and the handkerchief returned to his pocket. He pointed to his shoes. "They *are* good as new."

"Glad I could be of service."

"As am I, Miss . . . it is *Miss* Connors, is it not?"

She blushed. "For now."

"Excellent," he said, offering her his hand. "So, Miss Connors, may I have the pleasure of this dance?"

Dora glanced toward Lottie for her approval, but her attention had been diverted by two older ladies. Surely it was appropriate to accept Mr. Greenfield's invitation.

"Come now," he said. "It may be a bit of a challenge with the movement of the ship, but—"

"We'll counter it by making our own waves?"

"Haven't you done enough of that, Miss Connors?"

"Not at all. That, Mr. Greenfield, was only one attempt toward making a splash."

Where was this wit coming from? It was as though she'd been flirting her entire life. And Mr. Greenfield seemed delighted by her words.

The orchestra began a waltz, and Dora felt an inner swaying to the lovely music. She put her hand upon his and was led onto the dance floor. It didn't seem real. The glittering chandeliers, the scent of perfume and flowers, the sound of violins, and the touch of a gentleman's gloved hand upon her own.

And then upon her waist.

"Are you ready?" he asked.

"I should ask you that," she said.

He laughed and swept her into the swirling mass of silk and diamonds and tailcoats.

Dora stumbled the littlest bit, but within seconds found the rhythm of it. Mr. Greenfield was an excellent dancer, and with an exhilarating strength he took charge and led her round and round.

"You are radiant," he said, looking down at her.

"That's because I'm flying!" She tilted her head back to take it all in, fully confident in his leadership.

"Fly on, little bird," he said. "Spread your wings."

Dora remembered envying the soaring sea gulls. They had nothing on her now.

She let herself take flight.

⁂

Lottie crossed the dance floor in the arms of an ancient man twice the age of her father.

"You dance well, my dear."

She didn't answer. Her eyes were glued on Dora and her dance partner—her fifth of the evening.

Lottie eyed the cluster of men waiting on the edge of the dance floor. Waiting for Dora.

Lottie's partner—she'd forgotten his name—must have noticed the direction of her gaze, because he said, "The belle of the ball, that one is. Do you know her name?"

She's my maid. "She's my best friend. Miss Connors."

"I heard she has quite the wit. Spilling on Dr. Greenfield's shoes, bumping into him, then bringing him a handkerchief. A well-orchestrated bit of flirtation that was."

Lottie's thoughts divided. Firstly, Dora didn't know flirting from flying, and secondly, the name the man mentioned registered: Dr. Edmund Greenfield was the physician who treated the queen herself. No wonder Dora had dance partners. Once Dr. Greenfield gave Dora his approval, the other gentlemen would be quick to follow suit.

"Quite the dash in that young thing," the man said. "Quite the fire. Do you think you could introdu—?"

Lottie stopped dancing. "If you'll excuse me. I need to sit down."

The old man led her to a chair, offered polite concern, then was off with the others, watching Dora waltz into everyone's hearts.

It's the dress. My dress. That's what makes her so striking.

Then she remembered her dance partner's comments about Dora's gumption and wit. . . . Not one mention of her dress or jewels or even her dancing ability.

Lottie's dress, Lottie's jewels, and the result of Lottie's dance lessons . . .

A young woman was deposited in the chair next to Lottie as her partner left for some refreshment. Her face was flushed and she fanned herself furiously.

"Good evening," she said to Lottie.

"Evening."

"'Tis a grand ball, is it not?"

It is not. "Grand," Lottie said.

They were silent a moment as Dora and her partner waltzed by.

"Excuse me for the intrusion, but I saw you with that young woman who's in such high demand. I've heard she is a countess or a princess. Is that true?"

Lottie remembered the first time she'd let—she'd insisted—Dora try on one of her dresses. Dora had said she felt like a princess.

The young woman waited for an answer. "She's just an ordinary girl," Lottie said. *Masquerading as a lady.*

"Oh no," said the woman, shaking her head. "There's nothing ordinary about that one. She has the entire ship eating out of her hand. Would you be so kind as to introduce me to—"

For the second time that evening, Lottie interrupted a request for an introduction. She rose. "If you'll excuse me."

She'd had enough.

Lottie wove her way through the crowd with nary an eye to notice her passing. She headed back to their cabin.

No one would miss her, not when they had Princess Dora in their midst.

❦

Dora was escorted off the dance floor into a bevy of future partners—of all ages.

"Miss Connors, may I . . . ?"

"Miss Connors, please allow me to . . ."

"Miss Connors, you promised me . . ."

She laughed at their enthusiasm. "Let me breathe, gentlemen. Your eagerness to spend time on the dance floor makes me believe the ship must be low on cigars and brandy."

Their laughter fed her.

"I'll get you refreshment," said an earlier partner.

"Here, Miss Connors. Sit a moment and rest."

"Recuperate is more like it," she said, accepting the chair. She untied the fan at her waist and used it gratefully. A thought passed that the last time she'd been so glowing and spent was after she'd moved Lottie's winter clothes to the attic for spring storage. Traipsing up and down those stairs, weighed down with heavy garments . . .

Dancing was a far more enjoyable cause of exertion and exhaustion.

A glass of punch arrived, and without thinking, she drank the contents in three gulps. As she lowered the glass, she realized her error. Ladies did not gulp. They sipped.

"Don't stare at me, gentlemen—you who are the cause of my thirst. If you wish for me to continue, then I must be refreshed." She held up the glass. "In fact . . ."

"I'll get it this time," said a man she hadn't danced with as yet.

She wagged her fan at the older gentleman who'd been her last partner. His face was extremely flushed. "It looks as though you could use a bit of the refreshment yourself, Mr. Stoddard."

He twirled his mustache and grinned. "If you'll excuse me? Don't mind if I do."

The orchestra played the introduction to another dance, and her first partner, Edmund Greenfield, came forward. "I believe this dance was saved for me?"

"I believe it was." Dora accepted his arm, and they moved to the dance floor.

"If I may ask, what is your business in America, Mr. Greenfield?"

"My cousin lives there. I'm going to join him."

They danced past another couple, nearly too close. Dora felt her train brush against them.

"Do they have balls like this in America, I wonder?"

"Oh, I'm sure they do. Perhaps we could possibly . . ."

"Perhaps, Mr. Greenfield. America is full of possiblys."

Dora scanned the ballroom, looking for Lottie. The ball was over. People were leaving.

She tried to remember the last time she'd seen her but had to admit it had been far earlier in the evening.

"Miss Connors? Are you looking for someone?" It was a Mr. Stoker, who'd danced a quadrille with her.

"I'm looking for my friend. But it appears she's left already."

He held out his arm. "Would you care for an escort back to your cabin?"

"Please."

The witty banter she'd maintained all evening vanished as they walked. Dora was worried about Lottie. She prayed she was all right.

Mr. Stoker executed the key for her, then said his good-nights.

It took Dora's eyes a moment to adjust to the dim light of a single gas lamp. But in its glow she saw that Lottie was already in her bed, her back to the door, the cover pulled over her shoulder.

Dora tiptoed into the room and set her reticule and fan on a bureau. She began to remove her gloves when Lottie sat up in one swift motion.

"You frightened me!" Dora cried.

"Oh no, Miss Connors, for to frighten you, I would have to exist to you." Lottie plumped her pillow roughly before tossing it aside.

The evening flashed through Dora's memories. Unfortunately, tellingly, Lottie held no part in most of her recollections.

She finished removing her gloves and folded them with extra care. "Didn't you feel well?"

Lottie swung her legs over the side of the bed. "Oh, I felt well enough, abandoned enough."

Oh. That. But then she remembered. "I saw you dancing."

Lottie's laugh was bitter. "Once. Actually it was twice, though compared to you . . ."

Lottie was jealous! The knowledge nearly made Dora laugh, and it certainly quelled her concern. She began to unhook her necklace and earrings. "I'll admit I had a marvelous time. The gentlemen were very kind and solicitous."

"To you. Kind and solicitous to you. But to me and . . . and others?" Lottie stood and pointed in the direction of the ballroom. "Didn't you notice the scowls on the faces of the other women present? The women who didn't get to dance every dance? The ones who had to watch as the eligible men fawned over you?"

Dora held the earrings in her hand. She hadn't noticed such a thing. "I didn't do anything improper, did I? I didn't seek the attention."

"You did nothing to dispel it either." Lottie took the folded gloves and thrust them into a hamper of soiled clothing.

Dora felt her ire rise. "I thought you'd be proud of the way the ship's society accepted me, especially after my blunder last night."

Lottie didn't answer but held out her hand, wanting her jewelry back. Dora complied. Then she attempted to undo the back hooks of her dress, yet she knew it would be nearly impossible to undress without help.

Lottie pushed her hands away roughly and undid the hooks. "I admit it was amazing the way the men showed interest in you. I don't know what you said to make them gather round you so, but . . ." She sighed. "It *was* impressive."

Dora let out the breath she'd been saving. "I meant no harm or offense to anyone, Lottie. Please believe me. When Mr. Greenfield came up to me, teasing me about his shoes again, I—"

"*Dr.* Greenfield, the queen's physician," Lottie said.

Dora's stomach dropped. "A doctor?"

"A doctor to the royals."

And I called him "Mister" all night . . . Dora put a hand to her midsection. "I don't feel very well."

"Oh, stop it," Lottie said. "Obviously whatever title you called him— or called the others—they didn't care." The bodice was undone and Lottie moved around to Dora's front to remove it. After she did, she held it in her hands and looked at Dora, eye to eye. "How did you do it? How did you charm them so?"

"I . . . I made them laugh."

Lottie's eyebrows rose. "Laugh. You told them jokes?"

"No, not at all. I don't know any jokes."

"Then what?"

What *had* she done? "I guess . . . I teased them. I made fun of them. I made fun of myself. They seemed to like that."

Lottie unhooked Dora's skirt and train. "I'm not sure I could do such a thing."

"Then don't," Dora said. "Perhaps it wasn't the humor at all. Perhaps it was that I simply didn't know any better. I'm not versed at being coy and demure. I didn't know the proper niceties to say. I was just being myself."

"No one ever instructed me to be myself," Lottie said. "I was taught to be the daughter my parents expected, the ingenue society would greet with open arms, and the prospective wife that eligible men would want to marry. Being myself? I wouldn't know how to start."

The heavy skirt was lowered so Dora could step out of it. It was like stepping free from a lake where she'd had rocks tied to her waist.

Dora didn't know how to respond to Lottie's lack of confidence. How sad that what came naturally to Dora—what should have come naturally to any woman—had been squelched and bound into nonexistence.

"Here, now, let me help you get your hair undone," Lottie said with a sigh.

Dora sat at the dressing table, and Lottie removed the pins and embellishments. Dora reached back and touched Lottie's busy hand.

"I'm sorry you didn't have a good time tonight, but I can't say I'm sorry *I* did. I want to thank you for the entire evening, the entire voyage. Without you I never would have experienced any of it."

Lottie shrugged. "You're welcome. And perhaps next time I'll take your advice and try to let my true self shine through. Whatever that may be."

Dora wished her friend full success—and wished herself more of the same.

Chapter Seven

Dora opened her eyes, hoping to remove herself from the awful rocking and lurching of her dream.

She saw Lottie at the cabin window, looking out upon the sea. Without warning, Lottie gripped the edge of the window to gain her balance. A bottle of perfume skittered across the top of the vanity nearby, teetered on its edge, then fell to the carpet.

The rolling was not in Dora's dreams at all. The ship itself was swaying.

Lottie noticed she was awake. "We're in a storm. A bad one from the looks of it."

Suddenly it was as though the storm had moved from the outside to within. Dora lurched out of bed, grabbed the chamber pot, and gave up what was left of her dinner.

Lottie ran to her side, putting one hand upon her shoulders while the other gathered her hair away from her face.

When Dora was through, Lottie handed her a handkerchief. "Thank you." Dora had never felt so embarrassed. "It must have been the rich food."

"It's not the food," Lottie said, draping the chamber pot with a cloth and setting it by the door. "You're seasick."

"What's that?"

"The rocking of the ship makes your insides unbalanced."

That was exactly the way she felt. Lottie helped her back to the bed. Did it feel better to close her eyes? She wasn't sure. "What time is it?"

"Nearly time for breakfast."

Dora tried to get out of bed to get ready, but the dizziness forced her back to her pillows.

"You must stay in bed. When the time comes, I'll have something brought to you."

Dora realized the desire for food was not what propelled her to sitting. Before going to sleep last night, she'd thought a good deal about breakfast this morning—having nothing to do with the food but rather, the society. She thrilled at the idea of entering the dining room and being greeted by turned heads, smiles, and the good wishes from those who'd come to know her—and of her—last night at the ball. To miss that moment was nearly as excruciating as the churning in her stomach.

"Will you be all right while I'm gone?" Lottie asked.

Only then did Dora notice that Lottie was already dressed for the day. Lottie must have felt the intensity of her gaze, for she said, "Does my hair look awry? I tried to do the best I could on my own, but—"

"You look splendid," Dora said. "I didn't hear you get up, or get dressed, or . . ."

"You were worn out from the dance, no doubt."

There was still a hint of jealousy in Lottie's voice, but Dora was in no condition to counter it.

Lottie had her hand on the doorknob. "Will you be all right while I'm gone?"

Did she have a choice? "You might bring the pot closer, just in case."

"Let me get it emptied first." Lottie opened the door and Dora heard her flagging down a steward. She popped her head back in the cabin. "I've instructed him to knock and enter with the new pot. Be sure to ask him for anything else you need. I won't be gone long."

Dora fell back upon the pillows and closed her eyes. The bob and sway of the ship was disturbing, but perhaps if she likened it to the rocking of a cradle, she could find it soothing.

Or not.

A soft knock on the door was followed by the entrance of a steward. "For you, miss?"

Dora pulled the covers to her chin. "Over here, please."

He averted his eyes and brought the pot close, setting it on the floor beside her bed. "Perhaps some tea, miss? Chamomile?"

"Tea would be nice. Thank you."

He smiled and left her. The thought that he would return gave her comfort. It was disconcerting to be alone when she felt unwell.

While she waited she thought about Lottie entering the dining room and being seated at their table. Would people miss Dora? Ask after her? Or was she being prideful by imagining such a thing?

The ship road a swell and dove left, then right, and Dora reached for the chamber pot.

Unsuccessfully.

She was appalled by the mess she'd made and crawled from her bed to find a towel. She got on her hands and knees and mopped up as best she could.

Was there water in the pitcher and basin? She tried to stand in order to check, but the heaving of the ship brought her back to the pot.

At least this time she found it. When she was finished, she sat upon the floor and tried to lean against the bed, but the upright position was too much for her.

She fell onto her side and lay there, waiting for help—or death. She didn't care which.

※

The dining room had scant attendance. As Lottie made her way across the room, taking hold of the backs of chairs along the way as the tip and sway of the room demanded, she noticed that of the usual diners at their table, four were missing.

"Well, well," said Mr. Collins. "Miss Gleason, you must be commended for your resilience against the storm."

"And hungry," his wife added.

The waiter held her chair as she was seated. "Has the storm affected the others?" she asked, noting that every table had empty chairs.

"Yes, yes. Apparently many have given a reluctant offering to Neptune," a banker from Philadelphia said. "Has Miss Connors succumbed?"

Lottie found his word choice humorous but did not smile. "She is a little under the weather."

Mr. Collins laughed. "From the storm or her popularity at the ball last night?"

"I do enjoy seeing a young person truly enjoying herself," Mrs. Collins said. She looked longingly at her husband. "It makes me remember my own youth."

He patted her hand. "We were quite the pair in the Virginia reel, weren't we, my darling?"

The thought of the corpulent couple dancing was not an easy image.

Lottie felt the touch of a hand upon her shoulder and turned to find Dr. Greenfield at her side.

"Good morning, Miss Gleason." He nodded to the others at the table. "Ladies. Gentlemen."

The others murmured their greetings, then turned their attention upon each other, giving Lottie and the doctor the impression of privacy.

"May I?" He indicated the seat beside her.

She gave her affirmation, and he sat down. "How are you this morning, Miss Gleason?"

"I'm well."

He gazed around the room. "One of but a few, it seems."

She suddenly realized he had accosted her because he was concerned about Dora. She knew she should make things easy for him and not make him ask, but the seed of envy that had been planted last evening spread roots and she offered no information.

He cleared his throat. "Is Miss Connors attending breakfast this morning?"

Lottie shook her head. "It appears her constitution is weak against the waves."

He stood immediately. "I'll go check on her, see if I may be of service."

Lottie put a hand on his arm. "No, sir, I . . ." *What am I doing? Dora could use the assistance of a doctor.* But her lesser side won the battle. "She has been attended to. She's resting now."

He seemed appeased—though a bit disappointed. He took a fresh breath and said, "To her credit she created her own waves last night. Truly the belle of the ball."

She didn't look so belle-like throwing up in the chamber pot this morning.

Then Lottie got an idea. Perhaps she could usurp Dora's position in her absence. "Would you care to join us at our table, Doctor? There is obviously room. We would be honored."

He did not consider it long. "No, thank you. I must return to my dining partners." He rose. "But perhaps I will see you in the music room later?"

Lottie gave in to the inevitable. "Perhaps Miss Connors will be able to join us."

He beamed and offered a nod. "That would be wonderful. Please extend my sympathy on her discomfort and offer my services at any time. Tell her I wish her fine health in the near future."

"Fine health and calm seas."

He smiled and left them.

The others at the table had obviously heard every word and were quick to pull Lottie back into conversation. "It appears Dr. Greenfield is smitten," the banker said.

His wife poked his arm. "That is not for us to discuss, my dear."

"Well, then, whom shall we discuss?"

Mrs. Collins leaned forward, her eyes aglow. "Did you see Miss Connors dancing with the Duke of Hertfordshire? And then a member of Parliament, and—"

"A doctor, a lord, a duke, and a bevy of other gentlemen," said her husband. "I believe she earned herself a full house."

"At least," the banker said. "Or four of a kind."

The men laughed at their joke.

Lottie was not amused.

※

There was a light rap upon the door and someone entered. Dora didn't have the energy to look up from the floor to see who it was.

She heard the clatter of a tray being set down, and then a young woman in a maid's uniform came to her aid. "Oh, miss. Are you all right?"

"The rocking . . ."

"You ain't the only one indisposed. 'Ere, let's get you to bed agin."

Dora let herself be helped; she welcomed it.

"There, now," the maid said. "The steward said you were in need of some nourishment, but he didn't tell me you were all out on the floor. He shoulda helped you."

"He did help," Dora said as the maid arranged the pillows so she could sit up in bed. "I . . . it . . . after he left . . ."

"Well, I'm 'ere now, and I've brought you somethin' soothing."

She retrieved the tray she had set aside during her hasty entrance. "There's chamomile and I brought you some Carr's crackers."

Dora didn't feel like eating. "I don't think—"

"You must eat somethin', miss, or you'll be the worst for it when the drys come."

Oh. Those. Dora had been that sick only once in her life and did *not* want to repeat the process. She nodded, spurring the maid to pour the tea. The girl had to stand with a wide stance in order to remain steady.

"When will the rocking end?" Dora asked.

"When God says so. He's the one in charge out 'ere." She held the filled teacup for Dora and handed her a biscuit. "Just a little bite, like you's a baby."

Dora nibbled the cracker, then sipped the tea with the girl's help.

"There now, that'll help. Later, I'll bring you ginger cookies. The cooks're making a big batch. Ginger helps when people get the sickness."

"Thank you . . . ?" Dora said.

"Annie."

"Thank you, Annie." She imagined all the other people who needed assistance. "I know you have many to help this morning. I'll be all right now."

"Oh, I'm glad to be 'ere with you, miss. When Fred asked someone to help you, I offered right off."

"Why?"

"Because of the broken glass."

Did all the servants know of her fiasco? "I made a mess. I'm so sorry. I—"

The maid shook her head. "No, miss. The mess ain't it at all. It's the fact you got down on the floor in your fancy dress and helped with the cleanup. We've ne'er seen a lady do that before."

No one had. Which had been the problem.

"If you don't mind me saying so, miss, you're the talk of the ship. The Glass Lady, they're calling you. News of a nice one of your kind spreads fast." She suddenly put a hand to her mouth. "I don't mean no offense, miss. I meant—"

Dora knew exactly what she meant. "It's all right, Annie. I meant no offense to anyone either. The glass broke and I reacted without thinking."

"You reacted from a kind heart. That's what my kind are saying." She lowered her voice even though they were alone in the cabin. "Oftener than not when something gets broke, we're the ones 'oo get blamed, and no one lifts a finger to help or even looks up from their chatting."

"It's like you're invisible."

She smiled. "That's it, miss. You're a good one to understand like that. Why, you'd think you was once—"

The cabin door opened and Lottie entered. She took one look at the maid and huffed over to the bed. "Here, I'll take that." She took the cup of tea away. "You can go now."

Annie bobbed at Lottie, then nodded to Dora. "You need anything, you just call. And I'll bring you those cookies when they're baked."

"Thank you, Annie."

As soon as the door clicked shut, Lottie set the teacup aside. "Annie?"

"She was kind, bringing me tea and biscuits." She took another nibble of the cracker. "Did you know the servants on the ship call me the Glass Lady, and it's *not* in a bad way? They think it's wonderful I tried to help clean up the—"

"You should not get familiar with the servants, Dora. And you should certainly not take pride in being the subject of their gossip."

"It's not gossip. They simply appreciated that I helped and—"

"It doesn't matter. You have to keep your place and make sure they know theirs."

"But I understand what they go through. I—"

"You are no longer a servant. In the world's eyes you are a lady, and

103

you need to act like one." Lottie thrust the teacup forward, making it slosh onto the saucer. "Here. Drink. I'll take care of you."

Of the two, Dora would have preferred Annie's care.

Lottie returned from dinner to check on Dora. She opened the door to find a dozen notes pushed under it.

"What's all—?"

Dora was sleeping. Lottie had expected to see her up. There were many more in attendance at dinner, as the seas had finally calmed. But obviously, Dora was worn out.

Lottie collected the envelopes and saw "Miss Connors" written upon each one. Notes asking after her health.

She felt the swell of jealousy rise anew.

In an attempt to counter it, she tiptoed to Dora's side and adjusted the coverlet before exiting the room to join some acquaintances in the salon.

She passed a steward in the corridor and looked over her shoulder in time to see him slip yet another note under the cabin door.

Don't do that!

Lottie started to walk toward the salon, but at the last moment detoured and walked through a door to the outer deck. She was accompanied by an inner argument.

Go to the salon and have a nice evening. Without Dora there, you've a chance to have every man in the room gather round you and—

She shook her head, dispelling the notion. If she were the only woman in the room, the men would not flock to her side.

Well, perhaps they would. But more than likely they would assemble amongst themselves and talk of politics or money. For what man truly liked to converse with a woman? Most did so out of duty, because it was expected. She couldn't imagine any man chatting for the joy of it.

She couldn't say she felt much joy in her meetings with men either. At home she'd attended balls for pleasure and with the goal of finding a husband. Of all the suitable men, Ralph had been the only one who'd incited true interest, but she had to admit that even he had not swept her away like the heroines in her beloved fiction. Where was her prince? Was he in America? Was he Conrad?

Lottie strolled along the outer deck, wrapping her shawl close. She let her gloved fingers skim the railing and was alone but for the occasional couple, linked arm in arm, their heads tilted toward one another in mutual admiration. When passing, Lottie turned toward the sea . . . the inconstant sea.

No. That wasn't right.

The correct line from Shakespeare came to her: *O, swear not by the moon, the inconstant moon, that monthly changes in her circled orb, lest that thy love prove likewise variable.*

Inconstant moon . . .

She stopped walking and turned to the rail. Her eyes sought the moon and found it overhead and full.

Lottie disagreed with Shakespeare. She found the moon extremely constant. Yes, it changed in both position and orb, but it always *was*.

At home she'd counted it a friend, but when they made the annual trip to London she often lost track of it as it hid behind buildings or clouds. Yet Lottie knew it was there if she chose to search for it. She had been the one remiss; the moon was steadfast and dedicated to its function. And now, as she watched it follow her overhead, she felt comfort in the idea that it would retain its constancy in America—if only she looked for it. The moon seemed to be leading her. Surely it would glow brightly over all the land and be the link between her old and new life. It would watch over her.

I'll watch over you.

Lottie looked right, then left, as if the voice that had spoken was real.

And yet she knew it was not—not *real* in the sense of having been audible to anyone but herself.

She whispered the words, giving them reality. "I'll watch over you."

A warmth spread throughout her body, followed by a tingle, as if she had been touched—caressed—from within.

Lottie put a hand to her mouth and found tears far too close. "Please," she whispered. "Do watch over me. Please do."

She looked back at the moon. Its glowing ring pulsed as if responding to her attention. She repeated the words silently, prayerfully.

But then she heard a sound. Like a child crying. Lottie looked around, expecting to see a couple with a fussy child who didn't want to go to bed. But she was alone on the deck.

The sound seemed to be coming from her left. . . .

Lottie moved toward it, toward some stairs leading to the decks below. At the bottom of the stair was a chain forbidding the lower-class passengers from gaining entry to the first-class deck. But there between herself and the chain sat a little boy. Crying.

She walked down the stairs. "Little boy? What's wrong?"

He stopped his crying long enough to look up at her with pale eyes, a grubby face, and tousled blond hair. He looked to be four or five. "Do you know where me ma is?" he asked.

Lottie's heart melted, and she sat on the step beside him. "No, I'm afraid I don't." She could tell by his clothes he wasn't a child from first class. "Where was she when you last saw her?"

"Walking with me da. I was supposed to be asleep with me brother and sis, but I wanted to go with them. They walked too fast. I lost 'em."

Lottie had no idea how to find his parents, and the thought of proceeding to the lower decks was not appealing. "What's your name?"

"Sean."

"What's your last name?"

"O'Grady. I'm never going to find 'em, am I? They told me not to wander off, and I wasn't wanderin', I wanted to walk with 'em." He began to cry again. "They'll ne'er find me. They don' e'en know I'm lost."

Lottie put her arm around him. "Don't cry, now. I'll help you find *them*, all right?"

He sniffed loudly and began to wipe his nose with his sleeve. She stopped that motion and gathered a handkerchief from her purse. "Use this," she said. Sean wiped his nose, then handed it back to her. "You keep it," she said.

Then she noticed him shivering. "Where's your coat?"

"I dunno."

She removed her shawl and arranged it around his shoulders, tying it in front. "There. All better?"

"It's a girl's shawl."

"Don't complain, Mr. O'Grady. Maybe next time you venture out, you'll remember your coat." With the help of the railing she stood and held out her hand. "Come, now. Let's go find your parents."

At the bottom of the stairs, Lottie unhooked the chain and let it dangle. She and Sean walked aft, toward what she hoped would be a main deck.

Unlike the few strollers on deck in first class, many people were out and about on this level, taking a smoke, talking, even a few necking in the shadows. She approached one group after another, asking, "Do you know this boy? Do you know the O'Gradys?" She received odd looks and responses in languages beyond her comprehension. Didn't anyone speak English?

She also received many a look of another kind, glares from head to toe, judging her. Unlike the appreciative looks of the men on her own deck, these looks were either unfriendly or vulgar. She was an intruder into their world, and they didn't like it.

Neither did she.

Lottie walked faster, wanting to find Sean's parents and get back to first class, where she belonged. She was surprised to see that many a grouping had made a fire in a pot and were gathered round it for warmth.

Suddenly Sean shouted, "Ma!"

A woman and man turned toward the sound, and their eyes grew wide. The woman captured Sean as he wrapped his arms around her skirt. "Whatcha doin' outta bed, boy?"

"We told you to stay put."

"I wanted to walk with ya."

Mrs. O'Grady looked at Lottie for the first time. "You found 'im?"

"He was crying on the stairway."

Softening to her son, she caressed his hair. "There, there, now, Seany. We've got ya now."

The father saw the shawl and took it off Sean. "This be yours, I assume?"

"He was cold." She realized it was a stupid thing to say.

Mr. O'Grady took off his own jacket and put it on his son. "We thank ya for taking care of 'im."

Lottie nodded. "I'll be going now."

"Wait!" Mrs. O'Grady took a step toward her. "Get yerself warm first. Come sit by our fire."

The idea was absurd.

But Mrs. O'Grady took her hand and pulled her toward the grouping.

Lottie sat on a crate amid a crowd of a dozen.

"I loves yer dress," one woman said.

"Thank you."

"A lady I worked for 'ad dresses like that."

Lottie wasn't sure how to respond. "You were in service?"

"Twenty years. But enough of that. I'm going to the New World to 'ave me own house 'n' me own business."

There were nods all around, and Lottie was truly interested. "What kind of business would that be?"

"Don' know fer sure, but I ken sew and cook with the best of 'em. Maybe a bakery. I make a mean berry pie."

The man beside her patted his ample belly. "Don' I know it."

"What're you planning to do in America?" a man asked Lottie.

"Sit around and be pretty," another man answered.

Lottie felt herself blush and was glad for the darkness of the night. She knew that with one sentence she could silence them, tell them she was marrying one of the richest heirs in America. Yet instead she said, "I'm not sure what I'm going to do. I'm supposed to marry a man I've never met, but I'm having second thoughts."

Mrs. O'Grady sat beside her with Sean upon her lap. "Me Gregory and me've been married ten years." She looked up at her husband. "He's me other self."

"What a lovely thought," Lottie said. And before she could contain the words, she added, "I envy you. All of you."

There was laughter all around. "You? Envy us?"

She knew it must sound ridiculous—it was ridiculous. She, who sat among them in a dress that cost more than the whole of them made in a year, with a future dripping with wealth and social standing beyond measure, envied *them*? "Perhaps we're not as different as we look," she offered.

The first woman laughed. "Then gimme your dress and I'll give ya mine."

Lottie brushed a hand over the satin of her skirt. "I'd give it all up for a chance to truly love and be loved and to have a real purpose."

More laughter. "I'll help ya find your real purpose," said a man.

"Stop it!" Mr. O'Grady scolded. "This 'ere lady was kind enough to bring Seany back to us. Treat 'er with some respect."

The offender shrugged and left the circle.

It was time to go. "I should be getting back. I don't want to worry anyone."

Mr. O'Grady stood and helped her up. "I'll walk you back."

"That would be nice."

As Lottie started to walk away, Sean climbed off his mother's lap and ran to her, wrapping his arms around her legs. "Thank you, lady."

The feel of his embrace elicited unfamiliar feelings. She lifted his chin with a finger. "You do what your parents tell you to, all right, Sean O'Grady?"

"Yes, ma'am."

Lottie walked with Mr. O'Grady. It was a bit awkward, but she was glad for his company. "What are your plans once you arrive in America?" she asked him.

"To work hard."

"Doing what?"

"Whatever job I ken get. Hopefully one thing will lead to the next and we'll be happy."

"You weren't happy before?"

"We was settled, but that was all there was to it. America offers us the chance at somethin' more, a chance to choose our life, not live one set for us by others."

She was moved by the intensity of his assertion. "But it's a great risk, yes?"

"Better to risk an' fail than never try."

Lottie felt her throat tighten. She would have liked to talk to him longer, but they were back at the stairs. "There," she said. "I found Sean there."

Mr. O'Grady picked up the fallen chain. "That imp. He shoulda known better than go past 'ere."

"He was just exploring," Lottie said. "That trait should suit him well in America."

"Or lead him into trouble."

That too.

Mr. O'Grady held out his hand. Lottie hesitated a moment, then shook it.

"I thank you agin for takin' care of 'im for us. God bless you fer it, miss."

"God bless you too."

Lottie ascended the stairs to the first-class deck and looked back to see Mr. O'Grady reattaching the chain at the bottom of the stairs, a subtle line that wasn't to be crossed.

And yet . . . she was very glad to have crossed it.

Making her way toward her stateroom, she noticed the moon once more. The same moon that shone for her shone for the O'Gradys and their travel mates.

One moon.

One ship.

One goal. To start over, to start fresh, to risk everything for something better.

Suddenly Lottie stopped and turned directly toward the moon. "I can't marry Conrad. I can't settle on a life set for me by others."

The simple statement grew large in her mind, overshadowing the doubt and questions that had lingered for weeks. And as it gained strength and clarity, Lottie realized marrying Conrad would be settling for a lesser goal. Like Mr. O'Grady had said, *"Better to risk and fail than never try."*

Lottie felt a breeze pick up and was mentally transported back to her walk on the grounds of Dornby Manor after she'd accepted that she was going to America. She'd thought about running off on her own even then. It was her secret plan. She *could* be free.

Her mind skipped to an earlier memory, a handful of words said by Dora. *"If you don't want him, I'll take him."*

Conrad. They'd been talking about marrying Conrad.

Dora had passed it off as a joke, but . . .

Could it be something more? Could it be the solution to everything?

Could Dora take Lottie's place at the Tremaines', pretending to be Charlotte Gleason? She'd successfully come this far in playing the part of a lady; why not go one step further?

If Dora took Lottie's place, that would leave Lottie free to . . . to what?

On impulse Lottie removed her shawl and held its corners with either hand, lifting it into the air. It billowed above her like a sail, taking her to—

To?

A new life.

Could it be that simple?

She'd risk it. She had to.

Dora heard the door of the stateroom and opened one eye. Lottie entered, but didn't just enter—she burst into the room.

Dora sat up in bed. "What's wrong? Did something happen at dinner?"

"Forget dinner. But yes, something happened that will change our lives. Forever."

Her mind was hazy. *What is Lottie talking about now?*

Dora tried to stand and Lottie came to her aid. "Are you feeling better?"

She gauged her answer. "I believe I am. The ship . . . it's not rocking?"

"Not since early afternoon. The sea is calm."

Dora couldn't remember the last time she'd looked at a clock. "I've slept away the day?"

"As you should have."

Dora was horrified she'd slept so long. It was disconcerting to lose track of time. Plus, she was disappointed to have missed a day of her trip and time with Dr. Greenfield. To have experienced such a success at the ball, only to disappear . . .

Her disappointment faded to resignation. She'd enjoyed playing the part of the princess for one night. Most women never got that chance. "Here. Let me help with your dress," she told Lottie.

"Forget the dress, Dora! Didn't you hear me? Our lives are about to change forever."

She might as well listen. There would be no rest until Lottie had her say. "Go ahead, then. Tell me."

Lottie paced as she told some farfetched story of finding a lost Irish boy, going down to a lower deck to seek out his parents, and sitting on a crate by a fire. It was too fantastic to be true.

"Why don't you believe me?"

"You, who wouldn't even let me look at the people on the lower decks, went among them? Alone? At night?"

"A little boy needed help."

"Since when have you cared for children?"

"I care for children. Just because I haven't been around them doesn't mean I don't care—" Lottie stopped pacing and glared at Dora, her hands on her hips. "Let me finish. I haven't even reached the good part."

Dora gave her a by-your-leave wave.

"I told you all that to tell you this: *I* am not going to marry Conrad. You are. As me. Pretending to be me."

Dora stopped breathing for just a moment. Then she laughed. "Me? Marry Conrad Tremaine? Heir to one of the richest families in America? Certainly. Why not? Or perhaps I should marry one of Queen Victoria's grandsons and really have a good go of it."

Lottie perched on the edge of the vanity bench, her hand to her mouth, her eyes racing. Dora had seen that look before. A scheme was being hatched, and considering the failure rate of past plans, Dora was hesitant to hear more.

But Lottie had more to tell. "The idea just came to me like a bolt. Why don't *you* marry him? What if you took my place at the Tremaines'?"

"Me. Be you." It was absurd.

Lottie rose and resumed her pacing. "We look alike; people have always mentioned as much. And the only photograph Conrad has of me is very small, in a frame no larger than a compact. And not a very good one either. I wanted a new one taken, but Father . . ." Her eyes cleared. "He probably couldn't afford it."

Dora caught a glimpse of herself in the vanity mirror along with the reflection of Lottie pacing the room. There *was* a strong resemblance. Although her own hair was more strawberry than champagne, the distinction would not be apparent in a photograph. Nor would her extra inch in height be measurable. Nor her green eyes to Lottie's blue.

Stop it! It's a ridiculous idea. It could never work. "How did one stroll on the deck, finding one little boy, ever bring you to this idea?"

"It doesn't matter how; it only matters that it happened. And when I thought of it, I realized what a relief it was to set myself free of all that."

Dora wasn't about to give in to Lottie's fantasies so easily. "Then don't marry him. But why do you think I should do it?"

"Because you can. You, who've grown up with nothing, can now have everything. And if you'd like, you could even share that wealth—with your mother perhaps?"

Dora's thoughts raced. "Ma always wanted to get out of service and open her own little sweet shop."

"There you have it. With Conrad's money your mother can have a large sweet shop, packed full of clerks selling chocolates and pretty cakes."

Dora looked at her bed, assuring herself that she was fully awake. "Marrying a man like Conrad Tremaine would be a fairy tale. What girl wouldn't want to marry a rich heir?"

"Me," Lottie said.

Dora was skeptical. "You say that now, but once you get to New York you'll change your mind." And once Lottie did that, there would be pain involved. If Dora let herself accept this incredible dream even a little . . .

Lottie shook her head vehemently. "I won't change my mind. And where's your courage, Dora? If these people of lesser means can risk everything, so can we."

"They have less to risk."

"Do they?" She knew it was a complicated question, for surely the emigrants had fewer material possessions at risk. But then again, because they had no cushion to fall back on, perhaps their risk was even greater than her own. Or Dora's. "I want to find my own happiness, Dora. I want true love."

"So do I."

Lottie's eyebrows rose. "If you're thinking of Dr. Greenfield . . ."

Dora hadn't admitted as much to herself, but what Lottie said was true. "What if I am?"

"He's the physician to the queen."

"*Was* the physician. He's starting over in America, just as we are."

"Just because he's shown interest in you here . . ."

Dora was hurt. No, she was not entering America as a member of the social elite, but she *was* entering as Lottie's companion. Surely such distinctions could be blurred if she acted like a lady and earned the approval of society. What she'd accomplished on the ship could be continued on land.

Lottie persisted with her argument. "If things stay as they are and you're my companion at the Tremaines', Dr. Greenfield will have nothing to do with you."

"But I won't be your maid. I'll—"

"Forgive me for being blunt, Dora, but as Dora Connors you are not one of *us*."

And there it was. The truth that could never be denied no matter what fancy dress Dora put on. Back in England, high society was a closely knit group who linked arms at any attempt to breach their bastions. She had no reason to believe New York society was any different.

"There, there, Dora," Lottie said with a pat to Dora's arm. "You may not be able to have Dr. Greenfield, but I am giving you the chance at someone far more important."

Dora shook her head, incredulous. "So now Conrad Tremaine is a catch? A man worth marrying?"

"He was always *worth* marrying, Dora. I just didn't want to do it."

Once again it came down to the stalwart fact that Lottie never did what she didn't want to do.

Lottie handily set Dora's objections aside. "Don't you see? Since I've been virtually kicked out of my old life in England, once in America, with this new chance . . . I want adventure. I want to explore new worlds."

"You've never been anywhere alone."

"Then it's time for a change."

Lottie's quick answers were exasperating. "If you don't want to marry Conrad, then why don't you and I go off together and explore new worlds?"

Lottie hesitated a little at this one. "Because we would need money, and . . ."

"And?"

Lottie answered in a burst. "I do have my family's jewels to sell. I can survive on that, but I don't know if I'll be able to get enough to support two of us."

Money was an issue. Money was always an issue.

"There is another reason we can't go off together. I don't want my parents to worry," Lottie said. "If you take my place, they'll believe all is well, that I'm taken care of. Charlotte Gleason will be where she's supposed to be. If I tell them I'm heading off on my own, they'll be mad with worry. I don't want to do that to Mother. She has enough to deal with at home. Once I'm established and the need for worry is gone, I'll contact them."

There was a large flaw in her plan. "But once your parents know what's been done, won't they contact the Tremaines and tell them the truth—that I'm *not* you?"

"And create another scandal?" Lottie shook her head. "I think not. Besides, when I asked Father if the Tremaines knew about our family's problems, he said, 'What the Tremaines don't know won't hurt them.'"

"He said that?"

"He did. So you see, he's not beyond fudging the truth to suit his needs. If it becomes an issue, I might even write Father a letter stating that if he tattles, I will tell the Tremaines he misrepresented our financial strength as well as the precariousness of our social position."

It made sense—in a Lottie sort of way. And yet . . . "Isn't that blackmail?"

Lottie shrugged. "We are here, on this ship, because of my father. I am fleeing everything I know because of him. He owes me."

It still didn't seem quite right, but Dora had other questions. To begin with, "What if I don't like Conrad? What if he doesn't like me?"

"Then don't marry him. You and I will be in touch, and if the worst happens, you can come live with me." With a snap of her fingers, Lottie expected to make everything work.

"But *then* what of your parents?"

With a quick shake of her head the question was dismissed. "We'll deal with that when or if the time comes." She took Dora's hands in hers. "Come on, Dora. This is perfect. We'll each gain our own adventures and find happiness."

"Or not."

Lottie tossed Dora's hands away. "You *will* think about it."

It was not a question. "Yes, of course, but—"

Lottie showed Dora her back. "Help me off with this. I want to get to bed. We have a lot to do in the few days before we land. A lot to plan."

Oh dear.

❦

Sleep eluded her.

It was hard for Dora to comprehend the journey she'd taken. It had nothing to do with miles of ocean, but with the distance she'd traveled between being a lowly maid to having the chance to marry one of the wealthiest men in America. Along the way she'd dipped her toe into a refreshing pool of romance with Dr. Greenfield. . . .

Was Lottie correct in stating that she had no future with the good doctor? Unfortunately, Lottie's reasoning made sense. Once they reached New York, Dora would not be Lottie's equal, but her companion—her lesser companion. As the former physician to the queen, Dr. Greenfield would have nothing to do with her—whether he wished to or not. Society would not allow it.

An old hymn started playing in Dora's head. *The rich man in his castle, the poor man at his gate, God made them, high or lowly, and ordered their estate. . . .*

There was an order to things. If she wasn't good enough for Dr. Greenfield, how could she ever be good enough for Conrad Tremaine?

But I wouldn't be Dora Connors. I'd be Charlotte Gleason.

Her head ached from the clash of what could never be with what could, perhaps, maybe . . . She could never be Mrs. Edmund Greenfield, but she might be able to be Mrs. Conrad Tremaine.

If she could pull it off. If the moon and the stars aligned—and if God approved.

What did the Almighty think of this plan?

Thou shalt not lie.

The string of lies that had brought them this far was crooked and unwieldy and had started with Lottie's father. As Lottie had stated, his actions were the cause of their current situation. Would it be so horrible for Lottie to find her happiness beyond the scope of her father's plan, and for Dora to grab hold of this chance in her stead?

Dora wouldn't be the only one to benefit. If all went well, her mother could put an end to her life of servitude and find happiness running her own shop. Her mother had lost a husband and three children and had worked eighteen hours a day her entire life. Didn't she deserve a chance to be happy?

Wasn't it Dora's duty to try to provide her with that chance?

What about Conrad? What about the Tremaines? What have they ever done to be the recipients of such deceit?

Lottie's voice interrupted the darkness, and her thoughts. "Are you awake?"

"Of course."

"You can do this, you know."

Dora had said the very same words in the dark just a few days previous. She answered now as Lottie had answered then. "I know."

And with those two words, Dora shut away her doubts, her fears, and her conscience.

I can do this.

She had to try.

Chapter Eight

Lottie closed the lid on the last trunk. "There," she said. "I hereby bequeath to you these lovely clothes. May you wear them well." In spite of her bravado, she felt a stitch in her stomach. To leave these gowns with someone else . . .

Dora glanced at the much smaller trunk. "Are you sure you only want to take a few?"

No. Lottie was not sure. But she felt ill at ease presuming upon the hospitality of Dora's cousin with a bevy of luggage. Yet to make sure they did connect, Lottie had sent a telegram announcing her upcoming arrival. She prayed everything would fall into place.

In their final days on board, as Lottie expected, Dora had relinquished her impossible dream of pursuing a relationship with Dr. Greenfield and had agreed to *become* Charlotte Gleason. Once the decision was made, Lottie inundated her with the finer points of being a lady while coming up with her own plan. Once in New York, Lottie's first task would be to sell her jewels. With that accomplished, she would have money to live on.

As if reading her thoughts, Dora said, "I'm sad you're going to sell your good jewelry. You could also have these costume sets we've been wearing. I don't need to wear jewels of any sort."

"You most certainly do," Lottie said. "You can't wear my gowns without them or the Tremaines will think less of you. Until Conrad gives you presents of your own, you must wear the lesser jewels proudly. Remember, what they don't know, you don't have to tell." She stood erect, her chin held high. "It's all a matter of carriage, Dora. Act regal and people will perceive you as such."

Dora mirrored Lottie's posture but soon wavered into her normal unassuming stance. "I'll be on pins and needles the entire time. In spite of your patient teaching, I don't know what I'm doing. This isn't going to work."

"It will work." Lottie was not as confident as she portrayed. "Take heart, Dora. Your path is more certain than my own. You have a vocation to fall back on. I have no skills other than how to do needlework, play the piano, sing in a manner so as not to make listeners cringe, and read aloud with a certain flair. These menial talents are of little use to the world beyond the drawing room."

Yet Lottie felt good about making this decision. It was her one big chance. In her parents' house her opinions had counted for little. Although she'd spent a lifetime with every material whim met, her opinion on matters of the heart, mind, and soul had either been ignored, discarded, or cut off like a bothersome smoking wick. Once she landed in America, she would have to rely upon herself alone.

Sink or swim.

Amid all Lottie's bravado came the undeniable knowledge that her own worth had never been measured by anything she thought or achieved, but was mired in who she was according to society—a society that had proved to be dishearteningly fickle. What worth would she have in New York—away from the upper-crust life?

Dora put on a hat, securing it with a long pin. "I suppose I have little to lose. If I don't do this, I will always wonder what might have been."

"Precisely," Lottie said.

"And if we're totally wrong . . . I suppose God will forgive us and set us right again."

Lottie didn't like the sound of that.

There was a knock on the cabin door. The porters had come for the luggage. Lottie took charge. "Here they are. The trunks are ready to go."

As the porters left, a ship's officer knocked on the opened door. As soon as he saw Dora, he nodded a greeting. "Miss Connors. I trust your voyage was enjoyable?"

"You have all been most hospitable."

Lottie didn't like being ignored, especially since the purser was holding her box of jewels brought from the safe. "If you don't mind?" she asked.

He blushed at the sight of her, obviously realizing his faux pas. "Yes. Indeed. Miss Gleason. Here are your belongings, safe and sound."

She took them, feeling better for having the leather box in her possession.

He turned to leave. "I hope you have a pleasant stay in New York, ladies."

"Thank you, we—"

"I had a pleasant voyage too," Lottie said. "If you're interested."

His face reddened even more and he touched the tip of his hat and left them.

"Lottie, that was rude."

"Was it polite for him to ignore me and fawn over you?"

"He knew me. I'd met him. It was not a slight against—"

She was done with it. "Enough. Let's go on deck to watch the city rise before us."

"Hello, ladies." Lottie and Dora turned to see Dr. Greenfield coming up beside them at the rail.

"Good morning, Doctor," Lottie said.

Dora nodded a greeting, feeling her cheeks grow hot.

He looked directly at her. "I've missed spending much time with you these past few days."

"She's been busy with the details of our arrival," Lottie said. "*We've* been busy."

"How unfortunate. For now we arrive."

In a few hours this man would be gone, absorbed into the population of America. The thought made Dora incredibly sad.

"What are your plans in New York, Doctor?" Lottie asked. "You have been the physician to royalty. There is no royalty here."

He laughed. "Although Americans acknowledge titles, in truth they think them a novelty, an endearment of sorts. They consider titles . . ." He searched for the word. "Amusing."

"Perhaps they're jealous," Lottie said.

"Perhaps," he said. "Yet they did have the chance to create a monarchy. That they chose this other way . . ."

"They are stuck with it now," Lottie said.

He chuckled. "But to answer your question, royals or no royals, I've been bitten by the American bug. I'm going to join a practice here. My cousin is a doctor and well established. He offered me a position a few months ago, and I . . . I'm taking the plunge. It's quite exciting to start over."

"Yes, quite." It was the first time Dora had spoken, and her words were full of inner meaning. She gazed over the harbor that stood before them. The buildings of New York City stood shoulder to shoulder like children vying for the best view. And they on the ship followed suit and stood at the railing, awaiting a formal introduction. Or a harsh rejection?

"What is that, on that island?" Lottie asked, pointing ahead.

"That, dear ladies, is Lady Liberty. 'Tis a gift from France, just completed. They built the entire statue in a workroom in Paris, dismantled it, and reassembled it here."

It seemed odd to have one country give another country such a gift. "But why?" Lottie asked.

"To celebrate the friendship the French and Americans began during their revolution. Their revolution against us," he said.

"As a British citizen, I feel rather left out," Lottie said.

He laughed again. "The Americans owe much to the French. Without their help we would be landing in one of our very own colonies."

Dora leaned forward and looked at the lower decks that were lined with hundreds of people, entire families, coming to America with the highest hopes.

As was she.

"Miss Connors . . ."

The change in Dr. Greenfield's tone necessitated that Dora look at him.

"Yes, Doctor?"

"When we land, after you've had a chance to settle in, I was wondering if you . . ." He sighed. "Oh dear, you would think I were a schoolboy in this."

Dora guessed the direction of their exchange and panicked even as she felt intense satisfaction. He *was* interested in her! Yet she mustn't allow him to broach the question of seeing her. Once they landed, Dora Connors would no longer exist. She looked to her other side, hoping for Lottie's quick answers, but discovered her friend in conversation with another couple.

"Oh, let me just say it," he said in a rush. "I would enjoy the honor of calling upon you while you are in New York City. Would that be agreeable?"

Actually, a few days ago, or at any other time, in any other situation, it would have pleased her beyond measure. Dr. Greenfield had been her dashing prince who could whisk her away into a happy ending. That she had gained the attention of such a man was beyond her imagining. That she would have to shun him now . . .

There was no way around it. She and Lottie had made a pact. It was too late to abandon it now. "I'm extremely honored by your offer, Dr. Greenfield, and I've fully enjoyed your acquaintance and your kind attention on our journey, but . . ." She offered her own sigh and found it hard to get the words out. "In truth, I'm to be betrothed."

He looked aghast. "Betrothed? But you never—"

No, she had never. Doubts assailed her. Who knew what Conrad Tremaine would be like. What his family would be like. Or if she would even be able to carry off the masquerade. Dr. Greenfield liked her—as she liked him.

"I am truly sorry," she said. "I enjoyed our friendship and cherish the time we had together more than you'll ever know. That I didn't give you full disclosure as to my plans upon landing in America . . . that I may have hurt you in any way . . ."

He looked upon the busy harbor. "It is unfortunate."

She didn't know what else to say. This man had made her feel wanted, desired, and appreciated. He'd given her the gift of confidence when she'd possessed none.

"If the situation were different," she said, but could say no more.

He looked at her with a gleam in his eyes. "But . . . you aren't betrothed yet?" he asked.

She felt the faintest flutter. "No, I'm not, but—"

"Then permit me to be bold. Permit me to let my prayers and the decision of God finish our story."

Our story?

"Would you agree to giving me that much hope, Miss Connors?"

Give *him* hope? His words gave *her* hope, blessed hope. "I . . . I suppose."

A traveling companion of Dr. Greenfield joined them. "Excuse me, Doctor, but Mr. Bram Stoker wishes to speak with you before we land."

He turned to Dora and took her hand, bringing it to his lips. "Until fate allows," he said.

Dora watched him walk away and felt an awful panic. *Come back! Don't leave!* He was a wonderful, kind, appealing man and made her feel wonderful, kind, and appealing in return. That he would soon disappear amid the buildings that marked New York . . .

What have I done?

Lottie returned to her side. "Did you chase him off?" she asked, nodding toward Dr. Greenfield.

"He asked to call on me in New York."

Lottie's eyebrows rose. "But he can't."

"I know. But—"

"There are no buts," Lottie said.

But there were. "What if I don't go through with the masquerade? What if I remain myself?"

"And what of me, then?" Lottie asked. "When the Tremaines find no one at the dock, they'll contact my family and the alarm will sound. They'll come looking for me. Do you really want to cause such turmoil?"

And there *would* be turmoil. "But I like the doctor and—"

"We've been through this, Dora. If you remain Dora Connors, what will you do to make a living?"

"I suppose I'll be a maid."

Lottie snickered. "Do you actually think Dr. Greenfield will be interested in Miss Connors, the maid?"

Dora felt the breath go out of her. There was no way for their friendship to succeed.

"Push him out of your mind, Dora. He is not for you and you are not for him. Conrad is your future—is the future of Charlotte Gleason."

A phrase her mother taught her stepped forward, demanding her attention. *What a tangled web we weave, when first we practice to deceive.*

The image of a huge, hideous web spread across her mind. Dora prayed she wouldn't get caught in it. And eaten alive.

⁂

As the ship dropped anchor, everyone on board seemed to hold their breath. It was time. They had arrived.

Or had they?

"We're still in the harbor," Dora said. "How do we get to shore?"

They were anchored a good distance from land, nearer the island that held the Statue of Liberty than to the island named Manhattan. Their destination was a rounded fortlike structure that jutted into the water at the tip of Manhattan. It had a large, windowed cupola on top that sported an American flag waving in the wind. This was Castle Garden, where all immigrants started their American journey. She could see why they called it a castle, but could not see any gardens.

Lottie didn't know how they would get from the *Etruria* to shore but upon seeing smaller boats encircle the ship pretended she did. "There. They'll pick us up and take us to Castle Garden."

Dora nodded, accepting the guess as truth. The girl was visibly nervous and had nearly shredded a handkerchief. "But how will we get our luggage? There's an enormous amount of it. I don't want to lose all my beautiful clothes before I even get to wear them."

My beautiful clothes.

"It will be a long process, that's for certain," Lottie said. "With nearly fifteen hundred people on board—"

Dora looked aghast. "That many?"

"All told." Lottie liked knowing things Dora did not. "Five hundred first class, one hundred sixty in second, and eight hundred in steerage."

"How do you know that?"

She had always been good with numbers. "I made friends with the crew too, Dora. The first mate was quite attentive." Too attentive. He'd cornered Lottie on one of her strolls and had rattled off far too much information about the ship. She'd had to feign another engagement to be rid of him.

Dora's forehead continued to be furrowed with worry. "We telegraphed the Tremaines from the ship, but what if they come to the dock and it takes too long and they leave and—"

"They will not leave."

"Maybe they'll send a servant to fetch me. I would feel better if they're not put out, if only a servant is forced to wait."

Dora seemed to have little concept regarding her newfound position. "Firstly, you are not being *fetched*, Dora. You are not a spaniel or a cow in a pasture. Conrad telegraphed that he'll be there to meet you with his sister, Beatrice."

"At least it won't be his parents. I fear them the most."

"With good reason."

The panic in Dora's eyes caused Lottie to suffer a twinge of guilt. She should calm her friend's fears, not add to them. And yet, in these final hours, she couldn't help herself. The full implication of their plan was settling upon her shoulders and proved to be a heavy burden. "The Tremaines didn't gain their vast wealth by being stupid or ignorant, Dora. I expect them to be very savvy about people and situations."

"But I'm not savvy! They'll know something is amiss. They won't believe I'm you. I can't do this! Besides, it's not fair to them. They're expecting a real lady."

Dora was making a scene, talking far too loudly, causing the other first-class passengers to cast odd glances in their direction.

Lottie put a hand upon her back. "Shh. Do you wish to ruin your chances right here and now, before we've even assumed our new identities?"

Dora looked at the other passengers assembled close by. "I'm sorry," she whispered. "I just want it to be over. I won't be able to relax until I'm safely ensconced at the Tremaines'."

Merely being in the Tremaine household would only be the beginning of Dora's trials. But Lottie was merciful and didn't mention it.

Waiting. Life was waiting. It was not one of Lottie's strong suits.

The first-class passengers had been allowed onto the first boats to shore, and once on land had been subjected to a very brief medical exam. A woman with a bad cough was told to step aside and her husband accompanied her. Lottie was extremely glad she was in good health. What were they going to do with the woman? Send her home? Were only the healthy allowed to enter America?

They may have been first on the transfer boats and first through the medical exam, but once they entered the building called Castle Garden, they were first in nothing. The building was circular in shape with arched columns rising two stories. The center was open to the sun, letting a beam of God-light access to the floor. The floor had divisions built upon it, looking like animal runs and pens. A wide balcony rimmed with windows encircled the room, which was teeming with thousands of people. There was no first class here. All were equal upon coming to America. All were new, all were confused, and all were tired.

"We'll never get through this," Dora said.

Lottie had not expected the crowds. These weren't merely passengers from their own ship but also from ships that had anchored before them. Many ships, from the looks of it.

"Come on, now," a constable said. "Move it along."

"Sir? Where is our luggage?" Lottie asked.

He glanced at the leather box she held to her chest. She hoped he wouldn't ask to see inside.

"You'll get it soon enough," he said. "You have to register first. Then you change your money to dollars, arrange for transportation, and *then* you get your luggage." He pointed to the right. "English-speaking line's over there."

Thankfully, their line was far shorter than the other lines that accommodated foreign languages. Lottie couldn't imagine coming to a country and not speaking the language. The deficit would make a nerve-wracking experience nerve-shattering.

Lottie looked ahead to the men seated behind a long counter. Each had a large book spread open before them. She pulled Dora to the line on the left because the man looked nicer than the others. But as they neared their turn, Lottie wondered about her box of jewels. She didn't know if the registrar would ask about it, or even notice it. She didn't want her jewelry displayed for all to see, nor did she want to risk the chance that the registrar would see fit to help himself to a bauble as a form of toll. She held the box down, within the folds of her skirt.

Dora was first to step up to the man.

"Name?"

Dora cleared her throat. "Charlotte Regina Gleason." She glanced back at Lottie.

And that was that. Lottie was no longer Charlotte Gleason. Her name was gone. Forever.

"Spell the last name, please," the man asked.

Dora spelled it out, and each letter pronounced was like a clock ticking down the final moment when all that was Lottie was finished.

Step up and tell them you're *Charlotte Gleason. It's your last chance. Don't throw your life away!*

But it was too late. The registrant was on to the next question. "Age?"

"Nineteen."

He smiled at Dora. "And a pretty nineteen it is too, miss."

"Thank you."

He cleared his throat and went back to the listing. "Nationality?"

"British. I'm from Dornby Manor in Wiltshire."

He wrote it down.

"Ship name?"

"Etruria."

"And your final destination?"

"Here," Dora said. "New York City."

What is my *final destination?* Dora knew where she was going, but Lottie . . .

"Thank you, miss." He winked. "Next."

Lottie stepped forward.

"Name?"

And there it was. The moment when she would finalize the bargain. She drew in a fresh breath. "Lottie Hathaway," she said. Of all the names in the world to choose from, Lottie had decided upon a surname that had personal meaning. Eliza Hathaway had been her beloved nanny throughout her early childhood. She'd lost track of her these last few years, but using her surname now made the transition from Lottie's old life to this new one less painful. If she could become a woman as kind and good as her nanny, she would consider herself well done.

She answered the rest of the questions without incident. And then they were through.

Dora slipped her hand through Lottie's arm. "There," she said. "It is finished."

Lottie forced herself to take a deep breath, a new breath in a new country with a new name and a new life. Did she feel different?

She did. For here, now, there was no history to rest upon, no family name to signal her position and status, no relations or friends to offer a constant assurance of who she was in the scheme of living, and no timetable of what to do when, and how, and with whom.

All the familiar constraints and restraints she had accepted, tolerated, and complained about fell from her being like dust particles being swiped from a coat, only to dissipate into the air, invisible until they accumulated on the floor and were trod upon by a thousand footfalls.

Lottie should have felt free and renewed. Yet without the familiar structure of the *known*, she felt complete and utter panic.

What have I done?

"Block the view," Lottie said.

Dora was confused.

Lottie made a spin-around motion with a hand. "I want to put my new dollars and cents in with my jewelry and don't want the entire world to watch me do it."

Ah. Dora turned around so Lottie could fiddle with her jewelry box behind her. She'd let Lottie have all the money Mr. Gleason had given them. Surely the Tremaines would provide for Dora's needs. The transaction in Castle Garden had gone smoothly, yet almost too much so. With swift motions the money changers had taken Lottie's pounds and shillings and had handed her American money in return. Dora was pretty certain Lottie had been cheated, yet they were in no position to argue.

"There," Lottie said when she was finished with the transfer. "You can't be too careful. Now let's go claim our luggage."

Just as passengers had been ferried from the ship to land, so was the luggage. Dozens of sailors and dock workers moved the luggage from barge to dock, until a heap of suitcases, trunks, and parcels were spread before them. Moving around its boundary were dozens of people in all manner of dress and nationality, each with wide eyes searching the mountain for their possessions.

Dora approached an official-looking gentleman. "Excuse me, sir, but is this the luggage from the *Etruria*?"

He looked around the dock. "Not that pile over there, but this one, yes. This is the *Etruria*'s."

"How do we claim it?"

He tapped a pencil to a pad of paper on a clipboard. "You just points it out and my company will take it anywhere in the city." He showed her the letterhead of the top page. " 'The Castle Garden Express Company.' That's me."

A young man wearing odd shoes made from wood came forward and asked the official, *"Hoe krijg ik mijn bagage?"*

"Hey, now," the official said to the young man. "I'm helping the lady here. Wait yer turn."

The boy looked at Dora, then seemed to comprehend. He nodded and took a step back. An elderly woman wrapped in a plaid shawl moved to his side. Her hair was completely white and her face as wrinkled as a dried apple, and Dora wondered what had been so horrible in her home country that she would suffer a trip to a new one at her age.

"Here, now," the man said to Dora. "Do you sees yer luggage yet?"

"I do!" Lottie said. "Those six trunks with the red *X*'s on them, over there, and there."

"Good job with the *X*'s. Helps the process." The man began writing. "Now alls I need is an address."

"Addresses," Lottie said. She retrieved a paper from her reticule. "The five largest trunks go to the Tremaine residence at Thirty-fourth and Fifth, and the other one—"

"Hold yer horses. Let me get the first one down."

Dora let Lottie handle the addresses and kept her eye upon the trunks. The throng of humanity was astonishing. She had never known there were people of such diversity. She saw dark-haired people with brightly colored shawls and bundles of goods on their heads, and families of four and six children with matching fur caps pulled down low to their ears. There were others who were stranger still with deep brown skin, and others with odd eyes, and still others wearing clothes that looked to be made from wrapped bedsheets. And the languages . . . some guttural, some clipped, some fluid . . . and smells both foul and fruity, spicy and sour. It was as if the population of the entire world had decided New York City was *the* place to be, and had crossed half the globe to get there.

Lottie gave the man a few coins and handed Dora a slip of paper. "Keep this until they're delivered," she said. "I certainly hope your cousin is at home to get the delivery of my trunk."

"I certainly hope she's here to get the delivery of you," Dora added. "We're not entirely sure she's received the telegram of your coming."

133

"I can't worry about that now," Lottie said. "I'm here and I don't plan on stopping until I get to her address—with or without her to accompany me." She pointed to the left. "There. That's the way out."

They walked down the dock and sidestepped the Castle Garden building. A man thrust a piece of paper at them and said, "God's in America too, ladies. Don't forget Him!"

Dora looked at the paper and saw some Bible verses there along with the address of a church. She was glad for the man's reminder. Traveling so far from what she'd known, it *had* seemed as though she'd left God behind, that He somehow lived only in Wiltshire and had yet to catch up with her journey.

"God's in America too, ladies."

"Apples? Apples, a penny!"

An old woman sat alongside three bushels of apples. She looked right at them. "Ladies? An apple a day keeps the doctor away."

Dora immediately thought of Dr. Greenfield. If an apple would keep him away, she wanted nothing to do—

Lottie stepped forward, opened her leather box, and removed two pennies.

"Thank you, ladies. God bless."

Yes. Please, God. We need your blessings—and your protection. And direction. And mercy. And . . .

They entered a wide expanse of park with stone walls and benches that were occupied with people waiting. At least it was a beautiful October day. Where would all these people have gone if it were raining?

"What now?" Dora asked.

"Now you walk toward the street and look for the Tremaines. You've seen a picture of Conrad. And you know they'll have a fine carriage waiting for you."

Dora stopped walking and faced her. "And you?"

She pointed ahead. "There's an elevated train. If I don't see anyone holding up a sign with your name on it, I'll assume your cousin isn't coming and I'll ask which is the best way to get to her house."

"You've never taken a train alone," Dora said. "Do you know how to buy a ticket? Perhaps I should stay with you until—"

"I need to do things on my own now, Dora. Go on. Don't worry about me."

But Dora did worry about her—*would* worry about her. Lottie had never had to plan anything beyond how to spend a free hour or what to wear.

And yet . . . they'd come this far. Perhaps the excitement of this new beginning had awakened something in Lottie that had never been allowed to blossom. It was a hopeful thought.

Suddenly, through a break in the crowd, Dora spotted a carriage that outshone the other lesser hacks. A coachman stood at its side, holding a sign that said *MISS CHARLOTTE GLEASON.*

Her heart jumped the full length of her body before landing in its proper place. "They're here," she whispered. She pointed.

Lottie gently moved her hand downward. "It's not polite to point."

The litany of the do's and don'ts of polite society ran through Dora's mind. *Don't tink the edge of your teacup with your spoon. As a guest don't touch the piano or handle ornaments or furniture in the room unless invited to do so. Never wear gloves at the dining table. Always wear gloves when you dance. Address a boy under age fifteen by his Christian name, but do not call an older man by his Christian name until he tells you it's all right to do so. Do not—*

"It's time, Charlotte."

It was the first time Dora had been addressed by her new name. She liked the sound of it, and yet . . . she felt a bit wistful leaving "Dora Connors" behind. *Good-bye, Ma. Good-bye, Barney.*

"The Tremaines are waiting for you."

Yes, yes. She had to move forward. "Do I look all right?" She felt both tailored and feminine in her navy blue walking suit with its zouave-style cape and wood buttons. She appreciated Lottie's taste in adding a red feather to her bonnet.

"You look ready to greet the world."

If only she owned this outer confidence within.

"Come, now," Lottie said. "We must say our good-byes. You mustn't keep the Tremaines waiting."

Lottie extended her free arm, and Dora returned the awkward embrace. "I'll miss you, Lottie. We've known each other for so many—"

"I'll miss you too." Lottie pushed away and Dora saw tears in her eyes. "Now go," she said. "And wear the Gleason name with pride."

"Write to me?" Dora asked. "Send word that you've reached my cousin's, that you're safe and well."

"I won't be there long."

"Then send word of your whereabouts, wherever they may be."

"I will."

"I'll pray for you, Lottie."

"And I for both of us."

And so Dora—Charlotte—walked toward the carriage. *Don't look back. It will only make it harder for both of us.*

She focused on the carriage and saw two people inside. Was this her future husband? Her future sister-in-law? If only they would look toward her and smile. *That* would be a proper memory of this first meeting.

Instead the coachman took a step forward and tipped his top hat. "Miss Gleason?"

"Yes."

"Where is your luggage?"

Had she done something wrong? "I had it sent to the house."

"Hmm. Are there not two of you?"

Two!

He continued. "Did you not bring a companion with you?"

Lottie is gone. We're not together. What if she needs me? What if I need her?

"Miss?"

Charlotte remembered their agreed-upon answer to such an inquiry.

"My friend has decided to go her own way." She left it at that, and though the coachman looked as though he wished to ask more, he did not. It wasn't his place. Instead, he stepped toward the carriage door and rapped upon it with a gloved knuckle before opening it. Conrad stopped his conversation and looked up.

At her.

For a moment he looked surprised. Did he notice a visible variation from the Charlotte he'd come to know by her photograph?

She forgot to breathe.

But then his sister swatted his arm and said, "Come on, brother. Find your senses. Invite the girl inside."

He gathered himself and held out a hand. Charlotte found her own hands full with the apple and her skirts, so she handed him the fruit.

"Oh look," the sister said. "She's brought an apple for the teacher."

Charlotte had no idea what she was talking about but felt foolish just the same. She lifted her skirts enough to traverse the carriage steps and took a seat across from the siblings. She was afraid to meet their gaze. As the carriage pulled away from the curb she was lurched forward; her hand instinctively reached for balance and she touched Conrad on the knee.

"Oh. So sorry. Pardon me."

She saw him blush. The sister rolled her eyes. It was not a good beginning.

Charlotte was surprised when the sister spoke first. "As you probably surmised, I am Beatrice and this is my older—but not wiser—brother, Conrad."

Conrad's blush deepened. "It's very nice to finally meet you, Miss Gleason. Was your journey enjoyable?"

Charlotte thought back to the broken goblet, meeting Dr. Greenfield, being the belle of the ball, and suffering seasickness. *Enjoyable* was not a good summary. "My journey was an adventure."

"Oooh," Beatrice said with her eyes sparkling. "Do tell."

"Leave her alone, Beatrice. You've not given her time to breathe."

"Well, then. If you won't allow her to talk, I'll do the talking for all of us. Look out the window, dear, and I'll give you a tour of the city as we ride along. We're traveling north on Broadway, and if you think the traffic horrific here, you will see worse."

Charlotte was thankful for Beatrice's banter, although she didn't pay much attention to the sights. What she really wished to do was to look upon the Tremaines.

She knew Beatrice to be a few years older than herself, yet with a pinch to her facial features, Beatrice looked even older than that. If Charlotte hadn't known she was a lady of society, she would have guessed by her countenance that Beatrice was a headmistress in a very strict school. Her eyes were small and darting, but not in the way of someone who wished to observe the world, but rather of someone who wished to catch it at fault. Whether she wished to do so to condemn or ridicule was hard to tell, yet Charlotte had trouble imagining Beatrice with a full smile. Her looks were not beautiful, nor pretty, nor even particularly amiable. If pressed, Charlotte would have said—to be kind—that she was a handsome woman.

As for Conrad . . . Charlotte tried to study him a glance at a time, to gauge if she felt any physical attraction. He was not a handsome man, though not unhandsome either. He had a wide nose and a cleft in his chin, but her first impression was of a man who ate a bit too much and who was a bit soft in the muscle, with no need to exert himself with any means of physical labor. She couldn't imagine him a horseman either. Did New Yorkers ride for sport or have country homes where they could exercise with a fox hunt or a round of polo? His grandfather had started a dry goods store. Did Conrad work there? Was he a good worker? Would he be a good provider?

She risked another glance in his direction and found he was clearly looking at *her*.

She looked away and was decidedly disturbed when her thoughts suddenly detoured to Dr. Edmund Greenfield.

Would she ever see him again?

Such thoughts were absurd, indiscreet, impossible . . .

And undeniable.

⁂

Come back!

Lottie watched Dora get into the Tremaines' carriage. Not once had the girl turned around to see her one last time. Lottie had been ready to raise a hand for a final good-bye, but there'd been no need. With their one embrace, Dora had walked away from Lottie and had *become* her.

Just like that.

Lottie scanned the New Yorkers waiting for travelers. There were many handwritten signs, but not a one with Dora's name on it.

Dora's cousin wasn't coming.

Although Lottie had bravely told Dora she would take the train to the cousin's address, saying so and doing so were far different things. She looked at the elevated railway overhead. The noise when a train came past was deafening. She had no notion of where to buy a ticket, or where to get off or—

Suddenly she was knocked off-balance as a man ran into her full force.

"Hey!" she said as she tried to right herself.

But instead of making his apology, he snatched the leather box out of her arms and ran on.

It took her a moment to comprehend what had happened.

Then . . . "Stop! Stop that man! Thief!"

The people crowding the park looked up from their business, then down again. Her problem was of no concern to them.

Lottie spotted a uniformed man with a baton at his belt and ran toward him. "Sir, a man just stole my jewels!"

He removed the baton and looked in the direction she pointed. "I don't see any man."

They looked upon a hundred men. "He grabbed them out of my hands."

"You were carrying them, out in the open?"

"Not in the open. In a box."

He looked for the thief one more time, then sighed. "Box or no, they're long gone now."

"Aren't you going to run after him?"

He tapped his baton against his leg. "Bum leg."

"Aren't you a constable?"

"A police officer. Yes, I am."

"Then I demand you try to catch him."

His eyebrow rose beneath his hat. "Excuse me, missy, but you being new here . . . I don't think you've earned the right to demand much of anything."

It was hopeless. In the time they'd discussed the theft, the thief had gained too much ground. He was blocks away by now.

The strain of the day fell upon her. An arrival, a parting, a theft . . . What should she do now?

She began to cry.

"Now, now, no need for that," the policeman said. "Let's get you sitting down where you can collect yourself."

The absurdity of his measure of comfort pulled her out of her tears. It was laughable. Collect herself? She'd just traversed an ocean, run away from her family and her life, and had now lost her only means of revenue and survival.

Collect herself?

She jerked away from his leading arm. "If you can't—or won't—help me, then leave me be."

"Don't get huffy, missy."

"It's Miss Hathaway, and I'll do whatever I please." She faced him fully. "If this is the kind of welcome you give newcomers, then I think the whole of New York City will be losing more than a few by return passage."

"Fine by me." He waved his baton over the crowds around them. "Too many of you foreigners here anyways. No one would be happier than me if the bunch of you went back where you came from."

"Then we're agreed," Lottie said.

"I guess we are."

"Then . . . good day."

"The day it is, but good it ain't." He nodded and left her.

Lottie held her stance as long as she could, but the exertion took its toll and her legs grew weak beneath her. She stumbled to a bench and found a hand upon her elbow to ease her to sitting.

"Thank you," she said. "I'll be all right."

"*Quell'uomo terribile! Povera ragazza!*"

Lottie looked at her rescuer. It was a woman with dark hair pulled smoothly into a bun. She wore no hat and her clothes were plain. The language was not entirely unfamiliar, and Lottie guessed from her experience at the opera that the woman was Italian.

"Thank you for helping me. But I'm sorry, I don't understand."

The woman shook her head, then said, "*Scusi.* That man . . . horrible. You poor girl." She looked in the direction the thief had run. "I saw thief."

"He took . . ." She stopped before explaining more. Yet what would it hurt for the entire world to know the box contained jewels? They were gone now. "He took my jewelry." Lottie touched her earrings and put a hand to her neck.

"Ah. *Sì. Gioielli.*"

Lottie noticed the woman had come to her aid from a grouping of three immigrants who were gathered with miscellaneous satchels and trunks spread around them. "Thank you very much for helping. But I'm all right now." She pressed a hand to her chest. "Fine. All right."

The woman smiled. "*Sì.* All right."

She went back to her family, leaving Lottie alone.

Lottie had to regroup. Her jewels were gone. The first order of business was to get to the cousin's house, where perhaps she could get some advice. Before the theft, Lottie had been on her way to ask about the train. Surely it wouldn't cost too—

Lottie gasped. She'd put all her money in the jewel box!

Not only were her jewels gone, she didn't have a single penny.

How could this happen? She closed her eyes against the sight of this frightening and exasperating new land. If only she'd never left home. If only that man hadn't taken everything she held dear. If only Dora hadn't left her alone. . . .

You're not alone. God's in America too, Charlotte. Don't forget Him!

God was with her? If He was here, why would He let this happen to her? What happened to *I'll watch over you?*

America, with its streets paved with gold. It was laughable.

She was in a foreign country with no means of support. Was God having a good laugh at her expense?

Lottie pressed her hands against her face. "What more?"

There couldn't *be* more. God had already done His worst. Hopefully He would forget her and move on to His next victim.

Lottie had told Dora she would pray, but no more. From now on, Lottie would handle things herself. She certainly couldn't do any worse.

Chapter Nine

Scusi? Miss?"

Lottie took the last bite of her apple and looked up, putting her worries on hold. Just as well. They had no eloquence but were a jumble of words and thoughts that were unintelligible. It was the Italian woman. Her family was standing close by, ready to move on. "Yes?"

"You meet someone?"

"No."

Her dark eyebrows nearly touched in the middle. "You have place to go?"

Lottie removed the cousin's address from her reticule. The woman looked at it and frowned. "Far. Too far. You come with us? Send message? Yes?"

So the woman was not one of the immigrants just off the boat? "You live here?"

"Six years. I am Lea Scarpelli. *Mia familia* has come." She introduced the people behind her. "*Mia* sister Francesca, husband, Aldo. Son, Vittorio. From Napoli. A long—"

Suddenly a man wearing a vest and a bowler hat stepped between them and shouted at Lea. "Get away from her, you stupid crow. Can't you see she's a lady? She doesn't want to go with the likes of you." He turned to face Lottie in far too close a manner and grinned. He had two teeth missing and his odor smacked her senses. "Come on, pretty miss. I'll help you git wherever you want to go. I know this city better'n any I-tie ever will. I'll find ya a good place to sleep."

It was his final wink that settled it. Without a word, Lottie side-stepped the man and moved to the middle of Lea's family.

His grin faded to a sneer. "Fine. Choose them over me. I'm sure one of those *omettos* will be glad to take care of you. If they can." He laughed at his joke and sauntered away.

Vittorio stepped out of the group, raised an arm, and yelled, *"Cretino stupido!"*

Lea nodded at her nephew and smiled. "Our *protettore*." When Lottie didn't understand, she raised her fists as if fighting.

Ah. "Protector."

"Sì." The woman put a hand to her chest. "I am Lea, but you?"

"Lottie Hathaway." Lottie was amazed at how easily the name fell from her lips. Repeating the surname of her dear nanny gave her strength.

"Lottie Hathaway, come. You be with us tonight."

"I don't wish to be a burden."

Lea handed her a satchel. "Carry."

Lottie adjusted the leather handles. It wasn't that heavy. Once they got on the train—

"Come now. We walk."

"Walk?"

"You have money for train?" Lea asked.

She felt herself redden. "No."

"You have legs?"

An unbidden smile escaped. "Yes."

"We walk."

Lottie didn't dare ask how far.

The carriage slowed. "Here we are," Conrad said.

Charlotte looked out the window at a white marble building with a columned entry. It looked very much like a library or a building of state. Four stories, capped with a short curved roof that looked French in design, grew upon a carved foundation. Surely this couldn't be a home—their home.

She kept her questions to herself, not wanting to appear naïve.

The coachman opened the door and Conrad said, "After you, Miss Gleason." She was helped to the sidewalk. The building towered above her. The width of the house was over a hundred feet across its front and sat on a corner that sported signs that said *W. 34th Street* and *Fifth Avenue*.

Beatrice joined her, and finally Conrad. The carriage pulled away. "Well, now," Conrad said. "What do you think of our little home?"

Little? A laugh escaped and Charlotte pressed a hand to her lips. "Forgive me." Then she collected herself, sighed, and said, "It will do."

Beatrice patted her on the back. "A girl of gumption. How . . . charming."

Charlotte looked to Conrad. Did he appreciate her manner? He seemed less certain. Then he nodded toward the brownstone across the street. "Our house certainly outdoes the neighbors'." He leaned close. "Mrs. Astor lives there."

He made it sound important, as if she should know this Mrs. Astor. Charlotte feigned knowledge and offered an extended "Oh," as if she were impressed. The brownstone was quite dull compared to the Tremaine mansion, and a third its size. It reminded her of a larger version of the home where the Gleasons stayed when they went to London.

"Come inside," Beatrice said. "If we keep you out here much longer, Caroline will see you, and the whole city will know you've arrived before Mother has had the honor of spreading the news."

Conrad led her up the front steps. "Mrs. Astor *does* know you're coming. Mother made sure of that. One does not surprise Mrs. Astor."

The woman sounded formidable and someone Charlotte hoped she never had to meet.

A butler opened the door, and they came into an entry hall rimmed with fluted columns and populated with Grecian statues.

Beatrice gestured to a statue of a seated woman who was cowering with one arm bent above her head. "First you should meet Cousin Mildred. This is a statue of her reaction to Mother's insistence she learn to like trout."

"Stop it," Conrad whispered. He smiled at Charlotte. "Come this way. Mother is probably waiting in the drawing room."

Had Mrs. Tremaine been waiting long? Would she be angry because of the time it had taken Charlotte to pass through Castle Garden?

Beatrice took Charlotte's arm and pulled her back. "Mother can wait a bit longer, brother. Let the poor girl freshen up. She can meet our parents at dinner."

Conrad looked toward the drawing room, and uncertainty clouded his face. "Are you sure?"

His sister took Charlotte by the arm and led her toward a wide staircase. "You go in and tell Mother the plan just as I have stated it. She won't bite, Conrad. I'm proof of that."

Beatrice's grip was reassuring. She seemed to know what she was doing. "Thank you," Charlotte said. "I am rather weary."

"Of course you are. Sometimes my brother acts like a mouse afraid to grab the cheese. He's so concerned with pleasing our parents that he risks going hungry. He doesn't even realize that as the only son his place is secure and dripping with favor."

Charlotte guessed Beatrice did not hold the same position in her parents' esteem. There was something confrontational about her.

Beatrice patted Charlotte's arm as they ascended the staircase. "This house may look like a museum, Miss Gleason, but be assured its residents aren't really as cold and hard as the statues. In spite of all this fine frippery, our grandfather started his career selling Irish lace on the street. He opened his first store in 1846."

"First store?"

"Before the war. Of course the present store is huge by comparison—five stories encompassing an entire block over on Broadway."

"No wonder this home has such lovely things."

Beatrice laughed. "Oh, you won't find this kind of bric-a-brac at the store. These pretties were specially ordered from Europe and Asia." They turned down a long hall. "Perhaps we'll show you our art gallery after you've had a few days to acclimate." She glanced over her shoulder. "Do you have a talent, Miss Gleason?"

Charlotte knew her abilities to dress hair, listen to Lottie read her novels aloud, and mend Lottie's clothing were not what Beatrice was looking for. "Not really."

"Good."

Good?

"Here we are . . ."

Beatrice let go of Charlotte's arm and allowed her to enter the bedroom first. Charlotte took a few steps inside, then stopped. "This is my room?"

"If you have trouble sleeping with that chandelier looming above you, put a pillow over your face. That's what I do."

The golden chandelier with a dozen white globes was the least of it. The bed was massive mahogany with a headboard that rose halfway up the wall—which was at least fifteen feet from floor to ceiling. The ceiling was edged with intricate carving and painted flowers that complemented the pink and green of the floral carpet. The room was large enough to boast numerous dressers, a dressing table, a green satin couch, a dozen chairs, and a spattering of tables. It was the bedroom of a princess.

"Surely your trunks will arrive soon," Beatrice said, crossing the room. Suddenly Beatrice looked around as if something was missing. " 'Tis a shame about your companion. You never said what happened."

She reverted to the excuse she and Lottie had concocted. "I'm afraid I lost her."

"Lost—?"

She should act more upset. . . . "I saw a man approach her while we were waiting to claim our luggage. I thought it odd that she would talk with a stranger, but Dora was a friendly sort. And then, when I turned around, she was walking away with him. I called after her, but . . ." She took another breath. "She walked faster. Away. From me. With the man."

"Just like that?"

"She must have been planning to part company the entire time. It's quite disturbing. I thought she was a loyal friend."

"No one's loyal in this town, Charlotte. There are too many opportunities toward self-gratification. But how rude of her to leave you alone on the dock."

Charlotte was thankful the story had passed Beatrice's muster.

"So much for her," Beatrice said. "Now then. I'll send in Mary. When your trunks come she'll be thrilled to unpack your pretty things and help you with your toilette." Beatrice pointed to a clock on the mantel. "Dinner will be at eight. It would be best if you were down at seven, in the drawing room."

"What is the attire? I want to make a good impression."

Beatrice's eyes darted to the door, then back. "We enjoy full dress for dinner. Mother loves bare arms."

A ball gown for dinner when there was no ball? Americans must be more formal than back in England.

Charlotte eyed the bed. What she wanted most was a long nap.

Beatrice moved to the door, her short train swishing against the thick carpet. "Get some rest. You have the balance of your life to spend here, Charlotte. Gain what strength you can now. You'll need it."

What did she mean by that?

"There. City Hall," Lea said. "And courthouse."

Lottie was uninterested in municipal buildings and took little notice. What drew her eye was to their far right. "That bridge . . . it's huge." An enormous brick structure loomed castlelike above all the other buildings in the distance. It was pierced with high arches that reminded Lottie of pictures she'd seen of Roman aqueducts. But strung on top were great wires leading to the next higher edifice, and then to the next like intricate lace. She'd seen bridges in London, of course, but they were low-lying, while this . . .

"That Brooklyn Bridge. It finished three years now. Many men work hard."

"I can imagine. Can people walk across it?"

"Who has time? Or a penny." Lea pointed ahead. "We nearly home."

Lottie was glad for that. Her arms ached from carrying the satchel, and she'd spent much of her time changing it from one arm to the other. For the most part she'd not spoken with the Italians who walked with her, and they seemed content to chatter away. It was the first time she'd heard another language beyond short snippets, and she found it delightful. And animated. Vittorio was especially vibrant. His words popped and crackled like oil sputtering on a hot pan. Occasionally a term would surface that she could understand: *madre, padre, ristorante, appartamento, familia.* She took comfort in it.

But as they walked farther up Park Street, the buildings began to change. Most were five or six stories tall and made of brick, but some made of wood looked as if they could collapse at any moment. The tops of the buildings became obscured as they walked down the middle of a street full of litter, a street pressed from both sides with pushcarts selling fruit and kitchen utensils and hats. Awnings shaded whatever shop might be behind the carts, and the smells were unlike any she'd ever experienced: spicy and pungent and far too close.

The people were as fragrant as their wares. The street flittered with women—most older than herself. They wore their hair in simple buns and had much-used aprons covering their dresses. Shawls were tied around their shoulders or over their heads. A few had babies in a shawl-sling and showed no signs of being hampered by their presence.

A little boy wearing suspenders and a cap ran toward them with a piece of wood in his hands, as if broken from a crate. *"Legno da bruciare, signora?"*

Lea shoved him back. *"Vattene via!"*

The boy ran away to another group of people. He didn't appear upset by the rebuff. Did he do this all day long? How much money could he make selling a scrap of wood?

The noise hit her next. The voices. At Castle Garden, Lottie had heard a cacophony of unfamiliar languages, but here, it seemed everyone was Italian, as if she'd walked into a street in Rome or Florence and everyone was talking at once. She was familiar with the narrow streets in London, but the streets there were for carriages and horses. Here, it was as if the middle of the street was but a crowded sidewalk. If a carriage needed to pass, it would have to fight for the privilege.

She heard Aldo say something to his son, then noticed the two men move to the outer edges of their group of five. She was glad for their protection and hung closer to Lea. If the men felt threatened . . .

Most people gave them little notice except to offer their goods for sale, but when their eyes did land upon Lottie, they lingered, and their mouths drew down in distrust. Although her clothing was a simple traveling suit, the jaunty bow and feather on her hat, the striped green fabric of her bodice, and the drape of the bustle in the back singled her out as a stranger.

No one accosted her, no one pointed and said, "Get away! You do not belong here!"—in Italian, of course—but neither did they smile or nod a greeting as vendors in London would have done, hoping for her business.

"Not far," Lea said to her.

Although her feet and arms were glad to hear it, they were the only parts of Lottie's anatomy that appreciated Lea's words. Lea lived in such a place as this? They were traversing a gauntlet of the Italian masses, in a maze that seemed to go on and on and on. . . .

They approached an intersection, and Lottie took a deep breath, hoping that here, in this expanse, there would be a burst of fresh air to rid her senses of the claustrophobic presence of the crowd.

"This Five Points," Lea said. She repeated it in Italian for her family. "*Ciò è Cinque Punti.*"

They nodded and exchanged a few words, as if this had been their destination.

"Five streets," Lea explained, pointing to the five streets that converged at this place. "Worth, Park, Baxter . . ."

A squealing pig ran between them, making Lottie drop the satchel. When she went to pick it up, Vittorio took it for her and smiled.

"Thank you."

"*Prego.*"

Though younger than herself, he was quite nice looking, with an aquiline nose, soft brown eyes, and the promise of becoming fully handsome in a few years time. She could tell that he also appreciated her looks. Being able to subtly flirt with him had given her something familiar to do as one block progressed into another.

They continued up Park Street to the next intersection, Mulberry.

"There, up there," Lea said.

The street still swarmed with people, but these knew Lea and many ran to their group, chattering with the newcomers, greeting them as if they were expected.

Lottie was the only one unexpected and, as such, stepped to the edge of the group to wait. She was unused to the generous displays of affection going on before her. Her own mother hugged others only on great occasion, and she could not remember her father offering her anything beyond a nod or handshake.

A little girl came running, weaving her way through the crowd. "Mamma! Mamma!" Lea opened her arms, and the girl wrapped her arms around her legs. She made further introductions to her family. *"Mia figlia, Sofia."*

Sofia was five or six. She shared her mother's large eyes and lovely skin.

She spotted Lottie and pointed. *"Chi è lei?"*

"Amica." Lea looked at Lottie and smiled. "Friend."

The little girl's eyes were locked on Lottie's hat. On impulse Lottie knelt down and put a hand to the bows. "Do you like my hat?"

Sofia hooked a finger in her mouth but kept looking at it.

Lottie untied the bow under her chin, placed the hat on the girl, and retied the bow. The hat was a cheerful topping to the girl's faded dress. "There. Very pretty."

"Bella!" Lea said.

Sofia beamed and skipped away toward the ladies in the stall nearby. They oohed and aahed over her.

Lea touched Lottie's hand. *"Grazie mille*, Lottie."

It was then Lottie realized her bonnet was gone for good. She had never meant to *give* it to the girl.

And yet . . . to see the smile on Sofia's face, to watch the neighbor ladies adjust the bow, to see Sofia pull out the corners of her paltry dress and attempt a curtsy . . . the loss might have been gain.

"Vieni dentro la nostra casa," Lea said, gesturing toward stone steps. She looked for her daughter. "Sofia! *Vieni dentro.*"

They all followed her inside, and Lottie was immediately struck by the sudden darkness. Two of Lea's family bumped into the back of Lottie as she pulled up short in order to let her eyes adjust. Sofia ran around them all and raced up the stairs.

A lone gaslight flickered its meager offering. The air was dank and smelled of rotting wood and food, and places and people unclean.

They conquered the stairs single file—and a conquest it was. Each landing was piled with someone's belongings, and on the third flight, they had to step over a sleeping man sprawled across a pile of what looked to be garbage. Lottie heard babies crying, adults arguing, and children running in the hallways.

Floor after floor, step upon step . . . the group ceased their chatter and concentrated on the task at hand. Although Lottie heard the men puffing behind her, she seemed to be the most affected. After five flights she felt a painful stitch in her side. She had to stop. "Please. I. Can't. Breathe."

The Scarpellis halted and talked among themselves. She saw Francesca spread a hand upon her own midsection, then nod at Lottie's and say something to Lea. They were discussing her corset. It was the first time she'd noticed that the Italian women wore none. Their bodices were loosely bloused.

"I agree with you," she told the women. "In this, your way *is* better, and far more conducive to exertion."

The two women understood nothing but, just the same, exchanged more opinions.

Vittorio pointed up the stairs. *"Ci siamo quasi?"*

Lea pointed to the next landing. *"Sì."* She looked at Lottie. "Top. *Siamo lì.*"

Lottie nodded and stood straighter to capture another breath. "Go."

And so they accomplished the final stairs. Lea led them to a door on the right and opened it. *"Benvenuti."*

They entered a room that was crowded with furniture—makeshift and real. A young woman was working over a small iron stove. Another daughter? She greeted the relatives, who took turns taking her face in their hands and kissing her. It was obvious they'd last seen her as a child. *"Bella Lucia . . ."*

The girl looked at Lottie, then her mother, her face asking the question.

"Lottie Hathaway. *Immigrate. Non ha soldi, nessun posto dove andare.*"

"Irlandese? Inglese?" she asked.

"Non lo so."

153

Lottie understood one of the words. "Yes, British," she said. "Wiltshire."

"Ah." They all nodded.

Lottie wondered if it mattered, if there were some bad feeling of one culture for another. Surely not here in America, where all came together to start over.

The next hour was spent finding places for all the relatives' belongings, piling what was already piled even higher. Then they sat around the small table. Chairs were created out of crates and crude benches, but all found a place. Lea and Francesca helped Lucia with the food preparation—which smelled delicious. Lottie had not eaten anything but an apple since leaving the ship. Was that today?

As the dinner was ready to be served—it appeared to be pasta, hunks of cheese, bread, and greens—the door opened and a ruddy man with a mustache entered. The room was once again alive with greetings. This was the man of the house. Dante Scarpelli.

He kissed his wife and put a hand around her waist as he listened to her explanation of the stranger at their table. Dante nodded, and in the end looked at Lottie and extended an open palm from his chest outward. *"Benvenuta, Signorina Hathaway."*

"Grazie, Signore Scarpelli."

The room went silent for a moment, then burst to life with laughter and much talk, and pats on Lottie's back. *"Bene! Ben fatto!"*

Mr. Scarpelli took a second look at little Sofia's new chapeau. The girl nodded toward Lottie. *"Me l'ha dato."*

He looked at Lottie, brushed a thick finger across the brim, then winked. *"Molte grazie."*

She wished she had another hat to give.

※

Mary adjusted a curl to pin above Charlotte's right ear but fumbled it. Again.

"Here, I'll do it," Charlotte said. She took over and pinned it in place. The maid had absolutely no talent for dressing hair. It was as if she'd never done it before. It was not the first indication that Mary had little experience as a lady's maid. In fact, her chapped hands indicated she was more used to duties with pail and water than snaps and hairpins. Charlotte couldn't help but think Beatrice had something to do with Mary's present assignment, though she didn't want to imagine why Conrad's sister would do such a thing. Beatrice had acted friendly enough.

"You look beautiful, miss. The Tremaines will be very impressed."

That was the objective.

The clock on the mantel struck seven. "I'm going to be late!" Charlotte hurried from the room and headed toward the front stairs. She paused at the top of the sweeping steps to collect herself, then ran a hand along the pink satin that lay in folds at her hips and fell into an elaborate bustle and train edged in matching ruffles. The embroidered and beaded front panel culminated in silk pleats at the floor. A corsage of variegated roses balanced on the small band that crossed her shoulder. She felt pretty in pink. She hoped the Tremaines agreed.

She adjusted her long gloves and made her descent, with memories of Lottie's lessons on the rules of dining accompanying her every step.

"Firstly, Dora, you will enter the dining room in a specific order. The host will offer the highest-ranking woman his arm, and then the other women will follow on the arms of their partners in order of their status, with the hostess coming in last upon the arm of the husband of the woman escorted by the host.

"When going in to dinner, your escort will always offer his left arm. But don't hold tightly. Barely touch him. It's all a matter of show. We are led, but act as though we don't need leading. We are together, yet apart, all dolls upon display.

"The most prominent man sits to the right of the hostess, with the most prominent female sitting to the right of the host. The second in rank to their left, with the rest of the table alternating male and female toward

the center. You never want to be at the center of the table, for that is where the least important are seated."

If "least important" was a measure of visibility, Charlotte would be happy to fade into a center seat.

"Your chair will be pulled back and you will sit, pulling your train to the side.

"Remove your gloves and place them in your lap. Then take the napkin from the table and set it on top of your gloves. Occasionally the footman will place your napkin for you."

Occasionally? Not always? So should Charlotte wait or do it herself or . . .

Upon reaching the bottom of the stairs, the details of dining were replaced by panic. She was lost. Was the drawing room to the left or right?

She spotted the statue of the cowering woman that Beatrice had teased about and got her bearings. To the right. She prayed she wasn't the first one there, nor the last. Lottie had stressed the importance of proper timing—unfortunately, how to achieve such timing had not been discussed.

The drawing room doors were open and she heard voices. How many? She would know presently.

The intricacy of the room's architecture made her bedroom seem austere. Every surface of wall, ceiling, and floor was adorned. Two massive chandeliers sparkled with dozens of lights. Mirrors reflected—and doubled—the grandeur, and there were chairs and settees to seat at least thirty.

"Well now," Conrad said. "And here she is." He started to come to greet her, held back ever so slightly, then began again, taking her hand in his. His face was flushed—with pleasure or nerves? And why had a crease formed between his brows?

He led her to his parents. Mrs. Tremaine sat upon a settee, regal in a deep burgundy dress—with a high neck and full sleeves—but before Charlotte had time to assess the difference in the woman's gown compared to her own, Mr. Tremaine cleared his throat. He stood behind his wife, his hand hooked within the watch pocket of his evening clothes.

"Charlotte, may I present to you my parents, Mr. and Mrs. Martin Tremaine. Mother, Father . . . this is Miss Gleason, our Charlotte."

Mrs. Tremaine blinked, and Charlotte wondered if it was because of her son's use of the word *our*. That one blink was proof their engagement was not official. She was on trial here.

Charlotte managed a curtsy with only the smallest sway off-balance. "I am so pleased to be here. Thank you for your generous hospitality."

"Yes, well. It needed to be done." Mr. Tremaine flipped her gratitude away.

Mrs. Tremaine took over, and upon her first words, Charlotte knew this was the way of it. Mrs. Tremaine was the one to impress. "We trust your journey was agreeable? The accommodations on the *Etruria* were satisfactory?"

The Tremaines had paid for their passage—two passages. Had Beatrice told them the story about her "companion"?

"It was a delightful trip, but I am reluctant to inform you that my traveling partner was caught up in the excitement at Castle Garden and . . ." She sighed for dramatic effect. "She ran off."

"Ran off?" Mr. Tremaine asked. "To where?"

"I don't know. Perhaps she was lured away by a man making claims about a better life. I saw her talking with—"

"Castle Garden is full of men making claims." They all turned toward Beatrice's voice as she entered the room. "Sorry to be late. I shan't do it again."

"Until next time," her mother said.

She shrugged and Charlotte was immediately struck by her gown—which was of dark green velvet, with high lace collar and cuffs at her wrists. She felt like a fool in pink, and with bare arms and décolletage besides.

Beatrice found a chair. "What a lovely ball gown, Miss Gleason."

Charlotte felt her jaw tighten but withheld her anger. "Thank you. My dinner gowns suffered some damage with the crossing, so I'm afraid you'll have to bear with my state of overdress."

Beatrice offered a slight smile and nod, as if to say *touché*. It was quite evident she'd misdirected Charlotte on purpose. But why would she do such a thing?

Mrs. Tremaine's face softened slightly. Was she relieved there was *some* explanation for Charlotte's fashion misstep?

Conrad fiddled with his cuff links, as if he sensed there was something going on between the women but was uncertain what. He returned to the previous subject.

"Since your companion ran away, Miss Gleason, should we call the police and send someone after her? For her own good?"

"Pfupft," Beatrice said. "She's long gone by now. Do *you* want to dive into the immigrant slums and hunt her down? I surely don't."

Immigrant slums? Charlotte hated to sound ignorant, but . . . "What are you talking about?"

Mr. Tremaine answered. "A place with too many people, too many languages, and too little money."

"I hear they live under horrible conditions," Conrad said.

Mr. Tremaine shook his head. "They're fortunate to have a roof over their heads. If they work hard enough they can move elsewhere. In the meantime I imagine they find comfort in being with like kind."

"As do we," Beatrice said under her breath.

Her mother flashed her a scathing look. "What was that, Beatrice?"

Instead of backing down—as Lottie would have done—Beatrice repeated her words. "As do we, Mother. Isn't New York society all about being with people of like kind?"

"That will do, daughter."

"Au contraire, ma chère mère. I think it's only appropriate we let Charlotte know how things are here in New York. How can she be expected to be accepted in our society when she is unaware of its . . . foibles?"

"Beatrice . . ." Conrad looked at her imploringly.

Mr. Tremaine relinquished his place behind his wife and came round to address his daughter. "As a member of English society, I'm certain Miss Gleason is very familiar with the dictates and manners of proper intercourse."

Beatrice crossed one leg over the other, revealing an ankle. "Dictates . . . but does England have a dictator like we do? Or should I say, dictator-ess?"

"Cover yourself!" Her father nodded at her ankle. His face was florid.

She rolled her eyes but put both feet upon the floor, straightened her back, and clasped her hands in her lap. Charlotte couldn't imagine Lottie talking to her parents in such a fashion, or exposing herself in that way—and never in mixed company.

But Beatrice wasn't finished. "Have you told her about the Four Hundred yet, Conrad?"

"No, I . . . you know very well Miss Gleason and I have not had a chance to have a full conversation as yet."

"As yet," Beatrice repeated.

Seeing the look on Mrs. Tremaine's face, Charlotte was afraid the subject would be dropped, but she didn't want it dropped, for Beatrice had sparked her curiosity. "Mrs. Tremaine, if I may ask, what is the Four Hundred?"

The woman looked taken aback.

"I'm sorry. I shouldn't have—"

"No," Mrs. Tremaine said. "It's nothing, really."

"Not so, Mother," Beatrice said. "We've all heard Mrs. Astor speak of such a thing. She holds the keys to who's who on the list."

"There is no list."

"Oh, there's a list," Beatrice said. "If not on paper . . ." She tapped a finger against her temple.

Mrs. Tremaine's focus moved from her daughter to the doorway, where a butler declared, "Dinner is served, ma'am."

"Ah. So." She held out her hand and her husband helped her to standing. Conrad extended his arm to Charlotte, and the two couples paraded toward the dining room.

With Beatrice following behind.

Alone.

⚜

Dinner was a staid affair. Charlotte was used to eating with the other servants in the servants' hall or from a tray in her room. Although she had never attended a family meal at the Gleasons' in any capacity but to serve, she knew they spoke to one another. A little.

Not so the Tremaines. And what could have been accomplished in one half hour took nearly two. There were six courses—which showed Charlotte her standing. A dinner of three courses would signal she was of no consequence, and one of eight or ten would indicate they wished to impress. Six courses implied respect for her presence, but also a superiority.

Each course was ceremoniously accomplished and eaten while the Tremaines spoke *around* each other. Mr. Tremaine seemed content to let his wife initiate what little talk occurred, and Conrad was quick to nod in complete agreement with whatever his mother had to say. Only Beatrice offered any amusement, yet as most everything she said seemed to grate upon her family, Charlotte couldn't risk showing too much pleasure in it. Besides, Beatrice had shown herself untrustworthy. She was a woman to be watched. Carefully.

Mostly, Charlotte was relieved that the questions asked about herself were easily answered. Perhaps the Tremaines' reticence would be a blessing. Perhaps their general disinterest in deep discussion would prevent a verbal mishap on her part.

As one course faded into the next—some which looked appetizing enough but which Charlotte had no appetite to eat—she found her eyelids drooping, and the sound of Mrs. Tremaine's voice began to hum. . . .

"Miss Gleason!"

Her head jerked erect. Had she dozed?

"Is our company so tiresome?"

Conrad extended a hand upon the table toward his mother. "It's her journey that's been tiresome, Mother. Miss Gleason has had an exhausting day."

Charlotte was overjoyed at his defense—because the reason for her weariness was genuine, and because it was the first time she'd witnessed him showing some gumption. "I apologize," she said. "I do assure you my fatigue is not due to either the delicious meal or the fine company. My eyelids have simply mutinied and demanded their way."

Beatrice laughed softly, and Charlotte saw that even Mr. Tremaine smiled.

It was her way out and away, so she scooted her chair back and stood. "If you will please excuse this weary traveler, I promise to be bright-eyed tomorrow."

The men rose, and Charlotte assured them she could see herself to her room. She was relieved when no one followed. Each step upon the staircase was accomplished with effort. She leaned on the railing, hoping she wouldn't fall asleep right then and there.

Mary must have been alerted, because she came running down the hallway and helped Charlotte negotiate the final steps to her bedroom.

"My, my," Mary said, closing the door behind them. "You're as pale as a ghost."

"Bed, Mary. Please."

Charlotte stood in the middle of the room and let Mary release her from her fashion bondage. Free of the heavy drapery and finally the corset, she took several deep breaths before raising her arms like a child being readied for bed. She felt a soft nightdress being pulled into place, and with Mary's hand at her elbow, she negotiated the few steps to the bed.

The pillows swelled around her heavy head, and the covers Mary placed over her shoulders reminded her of the days when her mother had tucked her in.

Sleep rushed to meet her.

※

At the Scarpellis' the sleeping arrangements took Lottie by surprise. When she'd first entered their apartment she had assumed there were multiple bedrooms beyond. But no. There was only one very small bedroom. Windowless. Inside were a set of makeshift beds built upon stilts, creating one bed above the other. The upper bed was no more than a sling of fabric tied to posts. Using those beds . . . two could sleep top and bottom. But what about the rest of them?

Lucia tapped her on the arm, then pointed to her midsection. *"Togli il corsetto."*

Her corset? Lottie looked down at herself, then at Lucia. As she'd noted before, the girl was wearing a loosely fitting blouse. Yes indeed, it would be nearly impossible to sleep wearing her corset. And her travel suit was made of fabric too stiff to bend and bow. She longed for her nightgown.

But as Lottie glanced around the room, she saw that no one was donning a nightshirt or gown. They were removing their shoes, their suspenders, and their coats, and that seemed to be that. All were unencumbering themselves of their daytime clothing as best they could while maintaining some semblance of modesty in this communal space.

Lucia retrieved another blouse and skirt from a small dresser. *"Mettiti queste."*

The clothes looked clean enough, though the blouse was much faded from its original green. But this wasn't about fashion; it was about comfort. And sleep. Lottie longed for sleep more than she'd ever longed for anything.

She took the clothes from Lucia. *"Grazie."* She *did* like the way her tongue rolled the *r*. It was fun to say the word.

Lucia smiled. *"Prego."*

Lottie looked around the room at the people getting settled in for the night—Aldo and Dante were placing a thin mattress on the floor. . . .

"Where can I change?"

Lucia understood, for she grabbed a blanket, nudged Lottie into a corner, and held the blanket as a makeshift wall. It would have to do.

With difficulty Lottie unbuttoned her skirt, and once that was accomplished, she reveled as its weight fell to the floor. She stepped free of it, untied the bustle padding from her waist, and tossed it on top of the fallen skirt. The serge bodice was next to be sacrificed. The cool air against her skin was a relief. She unhooked the front of her corset from bust to hips, and with its first give of one inch, then another, let herself breathe fully. She always felt relief at the end of a day's fashion burden, but today above all others the release was especially sweet.

Lottie pulled Lucia's skirt over her petticoat, put the blouse over her camisole, and tucked it into the skirt. The light fabric was heavenly, almost like not wearing outer-clothes at all. Next, her shoes. She sat on a box against the wall and unlaced her boots. Her feet responded in a similar manner as her torso. The release, the freedom . . .

"All done," she said.

Lucia lowered the blanket enough to peek over it. "Good." She folded the blanket and placed it on the floor. "Bed." She handed Lottie another blanket and a small sack of rags to use for a pillow.

Lottie had never slept on a floor, but what choice did she have? Vittorio climbed into the upper sling, and Lucia and Sofia shared the bottom bed, which was barely wide enough for one. Francesca and Aldo huddled together on the skinny mattress that had been unrolled on the floor. And Dante and Lea . . . Lottie could hear them talking quietly in the main room. She hadn't noticed a divan or Chesterfield there, nor any chair that was in any way padded. Were the Scarpellis also lying upon the hard floor? She thought of her parents . . . what would they have done with too many guests?

They would never have invited them to stay. They certainly would never have given up their own comfort, especially to a stranger.

It was her turn to take a place on the floor. Her sleeping mat lay next to the sisters' bed. The folded blanket offered little relief. She turned on her side, but without a proper pillow, comfort was an impossibility. She turned onto her stomach. At least her arms could provide some measure of cushion. And at least she could breathe more easily freed from her corset and heavy clothing.

"*Dio vi benedica. Buona notte,*" Dante called from the other room. The family offered their own good-nights.

The oil lamp was extinguished and the room fell into complete blackness. The bedroom had no window, and though the main room had one, the building next door was so close the moonlight could find no entry.

Lottie's heart began to beat faster. This was the pit of hell. Such darkness, such closeness, such lack of air . . .

Be thankful for this.

Thankful for sleeping on a floor in an airless room full of strangers who needed a bath as much as she? She'd never been at ease in full darkness and was used to sleeping with a lamp or fireplace lit. How had she moved from her cozy bedroom in Wiltshire to this awful place?

These people fed you. They cared for you. Be thankful for this.

Sudden tears threatened. Tears of gratitude? Reflection? Frustration? Or panic? Whatever their cause, they demanded release. She dug her face into her folded arms and let them come.

Then she felt a gentle hand upon her back. In the darkness she could not see whose it was but heard little Sofia say, "*Non essere triste. Tutto andrà bene.*"

Lottie did not understand the little girl's words but felt their intent. She turned on her side, took the tiny hand in her own, and kissed it.

"*Dormi bene,* Lottie."

She returned the words as a whisper in the dark. "*Dormi bene,* Sofia."

Be thankful for this.

She'd try.

Chapter Ten

❧

"Ouch!"

"*Scusi!*"

Lottie was yanked from sleep by Aldo stepping on her foot. The room was still dark until Lea brought in a lantern, which cast light and undulating shadows over the crowded space.

"*Buon giorno,*" she said.

Vittorio sat up in his upper bed, hitting his head on the ceiling. "*Aiye . . . buon giorno.*"

Lottie had no choice but to arise with the rest and move her blankets out of the way. How could it be morning? She'd barely slept, what with the hard floor, the lack of a proper pillow, the stale air, and Aldo's snoring.

She needed to use the facilities, but cringed at the thought of traipsing down all those flights of stairs to the outhouses in the alley. Her excursion last night—after discovering that neither the Scarpellis nor anyone else in the building had indoor water closets—had made her wish such bodily functions were not necessary.

After folding her blankets, she tugged on Lucia's sleeve but had no idea what the Italian word was to explain her need. "I . . ." She looked around the room, hoping the men were not listening. She pointed outside and bounced twice. "W.C.?"

Lucia's eyes showed recognition. *"Toilette?"*

"Yes, *sì*."

Lottie was glad Lucia didn't point to the chamber pot in the corner. Privacy was impossible. Instead, she took Lottie's arm, walked through the main room—offering good-mornings to her family—then led the way to the stairs. At the end of the hall they had to wade through a queue of women carrying vessels to fill with water from the spigot on the wall. One spigot per floor. It was unfathomable. How she longed to wash her face and brush her teeth, but she sensed such personal use would seem frivolous compared to all these women trying to make breakfast for their families. Lottie would take a real bath once she got to the home of Dora's cousin. All this filth would be behind her soon. But not too soon.

As had been the case the night before, Lottie smelled the outhouses long before she entered the alley to use one. She put a hand to her nose, hoping to squelch the horrific stench. When necessity had forced her to come here last night, it had been dark. The place had frightened her, but she assumed it would be more tolerable with the daylight.

What daylight? The alley was narrow and the tenements high. She doubted sunlight ever reached this awful place. Why would it waste its rays here? But without its presence, shadows greedily consumed the alley. Windows dotted the side of the buildings like dark holes in a birdhouse. At least a dozen lines of laundry hung overhead, spanning the buildings. The clothes hung lifeless. There was no air.

They passed doors on the left, and just as Lottie was thinking these might be storage rooms of some sort, a door opened. Inside, Lottie glimpsed a tiny apartment full of children. People lived in these spaces? Here? With a dozen feet separating the place they ate and slept from the long row of outhouses that spanned the other side of the alley?

There were lines of people waiting to use the facilities—yet the term was far too sophisticated a title. Inside, the outhouses were little more than a few planks of wood spaced just far enough apart to . . .

She stayed close to Lucia's side. The men in line gave her looks of curiosity along with other looks that made her want to run upstairs.

Lucia let her go first. In the rickety outhouse, Lottie wasn't certain which sense was assaulted first. Her nose from the stench, her eyes from the absence of light but for the bit coming through the slits in the wood, or the sense of suffocation from lack of fresh air and lack of space to maneuver her skirt and underclothes. Necessity made her endure it all. She vowed that as soon as she retrieved her trunk, she would get out of these underclothes and burn them.

Lucia went next, leaving Lottie alone with the mostly male crowd awaiting their turn. The attention continued, with sly smiles and heads bent toward heads, talking amongst themselves. One man put his fingers to his lips and kissed them.

It was too much. "Stop it!" she said.

They laughed and their talking gained momentum and volume.

Since she was leaving this place, since she would never see these people again, and since they probably didn't understand English anyway, she decided to tell them what for. She placed her hands on her hips, raised her chin, and said, "My name is Charlotte Gleason and my father has more money than the lot of you will make in ten lifetimes. I've been presented to the queen of England and am only here because a thief stole all my jewels and money. So you had best leave me alone and go after women of your own station—whatever that is."

During her tirade a couple of the men mimicked her, with hands on their hips and bobbing heads. She didn't care. It felt good to have said it.

With impeccable timing, Lucia emerged from the outhouse just in time for Lottie to take her arm and escape into the building.

Lucia looked over her shoulder at the men they left behind. "What you do?"

"I gave them the scolding they deserve."

"*Cosa?*"

Lottie dropped Lucia's arm and made boxing motions.

Lucia laughed. "*Combatti.*" She made a fist and added a sound, "*Pwue!*"

"Pow!"

The five flights up didn't seem as strenuous with laughter fueling their way.

⁂

Charlotte squinted her eyes against the light. Mary was at the windows, pulling aside the heavy drapery. "Good morning, miss. I'm drawing your bath."

She sat upright, stirred by the thought. Yesterday, she'd seen the large claw-footed tub but had been uncertain as to the protocol of asking for a bath. She didn't want to cause anyone undue trouble. But to bathe in such a tub . . .

When she'd first started working at the Gleasons', they'd just added a bathroom on the second floor that contained a flush toilet, a sink, and a tub. They'd carved the space out of a guest bedroom. The servants hadn't shared the luxury and had continued to use hip baths in the kitchen and the outhouse in the yard. But the Gleasons' functional bathroom was primitive compared to the one off of Charlotte's bedroom. And communal.

The fact she didn't need to venture into the hallway was luxury indeed. The bath was completely tiled in white and was situated between her own room and another guest room. Mary had intimated that Mr. and Mrs. Tremaine each had their own baths (as well as their own bedrooms), and there was another facility shared by the other two guest rooms. Conrad and Beatrice had their own. There was also a W.C. situated on the first floor near the cloak room, and Mary bragged that even the servants had a complete set of indoor plumbing downstairs.

"I've brought some garments into the room for you, miss. And some towels are on the warmers."

Warmers?

There were a series of pipes coming out of the floor, forming a towel rack before returning to the floor again. They were spaced wide enough for towels to be hung upon them. Charlotte touched one and found it hot.

"There's nothing like a warm towel after a bath," Mary said.

"I can imagine."

And the bathwater itself was enticing, with steam rising . . .

Mary stood ready to help remove her nightdress. "I'm fine now, Mary. Thank you."

She bobbed a curtsy. "As you wish, miss. Would you like to wear the blue day dress?"

How many times had she made such suggestions to Lottie? But in this case, Charlotte wasn't certain. "I don't know what the Tremaines have planned."

"'Tis not for me to know, miss."

Unfortunately, Charlotte wasn't certain it was for her to know either. The blue dress would do—for a start. She assumed changing clothes was a frequent occurrence.

Mary left her and Charlotte made sure the door leading to the other guest room was locked. Then, just because she could, she locked the door leading to her own bedroom. At the Gleasons' there were no locks on the doors to any of the servants' quarters. Charlotte had been thankful Mr. Gleason was not the sort to take advantage, and she'd also been glad there were no Gleason sons. Keeping the hallboy at bay at Dornby Manor had been enough of a challenge.

She pulled her hair into an impromptu knot, then slipped into the bath. The water rose to her chin. A bar of soap sat ready at the side. Unlike the Pears soap Lottie used back home, this bar was shaped into a white rectangle. She brought it to her nose and inhaled a fresh scent that smelled . . . clean. Carved into the top of the bar was the word *Ivory*.

The tub was designed to offer support for her head. She closed her eyes. Never had she felt so indulgent. To loll in a hot bath, without a care . . .

On a whim, she slid completely under the water. She blubbered and spit and quickly rose out again, a bit afraid. She'd never been immersed like that. Was this what swimming was like? Emboldened, she took a breath, held it, and slid down once again. All sound ceased but the *bwom-boomp* of her own heart. She'd never heard it so, resounding through the water, ringing in her ears.

Unnerved, she emerged again, glad to be among familiar sounds. Pressing her soaking hair away from her face, she realized combing it would be a challenge. But as she leaned back she let such trivial worries fall away with the bubbles upon the water.

When she let herself fully relax, the experience became more than a mere bath. It was a cleansing of the past, a rebirth. A purification. It was the final washing away of Dora Connors and the transformation of that maid into someone important, someone with a place in society and a purpose beyond meaningless household tasks. It was a baptism marking a new life with a new name.

Through amazing circumstances, she was now Charlotte Gleason, and with due effort, determination, and God's help, she would become Charlotte Tremaine. With that one act her mother would have her sweet shop, Lottie would gain the freedom she craved, and Charlotte would live like a princess with a good man at her side.

What kind of life this would be!

※

What kind of life would this be?

Back in her own clothes—including her dreaded corset—Lottie finished her good-byes to the Scarpellis. Dante had already left for work with the men, and Lucia was leaving also. Lea encased her with a warm embrace. "Take care, *sì?*"

"*Sì.*"

"*Che Dio sia con te.* God be with you."

She was touched. "And also with you."

Sofia stood at her mother's side, and Lottie knelt to see her face-to-face. She adjusted a flower in Lottie's bonnet, which the little girl had donned upon rising. "Take care of my hat for me. You look very pretty. *Bella.*"

Sofia smiled shyly, then reached out and touched Lottie's cheek.

She'd better leave soon or she would cry.

There was one last Scarpelli . . .

Lottie stood before Lucia and took her hands. "I'll miss you." And oddly, it was true. Although they'd known each other only a few hours, although they'd only exchanged a few dozen words, they shared a bond that seemed instinctive, inherent, and strong. Yet perhaps not inevitable. For Lottie felt an attachment with this Italian girl beyond any fondness she'd ever felt in Wiltshire among the young women of her own set.

Lucia nodded at Lottie and her brows furrowed. Her chin quivered. "I miss you too."

Not knowing what else to say, Lottie put a hand upon her heart. Lucia did the same.

Lottie made a vow that once she was settled she would return to Mulberry Street to visit Lucia. Yet as she left the tenement and walked north toward the address of Dora's cousin, she was not sorry to leave the chaotic conditions of Five Points behind. She was used to order and cleanliness, with quiet and measured days, not this chaos, filth, and cacophony.

But while walking alone up the street, she heard a faint mental admonition. It was her mother's voice. *"A woman is not allowed to walk alone on the street until she's married."* Indeed, Lottie had never done so, and with greater thought she realized the times she'd walked at all were not to go anywhere or to achieve anything. She'd walked on the estate grounds for a diversion or to find a lovely place to read. In the village of Lacock she'd always been accompanied by her mother or aunt, and while in London they'd walked in parks to be seen. She and her mother had been the walking equivalent of the Gleason family jewels, brought out in fine weather to be noticed and appreciated, their worth assessed and noted for future reference.

How silly it now seemed and yet how safe. For they hadn't ventured onto the city streets for their promenade, but were taken by carriage to a location where other walking, breathing jewels were displayed.

What was more disturbing than the acknowledgment of this absurdity was the fact that Lottie had enjoyed it. Very much. The highlight of her week had been the stroll through the village or the park, especially when she was in possession of a new gown, bonnet, or parasol.

Now, on the other side the world, she also received attention and appreciation, but these stares and indecipherable comments were unwelcome. Although her traveling suit was not in any way ostentatious, it still made her stand out. If only she could have left her suit behind in exchange for the ease and anonymity of Lucia's skirt and blouse. But comfort had to be forfeited. Lottie had to be dressed well to meet Dora's cousin. Thinking of that coming event, she tugged at the sleeves of her suit and put a hand to her hair. She felt naked without her bonnet. No woman of bearing entered public without one. Oh well. It couldn't be helped. There was no way she could have taken her hat from Sofia.

In the first block she hugged the left side of the street, following the up and back of the pushcarts. Such close proximity left her susceptible to the occasional call of the owner to buy this or that, but also gave her a sense of security. If they believed she had money to buy, perhaps they would let her pass unbothered.

But her ploy soon failed as the children began to notice her. Many approached with something to sell—rags or a flower or a piece of bread—and others came boldly with their palms outstretched. The distinction between peddler and pauper was not noticeable, as all wore clothes that were shredded or holey or sized too big or too small.

None wore coats against the October chill, and a few, shockingly, were barefoot.

"No, no," she repeated. "I have nothing. I'm sorry, but I have nothing for you."

They were unfazed by her disclaimers, and the crowd of four children became eight, then a dozen. There were none older than twelve, and many should have been sitting on their mother's laps. Their eyes pleaded and cut into her soul. She felt a tug within that threatened to either strangle or snap and break her.

Where were their parents? Where did they live? When was the last time they'd eaten? Or bathed? Or been hugged?

A little girl of not more than four tripped within the gaggle and fell to the ground. Out of instinct, Lottie knelt to help her up. The children took advantage of her lessened height and pressed harder against her, their dirty hands grabbing, imploring, needing. . . .

Frightened, she pushed their hands away. "Stop it! Get away from me!"

Apparently taken aback by her shouts, they backed away, letting her pass.

She stumbled free of them, her breath ragged. Within a dozen steps she ran into the path of a man dressed in black with long ringlets at his ears.

"Umph!" he said, taking her arms to steady her. *"Obserwuj to!"*

She broke free of him and ran as fast as she could.

"Sí wy dobrze?"

Lottie didn't look back.

Mrs. Tremaine opened a notebook featuring various china and sterling flatware patterns. "I was thinking the Royal Doulton china would be the best for your party. And perhaps the Alvin sterling. I particularly like the Old Chippendale pattern."

Charlotte was still trying to get over the shock of hearing that the

Tremaines were giving a welcome party in her honor. Thirty of their closest friends.

Mrs. Tremaine took her hesitance to indicate dislike. "Or I suppose we could go with the Haviland and the Wallace."

"No, no," Charlotte said. "Your first choice is lovely. It's perfect." Charlotte glanced at Beatrice, who was shaking her head.

Mrs. Tremaine noticed her daughter's action. "You don't approve?"

"Oh, I approve," she said. "But isn't there a less stodgy way to introduce Charlotte to the clan?"

"New York society is not a clan, Beatrice. And no, there is no better way than a dinner party."

Beatrice sighed dramatically. "Plus, I suppose it is a chance for you to show off."

"Beatrice!"

She responded with a shrug. "Flaunting our fancies is the reason for the season, is it not, Mother?"

"Our best china and sterling are not 'fancies.' They are the finest dinnerware available, and they show our guests how much they are appreciated and—"

"And indicate how much *we* are to be appreciated."

Mrs. Tremaine took in a long breath, and Charlotte waited for a burst of anger, for surely Beatrice deserved it.

But instead of an outburst, Beatrice stood. "I will ease the tension in the way I know best: by leaving you two able ladies to plan the soiree without me." She nodded at her mother, then turned to exit the drawing room.

"What are your plans for today, Beatrice?" her mother asked.

The girl paused in the doorway, then turned half round to answer. "To be chaste and correct in every way, and to uphold the decorum and sanctity of the Tremaine name. Will that suit you?"

Her mother didn't answer but turned back to the book of tableware. "Then there it is; we'll use the Royal Doulton and the Alvin."

Although she wasn't certain it was proper, Charlotte reached out and skimmed the top of Mrs. Tremaine's fingers with her own. "I want to thank you for all you're doing to welcome me here," she said.

Their eyes met for a moment. Then Mrs. Tremaine pulled her hand away in order to turn a page. "Now, for the table linens . . ."

⁂

Finally.

Lottie checked the slip of paper against the numbers on the building. Yes. This was the place.

It was a better neighborhood than she'd left, but not by much. At this point, with her feet and back aching, she was not about to discriminate.

She walked up the stoop and was ready to knock on the door when she hesitated. Did this dwelling belong to one family or was it a tenement house?

Before she could find out, a window opened to her right and a woman leaned out to shake a rug. She saw Lottie. "You be wanting something, *Fraulein*?" The voice had a German ring to it. Lottie was sincerely glad to hear English of any kind.

"I'm looking for Mr. and Mrs. Twilerby."

She looked at Lottie skeptically. "And why would you be doing such a thing?"

Lottie was taken aback. It was not the woman's business.

"Be that way." She started to close the window. "I have no time for chitchat."

"No, wait!" Lottie said. "My name is Lottie Hathaway, and I'm just in from England. Mrs. Twilerby is a cousin of a good friend of mine. We wrote to her regarding my arrival. We sent a telegram. She's expecting me."

"Oh, she is now, is she?"

"I assure you, ma'am, that our association is legitimate and—"

She waved Lottie's words away like flies in the breeze. "Oh, you can assure me all you want, but that don't change the truth of it."

"The truth—?"

"Mrs. Twilerby died three weeks ago of a fever, and her husband moved west a week after that. Since the bridge got finished, Samuel couldn't find steady work, and with Ingrid gone . . . he moved to Iowa or Kansas, or someplace thereabouts."

"She died and he moved?"

"That's what I said, didn't I?" She put her hands on the window sash, readying to close it.

Suddenly Lottie remembered her luggage. "But wait! My trunk. I had it sent here from Castle Garden, to this address."

The woman hesitated, and just the way her eyes skittered left, then right, made Lottie fear for her property. She stepped closer to the window. "It was a trunk with brass fittings. Surely you've seen it."

The woman pursed her lips and said, "Come on in, then," and shut the window.

Hope returned.

Lottie entered the building and paused to let her eyes adjust to the dark foyer. Stairs led to other apartments. A door opened to the right and the woman came out. "This way."

She led Lottie down a dimly lit hallway, then used a key to open a door. Inside was a small room packed full of belongings. Lottie immediately spotted her trunk.

"We didn't know who it belonged to," the woman said. "And since the Twilerbys were gone . . ."

"That's all right," Lottie said as she stepped over a pile of clothes to reach it. "I'm just glad—"

She reached for the lock.

And found it broken.

She opened the lid and confirmed her fear. "My things . . . they're not here."

The woman shrugged. "As I said, we didn't know who the stuff belonged to and so—"

"You helped yourself?"

"If you're accusing me of stealing, I'll tell you to get on by, this very minute."

"But you took everything."

The woman backed out of the room and pointed down the hall. "I'll ask you to leave now. You're the one who sent your luggage to people who weren't even here. You're the one who made the mistake, not me."

She was right about that. Lottie never should have relied on strangers, but she'd been so keen on having someone in New York as her connection, her friend . . .

The woman called down the hall to someone, and Lottie heard a man's voice respond. If she wanted to avoid trouble, she needed to leave. Now.

She took one last look at her empty trunk and left the storage room.

"That's the way out, yes it is," the woman said. "Out that door and keep on walking. We don't need your high-and-mighty kind round here, making accusations against good, hardworking folk like us."

She passed a scruffy man with a long mustache. "Is this the troublemaker, Johanna?"

"She's the one, Grif. Accused me of stealing, she did. *Dummes Mädchen.*"

Lottie burst into the open air and rushed down the front steps. The man and woman followed after her, yelling and shaking their hands at her, causing everyone to look in her direction.

Lottie hurried faster, heading farther north, feeling as if imps were biting at her heels. She only slowed when her lungs demanded more air than her corset allowed. She ducked into an alcove and tried to catch her breath.

A woman with a bosom too prevalent for midday sauntered by, then returned to look some more. She snapped the end of her shawl at Lottie's arm. "This is my stand, bitty. My block. Getcher own."

Lottie gasped. Was this a woman of ill repute? And even worse, did she think Lottie was one of her kind?

"Pardon me." Lottie skimmed past the woman and out to the street again.

"Well, pardon *me*," the woman parodied in a high voice.

Lottie sped by other pedestrians on the sidewalk, keeping her head down. Yet where was she going? She knew no one. She had nothing. Not a penny to buy a crust of bread. Where would she sleep? Who would take care of her?

She thought of the Scarpellis and yet . . . they had a full house. They didn't need some stupid, inept Englishwoman taking advantage of their hospitality.

She reached an intersection and saw a street sign for Tenth Street.

The Tremaines live at Thirty-fourth Street and Fifth Avenue.

Dora was at the Tremaines'. Comfort was at the Tremaines'. The end to this horror was at the Tremaines'.

Thirty-fourth Street . . . she had a lot of walking to do, but she would do it.

It was her only hope.

※

"Ugh!"

Lottie looked back to the street she'd just crossed and realized she'd stepped in a pile of horse droppings. She hurried to the curb and dragged the sole of her boot over its edge, hoping to extricate—

"Hey! Stop that."

A man had come out of his shop and was pointing directly at her.

"Pardon me, sir, but where else would you like me to clean my shoe? And where are the crossing sweepers in this city?"

His eyebrows rose and his hands found his hips. "Well, aren't you the hoity-toity one? Want me to send my son out here to sweep the way clean for you, milady?"

Actually . . .

As others passed by, Lottie realized she had been rude cleaning her boot right in front of the man's store. "Actually, I do apologize.

Perhaps you have a cloth I could use to aid my foot in releasing its . . . bounty?"

He leaned his head back and laughed. "Now, that's a different way to put it. Sure, girlie. Come inside, and you can even sit down while you do it."

Sit? That sounded blissful.

Lottie walked into the store, putting her weight on her heel so as not to foul his floor. He offered her a chair and a rag, and she completed the nasty task, then washed her hands in a bowl he'd brought for that purpose.

As she was leaving, to be polite, she showed interest in the man's wares. "What kind of shop is this?" He had a wide assortment of items from musical instruments to luggage to jewel—

"That's my necklace!" She pointed at a ruby necklace in a glass-counter case.

The man looked at it, then at her, and she could tell he was appraising her as he would a jewel. Without a bonnet and wearing a traveling suit that was in much need of a good brushing, he would find her tarnished at best. "I don't think so."

"I know so!" Lottie said. "It was stolen from me at Castle Garden! My mother gave it to me on my last birthday." Then she knew what kind of shop . . . "Is this a pawnshop? Did you buy this from someone—from the thief who stole it from me?"

"Hey, now, girlie. I don't know where people gets the things they bring in. There's no way to know it."

"But it's mine and I want it."

"Then you'll have to pay for it."

She was taken aback. "I should call the police. That's what I should do."

He crossed his arms in front of his chest. "Go ahead and do that. But unless you can show me proof this is yours . . ."

"I . . . I have no proof."

"Then you can buy it same as any customer."

This was ridiculous. But she wanted that necklace back. "How much is it?"

"Five dollars."

"Five? It's worth five hundred at least. Those are real rubies and diamonds."

He smiled smugly. "I thank you for the information. Five hundred, then."

Why had she told him that? "I don't have five hundred dollars." Or five.

"Then I'm guessing this conversation is over."

She bit her lip. "If I want it back, the price is five dollars, yes?"

"For you? Why not?"

She looked around the other cases. "Did the man who brought that in . . . did he bring in other pieces? What about a sapphire ring and some pearl earrings, and—"

The store owner suddenly stepped from behind the counter and put himself between Lottie and the goods. "The transactions with my suppliers are confidential."

She tried to get around him, but he blocked her attempts. "Suppliers?" she said to his face. "That's an interesting word for thieves. Forget the five dollars. I'll get my goods back by calling the police."

He took her by the shoulders. "I won't have my business disparaged by some harpy off the street. Off with you."

"Get your hands off me!"

He pushed her out to the sidewalk, then stood guard in the doorway. "Go on now, or I'll be the one calling the coppers."

Seeing she had an audience of passersby, she smoothed her skirt and looked upward at his sign. "McCorey's Pawn Shop . . . I'll remember you and I'll be back."

"You get some cash 'n' I'll be waiting with open palm."

I bet you will.

A fine mist turned Lottie's trek from drudgery to despair. Her clothing grew heavy with damp, and she gripped her hands around her arms against waves of shivering. She walked north with head lowered, her consciousness mesmerized by the rhythm of her shoes upon the sidewalk. *Step, step, step, step . . . keep going, keep going, soon it will be over. Over. Over.*

Where the southern neighborhoods had been congested with people and carts, as she neared the Tremaines', pedestrians were few. Carriages passed by with their coachmen crouched low against the wet cold. The wheels splashed water, dirtying her already dirty shoes and skirt. The people she did pass walked beneath umbrellas and gave her a wide berth, as if her lack of such shelter made her someone to fear. All sane people were inside, where it was dry and warm.

Did that mean she was insane?

Oddly, during her march, she didn't ponder her predicament: no money, no luggage . . . Instead, her thoughts focused on her goal: the Tremaines'. There was no need to consider other alternatives. There were none.

Lottie glanced up to check her progress and saw an intersection ahead—what should be *the* intersection. A white stone building stood catty-corner, looming four stories. It reminded her of a library. The buildings on all sides were also formidable, some row houses and others larger than they, all in prime condition. Which house belonged to the Tremaines?

A man hurried across the street toward her, his umbrella raised high to accommodate his top hat.

"Excuse me, sir?"

He walked past her, then reconsidered. "Yes. Well. May I help you, miss?"

"If you please, which house belongs to the Tremaines?"

He pointed at the white stone building. "The servants' entrance is around back," he said.

Lottie barely managed a thank-you. Servant? He thought she was a servant? Only after the humiliation had its full say did she realize the Tremaines' home was the huge building she'd taken for a library. This was a home? For four people? She'd assumed their wealth to be above her own family's but had never imagined it could match the wealth of English royalty.

She crossed the street to the left and walked on the sidewalk directly across from the home. Her determination faltered.

How could she possibly knock on their door looking as she did—as a servant, or worse, a wet dog, drowned by the rain. Why, she wasn't even wearing a hat. She never should have given it to Sofia. She needed that hat. If only she had the hat—

The addition of the hat would not have changed her condition, for it too would have been soaked, its ribbons and flowers wilted and sagging.

If only it hadn't started to rain.

If only . . .

The list was too long.

⚜

"Thank you, Mr. Childs," Charlotte said to the butler as he helped her on with her cloak.

"'Childs' will do, Miss Gleason," Mrs. Tremaine whispered. To the servant she said, "The umbrellas?"

A footman and the butler retrieved two umbrellas, which they unfurled as soon as the front door was opened. A carriage awaited the two women, and they hurried down the front steps to get inside, with the two servants straining against the wind to protect them with the umbrellas.

Charlotte sat on the seat and brushed the wetness from her skirt. "It's a good day for flowers but not much else," she said.

"Happily for us, Thorley's House of Flowers has an enormous assortment inside for us to choose from for your party." The butler closed the door of the carriage, and it began to pull away. Mrs. Tremaine looked outside. "Oh my. Who is that slovenly woman there? I do hope Childs gets rid of her. Beggars are not acceptable in front of private homes."

Charlotte looked outside too and, as the carriage sped on, craned her neck to see more.

No. It couldn't be.

Was the woman standing in the rain Lottie?

She raised a hand, as if to wave.

"Do sit back, my dear. It's not polite to stare."

Her heart raced. Not polite to stare? Was it polite to assume another woman's identity?

Lottie had come to the Tremaines'? It could only mean one thing. She wanted to renege on their plan. While Charlotte and Mrs. Tremaine were at the florist's picking out flowers for her welcome party, Lottie would knock on the front door and say, "Hello, I'm the real Charlotte Gleason."

"Charlotte, I've been speaking to you."

"Yes. Sorry. What were you saying?"

It didn't matter what Mrs. Tremaine said or which flowers they might choose. China and sterling patterns, linen, guest lists, and gowns. None of it mattered.

It was over.

※

That's her! That's Dora!

Lottie raised her hand to wave as the carriage pulled away. She ran after it but tripped on the cobblestones and fell hard into a puddle.

Before she could collect herself, a man grabbed her forcefully by the arm and pulled her to standing. "There, now. Be off with you."

"But I know—"

"Mrs. Tremaine does not take kindly to vagabonds lurking outside her house. You get along now, or I'll call the police."

"But I'm not lurking, I'm Charlotte—"

The man turned to the other servant on the steps. "George! Go fetch the police."

The younger man nodded and ran down the street.

Lottie yanked her arm free. "Leave me alone."

"You're the one who needs to do the leaving."

"Fine," she said, walking toward the intersection. "I'm going."

"You be doing that." He pointed a finger at her. "And I'll be watching you until you're gone. For good, you hear? For good."

Lottie saw that the other servant had stopped in the next block and was waiting for her to move on. She had no choice but to walk away in the direction from whence she'd come.

≋

The firm stride that had brought her north abandoned Lottie, as did all determination. Her feet never left the sidewalk but scraped along, one step shuffling into the next. She was beaten. She was vanquished. She was through.

The mist turned to full rain. What couldn't get worse did.

She couldn't go on. She would sink to the ground in full surrender. At least she could rest.

A bolt of lightning lit the darkened afternoon, and she looked up and saw she was beside a church.

Sanctuary.

She held on to the stone railing, dragging her feet to follow her mind's lead. At the landing it took all her strength to open the thick doors, but once inside, the lack of rain offered immediate relief—which was soon replaced with an awful chill.

The narthex was unoccupied and she gained new hope that she could enter the sanctuary unnoticed. She paused at the doorway of the center aisle, noted no one present, then slipped inside. Faint light made the stained-glass windows glow in muted colors, and an intricate cross sat upon the altar, drawing her forward. Holding the pews for support, she bypassed the seats in the back and walked ahead, keeping her eyes on the cross.

Come unto me, all ye that labour and are heavy laden, and I will give you rest.

She stood next to the first row and stared at the cross. "Rest," she whispered. Then she turned into the pew, sprawled across the rich velvet cushion, and was instantly asleep.

You're safe now. I'll watch over you. You're not alone.

Mrs. Tremaine entered the house, immediately removed her gloves, and handed them to Childs. "It's disappointing that you developed a headache, Miss Gleason. Childs, make sure Mary gets Miss Gleason some medicinals."

"I'm disappointed too," Charlotte said. "I didn't mean to cut short our excursion. Please know that any flowers you choose will be lovely. I trust your taste completely."

"Hmm." To the butler Mrs. Tremaine said, "I'll be in my sitting room. Please have coffee brought in."

Charlotte was left alone with the butler. She handed Childs her gloves slowly, trying to study him at the same time. She awaited the proclamation *There was a woman come by who said she was you, Miss Gleason.*

But all he said was "I'll send Mary up to your room, Miss Gleason."

Had Lottie changed her mind? Was their secret still safe?

Apparently so, because as Charlotte headed to the stairs, she saw Childs go off to get Mary.

Charlotte counted her blessings.

And worried about Lottie.

Chapter Eleven

"Miss? Miss."

Lottie felt a hand upon her shoulder. Had Davies, the butler, come to wake her? Why wasn't Dora—?

She opened her eyes and shot to sitting.

"Now, now. Don't panic. You're fine," the man said.

He stood on the altar side of the first pew, dressed in clerical garb with a pastor's collar.

Pews, altar, cross.

The past raced through her memory in a flash. She pressed a hand against her damp hair, trying to pin drooping curls into place.

"Nah, nah, lassie. Don't trouble yourself. I see you've been out in the rain. It's the wondering why that's on my mind." He took a step to the side, gesturing for her to follow. "Come and get by a fire, and you can tell me all about it."

She wasn't going to tell him anything, but the thought of being warm enticed her to follow.

They exited the sanctuary through a side door leading to a room in the back. He hurried to the fire and stirred it to life, then added another log. As he motioned toward a chair, a woman came from another room.

"What's this?" she asked.

"We have a guest, Mattie. Get a blanket."

She shook her head and came to Lottie, leading her into the room she'd left. "A blanket won't be doing her much good, Douglas. She needs to get out of her wet clothes. I'll take care of her."

They entered an eating area and then a small sleeping alcove beyond. The woman took a skirt and blouse from a hook. "Here. Put these on." She pulled a curtain to give her privacy.

It had all happened so fast, Lottie found herself undressing before she was fully awake. Propriety begged her to go, but reality pressed her to stay. She needed help. That's all there was to it.

Removing her sodden clothes was a relief, as was the feel of dry fabric upon her back. She left on her undergarments but did remove the bustle and petticoats.

"You 'bout done?" the woman asked. "Hand me yer things and I'll get them to dryin'."

Lottie stopped buttoning the dry blouse and handed the woman the clothes through the curtain.

"Ey, these weigh a hundred pounds," the woman said.

Indeed, Lottie felt liberated. She finished her buttoning and passed through the curtain. The woman was spreading Lottie's garments on drying racks by the fire that served the kitchen. Her task complete, she turned to look at Lottie. "Well, now. They may not be fancy, but at least they're dry."

For the first time, Lottie spoke. "They're wonderful. Thank you."

"You're welcome. Now, go sit with me husband by the fire while I get you something to eat." When Lottie hesitated, she added, "He's a good listener."

Ah yes. She remembered his wanting her to tell him all about it.

Lottie went into the main room and saw the pastor seated by

the fire in one of two upholstered chairs, with another wooden chair brought close to make three. He rose and offered her the most comfortable chair. "Here, now. That's better. My wife has taken good care of you, hasn't she?"

"She has."

Lottie sat and was immediately warmed by the now roaring flame.

"So now." The man's receding hair glowed silver in the firelight. "I'm Pastor Weston, and that lovely woman in the other room is my wife, Matilda. And you are?"

It was a good question. The truth begged for release, but Lottie ended up saying, "I'm Lottie Hathaway."

He nodded once, as if satisfied the introductions were properly accomplished.

Mrs. Weston returned to the room with a tray. "Here, now. Some soup, bread, and coffee." She set the tray on Lottie's lap.

Smelling the food, seeing it . . . Lottie gave her hunger free rein. She hadn't eaten anything since early that morning at the Scarpellis', and now it was—

She finished chewing a bite of bread. "May I ask the time?"

Pastor Weston glanced at a wall where a clock hung. "Half past one."

She'd left the Scarpellis' at seven. No wonder she was hungry.

Lottie took a sip of coffee and found it less potent than the brew she'd had at the Scarpellis'. If only the characters from *Little Women* were with her now, enjoying a cup together. She could use their fine company.

"Soup," Mrs. Weston said. "Take some soup."

Lottie did as she was told. The soup was a balm.

Mrs. Weston sat in the other chair, and Pastor Weston took the hard one. They let her eat for a moment in silence. When she stopped to take a breath, the pastor asked, "So, Miss Hathaway. Why were you out in the rain without cover? What brings you to sleeping on a pew at Marble?"

She must not have heard him correctly. "Marble?"

"Marble Collegiate Church. Don't you know where you are, lassie?"

His wife swatted his arm. "Tact, Douglas, tact." She looked at Lottie. "You are fair welcome here, please know that. But we're concerned because you're obviously a lady of standing, and such ladies don't often enter the church in your . . . condition."

Pastor Weston looked at his wife. "Didna I just ask the same thing?"

"I did it better," his wife said.

Their banter made Lottie smile. She set down the spoon, tried to settle on how much to tell them, and decided a portion of the truth might be better than none. "I know someone who lives north of here. I went—"

"Who is it you know?"

This, she couldn't say. "Just a friend. But she wasn't able to receive me, and so I started walking home and—"

"And home is where?" the pastor asked.

Lottie found her mouth agape, unable to say. An awkward moment passed.

"Home is where the heart is," Mrs. Weston said. "Isn't that so, Miss Hathaway?"

She couldn't nod or even shake her head. Home was a foreign land that couldn't be reached by any means. Home was locked away in a past that forbid her reentry.

The pastor put a hand upon her arm. "So 'as a bird that wandereth from her nest, so is a man that wandereth from his place.'"

Tears sprang forward unannounced. "That's exactly how I feel," she said. "I'm flying around with no place to land."

Mrs. Weston stood and urged her husband to trade chairs with her. She took the tray from Lottie, then moved the wooden chair close and gave Lottie a shoulder to cry upon. "There, there. You've landed here. God's brought you here."

Had He? She remembered looking up through the rain and seeing the church. Had God led her to this safe haven and to these kind people? Even after she'd been mad at Him and vowed to do things her way?

The pastor handed her a handkerchief. "Your accent . . . you're English."

"Yes, I'm from Wiltshire. I just arrived . . ." She had to think. The answer was hard to fathom. "Yesterday?"

Their eyebrows rose in tandem. "You came through Castle Garden?"

"Yes."

"How did you end up here? 'Tis a long way north."

"I walked."

"Where did you spend last night?"

"With the Scarpellis. They—"

"Who are the Scarpellis?" the pastor asked.

"An Italian family. Mrs. Scarpelli was at Castle Garden to meet some family who'd arrived from Italy, and she saw when a man stole my jewels and money, took pity on me, and took me into their home, where I slept in a room with Aldo and Francesca and Lucia and Vittorio—and little Sofia. She held my hand, and I gave her my hat and—"

Lottie noticed the pastor and his wife looking at her, incredulous. She'd said too much, too fast.

"They were very kind to me."

The pastor recovered himself. "I'm sure they were, but where . . . where do they live?"

"Mulberry Street. Near Five Points?"

Their eyes grew wide. "You stayed in such a place? Alone?"

"I wasn't alone. They took me in when I had no one and nothing, even though they're struggling themselves." The comparison with their behavior and the reception she'd received at the Tremaines' was huge. Lottie thought of a Bible story, one of the few she remembered. "Like the poor widow who put all she had in the offering. Didn't Jesus declare her gift of more worth than the rich who gave only a little of their wealth?"

The couple looked at each other; then the pastor nodded. "You have humbled us, Miss Hathaway. For indeed you found a gem in the Scarpellis, a gem amid the horrors of Five Points. We haven't seen, but we've heard the stories."

"Is it as dismal a place as they say?" Mrs. Weston asked.

Lottie wanted to lie, to defend the place for the Scarpellis' sake, but the memory of the beggar children, the stench, the crowding, and the dilapidation could not—should not—be ignored. "It is horrible. Yet the people have found a way to carry on in spite of it. There's a strength there." It was unnerving that she hadn't acknowledged that strength until now.

" 'The Lord will give strength unto his people; the Lord will bless his people with peace.' "

"I'm not sure how much peace they have," Lottie said, "but they are strong."

Pastor Weston nodded. "It appears God provided for you twice— through the Scarpellis and through your visit with us here."

Lottie was taken aback. Was it true? Had God helped her both times?

Mrs. Weston returned the tray to her lap. "Eat some more. You need your nourishment."

The pastor sat back in his chair and crossed one leg over the other. "Are you going to try to see your friend again?"

"You could stay here with us tonight and try tomorrow," Mrs. Weston said.

Lottie looked toward a window. The storm had passed, and the sun was attempting to shine. She didn't want to burden this couple any longer. "The rain has stopped. I must be moving along."

"Let me get you a hack," Pastor Weston offered.

She began to object, but he'd already left the room. Mrs. Weston said, "Let us do this for you, child. You've walked enough these two days. Now, finish your soup."

Lottie did so quickly, and with Mrs. Weston's blessing took the bread for later. Mrs. Weston helped her get dressed again, and Lottie reluctantly put on the restrictive bustle and petticoats. She was ready when Pastor Weston returned.

"A hack is waiting outside." He pressed some coins into her hand. "For the fare."

Again, Lottie wanted to refuse, but now wasn't the time to be proud. Instead she said, "Thank you. Thank you both."

Mrs. Weston embraced her and looked deeply into her eyes. "You know where we are."

Lottie kissed the woman's cheek and left quickly before the threat of tears gained momentum. She backtracked through the church to the street. A hack sat ready to take her north—to the Tremaines'.

You can't go there. You're not welcome.

And then she knew where she must go.

"Miss?" the driver said.

She felt the weight of the coins in her hand. It was the only money she had. "I've decided to walk."

He looked perturbed but gave the reins a shake. "Suit yerself."

As the hack headed north, Lottie began to walk.

South.

Charlotte recovered from her headache in time to suffer through the midday meal. The food was flavorful but the company bland. It being Saturday, Mr. Tremaine and Conrad were present, which logically should have made the conversation of more interest—but was otherwise. Did this family ever just *talk*? And when would she have time alone with Conrad? How could she be expected to marry the man when the only time she saw him was together with his entire family?

Beatrice was the one distraction, yet Charlotte found herself tightening whenever she spoke because of the certain conflict that followed. Beatrice showed no concern for the effect she had on others, and in fact seemed to thrive upon it.

Charlotte wasn't sure how to feel about the girl. When she'd first heard Conrad had a sister, she'd imagined a confidante. But Beatrice had already proven herself to be unsuited for such a bond. And since she'd also shown herself to be completely contrary to her parents, Charlotte wasn't sure a further closeness was a good idea even *if* Beatrice could be trusted. Charlotte might be called upon to take sides between Beatrice and Mrs. Tremaine. And if so, Mrs. Tremaine needed to win. It was a question of who had the power. Power—or the lack thereof. That was the source of both girls' discontent.

She wondered why Beatrice wasn't married yet. Charlotte could think of no tweak of society that would prevent the younger child—if there were no other daughters—from marrying before her older brother. Had Beatrice's penchant for confrontation held her back? No man would be attracted to a woman with such strong opinions, especially if she slapped the face of the prevailing social order.

And honestly, it could have been due to Beatrice's lack of beauty. From Charlotte's observations of the social set back in England, it wasn't unheard of for a plain woman to marry, but her goal was certainly harder gained. And in Beatrice's case . . . when pensive, when unoccupied, her face wasn't without appeal. There was a strength in her chin, and her cheekbones offered a stately shape to her face. But alas, the moments of peace were few, and the rest of the time Beatrice's face hardened with a defensiveness that made one wish to recoil rather than engage.

"Are you worried about something, miss?"

The meal was long over, and Mary stood behind Charlotte in her room, adjusting her hair for a summons to Mrs. Tremaine's morning room.

Just everything. Yet Charlotte gave the correct response. "No, of course not. What do I have to be worried about?"

Mary nodded, but her eyes took on their own worry—which added to Charlotte's. If her maid knew enough to worry . . . Servants often knew more about what was going on in the house than its residents. Had Mary heard tittle-tattle through the servant grapevine about what the Tremaines truly thought of her?

Charlotte reached a hand upward and stopped Mary's movement. "If you hear anything you think I need to know, Mary . . ."

"I'll tell you. I promise."

Sending her maid to be a spy. Had it already come to this?

"There you are."

The implication from Mrs. Tremaine was that Charlotte had lingered too long upstairs. "I'm sorry to make you wait, ma'am."

"I have plenty to accomplish without waiting upon you, but when I request your presence, it would behoove you not to dally."

"Yes, ma'am."

"I am not your mistress. Mrs. Tremaine will do."

Charlotte's chest tightened at the slip. "Yes, Mrs. Tremaine."

The woman was seated at a dainty but intricately carved desk. She set her pen in a stand and sighed. Had she had enough of Charlotte already?

"It's appropriate for you to send a letter to your parents, telling them of your arrival."

Charlotte was taken aback. "We—I—sent a cable upon my arrival. They know I arrived safely."

"So your responsibility to your parents is through? With a mere cable?"

She felt herself redden. "No, no, of course not. You're right, of course. I'll go upstairs and write to them directly. They'll want to hear of your generous hospitality and—"

Mrs. Tremaine retrieved paper and pen. "You may do so now."

"Here?"

Her eyebrows rose. "You find my morning room lacking?"

Oh dear.

Mrs. Tremaine pointed to a small table with a chair beside it. "There. Sit there and compose your letter while I continue my work."

Charlotte took a seat at the table, her mind racing. It wasn't that she couldn't compose a letter to Mrs. Gleason. On the ship she and Lottie had talked about which terms of endearment to use, and Charlotte *had* planned on corresponding in Lottie's stead. But the samples of Lottie's handwriting were upstairs in her bedroom. She'd practiced copying the style of the script, but since Lottie was left-handed, the angle was hard to appropriate. Not that Mrs. Tremaine would notice the difference, but Lottie's mother surely would.

She really needed one of Lottie's letters to look at while she wrote.

It wasn't to be. Mrs. Tremaine brought her some stationery and a pen. "I would be remiss if I didn't encourage your correspondence. I would expect as much if Beatrice were in some other family's care."

Charlotte nodded and took up the pen. She remembered her practice sessions when she'd found that turning the paper in the opposite direction from the norm had made it easier to accomplish the left-hand slant that was the most noticeable feature of Lottie's script.

Mrs. Tremaine returned to her desk, but not her work. "What are you doing?" she asked.

"Excuse me?"

"You turn your paper . . . backward?"

Charlotte thought fast. She'd never expected to write letters in front of others. "I . . . I started writing like this as a child and never changed."

"Your governess never corrected you?"

Charlotte remembered Lottie telling her that as a young child her nanny had tried to get her to do things with her right hand, but with no success. "I'm afraid she indulged me."

"Spare the rod, spoil the child."

"Yes, you're right."

With a nod Mrs. Tremaine said, "To work, then."

As she began to write, Charlotte chastised herself for not writing a letter beforehand. During the last day of the voyage, Lottie had suggested she do as much, but Charlotte had put it off. This entire situation could have been avoided if she'd been able to tell Mrs. Tremaine she already had a letter ready to post.

She thought about writing nonsense and writing a real letter later, but the threat of Mrs. Tremaine rising from her chair and coming to check her progress was enough to make her create real sentences. *Dear Mother* . . .

The content wasn't difficult. Charlotte knew the relationship between Mrs. Gleason and her daughter was formal, so the writing flowed and soon she was done. She signed her name, *Your daughter, Charlotte*. She sat back in the chair and realized she'd been holding her breath during the entire ordeal.

"Are you finished already?"

Finished with this draft. While writing she'd decided she would retire to her room and recopy it with Lottie's handwriting samples close by. "Yes, Mrs. Tremaine."

"Mmm." She put her own pen aside. "By the way . . . isn't your mother a cousin of Lord Mortonbridge?"

What? Charlotte had no idea. Yet she had to assume Mrs. Tremaine wasn't trying to trick her. "Yes, I believe that's true."

"Your mother's maiden name was Caste . . . Caste . . ."

"Castenet." It was the first name that came to mind.

Mrs. Tremaine raised an eyebrow. Then she rose from her chair. "Give me your letter and I'll post it for you."

"But I can post it myself. You needn't bother."

"Nonsense." She held out her hand, and Charlotte had no choice but to relinquish the letter. Mrs. Tremaine gave it a cursory look, put it inside an envelope she had already addressed, and set it on her desk. "Now, go amuse yourself for a short while. At three o'clock a few acquaintances will arrive that I want you to meet. I'm going to check with Mrs. Dyson about the refreshments."

Charlotte eyed the letter. *I need it back.*

"You are excused."

Charlotte got an idea. "May I have a few pieces of stationery to bring up to my room in case I'm inspired to write further letters?"

Mrs. Tremaine opened the center drawer of her desk and handed Charlotte a stack of six or seven sheets. "And take the fountain pen along for your use."

"Thank you." Charlotte left the room. On the way upstairs, interrupting her panic about the letter, she suddenly stopped.

"Castalan!" she whispered. *Mrs. Gleason's maiden name was Castalan, not Castenet!* Charlotte looked toward the morning room. Had Mrs. Tremaine noticed the mistake? She hadn't said anything . . .

"Is something wrong, miss?"

Mary stood at the top of the stairs, a stack of fresh laundry in her arms.

Charlotte's thoughts returned to the letter—the letter that must not be sent. Perhaps Mary could help.

She hurried up the stairs. "Come, Mary."

They entered her room and Charlotte closed the door behind them. "I need you to do something for me."

"Anything, miss."

How would she explain it? "I need you to do as I say and don't ask questions. Understand?"

Mary's brown eyes grew wary, but she said, "Yes, miss."

"There's a letter in an envelope on Mrs. Tremaine's desk. It's addressed to my mother, Mrs. Thomas Gleason, in Wiltshire. I need you to retrieve that letter for me."

"Steal it?"

"It's my letter, but I wish to write a better one and replace it for the letter currently inside." She thought of a key point. "Without Mrs. Tremaine knowing it's been done."

Mary bit her lower lip.

"You have a pocket in your skirt, yes?"

She put her hand inside to show the affirmative.

"Slip the letter inside and bring it up to me; then I'll insert the new letter and you can return it to the desk. Mrs. Tremaine told me she's checking with the cook about refreshments for a visit from friends. The room should be unoccupied." When Mary didn't respond, Charlotte added, "It's very important, Mary. Can you do that for me?"

With less hesitation than expected, Mary nodded and headed for the door.

"Discretion, Mary. Discretion is essential."

"I understand, miss."

Charlotte hurried to the bureau and removed a stack of papers she'd brought with her from London. She found the examples of Lottie's penmanship and set to work writing a new letter to Mrs. Gleason in much better form than the one she'd created downstairs.

Haste prevented perfection, but Charlotte was glad for the chance to redo the letter, as she'd forgotten Lottie's unique way of writing her g's at the end of words, with the bottom loop originating from the left, not the right.

She'd just finished the letter and was looking it over when Mary slipped into the bedroom.

"Did you get it?"

She drew it out of her pocket.

Charlotte released the breath she'd been saving, then folded the new letter in half and replaced the old letter in the envelope. How fortunate Mrs. Tremaine hadn't sealed it.

"Here," she said, handing it to Mary. "Back to the desk it goes."

And she was gone. Charlotte fell onto a chair, drained from the effort. Her life was a deception. How could she ever keep it up? And how could any good come from it?

She covered her face with her hands and let the tears come. Mary slipped back in the room and was immediately taken aback. She hurried to Charlotte's side. "It's all right, miss. I did it. The letter is back on the desk. I saw Miss Beatrice in the entry, but I don't think she suspects anything. It's done. No need for tears."

Oh, there was plenty of need for tears. Should she end it all now? Just tell Mary she wasn't Charlotte Gleason, but merely a maid like herself?

Before she could talk herself out of it, she heard herself saying, "I'm not who you think I—"

A knock on the door saved her from herself. Or had it prevented her salvation?

Mary spoke with someone at the door, then returned to Charlotte's side. "Mrs. Tremaine's maid said the coffee has been postponed by half an hour. It will begin at half past instead of on the hour."

The chance for disclosure had passed. "Thank you, Mary. That will be all for now."

Mary looked at her askance. "Are you sure you're all right?"

"Perfectly. I simply felt a wave of homesickness."

Left alone, Charlotte breathed in and out, quite willing to let God spur her to go after her maid and reveal the truth, or . . .

She felt no nudge to go after Mary.

It was a relief.

⁂

"And this is Mrs. Charles Sonomish, Mrs. Thomas Standish, and Mrs. Reginald Byron."

Charlotte executed a curtsy. "I'm pleased to make your acquaintance, ladies."

"My, my, Gertrude, she is a lovely thing."

"Conrad should be very pleased."

"To think you found her across the pond. How extraordinary."

It was as though Charlotte need not even be present. She felt like a pretty bauble, acquired to be admired.

"She has good teeth too."

All heads turned in Beatrice's direction.

"That will be enough, Beatrice."

She shrugged as the ladies settled into the chairs of the music room.

Mrs. Sonomish removed her gloves and tucked them between skirt and chair. "I'm sure it is a delight for you to have another young woman in the house, Beatrice."

"Oh yes," she said with an intensity that negated whatever she would say next. "I've always wanted a sister."

She offered Charlotte a pulled smile that surely revealed its duplicity to all in the room.

Mrs. Tremaine began pouring the beverage. The smell of coffee permeated the room. "Before the season fully begins, we're having a proper party for Miss Gleason to introduce her to society, but I wanted you ladies—being my special friends—to meet her first." She gazed at Charlotte. "I don't know how such things work in Wiltshire, but here in New York the season begins on the fifteenth of November and ends on January fifteenth."

"Of course, the late winter is then consumed by charity balls," Mrs. Sonomish said. "Are you good at needlework and such?"

Charlotte was relieved she could honestly answer in the affirmative. "I can sew a bit."

"Good, for during charity season there is an endless need for items to sell at the events."

"As if the world needs another doily or pillow sham," Beatrice said.

Her mother flashed her a look.

"In the summer when the heat gets oppressive here, we all go to Newport for their season," Mrs. Byron added.

"Heaven forbid we miss a ball," Beatrice said under her breath.

But for a spare glance the ladies ignored her.

Mrs. Byron returned her cup to her saucer. "Tell me, Miss Gleason, do you miss your family back in Hampshire?"

"Wiltshire," Charlotte corrected.

"Hampshire, Wiltshire . . ." Beatrice said. "Miss Gleason doesn't miss her family because she keeps in vigorous touch with them. Didn't you send them a letter this very day?"

The way she looked at Charlotte . . . Mary had mentioned seeing Beatrice in the hall when she was switching the letters. Did Beatrice know more than she let on?

Mrs. Tremaine answered for Charlotte. "Indeed. Miss Gleason is a good daughter and wrote a letter to her parents."

"That is indeed commendable," Mrs. Standish said. "It's of utter importance for a daughter to be on amiable terms with her parents." Her eyes passed over Beatrice.

The point was made and acknowledged. Charlotte hoped Beatrice would remain silent—and for once, that's just what she did.

Mrs. Tremaine offered a plate of shortbread cookies. "Miss Gleason is an accomplished pianist. That's why I decided to have our soiree here in the music room."

"Oh, do play for us," Mrs. Standish said.

Charlotte felt the blood drain from her face. Lottie Gleason *was* a pianist—though far from accomplished, but Dora Connors couldn't play a note.

"I would love to hear something by Liszt," Mrs. Sonomish said.

"I'm afraid I've not heard—"

Mrs. Sonomish put a hand to the lace at her neck. "Franz Liszt? The Hungarian composer? Why, he's the world's most accomplished pianist."

"Didn't I read in the newspaper that he died recently?" Mrs. Tremaine asked.

"Yes, I believe he did," Mrs. Byron said. "Such a loss. But fortunately we still have all that wonderful music he composed." She turned to Charlotte. "Who is your favorite composer, Miss Gleason?"

Flee! Fall down. Break an arm. Pray the earth opens up and the house falls into a crevasse, stopping all talk of—

Beatrice set her cup and saucer upon her lap. "Perhaps our guest's talents were . . . exaggerated?"

Oddly, within the snide remark was a way out. Although unappealing, it was *something*. "I'm afraid Miss Tremaine is correct. My parents may have overstated my musical abilities." Charlotte sighed for effect and to calm her nerves. "A child off the street has more musical talent than I do."

The ladies' disapproval hung in the air between them. "Your parents shouldn't have done such a thing," Mrs. Byron said.

"You're right," Charlotte agreed.

"At least you told the truth now," Mrs. Standish said.

"Had no choice but to tell the truth . . ." Beatrice mumbled.

"What did you say, daughter?"

"I was merely of the same opinion, that Miss Gleason's character is heightened by her honesty." Beatrice clapped her hands softly. "Bravo, Miss Gleason."

Beatrice's attitude suggested the worst: she knew the truth, or at the very least, suspected something was amiss.

Mrs. Sonomish sipped her coffee, then said, "It's not a crime not to have musical talent. Either one does or one doesn't."

"Exactly," Mrs. Tremaine said.

"Do you paint perhaps?" Mrs. Bryon asked.

"I'm afraid I'm without that talent too."

Mrs. Standish put a finger to her lips. "Beatrice . . . you paint, do you not?"

"Yes, I believe I do." She stood. "Would you like to see one of my paintings?"

Mrs. Tremaine shook her head. "I don't think—"

Beatrice ignored her and left the room.

As they waited for her return, the ladies chatted about various events of the upcoming social season.

"We just returned from Newport, though it's taken me a good while to get the house back in shape again," Mrs. Byron said. "We pay the servants to maintain the premises while we're gone, yet I swear they do nothing but eat our food and play pinochle. My Reginald found two decks of cards missing from the game room."

"Did you find the culprit?" Mrs. Standish asked.

"No, but we will. 'Steal and be gone' is our motto."

"It's so hard to get good help, loyal help," Mrs. Sonomish said. "We have a hard time keeping servants beyond a year."

"They get restless," Mrs. Tremaine said. "Do you find that a problem in England, Miss Gleason?"

Not at all. The Gleasons' servants had all been employed for years—until they were let go due to the family's financial difficulties. She knew it would be simpler to agree, but a dose of pride welled up and she said, "We rarely have such problems—at least not in the Gleason household. My lady's maid, Dora Connors, has been with me since I was twelve."

"Commendable indeed," Mrs. Byron said.

Beatrice entered the room with a canvas. "Here is my latest attempt."

The women gave it their full attention and motioned her closer for a personal look. "My, my," Mrs. Byron said. "It's . . . lovely, Beatrice. You show true talent."

Charlotte noticed Mrs. Tremaine raise her eyebrows, as if surprised. "We are very proud of our daughter."

It was Beatrice's turn to raise an eyebrow.

Mrs. Sonomish held the painting upon her lap. "The use of color to distinguish the flowers while keeping them indistinct upon close inspection . . . it's very interesting."

"The style is called Impressionism," Beatrice said. "It's all the rage in France. Monet, Manet, Degas, and even a woman, Berthe Morisot."

"A woman *known* for her painting?"

"She deserves recognition," Beatrice said.

"Does she attempt to make money at it?" Mrs. Standish asked.

"I assume so. Isn't the worth of art usually determined by the price people are willing to pay for it?"

Mrs. Tremaine stood and took the painting away, setting it on the floor by a music stand. "Be assured Beatrice does not paint for income—or show. I can't imagine going to an exhibit of art painted by females."

"I can't imagine there ever being such a thing," Mrs. Bryon said.

"But why shouldn't there be?" Charlotte had held her tongue as long as she could. She knew the way of the world; she knew women of bearing were not to have a career of any sort, but during the discussion she'd watched Beatrice's expression fall, then tighten, and had seen a crease form between her eyes as if she was desperately trying to hold her emotions in check.

The women tittered between themselves, defending the right and privilege of women of worth to be deemed the "leisure class." They were proud of their duty to do nothing and considered it a sign of their status and station.

Beatrice returned to her seat. Charlotte caught her eye for just a moment and in that one look saw a glimmer of gratitude.

❧

"Lottie!"

Sofia ran toward her—ran into her—wrapping her little arms around Lottie's legs. She looked up and offered a long string of Italian words, of which Lottie understood none.

And yet . . . she understood everything. And felt the same way.

She cupped Sofia's chin in her hand. "I'm very glad to be back too, Sofia." She resisted the urge to swipe a handkerchief over her grimy cheeks.

If she had a handkerchief.

Which she didn't.

Besides, her own face was probably none cleaner.

"Mamma?" she asked.

Sofia took Lottie's hand and pulled her inside the Scarpelli tenement and up the stairs. She chattered the entire time, which was an unexpected salve to Lottie's nerves.

Finally on the top floor, Sofia burst into her family's apartment, causing her mother to put a hand to her chest.

But when Lea saw Lottie, her surprise became joy and she too embraced her.

"Meraviglioso! Benvenuta, Lottie!"

In the woman's ample arms, Lottie began to cry.

Lea didn't let go. *"Famiglia . . ."* she whispered in Lottie's ear.

Lottie was done flying. It felt good to land.

Chapter Twelve

Lottie wasn't sure about this, not one little bit.

Yet she couldn't very well stay behind when the Scarpellis went to church Sunday morning. Church was nothing new to her. She went every Sunday with her parents. In the village church in Lacock they had their own pew.

Her trepidation involved going to a Catholic church. St. Patrick's. She already felt like an outsider among the mass of Italians that entered the church, but to sit through a *mass* itself . . .

It was all so new.

Everyone had put on their nicest clothes, and the women covered their heads with shawls or pretty pieces of lace. Lottie was lent a piece to cover her own hair. Little Sofia wore Lottie's hat. One feather leaned precariously until Lottie tucked it back into place.

The cathedral was on Mulberry Street, just a few blocks away. They walked. Upon entering, the men removed their hats and they all dipped their hands in a vessel of water in the narthex and bowed at the aisle, touching their heads and chest with their hand. Lottie had no idea what they were doing, but it seemed to be a gesture of respect, so she did the same. Then she walked down the aisle between Lucia and Sofia and went into a pew. They did not sit at first, but knelt in prayer.

Lottie's prayers were an assortment of need, gratitude, and fear. Her life was in a shambles. She had no possessions, only the dime Pastor Weston had given her for the hack ride, no permanent place to stay, and no plan. Yet *because* her jewels and money had been stolen, she'd met the Scarpellis. Which meant she wasn't alone. That was worth something.

During her long walk from Pastor Weston's back to Mulberry Street, she'd had plenty of time to think. What would have happened if she'd somehow arrived at the house of Dora's cousin without ever meeting Lea and her family? What would have happened if she'd arrived *with* her money and jewels intact? Either way she would have been alone. Completely and utterly.

The idea of being alone in New York City had not fazed her when she was on the ship with Dora, but now that she was here and had experienced firsthand the complex and mysterious ways of this city and its inhabitants . . . money was the least of her problems and even her needs. Being completely alone would have been devastating.

Yet God had taken care of that, right from the start.

Lottie glanced to her right, at Lucia's bowed head. Her lips offered soft murmurings of prayer. In that one glance Lottie's heart pulled with a tenderness that was a bit disconcerting. In her old world, she would never, ever, ever have had anything to do with someone like Lucia, and yet now, in the midst of her new life, a friendship had formed between them that could not be denied. Since the door linking herself to Dora had been so harshly closed, had God opened a window with Lucia? Did He understand how much Lottie needed a friend—even more than she realized that herself?

Lottie was thankful for the Scarpellis, for a roof over her head, for food in her stomach, and . . . for the hope of a job. Lucia promised to take her to the garment sweatshops in the morning.

The idea of working . . .

Was Lottie a good worker? She'd never worked. She'd never needed to. Yet could it be that she *did* need to work, that everyone needed to work? If not to earn a living, perhaps the act of working served some other purpose?

The congregation began to sit, and Lottie looked at the altar and beyond. A large crucifix was displayed at the front with Jesus suffering on the cross. She'd never thought much about His pain, and it was difficult to look at Him. She was more at ease thinking about Christmas and Easter, His birth and resurrection.

A priest came in behind a young boy, both clad in white, their hands held before them in supplication. Words were said, prayers prayed, but it took Lottie a few moments to realize the service wasn't being said in English, or even Italian, but in Latin.

She glanced at Lucia. Did she understand Latin? Did all these people—most of whom were not educated—know Latin?

Yet the look of peace upon many of the faces . . . peace and awe. Perhaps their faith wasn't dependent upon words heard or words said but stemmed from an inner need fulfilled.

She closed her eyes, letting the cadence of the Latin wrap around her as she attempted to open a place in her heart and mind where *her* faith lived. *God? Are you here with me?*

The priest began to pray. "*Pater noster, qui es in caelis, sanctificétur nomen tuum: advéniat regnum tuum . . .*"

Although Lottie didn't understand the words, she had an odd notion that she *did*. The cadence of the prayer seemed familiar. Was it the Lord's Prayer? The prayer prayed in her own church, in every church? No matter what their differences might be in ceremony or language, they had *this* in common.

Suddenly the miles between here and home fell away and she was seated next to her mother and father in their own church: *thy will be done on earth as it is in heaven . . .* Lottie said the rest of the prayer on her own and felt a strength and security accompany the words.

She looked up at the cross, to Jesus suffering. For her sins.

And there were many. Oh so many.

Lottie bowed her head, ashamed. She'd deceived her parents in order to do what *she* wanted to do. They needed to know she was safe and that she was sorry for lying to them.

I'll write them a letter.

But what about Dora? If Lottie's parents knew Dora had assumed her identity and was at the Tremaines' with the hopes of marrying Conrad . . .

Lottie shook her head in short bursts. No. Although she'd tried to end the masquerade, it wasn't her place to ruin Dora's chances of a happy life. If Dora and Conrad didn't find each other amiable, there would be no wedding, and Dora would leave the Tremaines' and continue her life elsewhere. Love would determine Dora's fate. Since all of this had been Lottie's idea, she wouldn't humiliate her friend or the Tremaines with exposure. There would be no more visits to the big marble mansion.

But she *could* ease the burden of her own deception by writing a letter to her parents with lesser disclosure.

Or could she?

She had no address to give them. No job. If she told her parents she was doing well, it would be yet another lie. And if she told the truth? She didn't feel up to using the piece of blackmail against her father—that he'd better not inform the Tremaines that it was a mere maid living in their home or Lottie would reveal the Gleason family scandals. Who was she to use extortion against her own parents? She, who had already deceived so many. Was she any better than they?

Sofia leaned against Lottie, dozing. Lottie raised her arm, letting the little girl in. The hat tipped precariously and Lottie carefully untied the ribbons beneath Sofia's chin and removed it, allowing her the freedom to burrow her head against Lottie's breast.

Lottie stroked her hair. Such a child . . . such a dear child . . .

The priest kissed the altar and said, *"Pax tecum."*

All replied, *"Et cum spiritu tuo."*
Amen.

Going to church with the Tremaines was a production Charlotte was used to. Back in Lacock she'd been expected to accompany the Gleasons to church on Sunday. The only difference was in where she sat today—in the family pew up front, rather than a few pews behind with the other servants.

But also not in the first pew.

Charlotte wondered about the identity of the families seated in the pews in front of them. Did the ranking of society continue in church? If so, which families were more important than the Tremaines? Whoever they may be, she was also disappointed to be seated between Beatrice and Mrs. Tremaine. Would she never get time alone with Conrad?

The organ played a song to remind everyone that God had arrived, and the pastor took his place in the pulpit. He was a squat man with receding silver hair. He had a ruddy Scottish look about him—which was confirmed when he spoke. The lilt of his voice was a comfort. Were the Gleasons in church this very day, praying after the safety of their daughter? *Was* Lottie safe?

Charlotte closed her eyes and offered her own prayer.

The pastor cleared his throat. "One day Jesus saw a rich man putting money in a collection plate. Then he saw a poor widow put in two small coins. This caused Him to make an observation as to which offering counted the most. The donation from the rich man who would never miss his offering? Or the gift given by the poor woman who'd sacrificed all she had? Jesus declared that her offering was worth more than all the rest."

The pastor put a hand upon the Bible and looked at his congregation. "Yesterday I came upon a young woman sleeping in these very pews, wet and cold from the storm. She had nothing and had nowhere to go. Yet she was full of wisdom as she reminded my wife and me of this very story and . . ."

Charlotte shivered as a thought coursed through her. Yesterday she'd seen Lottie standing in front of the Tremaine mansion, soaking wet from the rain. Had Lottie taken sanctuary in the church?

Charlotte looked down at the red pew cushion upon which they sat. Had Lottie been lying right here when the pastor found her? Had she been the inspiration for his sermon? If so, where was she now?

Without trying to look obvious, Charlotte scanned the chancel, hoping the pastor would produce his inspiration in person. Unfortunately, it was impossible to peruse the congregation without turning around.

Lottie, where are you? How are you?

Once again Charlotte was forced to recognize she had nothing to offer her friend but her prayers.

❧

They stood in line to shake the pastor's hand. More than anything, Charlotte wanted to ask him about the girl in his sermon but wasn't sure how to do so while surrounded by the Tremaines.

She overheard Mr. Tremaine grumble to Conrad, "All this talk of the poor woman's offering being worth so much . . . so our money isn't good enough? Perhaps Pastor Weston would like to see what the offering plate is like without our beneficence."

"Shh!" Mrs. Tremaine said.

It was their turn to shake hands. When it was Charlotte's chance, she said, "Excuse me, but I was interested in the woman who—"

Mr. Tremaine stepped forward. "Pastor, I would like to introduce you to Miss Charlotte Gleason, visiting us from England."

The pastor looked confused as he shook Charlotte's hand. But then his gaze grew intense. He was studying her.

What had Lottie told him? Did he recognize her name? Had Lottie told him that *she* was the real Charlotte Gleason?

Instead of wanting time to talk with the pastor, Charlotte suddenly wanted nothing more than to be down the steps and away.

"Nice to meet you," she said, and let the rest of the family take their turn.

But once she got in the carriage, she looked back at the church and saw him watching her. What did he know?

Charlotte sat back to hide from his gaze.

Charlotte wasn't sure how to accomplish it, but she knew she had to try.

At the noon meal, she broached the subject.

"Excuse me, but I was wondering if it would be possible to visit the church this afternoon? I would like to speak with Pastor Weston."

"Whatever for?" Beatrice asked.

Charlotte had thought of an answer. "I wasn't brought up in your denomination, and I would like to speak with him about the differences."

"You were brought up Church of England, correct?" Mr. Tremaine asked.

"Yes."

"Then there is no need for such a meeting."

"But—"

"Besides," Mrs. Tremaine said, "Conrad has plans for you this afternoon, don't you, son?"

Conrad had plans?

Put on the spot, he blushed and appeared ruffled. "Yes, I . . . well, I thought the two of us could take a . . . It's such a beautiful day—"

"He wants to take you for a walk in Central Park," Beatrice said.

Her parents flashed her looks of reprimand.

"What? I was simply trying to help. After all, I'm to be their chaperone."

Conrad cleared his throat and turned his eyes upon Charlotte. "Will you accompany me, Miss Gleason?"

Finally! She'd been wanting some time with him. "I'd be delighted."
Her quest to talk to Pastor Weston would have to wait.

⁂

They rode in the carriage some blocks to the north, to a large green
area on their left. It continued on. And on. And on.

"Is this the park we're going to?" Charlotte asked.

"Yes indeed," Conrad said. "It's called Central Park and is comprised
of eight hundred forty-three acres. Two good friends of ours designed
it: Frederick Law Olmsted and Calvert Vaux. They had ten million
cartloads of debris removed and brought in a half million cubic feet
of topsoil and—"

Beatrice covered her ears. "Enough, Conrad. We did not come for
a history lesson."

Actually, Charlotte would've liked to hear more. She missed reading
the Gleasons' newspaper or books borrowed from Lottie. Ever since
arriving at the Tremaines', it was as though she'd stepped into an intel-
lectual abyss. Not that she considered herself educated or wise, but
she *had* prided herself on being informed.

She looked at Conrad, intending to give him a supportive smile,
but he was looking out the window and then rapped on the carriage
to alert the driver to stop. He exited the carriage first and then helped
the ladies out. After offering Charlotte his arm, they joined a busy
procession of beautifully clad New Yorkers entering the park. The men
wore derbies or top hats and cutaway coats in many shades of brown.
The women were in brighter colors in deep hues, as though the cool
winds of autumn had expelled all memory of the pastels of spring and
the vivid shades of summer and happily called to the fore a completely
new palette: intense and bold, with a hint of the musky flavors and
aromas of the season.

Before coming to the park, Charlotte had liked her own costume,
but now she found its layers of black chantilly lace too mournful, the
glimpses of burgundy decoration too few. She much preferred Beatrice's

213

ensemble, which combined a gray-blue cashmere with Turkey-red borders and bows. Even Beatrice's parasol was adorned with a red bow. Charlotte's was solid black.

"I look like I'm in mourning," she whispered to Beatrice, who walked beside her on the right. "The colors here are full of life."

"I didn't wish to say anything to you, my dear, but as you see, the bustles in fashion are a bit higher than what you're wearing."

Charlotte had never noticed it before, but did so now. Indeed, the bustles of the women around her extended behind at waist level, almost like a shelf. "Their bustles give the appearance of the hind quarters of a horse."

"Excuse me?"

She'd given offense. "I'm sorry, it was merely a first impression."

Conrad chuckled. "An apt one, to be sure. I have no knowledge of women's couture, but I admit to wondering about the logic of the bustle in general. I believe I much prefer the bell-like shapes Mother wore when I was little."

"You liked them because there was more skirt to hide behind when I chased you."

Conrad changed the subject by drawing them to an intricately carved balustrade from which they looked down upon a fountain and a lake beyond.

The view took her breath away. "It's beautiful," Charlotte said.

"This is Bethesda Terrace."

The scene below them was lovely, with boats serenely floating on the lake and smart couples strolling beside the fountain and on the grass. It reminded Charlotte of home. She didn't realize she'd missed the green expanse of the Wiltshire countryside until now.

"The fountain was created by a woman sculptor," Beatrice said.

"Really?" Charlotte was genuinely surprised, for she'd never heard of a woman artist of any sort until Beatrice had mentioned a woman painter in France. She tried to determine what the sculpture was. A woman? Or an angel?

"You wish to see it closer?" Conrad asked.

"Please."

They walked down the stone stairs to see the fountain firsthand. "It's called the Angel of the Waters," Conrad explained. "See how she blesses the water with one hand, while holding a lily, the symbol of purity, with the other. Do you like lilies, Miss Gleason?"

She didn't know many flowers by their names, but looking at the flower in the angel's hand she could easily say, "Yes, yes I do."

Suddenly, Beatrice gripped her arm. "Oh dear. Oh no. There's McAllister."

"Who's—?"

"Shh. Smile."

Charlotte could feel the muscles in Conrad's arm tighten. With a glance she saw his jaw do the same. Who was this McAllister?

"Ward," Conrad said, tipping his hat to the man. "A lovely day, is it not?"

The man's gaze fell upon Charlotte like the keen eyes of a vulture finding its prey. "A beautiful day, to be sure." He seemed to remember his manners and looked to Beatrice. "Miss Tremaine."

"Mr. McAllister."

Conrad dropped his arm, forcing Charlotte to stand alone. "I would like to introduce you to our visitor from England, Miss Charlotte Gleason."

The man took her hand and drew it to his lips. The thought of touching either his shock of a beard or his long mustache was distasteful, and Charlotte was glad for her gloves. "*Enchanté*, Miss Gleason. The whole of the city has been awaiting your arrival."

She withdrew her hand, bobbed a curtsy, and said, "You are too kind."

"I hear there is a welcome soiree planned soon?"

"You are planning to attend, are you not?" Conrad asked.

His eyes still leered at Charlotte. "I wouldn't miss it."

She cringed at the thought of seeing him again.

He made his good-byes and left them.

Charlotte was glad when they began to walk. "Who was that horrid man?"

Beatrice laughed. "I commend you on your instincts. *That* is Ward McAllister, the self-appointed czar of New York society."

Conrad patted her hand, which was once again upon his arm. "He isn't so bad."

Beatrice stopped their walk to confront her brother. "You can only say that because you are not a woman."

Conrad began to speak but remained silent.

"Is he married?" Charlotte asked.

Beatrice laughed. "As if that matters to cretins such as he. Yes, he is married. Poor woman."

"Beatrice, please . . ."

Beatrice put a hand to her chest in mock surprise. "Are you implying I've shocked our dear Charlotte? Do marital infidelities not occur in England?"

Charlotte felt herself redden. Yes, she knew they did occur, and had occurred since time began, but she didn't appreciate Beatrice being so open about it. The subject hit too close to home.

"Enough, Beatrice," Conrad said. "Let's take a stroll down the Mall."

Beatrice began to come along, but then met a friend and stopped to chat. Charlotte finally had some time alone with Conrad.

But what to say?

She looked up at the trees that canopied the lane leading away from the fountain. "It's beautiful here."

"Mmm," he said. "When I need to think, this is often where I run to."

Run to? "You feel the need to run away often?"

"Oh no, not run away. Assuredly, my life is full. I have no right to— I have no complaints."

Charlotte sensed a need in him, a yearning, an absence. Instead of causing her to think less of him, she felt a desire to draw closer, to draw *him* closer. "Discontent knows no class boundaries," she said. "Even a king can be discontented."

His walk slowed. Then stopped. He plucked a yellow flower from along the path and handed it to her. "A token." Then he motioned toward a bench. "May we sit?"

Charlotte lowered her parasol. Whatever sun dappled through the leaves overhead was a pleasant counter to the cool air.

When Conrad didn't speak right away, she was alarmed. Had she misinterpreted his comments? Was the issue *not* discontentment? Had she misspoken?

"I'm sorry if I said too much," she began. "I meant no—"

"No," he said, shaking his head vigorously. "You did not misspeak. You perceived my situation quite rightly." He looked at her. "Quite wisely."

The sincerity in his words was evident in his face and made her throat tighten. At last they'd found a connection, a bridge between him and her and back again. She found she wanted nothing more than to listen to his concerns and worries and thoughts.

"Is . . . is it difficult being the eldest child? The only son?"

A soft explosion of air escaped and he smiled. "How do you do that?"

"Do what?"

"Know my thoughts? Sense the issues that plague me?"

She shrugged. "I don't know."

He grew serious again and took her hand in his. "God has brought you here, Miss Gleason, and if we never spoke another word, by the words we have spoken here today I would somehow find the courage to be content, for I have now experienced the joy of knowing that one other person on earth understands me. And cares."

Charlotte put a hand to her mouth. No one had ever spoken to her like this. No one had ever given her credit for merely listening.

"I've upset you."

She shook her head. "I'm just moved by your words, for they . . ." Would it be too forward to say it? "For they reinforce a new feeling that has also been borne in me today."

Relief washed over his face, and with his smile he looked far younger than his years. "It's a good beginning, yes?"

"It is."

Their moment was interrupted as Beatrice approached. "There you are."

Interrupted but not completely over. For before they stood to join his sister, Conrad squeezed Charlotte's hand, as if securing the new bond between them.

Charlotte squeezed his hand in return, put the flower to her cheek, and looked up at him. The gleam in his eyes sealed the moment.

Forever.

Sunday afternoon on Mulberry Street transpired—on the street. The stalls and shops were closed for the Sabbath, leaving more space for the children to run and the families to gather on the steps and on chairs brought into the open air.

After coming home from church with the Scarpellis, Lottie took Lucia's suggestion and slipped out of her tight clothes and into the freedom of one of Lucia's blouses and skirts. Then she joined the rest of the family on the street, nearly feeling like one of them but for her blond hair among the mass of raven heads.

Lottie sat upon the chair Vittorio brought for her. *"Grazie,"* she said to him.

He winked.

It felt wonderful to have learned a few basic words. And sitting beside Lea, with the rest of the family coming and going, with the refreshing air filled with the leftover smells of the noon meal wafting from the open windows, surrounded by a symphony of foreign but melodic words . . .

Lottie realized she was happy.

"Huh," she said to herself.

"Mi scusi?"

She felt herself redden. "Nothing. I'm just . . ." How could she explain? She spread an arm across the scene. "Lovely."

Lea nodded. *"Bella. Splendida."*

"Splendid. Yes it is."

Sofia ran toward them and presented each woman with the petal from a flower left behind by yesterday's flower carts.

Lea kissed her on the head and Lottie touched the tip of the girl's nose. Then Sofia surprised her by climbing upon her lap. Lottie made room and reveled in the touch of another person, the warmth, and the exquisite sensation of the child's cuddly body submitting to her own. Impulsively, she gave the little girl a hug.

Sofia glanced back at her and smiled, and Lottie felt her heart expand to a new size. She opened her hand—which still held the petal—and whispered in Sofia's ear. "I treasure this petal as if it were the finest rose."

The dip in Sofia's brow showed she didn't understand, but that was all right.

Lottie remembered her family's home being filled with flowers— vivid arrangements from the garden or flowers sent as a thank-you by guests. She'd taken them for granted and was surprised to find them only a vague recollection. None held a place in her memory as lovely as this one petal.

There was a sudden break in the momentum of the street. Conversations stopped, and heads turned to the right.

What was going on?

A man was walking through the crowd, coming toward them. He looked northern European in descent, with fair skin and fairer hair. He wore a suit with a blue and gray plaid vest, and over his shoulder he carried a wooden stand of some sort, with a box attached to the top—

Was it a photographic camera? Lottie and her family had had their photograph taken a few times but always in a studio. She'd never seen a camera outside in the open air.

He tipped his hat as he passed the families and received greetings in return. Then he looked in their direction. And stopped. And stared.

The attention made Lottie feel uncomfortable. She didn't know this man, and she wished he would look elsewhere.

"You're being rude, sir," she told him.

He blinked, breaking his gaze. "Forgive me, miss. I meant no disrespect."

She'd been right about his heritage. His words owned a Scandinavian inflection. Lottie's family had employed a gardener from Copenhagen once, and he'd also owned the up-and-down cadence of the northern countries.

She expected him to walk on, but instead he came toward her. "If it would be all right with you, miss, and you, *signora*, I would like to take your photograph."

Sofia wriggled in Lottie's arms. *"Giù."* She wanted down.

"No, no," the photographer said, waving his arm toward the girl. "Please stay, *piccolina*. I want the three of you. Three lovely ladies on an autumn day."

Lea said something to her daughter, and the little girl sat still.

It took only a few moments for the man to set his camera and its stand in place. He put a square plate inside its back, looked through the box, and covered his head with a cloth while holding on to the lens in front. "Hold it!" He removed the cover on the lens for a few seconds, replaced it, and then unfurled himself from the contraption. "There!" he said. *"Grazie."*

He'd gained an audience with his work and immediately had a swarm of people accosting him, tugging on his shirt, wanting their own photograph to be taken. Men removed their hats and smoothed their hair, shirts were buttoned, and aprons removed to reveal a cleaner skirt beneath.

"Whoa, now," he said, trying to contain the crowd. "I'll take a few more, but I don't have enough plates to take pictures of all of you."

A young boy snatched the wooden-edged plate from the man's hands and started to run away with it. Lottie reached out and grabbed the boy's arm as he tried to sneak behind the women. "Oh, no you don't." She took the plate back and returned it to its owner.

"A quick hand!" he said. "Thank you. The photograph is on there, waiting to be revealed."

"You need more than my help," she said. She spotted Vittorio, Aldo, and Dante close by and called their names, then added, *"Per favore. Aiuto."*

Lea also came to the rescue and instructed the men of her family into action. Soon the crowd had parted enough for the photographer to breathe.

Which he did—in one long sigh steeped with relief.

"Thank you," he said to Lottie. *"Grazie,"* he said to the Scarpellis. He righted the tripod, which had been on the brink of destruction just moments before. "I try to be unobtrusive, but with the weather so fine . . ." He set some of his equipment down and extended his hand. "My name is Anders Svensson, but everyone calls me Sven."

She shook his hand. She couldn't tell him her true name. She didn't know him. "I'm Lottie Hathaway, and your rescuers are the Scarpelli family."

He lowered his voice. "Are you staying . . . ?" He started again. "Hathaway isn't an Italian name."

"Neither is Svensson."

He laughed.

His laughter led her to explain. "I'm new here and had everything stolen at the dock. The Scarpellis have kindly taken me in."

"You're from England, then?"

"Wiltshire."

He nodded. "I came from Denmark nine years ago."

Sofia came toward them, holding a cup of water in her hands.

"Grazie, piccolina," Sven said. "I could use that."

He drank it and handed her the cup. She ran back to the safety of her mother's lap.

Sven's eyes scanned the street. "The children are so precious. I mourn for the way many of them live."

"So do I," Lottie said. "Yet there is a strength here, in spite of everything against them."

He cocked his head as if surprised by her insight. "Do you think we could sit on the step a while? I need to rearrange my equipment, and I'd enjoy talking with you."

Back home Lottie would never have considered such a thing. Sven was far below her station—a tradesman. Women of society didn't speak to such men.

But, as was abundantly clear, this wasn't home, and to chat with someone who spoke English would be wonderful. So she nodded and they moved to the step of the Scarpellis' tenement. He took her hand and helped her sit down. She expected his hand to be rough, but it was smooth. And strong.

"So, Miss Hathaway. Tell me more about how you came to be here, in this place."

Before she had time to create a story, she told the truth. "I'm from a family of standing back in Wiltshire."

He shook his head.

"Have you heard of Salisbury Cathedral? Or Stonehenge?"

"Ja. Sure."

"They're in the county of Wiltshire. I lived on an estate near the tiny village of Lacock. I—"

"Lacock? I've heard of that town."

"I don't think so."

"Henry F. Talbot. A pioneer of photography, of negatives. Didn't he live at Lacock Abbey?"

Lottie was amazed. "He did."

"Small world."

Minuscule.

"So, Lottie from Lacock, why are you here, across the world?"

"My parents wanted me to marry an American entrepreneur. I came here to do that, but—"

Sven laughed. "It appears you took a wrong turn somewhere."

She didn't like him laughing at her. "I decided not to go through with it. In fact, I sent my maid in my place to the Tremaines'. She will marry the man. I'm not who people think I am."

"Few in Five Points are who they expected to be when they came to America. If wishes were horses, beggars would ride . . ."

"No, I didn't mean it that way . . . I only meant that I'm free to do as I wish."

He did not laugh this time but looked up and down the street. "I would guess this place, among these people, isn't what you had in mind."

Lottie's defenses sparked. "Do not disparage them, Mr. Svensson. If not for their kindness, I would be in dire straits indeed."

His countenance softened. "I mean no disrespect to the Scarpellis or any who find themselves living around Mulberry Bend. And I know that this—" he swept an arm from left to right—"this wasn't what any of these people had in mind when they came to America in search of a dream." His eyes dropped to the dirt, litter, and horse excrement that masked the ragged cobblestones. Then his gaze turned upward, toward the slice of bright sky that seemed to mock the dark, drab colors of the world below. "These homes—which have no right to be called as much—shut out the sky and are criminal. Some could nearly crumble at a touch, and others are built behind these, and others behind those, so that many rooms are without light or air. Did you know dozens of babies die each year by suffocating in these so-called homes?"

Lottie felt her throat tighten with her own memories of the airless room where six of them slept each night. "They die?"

"Oh yes," he said, his face tight with anger. "Babies die inside—and out. Babies are left on the street when their parents can't take care of them, and a great number of the children you see running about have no home at all. No one to watch over them, no one to feed them or hug them or love them."

Lottie lowered her head, the threat of tears an embarrassment. The thought of other children as sweet and innocent as Sofia left to fend for themselves . . .

He reached over and gently touched her arm. "I'm sorry. I didn't mean to make you sad. But I'm passionate about revealing the inequities of this place. For these people to leave everything behind and come here to *this* . . ." He withdrew his hand and sighed deeply. "That's why I take their photographs and sell them to the papers. To show the world, to show the powers that be the atrocities here. There must be change. There must be reform." As soon as he finished his declaration, he looked at Lottie and blushed. "Forgive me. It's a lovely day. You don't need it darkened by my opinions."

"On the contrary, I am moved by your zeal, and from what I've seen so far, what you state are not opinions but fact. It's commendable of you to use your talent toward the good of others."

He opened his mouth to say something, then closed it and instead said, "Thank you."

They watched as two boys played leapfrog down the street in front of them. "And still they play," she said.

"The human spirit shows great resilience and strength to endure, and the desire for normalcy turns horrible conditions nearly tolerable."

Lottie thought of the Scarpellis' apartment. "I've seen that. Mrs. Scarpelli has little space in their apartment yet has hung some fabric as curtains and has family photographs on the walls."

Sven nodded, then raised an arm. "These people will go far; they'll rise above. I've seen it, and I predict more of it in the future. These immigrants did not come here to sit and wallow; they came to work and better themselves. In return they'll better this country."

Lottie felt something new ignite. Pride. She'd always been proud, in a haughty sort of way, but now she felt pride far differently. She was proud of her ability to survive thus far, and looked forward to future accomplishment and the possibilities that lay before her. She recognized this as a better form of the trait, one steeped in endurance rather than arrogance.

"I'm getting a job tomorrow," she said out of the blue.

He raised an eyebrow. "So you're not going back to your maid and demanding your place?"

She shook her head as if offended, then stilled it. "I've already thought of that, tried that to some degree."

"Ah."

"I went to Thirty-fourth Street and stood before the house that could have been mine." She sighed. "'Tis a very fine house."

"Did you go inside?"

"I saw my maid exit with an older woman, and—"

"Did your maid see you?"

"She did."

"You could have ended it right then. You could have stepped forward, admitted the deception, and claimed your rightful place."

Lottie lowered her head. She noticed her clenched palm and opened it to find the rose petal still there. "I couldn't do it, because the entire scheme was my idea; I was the one who forced the plan upon Dora. She deserves the chance for such a life. Dora is like a sister to me and—"

"You love her."

Although she'd never said the words aloud, she knew them to be true. "I love her, and I want her to be happy." Lottie suddenly laughed at herself.

"You find this funny?"

"I find it ironic that I, who have never thought of anyone beyond myself, have found a dose of compassion. Here."

"Perhaps the crossing involved more than just the sea?"

She liked the way he thought, the way he expressed himself. "Perhaps."

NANCY MOSER

Sven looked skyward, squinting against the light. "I best be moving along if I'm to do my work. The light is turning against me."

He stood and offered her his hand. She rose beside him and, for a moment, found she didn't want him to let go. He must have felt the same, for when he pulled his hand away his face reddened. He tipped his hat to her. "Thank you for the pleasure of our conversation. I'll come this way again, and when I do—"

Their discussion was interrupted when a violin began to play. On a stoop across the street a man stood proudly and drew his bow over the strings, calling people to attention. He paused long enough to shout, *"Danza ed essere felici!"*

The crowd cheered and jumped to their feet.

Another man joined the first, carrying an odd stringed instrument that he strummed on his lap. And then a wooden flute was added. The violinist stomped his foot, creating a beat. *"Uno, due, tre . . ."*

A lively song began and the people in the street wasted no time finding partners. Man and woman, child and child, grandmother and grandmother.

"Meraviglioso!"

"Favolosa!"

Vittorio rushed toward her. *"Danza venire con me, Signorina Lottie."* His hands were waiting to take hers.

She looked at Sven. He set his pack down and leaned on his tripod. *"This* I must see."

"Don't be rude. I'll have you know I'm a good—"

Vittorio grabbed her hands and drew her into the melee. "I don't know this dance. I don't know—"

It didn't matter. With a hand upon her waist he led her right, then left, then right in a glorious sashay. *One and two, one and two, one and two . . .*

He expertly traveled amid the other dancers, turning her round and round, back and through. They flew across the cobblestones, the music and clapping urging them on, as if pure joy fueled them all.

The strict regimen of the society balls that had permeated Lottie's life seemed like staid and stodgy wakes compared to this spontaneous outpouring of inner delight. She never wanted it to end.

Lottie's hair loosened and strands teased her face, but she dared not let go to secure it. Only rarely did her gaze meet Vittorio's. His attention—by necessity—was focused upon getting them safely through the maze of fellow dancers. Through it all, he beamed from within, as if his troubles had been frightened away by the noise and movement.

Perhaps they had—for this moment. For while the music played and the people danced, the horrid tenements of Mulberry Street disappeared and Lottie could imagine similar dances back in Italy. For the moment all were home among friends. Life was good.

Lottie spotted Sven along the edge of the dancers. He'd set aside his equipment and was dancing with Sofia, like a father dancing with his child.

He spotted Lottie and winked. And the music carried them away to a better place.

⁂

I'd rather peel onions than be so bored.

After dinner the Tremaines gathered in the drawing room. The silence that permeated the meal continued on. It was excruciating. Charlotte wondered if there was a set amount of time a family of breeding was required to gather each evening before they could make their excuses and go their separate ways. Perhaps a time delineated by Mr. McAllister?

Charlotte sat on the settee, a volume of Jane Austen's *Emma* in her hands. She'd found it in the Tremaines' library and had grabbed hold of the book, finding comfort in the familiar story that Lottie had loved so much. She escaped into the story of Emma's matchmaking efforts . . . *There does seem to be something in the air of Hartfield which gives love exactly the right direction, and sends it into the very*

227

channel where it ought to flow. "The course of true love never did run *smoo—*"

"This isn't a very good likeness, Miss Gleason."

She looked up to see Beatrice holding a small framed photograph in her hand. Mr. Tremaine looked up from his newspaper, Mrs. Tremaine from her needlework, and Conrad from his book of maps.

In the silence that followed, Beatrice walked the room, making sure everyone saw the photo—of Lottie. Everyone except Charlotte.

She couldn't remember the photograph the Gleasons had sent to America when talk had initially begun about a match between Lottie and Conrad. She remembered Lottie assuring her it wouldn't be an issue, since their faces were similar and the slight differences in the hue of their blond hair wouldn't be exposed in sepia and white.

Something must be said. Immediately. Charlotte smiled and held out her hand. She perused the likeness quickly, then made a face. "I never did like this photograph, but it was the only one Mother would part with. I look a little like a disgruntled dog, do I not?" She held the frame outward to show the others.

Mr. Tremaine raised his newspaper again. "The new photos are far superior to the old ones when we were forced to remain still for endless minutes. No wonder no one smiled."

Charlotte held the frame toward Beatrice and noticed an unfortunate quiver in her hand as she did so. Beatrice took it, her face tight.

"How convenient," Beatrice said.

"Pardon?"

Although Charlotte knew retreat wasn't the best option, she found herself closing the book, standing, and saying her good-nights.

On the way out of the room, she spotted a footman by the doorway. He broke his statuelike stance to look at her.

Charlotte hurried to her room.

Escaped.

They know; they all know!

"Did something upset you, miss?" Mary asked as she unbuttoned Charlotte's gown.

"Yes, no. I'm merely finding it hard to fit in."

"Of course you are. If you don't mind my saying . . . Mr. Tremaine's a rock and the missus is moss—she wouldn't be nothing if it weren't for him."

Charlotte smiled. "How about their children?"

Mary continued her work but answered immediately. She'd obviously thought about this before. "Miss Beatrice is a bird, landing on the rock, pecking at the moss, but flitting away when she realizes she's getting nowhere."

"And Mr. Conrad?"

"Mr. Conrad is a bug crawling up the rock, across the moss, hiding from the bird. He's going to get eaten one of these days. Or squashed."

Unfortunately, it seemed an apt description.

"Don't you get squashed, miss. I was hoping you and Mr. Conrad together might . . ."

"Hide better?"

"Run away."

Charlotte couldn't imagine Conrad ever leaving his family or his life here. And he wouldn't have to leave, not if he found a way to be strong.

She was willing to help him, but . . .

She thought of the mistakes she'd already made: Mrs. Gleason's maiden name, her inability to play the piano, the letter fiasco, and tonight, the photograph. If Charlotte's true identity were found out, her best hopes for Conrad would be for naught.

There was so much at stake.

Too much.

Charlotte remembered her brave talk about finding another job as a maid if things didn't work out at the Tremaines'. What an ignorant fool she'd been to assume anyone would hire her after she was responsible for the subsequent scandal and humiliation of one of New York's finest families.

The thought of hurting Conrad . . . why had she and Lottie never thought about him when they'd developed their scheme? He was a good man who deserved a good woman.

Could she be that woman?

If things didn't work out—

There was no "if." This had to work. For everyone's sake.

Chapter Thirteen

Lucia nudged Lottie's shoulder. "Up. We go to work."

Lottie opened her eyes to see if the sun was up, but was immediately reminded there were no windows in the bedroom she shared with five others.

A lamp was lit and its flame fluttered from the movement of the household. Only Sofia could return to sleep, rolling over on the now spacious cot she usually shared with her sister.

Lottie could hear Lea and Francesca preparing the morning meal, as well as lunches for the workers to take with them.

The three men buttoned their shirts and adjusted their suspenders as they discussed the day to come. Aldo and his son, Vittorio, from Italy had found work on the docks with Dante, and Lucia would do her best on Lottie's behalf in the garment sweatshops. As for Lea and Francesca? They would stay home with Sofia, and all three would work on making artificial flowers for ladies' hats. No hand was idle. Not if one wanted to eat.

Lottie laced her boots and thought of the times Dora had laced them for her: she, sitting like a queen on a throne, waiting to be dressed by another. It was a bit embarrassing to think of how helpless she'd been—or had pretended to be. She'd usually slept until late morning and had spent much of her day changing clothes for various social interactions that involved sitting, smiling, and making polite conversation. To work, to physically work . . . was she capable of such a thing? She had no skills—unless someone would pay her for playing Chopin or needed to know the name of the insipid cousin who proposed to Elizabeth Bennet in *Pride and Prejudice.*

Lucia must have seen her apprehension, for she put a hand on her arm. "You said you know sewing, yes?"

"I know needlework." But Lottie wasn't very good at it. Her mother often made her tear it out and start again. And never had she been allowed to work on her mother's cherished seat cushions. "I've never sewn clothing."

"Not even button?"

"Not even button." How pitiful it sounded. Was.

A crease formed between Lucia's brows but vanished with her smile. "It will be all right. I help you."

It had to be all right. It was imperative Lottie earn a living for her own sake, but also for the sake of the Scarpellis. Although she sensed they would let her stay indefinitely, she knew their resources were already stretched by the influx of their family from Naples. She had no right to intrude any longer than necessary.

Lucia dug in a felt box and pulled out a small pair of scissors and two needles stuck in a piece of fabric. "Here. You will need."

"They don't supply—?"

"They charge. Better to bring your own."

Bread and coffee were quickly consumed and kisses were given in parting. Even though the sun had not yet found its way past the buildings, Mulberry Street was fully awakened with workers leaving and peddlers opening their shops for the day's business. The men of the family headed south while Lucia and Lottie headed north.

"What if they won't give me a job?" Lottie asked.

"They will. One girl left to have baby. You take her place."

"Will she return?"

"Not today." Lucia shrugged. "Do not worry. One foreman, Mr. Silverman, he like me. I will smile and get my way."

Lottie had done more than her share of smiling to get her way. She didn't like the sound of that. "Don't do anything that will—"

Lucia understood. "No, no. *Non sia mai.* Mr. Silverman good man. Other foreman . . . he not so. Mr. Silverman help. You will have job today."

Lottie hoped so.

❦

"Look!"

Lottie ran toward the shiny object she'd seen on the ground. She was right! It was a coin!

"How much?" Lucia asked.

She looked at the woman's face on the front side and recognized it from the coins she'd received at Castle Garden. "It's a dollar!"

"That more than day's wage!" Lucia said.

Lottie felt rich. To have a dollar to add to the dime from the pastor . . .

"What you buy?" Lucia asked.

What could she buy with a dollar?

Thoughts of buying food or putting it toward her own apartment were quickly usurped by the memory of her ruby necklace at the pawn-shop. Perhaps if she took the money to the owner and put it down toward the purchase . . .

She slipped the dollar into the pocket of her skirt. It was a sign. Things were looking up.

❦

Lottie had expected . . . she wasn't certain what she'd expected, but the building they entered to go to work looked little different than any

233

of a hundred tenements they'd passed. The pale sunlight of the early morning was sorely missed once the front door was closed and they traipsed up endless dark stairs, higher and higher. Lottie moved upward completely by the feel of the railing in her hand. She even closed her eyes once, just to see . . . There was little difference between no light and the light available.

After six flights they entered a huge room. It was as though the entire floor had gobbled up the existing apartments, knocking down the walls but for an occasional column holding up the ceiling. She hoped it was holding up the ceiling.

The room was consumed by rows of long tables with women sitting shoulder to shoulder on both sides. Some were already at work.

Lucia slipped her hand through Lottie's arm and led her toward two bearded men at the front of the room. She whispered in her ear, "Smile."

That she could do.

The men looked up when the girls approached, and one smiled back. He must have been Mr. Silverman.

"I have new worker, sirs."

"We don't need a new worker," the other man said.

"To take Maria Romano's place?" Lucia offered.

"Who?"

Mr. Silverman nodded. "The one having the baby." He looked at Lottie. "Can you sew?"

Lottie didn't hesitate. "Yes." She refrained from adding "Of course."

The other man was distracted when a woman brought him a sleeve for approval. He eyed it closely, then barked, "Not enough stitches!" Then he yanked at the sleeve, ripping the lining from it. "Do it over!"

Mr. Silverman looked at the girls, his eyes showing some embarrassment at the behavior of his co-worker. "Get to work, then. Don't let me down, Miss . . ."

"Hathaway."

Lucia hurriedly sped her past a barrel of sleeves, grabbing two, then led Lottie to the middle of a middle row. There was only one chair here and one there, but Lucia said something to the women, and a place was made for Lottie next to her friend.

They got out their needles and scissors, and Lucia handed Lottie a spool of black thread.

Thread a needle. She could do that.

But not easily. The light originated from a few gas lamps and whatever light came through the windows on either end of the room. But it was a cloudy October day and the sunlight that reached the middle of the room was played out and dim.

She pricked her finger. "Oww!" She immediately put it in her mouth. The other women glanced at her, shook their heads, and made soft comments to their neighbors—most likely about the novice who thought a pricked finger was something to exclaim about.

"Here," Lucia said softly with a glance toward the other foreman. "You pull the lining so and stitch into wool like this . . ." She expertly sewed three stitches. "Only this little bit shows, see?"

A blonde across the table spoke up. "And make sure it's flat, dearie, or the Beast'll make you rip it out."

"He rip for you," said a girl with a guttural accent.

Yes indeed, she'd already witnessed that.

⁂

"No thank you."

Mrs. Tremaine looked at Charlotte askance. "Don't you like oatmeal?"

No, she did not. The texture reminded her of the awful gruel Mrs. Movery served on cold days. "I'm not very hungry this morning." She was still worried they were on to her. The photo confrontation the night before had plagued her sleep.

Conrad's bowl was filled to the top. "Mother is an avid purveyor of Quaker Oats. It's quite new—though it is a bit bland." He smiled and reached for the sugar bowl. "But I do like it with brown sugar and milk."

"You always did have a sweet tooth." Mr. Tremaine made the statement as though it were equal to a flaw in his son's character.

"Sorry, Father." Conrad passed the sugar bowl on. "See? I'll try it without today."

What did oatmeal matter when Charlotte's life was teetering on the edge of a precipice?

But in the silence that ensued, her self-concerns were replaced with concern for Conrad. She hated how he kowtowed to his parents over the smallest things. It went beyond respect and revealed a weakness. Or fear. Or even laziness. For wasn't it easier to give in than stand tall?

She thought about taking some oatmeal anyway, yet wouldn't that be her own act of desperate deference? The decision was taken from her when the servant moved on to Beatrice, who took an extra large helping. What did that say about *her* temperament? And who would have thought the transaction of breakfast food could reveal moral fiber?

"So, Mother," Beatrice said, "what are the plans for today?"

Mrs. Tremaine poured cream into her coffee. "Mrs. Devereau is coming to fit us for the gowns for Charlotte's party."

A gown? "You're having a gown made for me?"

"Of course, dear. We didn't want you to have to rely on the gowns you brought from home."

"We couldn't risk them being smart enough," Beatrice said.

"Beatrice!"

The girl put a hand to her mouth in a practiced attempt of acting contrite. "Forgive me. I meant no offense."

Of course you did.

Mr. Tremaine rolled his eyes. "Gowns?"

His wife made her defense. "You expect us to wear something old to such an event?"

"I do own a department store, my dear. There are plenty of gowns there, and it might behoove you to patronize our own establishment."

Charlotte recognized a way to gain favor. "I would be happy to wear a gown from your store, Mr. Tremaine. Perhaps Conrad could take me there today and—"

Mrs. Tremaine set her coffee cup on its saucer with a clink. "You will do no such thing!"

The woman's ire was unexpected. "I'm sorry. I—"

Conrad turned to his father. "I would be happy to take her, Father."

"She has an appointment here," his mother said.

"Oh," Conrad said. "That's right."

Charlotte found the discourse ridiculous when both parties *could* be appeased. "Perhaps we could see Mrs. Devereau today and go to the store tomorrow?"

"I have a meeting tomorrow," Conrad said. "But I could take Miss Gleason with me today."

Mr. Tremaine looked at his wife. "Call the dressmaker and have her come tomorrow."

The look on his wife's face exposed a realization she'd lost the argument—and was not happy about it one little bit. "Yes, Martin."

"Then it's settled," he said.

They ate the rest of the meal in awful silence. Charlotte tried to eat slowly because she was certain there had to be a rule about not finishing a meal before her host and hostess. But it was hard to make a piece of bread and jam last interminably.

Finally Mr. Tremaine put his napkin on the table. A footman came to his aid, pulling his chair from the table. "Good day, all."

And he was gone.

Just as Charlotte was feeling her first breath of relief, full release came from an unexpected source.

Conrad looked at her, then at her plate. "Are you finished? Because if you are . . ."

She set her napkin on the table. "I am." She looked to Mrs. Tremaine. "If I may be excused?"

Mrs. Tremaine flipped a hand and Charlotte and Conrad made their exit. As the footman closed the dining room door, she heard Beatrice say, "Well, what do you expect from her sort?"

For a moment Charlotte's stomach grabbed. Her *sort*?

But her attention was drawn to a jubilant Conrad.

"I can't believe I did that," he whispered.

"Did what?"

"Stood up to Mother."

If he thought *that* was equal to taking a serious stand . . . "I'm very proud of you," Charlotte said. "And I'm excited to see the store."

He held out his arm. "As I am excited to show it to you."

Tremaine's Dry Goods encompassed one full city block and was five stories in height. The street outside was bustling with carriages and pedestrians, all going somewhere, wanting to buy something.

Charlotte and Conrad were let off near the main entrance, and Charlotte could sense his eagerness. He paused on the sidewalk and looked up. "This is it. The source of our good fortune." He caught himself and looked down at her. "Our God-given good fortune."

"Your clarification is duly noted."

He always seemed so relieved when she spoke to him, as if her words countered a prevailing ring of doubt that threatened to strangle him. She was glad she could help, and vowed to do as much as she could to release him from his restraints.

He turned her to the north. "Here is the Ladies' Mile."

"Ladies'—?"

He pointed up the street. "It's Broadway. It's the entire world laid at the feet of all who come to shop, to dine, to flirt, to find amusement, and to meet acquaintances."

She'd never seen anything like it. To think of it: store after store, catering to women . . .

Instead of going inside, Conrad led her farther up the street, showing off the huge windows that showcased the goods inside.

In a way.

The clothing was displayed on dress forms, and other goods to purchase—such as bedding and house furnishings—sat willy-nilly amid the dresses. There was no continuity, no stimulation, no incentive to buy.

"What do you think?" Conrad asked.

She hesitated. His ego was delicate. Would she do it damage by telling him the truth? "The displays are very nice."

"Ah."

She risked a glance. "But they are a bit . . . dry."

His eyes lit up as though she'd told him they were exquisite. "Really? You really think so?"

"Why, yes."

"I'm so glad it's not just my opinion. Father insists on a strictly functional displaying of the wares, but I think it could be improved with a little creativity, a little more color and arrangement." He motioned to the steady stream of people walking by. "See how they glance but don't stop to look? That's because we give them nothing to look *at*, nothing to engage them."

"Nothing to make them *have* to go inside and buy."

"Exactly!" He paused a moment to look at her. "You understand."

"I'm trying to."

"No," he said, his voice softening. "You really understand me. No one understands me."

The way he looked at her made her nervous even as it made her heart race. "Perhaps I understand you because I'm much like you." *And I like you.*

With new purpose he led her toward the entrance. "You deserve something very special today, Miss Gleason, and I intend to give it to you."

Charlotte's first glimpse of the store's interior elicited unrestricted awe. The entire first floor was as ornate as the Tremaines' home, with arches and filigree, ornaments and carving. A marble staircase swept down from an open mezzanine above and was flanked by two enormous lampposts that boasted a dozen white globes of light.

As they walked past the millinery department on their left and men's clothing on their right, Conrad was accosted by clerk after clerk after clerk.

"Good morning, Mr. Tremaine."

"Nice to see you this morning, Mr. Tremaine."

"Wonderful weather today, eh, Mr. Tremaine?"

Although Charlotte could imagine employees offering salutations out of duty or to satisfy personal ambition, all who extended greetings seemed to be doing so from a genuine fondness.

And how could she think otherwise? During their short acquaintance, Charlotte had found Conrad to be affable, kind, and true.

And insecure, weak, and fearful.

Perhaps she could help. If only she could. She'd spent her entire life in service, helping others, sensing their needs even before they were recognized.

They ascended the grand staircase. "We have an elevator, but I like the vista from the stairs. Are you all right to walk?"

She nodded and carefully lifted her skirt so as not to trip. "I also enjoy the view." And she did. Walking up the staircase afforded a splendid view of the first floor with its shoppers, clerks, and displays. But there was another reason Charlotte preferred to walk. Although she had been in an elevator in London, she still was not used to such an enclosed space, nor used to trusting a machine for her safety.

Conrad led her through counters heavy-laden with all sorts of enticing goods of every color and sort: parasols, gloves and lace mitts, shoes and—

She stopped in front of a display. "What are these?"

Conrad looked embarrassed and nodded to a clerk to come forth. "These are hair goods, miss," the girl said. She brought forward a pile of very curly hair. "This is a 'Langtry bang' after Lillie Langtry, the famous actress."

Charlotte nodded in awe. Everyone in England had heard of Lillie Langtry, the mistress of the Prince of Wales. She was embarrassed to ask the next, so leaned forward a bit. "How does it . . . work?"

The woman placed it on a cloth form, on the crown of the head. "See how the frizzy curls frame the face? Mrs. Langtry was the one who started the style." She quickly moved to another display of a hairpiece with a part in the center that fell into masses of tight curls. "And this is called the Empress. It's ventilated for comfort."

She must have seen the gleam in Charlotte's eyes, because she moved to yet another display of long extensions. "This is our chatelaine twist. You just place it up under your own twist in the back. All of our hair is real and matched to your . . ." She stopped, her eyes on Conrad.

Charlotte looked over and saw that Conrad's face was almost comical in its curiosity. "These are quite amazing," Charlotte told him. "I assure you I've never seen anything like these in England."

Realizing his interest had drawn their attention, he shuffled his shoulders and took out a pocket watch. "At Tremaine's we aim to please," he said.

"We must be going," Charlotte said to the clerk. "But thank you for showing me." She smiled and lowered her voice. "I hope to be back." She took Conrad's arm and they walked away. "I'm impressed, Mr. Tremaine. The variety of goods you offer is astonishing. A woman wouldn't know where to start."

"Or finish," he said. "We often have ladies come in for the entire day. And we also cater to the rural customer who is weary of country stores that offer inferior goods at high prices. We even have a day parlor just for their use and special transportation to the train or ferry station."

"How innovative."

"I suggested as much to Father five years ago, but he was against it until Bloomingdale's started offering the service."

"At least he finally listened to you."

Conrad shook his head. "Listened to a competitor."

It saddened her to learn the father ignored his son's ideas. "But you thought of it first."

He shrugged, then brought her through a columned portico. "This is the women's emporium."

It was like walking into a female heaven. Luscious dresses and suits were displayed on mannequins like a contingent of mute well-wishers luring her inside.

"Ooooh."

Conrad laughed. "I'm glad you like it."

"Back home Lott— I had my clothes made by a dressmaker, which was often a hit-or-miss proposition. The dressmaker's vision didn't always match my own. But to see the ensembles ready-made is a heady prospect."

Conrad raised a hand and a middle-aged woman rushed to his side. "Yes, Mr. Tremaine?"

"Madame Foulard, I would like you to meet Miss Charlotte Gleason, just here from England."

She bobbed. "A pleasure, mademoiselle."

"Miss Gleason has shown interest in our little store here, and I thought it would be a glorious idea if we treated her. I would like you to personally assist her in trying on whichever—and however many—of your lovely costumes please her."

Madame's eyes lit up, and Charlotte felt her own heart flutter with excitement. "I get to try these on?"

Conrad removed his gloves and hat and sat upon a plush lavender sofa. "And I will be your delighted audience."

Madame Foulard extended an arm toward the offerings. "Come, Miss Gleason, come show me what pleases you."

It was a dream, a lovely dream. It had to be. The clerk showed Charlotte one dress after another. Charlotte couldn't help but touch each length of fringe or ruffle of exquisite lace and marvel at the visual depth of the velvets, the sheen of the satins, and the ever-changing watered pattern of the moirés.

"This gown exhibits some of our newest colors," Madame said. "This Congo tone. . . . isn't it superb next to the Palestine color?"

Charlotte had never heard of colors by those names, but liked the coppery color of the Congo combined with the mauve tone of the Palestine. "It's truly lovely. I'm having a difficult time deciding."

"Then let me do that for you," Madame said. She escorted Charlotte into a large dressing room lined with mirrors. A young girl in a maid's uniform was waiting for her and bobbed a curtsy. "This is Bridget. She will help you undress."

It was a bit awkward disrobing before a stranger, but Bridget was very attentive and by the time Charlotte was down to her under-garments, Madame Foulard came in with her arms heavy-laden with two gowns.

"This one first, I think," she said, handing Bridget a red reception dress.

Together, the two clerks ably helped Charlotte into the dress with Madame offering a running commentary of the gown's attributes. "This costume is made of grosgrain satin with six bands of jet gimp. Since the fabric is stiffened, the front is flat and the back bustle is folded rather than draped. This is the garnet color, but we can get it for you in navy, brown, or black."

Charlotte looked at herself in the mirror. "I like the garnet very much."

"It is very striking on you, mademoiselle."

They all started when there was a rapping on the door. Madame Foulard pulled the door ajar, spoke a few words, then returned. "Monsieur Tremaine wishes to see you in the gowns." She said something in French to Bridget, who was finishing the final touches on the bustle.

Charlotte was not at all certain it was proper for her to model in front of Conrad, but she was in no position to argue. She looked in the mirror, smoothed her hair, and exited the dressing room.

As Charlotte approached the sofa, Conrad stood, his face awash with awe and admiration. "You look stunning, Miss Gleason."

"Is she not?" Madame said. "The dress fits as though it were made for her."

"Turn round," Conrad said. "If you please?"

Charlotte felt sheepish doing so, but she walked a tight circle to show Conrad the full effect.

"You are like a canvas with the gown as your paint, Miss Gleason. In its grasp you become a work of art."

Madame put a hand to her chest. "My, my, Mr. Tremaine. You are so gallant."

And kind. And eloquent. And—

"We'll buy that one," he said.

Charlotte was surprised. "You don't have to do—"

"I want to. Now another one. Suitable for a walk in Central Park."

"*Absolument.*" Madame's eyes glittered with excitement. "Come, come, I know just the one. In a lovely brown, I think."

"I prefer green. To match Miss Gleason's eyes."

Madame's eyes widened. "Certainly, monsieur."

What transpired was a fairy tale with Charlotte the princess royal. Before the excursion was over Conrad had purchased the garnet reception dress, a forest green and ivory walking costume, a robin's-egg-blue day dress, a rust and brown seersucker suit, and a yellow topaz dress with Egyptian lace—along with a gown first seen in brown velvet, and the Congo-colored brocade silk. All with matching shoes, parasols, gloves, and bonnets, of course.

Madame went over the checklist with Conrad. A few stray hairs had broken loose from her coiffure, evidence of her hard work—her lucrative work. Did she receive commission on her sales? Charlotte hoped so.

"I'll have them sewn immediately. And I do think the scalloped trim on the blue gown will be better than the lace. You have a good eye, Monsieur Tremaine."

Conrad blushed. "Yes. Well . . ."

"I'll have them delivered within the week. Will that be soon enough?"

He looked to Charlotte. "Will that be soon enough?"

She was confused. She'd purchased the dresses, but Madame spoke of having them sewn. "They are made from scratch?" she asked.

"Oh yes, mademoiselle. We have our own workroom of nearly fifty seamstresses. When an order is made we create a custom dress according to the customer's particular specifications and preferences. You could have had the gowns in a variety of colors." She cocked her head. "Do you wish to change the order?"

Charlotte couldn't imagine changing a thing. "I'm very happy with the ensembles as they were presented."

Madame Foulard's smile was tinged with relief. "Then within the week it will be accomplished. Good day, mademoiselle. Monsieur Tremaine."

Charlotte took Conrad's arm. As soon as they were alone she said, "Your generosity is overwhelming, Mr. Tremaine."

"Not at all. I did it for me as much as for you. I've never had such a delightful time."

Charlotte couldn't imagine any man having an interest in women's clothing. "You are definitely a man among men."

He suddenly stopped and pulled her to the side, out of the way of the shopping traffic. "Dear Charlotte—may I call you Charlotte when we're alone?"

The look in his eyes was so intense, so sincere. "Of course."

"We've only known each other a short time and yet . . . I must say . . ." He glanced at the people strolling past. "Perhaps this isn't the place to say . . ."

She wanted him to say it. "Please."

"You make me happier than I have ever had cause to be. Just seeing you smile fills me with . . . with . . ."

"With?"

He was still searching for the word but suddenly said, "Joy."

She nodded. "'Tis a good word."

"'Tis a good feeling. Do you feel it too?"

"I do."

There was a moment of silence between them, and Charlotte wondered if Conrad was thinking—as Charlotte was thinking—of a future time when those two words might have even greater meaning.

"Come now," he said, breaking the moment. "Let's go home."

Home. I do. And *joy.*

Glorious words indeed.

There was no clock in the room, and it seemed as if they'd been working for days. But for an occasional trip to the outhouse—six floors below—and ten minutes to eat lunch, there'd been no breaks. What kept Lottie going was thinking about the money she was earning, the dollar she'd found, and how triumphant she would feel when she went to the pawnshop and got her jewels back.

Her aching body interrupted her fantasy. She closed her eyes, arched her back, and moved her neck, trying to relieve the pain. If only she had a back to her chair. Some women did, but she guessed they guarded them with their life.

She heard the voice of Mr. Cavendish—the name of the "Beast"—and immediately got back to work. Lucia was turning in a sleeve to Mr. Silverman; he was inspecting her work.

Lottie looked at her own sleeve. She'd only finished two that met the satisfaction of the foreman. Two sleeves—twenty cents. And her eyes . . . no matter how often she blinked or rubbed them, they would no longer focus. And her fingers were raw with prickings.

"How much longer?" she asked Maggie, the blonde.

With a look toward the Beast, Maggie took a watch from her pocket. "It's nearly two. Five hours more."

Five hours! Lottie's heavy sigh made a few of the women laugh—

softly, for the Beast didn't abide laughter. Even conversation was frowned upon.

"You 'ave a husband, dearie?" Maggie asked.

She shook her head. "I live with Lucia's family."

"You a lodger or a boarder?"

Lottie was confused. "I'm sorry but . . . what's the difference?"

"A lodger makes their own food and a boarder gets breakfast."

"A boarder, then."

"How much you pay 'em?"

Nothing yet . . . She glanced at Lucia, who was still talking with the foreman. "How much should I pay them?"

"Fifty cents a week." Maggie looked to the other women. "Yes?"

Another woman with glasses perched on her nose said, "My family charges forty, but our boarder has been with us for three years."

"Aye, Mr. Tim. I've heard ya talk about that one." Maggie raised her eyebrows suggestively. "Why don' you jus' marry the man?"

"He's fifty to be sure."

"You 'ave a better offer?"

"Maybe," the girl said.

Maggie laughed.

"Enough squawking!" the Beast yelled.

Fifty cents a week?

There went her dollar.

⁂

Lottie clung to Lucia's arm, her legs leaden. She stumbled on the cobblestone street. It was an effort to keep her head erect. Each stoop they passed tempted her to rest. She didn't need to get to the Scarpellis'. She would sleep right here in the open.

Lights were on in the buildings around them, but instead of finding comfort in their glow, Lottie was disheartened. "It was dark when we went to work, and now it's dark when we go home."

"This time of year hard," Lucia said. "Days short. Nights long."

The darkness may have been long, but Lottie feared this night would be too short.

She spotted a woman dumping a basket of rags and refuse in a garbage heap on the curb. The smell of rotten food wafted over them as they passed by.

But then, without warning to herself or Lucia, Lottie stopped walking and returned to the heap. There, amid the trash, was a blue blouse.

She held it up for inspection. The sleeve was torn from the bodice and it was missing a few buttons. But it looked the right size.

"Lottie, no! Put back!" Lucia made a face.

I can mend this.

Lottie rolled the blouse into a bundle and caught up with her friend. "I need another blouse. I can fix it. And wash it."

Lottie was glad her parents weren't there to see her.

Or Suzanna, or Ralph, or especially Edith Whitcomb.

🐎

For the first time since their arrival, Charlotte was eager for the evening meal. She was looking forward to letting Mr. and Mrs. Tremaine know she fully enjoyed the family's store.

Yet as usual, conversation was sparse. She kept hoping Conrad would tell his parents about their shopping excursion, but old habits were apparently deeply rooted.

Finally, after enduring some horribly tough roast beef, Charlotte took a chance. "I had the most delightful trip to your store today, Mr. Tremaine, and I can honestly say it's the most magnificent establishment I've ever visited."

He seemed pleased. But instead of answering her, he turned to his son. "So you *did* take Miss Gleason to the store?"

Conrad set his fork down. "I did, Father. She'd expressed interest in the apparel we offered and so we . . ." He looked to Charlotte and smiled—a smile that faded when he looked back to his father. "I ordered Miss Gleason a few costumes. Madame Foulard assisted us."

"Hmph." The snicker came from Beatrice.

"She was very helpful," Charlotte said.

"She's a pretender," Beatrice said. "I doubt she's even French. And to think she knows anything about fashion . . ."

Any plan Charlotte had to impress the Tremaines was extinguished. Until . . .

"Don't be a snob, Beatrice," Mr. Tremaine said. "Your life of privilege is directly related to the clerks I employ at the store. And your contempt for the fashion we sell there is unconscionable."

Beatrice looked to her mother as though wanting an ally.

But Mrs. Tremaine disappointed. "Your father is right, Beatrice. It's not right to look down upon the merchandise your father has painstakingly chosen for the store."

"But—"

"I know what I'm doing, young lady," he said.

Her posture deflated as if her core had been undermined.

"Forgive me, Father. I meant no disrespect for the merchandise, but—" she looked at Charlotte—"but I can't stand people who pretend to be something they're not."

Charlotte mishandled her water goblet and it tipped, spilling water upon the lace tablecloth. "Oh dear! I'm so sorry. How clumsy of me."

The footman attended to the damage and she was assured it was nothing, but when Charlotte glanced at Beatrice, the girl's face held a haughty contempt that served as a warning that the real damage was yet to come.

⁂

There was a knock on the door. Charlotte hesitated because she'd just gone to bed. But she went to the door and cracked it open.

"Beatrice. Is something wrong?"

Beatrice pointed a finger at her. "If you think you can ingratiate yourself into this family by ordering a few dresses from the store, you're wrong."

Charlotte was stunned. "I don't think any such thing, nor did I order the dresses with—" She stopped herself. While ordering the dresses she *had* considered what the Tremaines would think. "Truly, Beatrice, I didn't intend to offend anyone."

"Well, you did." Beatrice turned on her heel to leave, then turned back. "I saw Mary switch the letter to your mother. I don't know what you're up to, but it *will* come out. I'll see to it."

Charlotte closed the door and rested her forehead against it. This wasn't going to work. The masquerade was coming to an end. It was just a question of how soon she would be unmasked.

Chapter Fourteen

"Shh, lei dorme."

"Povera ragazza."

Lottie heard the voices of Lucia and Lea but didn't have enough energy to open her eyes. She sensed she still held the blouse she'd been repairing in her lap, and wondered after the needle.

She slept . . .

There was a draft. Lottie pulled her blanket tighter. Then she turned her head and suffered a decided crick in her neck. The pain pulled her from sleep and she sat upright. Sat? She was seated on a chair. Someone had put a blanket over her shoulders.

Lottie looked around the main room of the Scarpellis' apartment, where she'd spent the night. Lea was stoking the fire in the stove, talking softly to Dante as he folded their bedding. Sofia shuffled into the room from the bedroom, her hair ruffled from sleep. Lea picked her up and the girl cuddled in her mother's arms. Sofia whined a bit and Lea put a hand to her forehead.

I slept in here last night? In this chair?

Then she remembered. Last evening she'd sat near the lamp in order to mend the blouse she'd found in the trash. She'd been so tired, she remembered putting her head in her arms—for just a moment.

She must have fallen asleep there.

Lea noticed Lottie was awake and handed Sofia to her father. *"Buon giorno,* Lottie. You sleep good?"

She rubbed the back of her neck. "I slept. I'm sorry I was in your room."

"Nessun problema. First day job hard."

And the second day won't be any easier.

Lottie looked around for her blouse. "Do you know where my blouse—?"

"Here," Lea said, showing the blouse draped over a chair near the stove. "I wash last night."

Lottie moved to the stove, walking like an old woman with a stiff back. The blouse was nearly dry. Its color was still a faded blue, and it was horribly wrinkled, but to have it clean . . . *"Grazie.* You didn't need to do that."

Lea shrugged. "You work hard on it. Now clean."

Impulsively, Lottie embraced the woman. It was awkward at first—Lottie wasn't prone to hug others—but once in Lea's grasp, once encircled by her warm, soft arms . . .

Lottie melted. And began to cry.

"Oh, no, no . . ." Lea said. *"Non piangere, cara ragazza mia. Shhhh."*

This was becoming an embarrassing habit. To succumb to tears, to show such weakness in front of others . . .

There was nothing else she could do.

🦁

"There, my dear. What do you think of it?"

Charlotte looked at herself in the massive mirror in Mrs. Tremaine's bedroom. "It's lovely. Truly lovely."

She wasn't lying. Exactly.

The gown Mrs. Tremaine had ordered made for Charlotte's party was a complicated affair in rose and green. Its lower skirt was layered with odd pointed flounces that hung like pink petals. Covering the hips and creating a bustle was silk drapery that was pleated in scarves and held in place with bows and loops of green velvet ribbon to which two huge bouquets of multicolored flowers were added—one for each hip. The dress had short puffed sleeves and a center bodice panel made from rows of lace and edged with a wide band of the velvet ribbon. It looked as though the seamstress had utilized every style, every trick in her book.

"She doesn't like it, Mother," Beatrice said.

Charlotte chastised herself. She knew her face revealed far too much. The dress was extravagant—though not in a good way.

"Is Beatrice correct, Charlotte? Do you dislike the dress?"

Like it or not, now wasn't the time for the truth. Charlotte willed herself to smile and say, "It's far more elegant than I deserve. Perhaps . . . too elegant?"

Mrs. Tremaine stood beside Charlotte and peered into the mirror, her eyes meeting Charlotte's in this indirect manner. "The Tremaine family is presenting you to New York society. *We* know the degree of elegance that is required. Or do you believe you know best?"

Charlotte's throat turned dry. "No, of course not, Mrs. Tremaine. I . . . I was just a bit overwhelmed by . . . ." She ran her hands over the bouquet of flowers balanced upon each hip.

"Its perfection?" Beatrice offered.

Although Charlotte knew Beatrice meant it sarcastically, it was an ample word. The only word she had at present. "Exactly," she said. "Its perfection."

The seamstress sat on a low stool and checked the length. "I do think it's a tiny bit short. I'll add some fringe at the bottom perhaps?"

Fringe. Why not? All she needed now was an ostrich feather in her hair and she could be the opening act in the burlesque show at the Gaiety in London. Barney had offered to take her there once, but she'd declined.

The image of Barney, the butcher's assistant, assailed her. If she'd stayed in Wiltshire, she would have married him. What would he think of her now? His parting words were plucked from her memory: *"You and your fancy ways and proper talkin'. The Gleasons 'ave done you no favors making you think yourself better than the rest of us clods."*

Did she think herself better now? She looked at her dress and the luxurious gowns on Beatrice and Mrs. Tremaine. Who was she to judge its beauty, or even to wear it? She was Dora Connors, a maid. She wasn't a society woman; she wasn't an equal to the likes of the Tremaines. She was a phony.

She remembered what Beatrice had said about hating imposters . . .

"Are you all right, miss?" asked the seamstress.

Suddenly Dora—Charlotte—knew she wasn't all right. The weight of the dress was nothing compared to the weight of her guilt. "I don't feel very well."

"Another headache?" Mrs. Tremaine asked. There was little sympathy in her voice.

Oh dear. She *had* used that excuse before. Yet the door offering release from the moment had opened, and she wasn't about to let it close. "Yes," she said. "I'm afraid so."

The seamstress stood, assessing Charlotte's dress one last time. "I believe I have the measurements I need."

Mrs. Tremaine waved a dismissive hand. "Then get her undressed." She turned to her maid and said, "Go tell Mary Miss Gleason needs her assistance."

"I'm so sorry," Charlotte said as the train and bustle were removed. "I know I'll feel better soon."

"That *would* be best," Mrs. Tremaine said.

Apparently infirmities were yet another thing not well tolerated in the Tremaines' world.

She should keep a list.

"You and your fancy ways and proper talkin'. The Gleasons 'ave done you no favors making you think yourself better than the rest of us clods."

Suddenly Barney grabbed hold of the flowers perched on her hips and yanked hard. A thousand petals scattered to the ground and—

"Miss? Miss!"

Charlotte was shaken awake by Mary. "What? What is it?"

"A doctor is here to take a look at you."

She pushed herself to sitting on the bed. "I don't need a doctor."

"Mrs. Tremaine thinks you do." Mary began to adjust the afghan she'd placed over Charlotte when there was a rap on the door. A doctor entered.

He looked at Charlotte and—

Pulled up short. "Miss—?"

Charlotte's heart leapt to her throat. "Dr. Greenfield?"

He appeared confused, a condition that wasn't eased when Mrs. Tremaine entered.

"There you are, Charlotte. I called our physician to come right away, and he sent his new partner, a Dr. Greenbaum?"

"Greenfield, ma'am."

"Yes. Well. See to Miss Gleason. This is the second debilitating headache she's had in a few days. Her welcome party is approaching, and we need her well."

"I'll do my best."

Mrs. Tremaine stood by the door. Charlotte wished she would leave. She had to talk to Dr. Greenfield alone, to greet him, to revel in his presence. To explain.

To try to explain.

The doctor got his bearings and approached the bedside. "Well, Miss . . ."

"Gleason," she said.

"Miss Gleason. Describe the sort of pain you're experiencing."

Her headaches were nothing compared to the pain in her heart at seeing him while knowing their situation was untenable. "It's—"

Mrs. Tremaine stepped forward. "She's missed an appointment with the florist and had to cut short a fitting for her gown. Such interruptions cannot be tolerated, so I implore you to get to the bottom of her infirmity."

Charlotte knew her facial expression wasn't doing her any favors. She kept looking at Mrs. Tremaine—willing her to leave, then back at Dr. Greenfield—willing him to understand.

There was a knock on the door. Mrs. Tremaine answered, spoke a few words, then turned toward the room. "If you'll excuse me. It appears Mrs. Dyson has some questions about dinner."

Charlotte's heart beat once again.

"Can I get you something, Doctor?" Mary asked.

Mary. They still had Mary in the room.

"If you could bring Miss Gleason some chamomile tea, I think that will be a good start to her recovery."

"Of course, sir."

As soon as the door clicked shut, he turned to Charlotte. "Charlotte Gleason? Wasn't that the name of your friend on the ship?"

"Yes, but . . ."

"So is your name Dora Connors or . . . ?"

"It's Dora, but . . ." She wanted him to take her hands, to smile at her, to tell her how happy he was to see her.

Instead he pulled a chair to the side of the bed and sat. "Perhaps you'd better explain."

The truth that had been pounding on the door of her conscience since they'd landed in America burst into the open. Her words spilled out until the room from whence they'd come was empty.

"So that's the lot of it," she said.

He sat in silence a moment. "No wonder you have headaches."

"I'm not good at lying."

"Apparently you're good enough. The Tremaines don't suspect?"

She looked toward the door. "I think the daughter suspects something, though I don't think she's determined exactly how it fits together as yet."

"A credit to your acting ability, no doubt."

There was an edge to his voice. Did he think she'd been acting on the ship in regard to her feelings for him? "I am no actress. I can only take on this role because I know the real Charlotte Gleason like a sister. We've been together since we were children."

"Regarding that . . . where is your mistress—she now goes by Lottie Hathaway, you say?"

Charlotte nodded. "I don't know where she is. I saw her once, briefly, standing in the rain outside this house."

"So she wanted to end the charade?"

She hesitated. "I don't know."

He gave her a stern look.

"Yes, you're right. I can't think of any other reason for her to be here. But she didn't do anything toward that end."

He looked pensive. "Do you know where she's living?"

"No." She thought of something. "During the sermon on Sunday the pastor at the Tremaines' church mentioned a woman who'd stopped there the same day I saw Lottie, and . . . he might know where she is, but I haven't been able to get free of this place to go back and ask him."

Dr. Greenfield stood and put the chair in its place. "I could go to him."

"Would you?"

"I will. But if she can be found . . . what then?"

Charlotte had no idea. She'd grown fond of Conrad. But sitting in front of her was Edmund Greenfield. She felt something for him too. If she offered Lottie the chance to resume her proper place . . . would that be a good thing? Or . . . ?

"I don't know what *then*," she said.

"Perhaps you should think some on it."

There was one thing she did know. "I need to find out if Lottie's all right. I miss her. We've spent every day together since we were young girls. To be apart and to not know . . ."

Mary returned with the tea, and Dr. Greenfield moved to the door. "I'll check back with you, Miss Gleason. In the meantime, mind you don't stress yourself." He let himself out.

"Here, miss." Mary handed her a cup of tea. "The doctor's right. Chamomile soothes a body well. I know that for a fact."

Seeing Dr. Greenfield again, having him know the worst about her, having him look at her in a way far different than he had on the ship . . . All that, added to the uncertainty of her future.

It would take more than tea to soothe her now.

Lottie sensed rather than felt the presence of the Beast coming up behind her. She'd known the man for only a day, yet she already knew he was without honor, a man to avoid. When she was finished with a sleeve, she made a point of waiting until Mr. Silverman was free to check it. She wasn't alone in this, which unfortunately gave the Beast more free time to roam the workroom like an infection in search of a weakened host.

Feeling him close, she did not look up but hunched over her work even more, hoping he would pass her by.

The sound of his boots upon the floor ceased. Across the table she noticed that Maggie's and Helga's hands faltered in their stitching. All conversation around her stopped.

As had the Beast. Behind her. She could smell the stench of his stale clothes and the tobacco on his breath.

Still she didn't look up. *Please go away. Leave me alone.*

"Well, now." She felt his breath upon her hair. "How is our lovely new Brit doing?"

Lottie felt an involuntary shiver course through her. She hoped the Beast didn't notice. "Fine, sir."

She worked on.

"I saw that Mr. Silverman made you redo one of your sleeves three times yesterday."

"Yes, sir. I was learning. It wasn't right—at first. I know how to sew them properly now."

He leaned to her ear, his breath hot. "If you bring your work to me, I'll see it gets passed. I'm certain we can make an agreeable arrangement."

She closed her eyes and clenched her jaw. This man was appalling. A disgrace. "Thank you, sir, but I prefer to get it passed on its own merit. You'll need to make an arrangement with someone else."

Suddenly he put his hands on Lottie's upper arms and lifted her to standing. "Up! Come with me." He dragged her down the narrow space between the rows of chairs, causing women to be bumped and hairdos to become disheveled.

"Stop it!" she yelled. "Let go of me!"

Lottie caught sight of Lucia's look of alarm, but she knew that neither she nor the other women could risk speaking out.

Where was Mr. Silverman?

She glanced toward his normal station, but he was gone. No wonder the Beast chose this particular moment to do his dirty work.

Which constituted what, exactly?

"Ow! Get your hands off me, you brute!"

"Shut your trap, missy, or you'll get the worst of it."

What was *it*?

He dragged her out of the workroom, past the landing, and into another room. He shut the door and blocked her exit. "There, now. This is better, ain't it?"

I'm in such trouble. Horrible trouble. Please, God. Save me!

She sensed he fed on fear, so she gathered all her strength and lifted her chin. Then she smoothed her skirt. "I'd like to return to work now, Mr. Cavendish. I'm behind on my quota and—"

He strolled toward her. "Which is why I've brought you here, Miss

Brit. You ain't a fast worker, I can tell that already. You'll never catch up with the other girls. Unless . . ."

She took a step back. "I'll catch up."

"Which is why I'm giving you the chance to ease your mind and your load. You ain't like those other girls in there, those I-ties, Krauts, and Jews. You've got good blood in you. I can tell." He walked toward her, forcing her to back up against the wall. His right arm was outstretched, his hand heading toward her waist.

Anger swelled and demanded release. And patience. When he was finally close enough . . . Lottie heaved her knee into his groin. To her surprise, he buckled over and fell backward.

Run! Run!

She ran to the door and threw it open. Through the opened door to the workroom she spotted Mr. Silverman speaking with Lucia, but she didn't dare stop. Instead she lurched down the stairs, her spine prickling with the anticipation of hearing the footsteps of the Beast behind her.

Finally at the bottom of the last stair she ran out to the street and—

Tripped on a horse lying in the gutter, falling on top of it.

Appalled, she scrambled away on her hands and knees. *No, no, no, no!* Three little boys gaped at her, sticks in their hands. Had they been poking the horse? Was it dead?

A man took her arm and helped her up. "Miss Hathaway? What's wrong? What happened?"

It was Mr. Svensson, the photographer.

She pointed up the stairs. "That man, the Beast . . . he tried to . . ." She couldn't speak of such a thing.

Sven looked at the building. "There's a sweatshop up there?"

"I was working there until he . . ." She put a hand to her mouth, then, realizing it had touched the dead horse, wiped it on her skirt. "I can't go back to work there. I just can't."

"You don't need to."

Only then did she notice his camera set up on the street, aimed at the dead horse. "Actually, I could use an assistant. The boy who's been helping me got a better job with a blacksmith. Would you care to take his place?"

Anything, yes, anything would be better than the sweatshop. Lottie checked for the Beast again, but so far he hadn't followed her down. She gathered a new breath. "I don't know anything about photography."

"Did you know anything about sewing?"

She turned her pricked fingers under.

There was only one choice. "Yes, I'll help you." Her newly honed practical nature came to the forefront. "But I need to be paid a fair wage."

He shook his head, incredulous. "Demanding higher pay before you've even started?"

She gasped at her own effrontery. Where were her manners?

Back in England.

"I'm . . . I'm sorry. And a bit embarrassed. I know I have no right, but—"

He sighed. "You've just hit upon the problem with the entire system, Miss Hathaway. No worker has any rights here."

She felt strengthened by the fact that he hadn't chastened her. "So what *will* you pay me, Mr. Svensson?"

"Just Sven." He stepped back to his camera, shooing away the children who were paying it too much attention. "What did you get paid at the sweatshop?"

She considered lying, then told the truth. "Ten cents a sleeve."

"And how many could you do a day?"

She hesitated. "Not many now, but Lucia can do six, and I was getting better, and—"

"How about ten cents a photograph?"

"How many do you do a day?"

"We'll work toward six. How does that sound?"

She held out her hand for him to shake. "It's a deal, Mr. . . . Sven."

"Agreed." They shook on it.

Just then Mr. Cavendish burst onto the street, followed by Mr. Silverman. "There she is! You get yourself back to work, you hussy!" He rushed forward and tried to grab her arm, but Lottie hid behind Sven.

Mr. Silverman put a hand on his arm. "Joe . . . that's not the way."

"Leave her alone, man," Sven said. "And don't go calling her names. You're the one who—"

"Get out of my face, blondie! Who do you think you are to interfere? This has nothing to do with you."

"But it does," Sven said. "Miss Hathaway is my employee."

Cavendish let out a huff. "Since when?"

"Since now. So I'd advise you to go back to your sweatshop. And if I hear of you bothering any of the other girls, I'll call the coppers on you. Or perhaps you'd like me to take a photograph of the conditions there?"

Cavendish made a move toward Sven, but Silverman drew him off. "Upstairs, Joe. Come on. It's over."

The two men went back inside. Suddenly applause rained down from above. The windows on the street side of the sixth floor were filled with Lottie's fellow workers, who'd watched the entire exchange.

"Good going, Lottie!" Maggie yelled.

A few of the girls looked toward the room and seemed to decide it would be best to get back to their places before the bosses returned. Lucia waved. "You all right?"

Lottie called up to her. "I'm fine. I'm working for Sven now. I'll see you at home tonight."

With a glance toward the workroom, Lucia nodded and disappeared inside.

For the first time since the entire incident had begun, Lottie took a deep breath, then let it out with deliberation. "Well then. This isn't how I expected to end my day."

"End? I think not," Sven said. "The day's far from over. Come and hold my pack while I take a photograph of the horse before they haul it away."

Lottie complied. Gladly.

⁂

Sven was really quite handsome in a refreshing Nordic way. It was as though a constant wind tousled his hair and a biting cold ruddied his cheeks.

Lottie found it odd to scrutinize his looks while they moved through the horrors of the slums, but she couldn't help it. And perhaps it was self-preservation. For if she allowed her thoughts and feelings to fully acknowledge the revolting things she was seeing, she feared the burden would press upon her shoulders, pushing her down. Down. Down, into hopelessness.

Besides, flirting was what she did best; it's what she'd been groomed to do. From earliest childhood she'd learned that the right smile, the right tilt of her head, and the appropriate look of yearning in her eyes could get her whatever she wanted. At first she'd used her talent upon her father (and the occasional male servant who'd hesitated to give in to her whims) and then had broadened the scope of her power beyond the household and into society, where she was thrilled to find that boys (and then men) would do her bidding with little effort expended on her part.

She remembered one particularly momentous time when she'd been fourteen and her mother insisted she have piano lessons. Herr Baumgartner had been a lovely German man. During the first few lessons he'd sat on the piano bench beside her, helping her find the F-sharp and the D-flat when she faltered—and falter she did, for she knew exactly what she was doing. He had the deepest brown eyes.

Yet during the next lesson Herr Baumgartner remained standing, a position he adopted for the next six months, until her interest waned. Interest in the piano waned.

The interest in her own power of flirtation had just begun. In the years between then and now, Lottie had honed the skill into an art. If she desired a man's interest, she could get it. That her skills occasionally elicited the attention of an unwanted male was a drawback she'd learned to live with. There'd been one young gent who'd not been put off by her rebuff and she'd had to take slightly harsher methods to be rid of—

"There now," Sven said, pulling her to a stop. "Stand here a moment and let your eyes adjust."

Here was the entry to an alley so narrow they could only pass single file. Two tenements rose on either side, and as Lottie looked up she saw an arm extend out a window in one tenement handing something to an outstretched hand in the window across the way. To have a neighbor so close was unimaginable.

The window situation was soon forgotten when they reached the back of the alley.

"Perfect," Sven said to himself as he eyed his next subject.

Perfect? The back of one row of tenements met the back of the tenements from one street away. Sandwiched in the small space between the two were ramshackle hovels.

"People live here?" Lottie said.

"Rear tenements. Back shacks. They have no ventilation, no water, no toilets. It's inhuman."

And unnatural. Lottie thought longingly of the great expanse of green that comprised the land surrounding Dorby Manor: the full sky, the sound of the breeze in the trees, the smell of flowers and grass. She'd taken so much for granted. She missed *green*.

Lottie spotted movement to her right and saw an ancient man curl upon the ground, his arms hugging a ragged jacket to his body. On any exposed skin were open sores. When he looked at her, his eyes appeared dead. It was only a matter of time before the rest of his body would follow.

Sven nodded toward the man. "Most are happy to be picked up by the police, for at least there they'll get a bed and some breakfast."

A woman and her child walked by. Even the child gave the man no notice.

Lottie squealed when a bird flew from an upper perch and pecked at the man before rising into the air as if biding its time for a full meal. She shuddered and turned away but immediately felt Sven's hand upon her arm. "Don't avert your eyes, Miss Hathaway. Open them and be a witness. This is why I take photographs for the newspapers, to make people see. And hopefully act."

The man held out a hand. More than anything, Lottie wanted to give him something, wanted to help him. But she had nothing to give. Not a penny, not a blanket. Nothing.

You have the dollar you found . . . and the dime . . .

But she couldn't give it to him. It was all she had, and she owed the Scarpellis rent and . . .

No wonder the mother and child had kept their eyes averted. To continually see and not be able to help . . . What did such a conundrum do to hearts longing to feel compassion?

Sven set up his camera. "Go to the front door of that shack and see if the inhabitants will come outside to have their photograph taken."

The thought of approaching such a structure was revolting. It was little more than a shanty built with scraps of building material somewhat—somehow—attached to the building behind. That people actually lived there was hard to comprehend.

Sven looked up from his work. "What if I dock your wages for the times you refuse my direction? I can hire another boy off the streets, one that won't complain."

"Surely you understand my hesitation? I'm not used to being around these conditions."

"Who is?" he said. "Now, go. Do as I told you, Miss Hathaway. Smile to get your way with them the same as you do with me."

She felt her face grow red. "I don't smile to get my way with you."

"Go."

She had no time to defend herself more—if there was anything that could be defended.

The hut was a slapdash affair of boards, sheets of tin, and even cloth. The door didn't fit the opening but left a gap of three inches along a side and across the top. She imagined snow blowing through the gap and accumulating on the floor.

Lottie walked toward the structure, stepping between piles of stinky garbage. Sven would owe her extra for this one.

She readied her fist to knock but hesitated. The idea of any part of her body touching this—

She jumped back when a rat squeezed through the gap in the door. "Sven!"

"Go on. Ask them. I need this picture."

With one hand she took a wad of her skirt to hold it above the ground, and with the other she knocked on the door.

A woman—very visibly pregnant—opened the door. Her eyes were dull, as if they hadn't seen anything to brighten them for far too long.

Lottie pointed to Sven. "Mr. Svensson is a photographer. He'd like to take your picture out front—and pay you for your trouble."

The woman studied Sven a moment, then looked back to Lottie. "I had a photo taken once. For my wedding."

The idea of this woman being dressed in a bridal gown was incongruous.

"I'll be right out," the woman said. She closed the door.

Lottie immediately stepped away, much preferring the proximity nearer Sven.

In less than a minute the woman emerged with a grubby little boy wearing pants that were far too short and a man's vest that made his torso look as though it began at his knees. His hair had been slicked to the side. The mother attempted to secure the loose strands of hair that had fallen from her bun.

Such a gesture was ridiculous. She cared about her appearance? What about the shack where she lived? How did a woman who had enough money to have a photograph taken to commemorate her wedding end up in a hovel like this? How could she raise a child and give birth to a baby in such a place? Since there were no answers, Lottie tried not to think about it.

Sven directed the duo, and Lottie guarded the pack that contained the plates Sven fit into his camera—those new and those used and ready for him to develop elsewhere. The photograph was taken, and Sven handed the woman a few coins.

Lottie was glad to leave. That was four photographs so far today. Only two more. "Where to now?" Lottie asked as they made their way toward the alley.

"I've heard of a stale beer dive where men pay two cents to drink deadly stuff and sleep in a chair. I'd like to photograph it, but it's far too dark in there. If only there was a way for me to provide my own light."

Lottie was glad there wasn't. "How can people stay in such places?"

"They sink to the level of their necessity," he said. "One half of the world has no idea how the other half lives."

She'd never thought of it that way, but it was probably true. As a rich girl Lottie had had no knowledge of the poor, and the poor probably had no knowledge of the rich. They lived in separate worlds. Wasn't it better that way? They passed the man huddled against the cold and she wondered.

They walked back through the alley onto the main street, and Lottie relished the increase in light and air. Sven turned south, and they wove their way through the peddlers' stalls and people milling about. People. Everywhere people trying to eke out a living.

She thought of the job she'd given up at the sweatshop. How many of those women had suffered the treatment she'd experienced with the

Beast? Or worse? And how many had quit that sort of job hoping in vain for a better one? How many—?

Lottie heard a baby's cry. It wasn't a foreign sound, for there were children and babies in abundance, but this cry was different because it continued without comfort. Its intensity heightened.

She looked to her right, toward the sound, and expected to see a woman rocking a child in her arms.

Instead she saw a bundle on the cobblestones, placed against a building.

She looked right, then left. No one ran to the baby's aid. No one even looked in its direction.

She pulled on Sven's arm. "Stop. There's a baby on the ground over there."

He looked in the direction where she pointed. "Poor child."

He just looked at it.

"Aren't you going to do something?"

"I did something the first time I found an abandoned baby. And the second. And the third. I picked them up and held them and tried to find their parents. But it's the parents who put them there. Too many mouths to feed and women constantly with child, making more babies who can't survive. Five hundred a year abandoned, at least a hundred found dead." He shook his head.

The baby's cries were plaintive and panicked. Lottie picked it up and cradled it in her arms. "There, there. Shhh. You'll be all right."

"Don't make promises . . ." Sven said. "Put it back. I'm losing the light."

Lottie was appalled. "How can you care about light when this baby needs our help?"

"Your help, not mine," he said. "Although I admit it's a tragedy beyond bearing, it's not our business, Miss Hathaway. You and I have only four hands between us, and there are thousands upon thousands in need."

Suddenly a fire sparked within her. She'd had enough of walking on by. "So we don't even try to help? What happened to your high-and-mighty talk about being a witness and getting people to act? Have *we* no responsibility to act?"

He shook his head. "You're right, of course, but . . ."

"But nothing." Lottie looked at the baby in her arms. He'd quieted now and gazed up at her with deep brown eyes. Was he Italian in descent? There was that look about him yet also something else. Something different. Sven had said there were a lot of Romanians here. . . .

Lottie realized she'd called him *he*. Although the baby appeared to be just a few months old, there was a distinguished look about him. This baby was not a girl. And though there was a certain way to find out, Lottie recoiled from the idea of changing a diaper—if the child even wore one.

Yet as the boy adjusted himself in her arms, seeking comfort and finding it, she knew she would do that awful duty and many others for his sake.

"Come on now, Miss Hathaway. We have to keep going."

She looked at Sven with a new determination. "I'm not leaving him here."

"Him?"

"It's a boy."

"How can you tell? I mean . . ."

"I just know."

"You can't take him."

"I can and I will."

Sven ran a hand over his face, clearly exasperated. "Do you always expect to get your way?"

She cocked her head as if considering, but there was only one answer. "Yes."

"Fine, then. Take him with you. We're a few blocks from the Merciful Child Foundling Home. You can take him there."

But as they walked east, as the baby fell asleep in her arms, as it wrapped its tiny fingers around hers . . .

No! Don't be ridiculous. You can't keep the child. It's impossible.

Had *impossible* ever stopped her before?

When they paused to let some horses pass, Lottie made her pronouncement. "I'm not turning him in. I'm keeping him."

"You can't do that."

She remembered her talent for getting what she wanted and implemented it now. She smiled at Sven, and as she rocked the baby, she turned him toward the photographer. "See how he senses my concern for him, my caring?"

"No one is disparaging your compassion, Miss Hathaway. Only your sanity."

"Finding a baby abandoned in the street is the essence of insanity." A thought came to her. "God placed this child in my path so I'd take him and keep him safe."

"I'm not going to argue God's ways with you, but if I were Him, I would've at least placed the child in the path of someone who has a home and a husband with a well-paying job."

His logic annoyed her. "Perhaps He did, but *that* person chose not to take him."

"So you're God's second choice?" He looked far too amused.

"Never, Mr. Svensson."

"I thought not."

"But second choice or no, I'm not giving up this child. He's mine." The passion of her declaration shocked her. But before she could rationalize the situation, she pressed forward. "And his name is Fitzwilliam."

"How do you know that?"

"Because I just named him after Fitzwilliam Darcy from *Pride and Prejudice.* I'll call him Fitz for short."

Sven set his tripod down, resting it against his hip. "You are one determined woman."

"I'm glad you finally figured that out."

"What is the family you're living with going to think about this—about Fitz?"

The image of herself sleeping on the floor with Fitz beside her initiated a smile. "The Scarpellis are a loving family. They won't mind."

"I think you overestimate their generosity—or the generosity of any family."

"I'll take my chances."

Yet as she held Fitz close and pressed her lips against his tiny head . . . what was she doing?

Charlotte waited for Dr. Greenfield to return from speaking with Pastor Weston. And waited. Her headache—which had never been worthy of a doctor's care—went away, but she remained in her room. She didn't trust her ability to act as if nothing was amiss.

And nothing was amiss. Not really. Dr. Greenfield—her Edmund Greenfield from the ship—was privy to the truth, or rather, privy to Lottie's and Dora's lies. That he hadn't marched down the stairs and declared to the Tremaines that an imposter lay abed in their house was a relief beyond measure. That she was still attracted to him was a dilemma that had no resolve.

Charlotte couldn't remove him from her mind, and much of her time feigning illness was spent remembering the way she'd felt on the ship when they'd danced and walked and talked, and the look of his smile when she'd first given him her handkerchief because she'd spilt upon his shoes.

What had he said upon parting—when she'd hurt him by telling him of her upcoming betrothal?

"Permit me to let my prayers and the decision of God finish our story . . . until fate allows."

She sat upright. "Until fate allows . . . What are the chances that Dr. Greenfield would come into *my* room, to attend to *me*?"

The answer was unspoken but was, at the least, astronomical. The only explanation came from Dr. Greenfield's own words. Was God finishing their story? Did He wish it to be finished? Together?

There was a knock on the door, but instead of Mary entering as she always did upon announcing herself, it remained closed.

"Come in."

It was Conrad, carrying a tray. "I heard you weren't feeling well. I had Mrs. Dyson prepare a tray for you."

Guilt washed over her. To think she'd spent the afternoon dreaming of Dr. Greenfield, when all the while there was a man in this very house who cared for her—who deserved to be cared for *by* her.

"You are too kind, Mr. Tremaine. Thank you."

"Conrad. Please."

"Conrad."

He looked about the room for a place to set it, but paused for a moment, his eyes upon the dressing table. "You kept my flower from the park."

Yes indeed. She'd had Mary find a small vase, and there it had remained since that outing.

Charlotte left the bed and pointed to a table near a grouping of two chairs. "There, I think," she said.

"Should you be out of bed?"

"I . . . it's good for me to move about a little." She moved a bird figurine so there was room for the tray. He adjusted the table to her reach from a nearby chair.

"This looks marvelous," she said, perusing the tea, soup, bread, and slices of ham and cheese.

"Mother wouldn't say exactly what was wrong, so . . . ." He blushed. "So I told the cook to make it soothing."

"You are very kind." Too kind.

He stood by, a bit awkward.

"Do sit, Conrad. Give me some company while I eat."

He seemed relieved to do so. "I was told the dressmaker was here today. Do you like your gown?"

His face was so hopeful, she couldn't tell him the complete truth. "I liked the gowns you bought me at Tremaine's better."

"Then, wear one of—" He stopped himself. "Thank you for the compliment, but I think it will be best if you wear the one Mother had made for you."

His acquiescence made her sad, and yet he was right. "I agree."

His sigh secured the decision.

Another knock on the door and Mary entered, carrying a note on a silver tray. "This just came for you, miss."

The envelope was addressed to Miss Gleason. "May I?" she asked Conrad.

"Please."

She opened it, saw it was from Dr. Greenfield, and hungrily read his words: *I'll visit tomorrow morning. Hope you're feeling better. E.G.*

"Good news?" Conrad asked.

Her face must have revealed as much. "Dr. Greenfield will return to check on me tomorrow morning."

"That's good of him. But Greenfield? What happened to Dr. Carlton?"

"I believe they are cousins and partners. Dr. Greenfield recently arrived from England."

"Ah. So." He pressed his hands to his thighs and stood. "I best not tax your strength. I do hope you are well by morning and have no need of the good doctor."

No need. Much need.

It was getting complicated.

※

Because of the baby they took no more photographs that day. Fitz demanded Lottie's attention, and Sven even paid for some condensed milk, a feeding bottle, and some rags for diapers before walking her back to the Scarpellis'.

I still have my dollar. . . .

"I'm so sorry for cutting the day short," she said. "You don't have to walk me back. I could find my—" Fitz began to fuss. "Shh, say there. It's all right."

But Fitz wouldn't be appeased.

Sven stopped walking and set his equipment down. "Let me take him."

"It's all right. I can handle—"

He held his arms out. "Please."

She handed Fitz over. Instead of cradling him as Lottie had done all day, Sven set the boy upright against his shoulder. Fitz immediately stopped fussing. "See? He just wants a chance to see what's going on."

Fitz's bright eyes peeking over Sven's shoulder proved him right.

"You're very good with children," Lottie said.

"So I've been told. I've learned by experience."

Just the way he said it implied . . . much.

Sven was married. Why had he never said anything before now? She should have known something was amiss when he didn't respond to her flirting. Lottie felt herself strangely disappointed. Not that she'd ever be interested in such a man, but—

"Here," Sven said. "You can have him back now. You need to get him home. The day's turning nippy."

Yes, cold. Very very cold.

❧

What would the Scarpellis say about Fitz?

As they neared Mulberry Street, the question plagued Lottie's thoughts. Yet every time she looked at his lovely face, she knew she'd done the right thing.

At the door to her tenement, Sven pressed forty cents into her hand.

"No, I can't accept this. You've already paid for—"

"It's your pay, Miss Hathaway. Four photos, forty cents." He placed a gentle hand on Fitz's head. "You're a good assistant—or were so before this one grabbed your eye. I'm sad to see you go."

"Go? I'm not going anywhere. I'll work with you tomorrow and the next day—if you'll have me."

"What about Fitz?"

She'd thought it through. "Hopefully Lea and Francesca will take care of him. I'll pay them something for the service. And Sofia will help. Little girls love playing with babies. The arrangement has to work so *I* can work."

He looked skeptical. "If it comes together as you hope, meet me at the corner at seven o'clock. Don't be late."

"I'll be there."

Lottie received many curious looks as she ascended the stairs of the tenement. Those who knew her as the British friend of the Scarpellis wondered about the sudden appearance of a baby.

"Bambino?"

Although she wasn't certain they'd understand, she said, "His name is Fitzwilliam and he's mine now."

He's mine now? As the last flight of stairs drained her remaining energy, the question remained.

Oddly, the door to the Scarpellis' apartment was open, and the front room was filled with women. Lottie entered, looking for Lea.

A woman recognized her, glanced at the baby, then gestured toward the bedroom. *"Sofia è malata.* Sick."

Sofia?

She entered the bedroom and saw Lea and Francesca kneeling on the floor beside Sofia's bed. Lea had a cloth to Sofia's forehead. The little girl lay deathly still.

"Lea?"

Lea looked up, then rose from her knees, handing the cloth to Francesca. "Sofia sick. *Febbre*."

Fever? Sofia's face was flushed. "But she was all right this . . ." Lottie thought back to the morning and remembered seeing Sofia in her mother's arms. "Have you called a doctor?"

Lea looked at Francesca and repeated the word in Italian. "*Medico*." They shared a sarcastic laugh. "No doctor come here."

Only then did Lea's eyes light upon Fitz. "*Bambino?*"

"Baby. Yes. I found him abandoned in the gutter. I couldn't leave him there."

"*Fuori! Vattene! Via con quel bambino!* Out! No baby!"

Lea was right. Fitz couldn't be around Sofia. But where could they go?

Lea frantically spoke to the other ladies. All eyes turned on Lottie and Fitz, then back to Lea. When she finished speaking, there was a pause. Then, reluctantly, one woman raised her hand.

"*Grazie,* Maria." She turned to Lottie. "You go with *Signora* Rossi. She take you till Sofia well."

Mrs. Rossi motioned for Lottie to follow. What choice did she have?

The Rossis lived on the third floor of the same building in an apartment smaller than the Scarpellis'. Although at the moment it was only occupied by a very elderly grandmother, a young woman holding her own baby, and Mrs. Rossi, Lottie had no idea how many would join them once evening fell.

Mrs. Rossi made introductions, and Lottie heard her name among the string of Italian words. The grandmother shrugged, then returned to her nap. The young mother gave Fitz a cursory glance before giving her attention to her own baby. Neither woman showed any real interest in him. And why should they? Babies were plentiful in the tenements and grew up—if they grew up—to be children who demanded more care, more food, and more space.

Unless they got sick and died.

Sofia. Lottie longed to be upstairs with her. But with Fitz in her arms, and with none of the Rossis showing any willingness to take care of him, she couldn't risk it. Instead she sat on a chair in the corner and rocked him—as she rocked herself.

Amidst her need for comfort she found herself praying: *What should I do?* alternated with *Make Sofia well*.

She believed God was listening.

But how would He answer?

Chapter Fifteen

A baby cried.

Lottie ordered the sound out of her dreams. *Shh. I'm trying to sleep.*

The cry persisted.

A male voice barked, *"Silenzio!"*

Another said, *"Fache il bambino smetta di piangere!"*

She opened her eyes—and, with the help of the moonlight, remembered where she was. She'd fallen asleep in a chair in the Rossis' apartment, her head resting against a wall.

Fitz lay sprawled upon her lap, fallen from the comfort of her arms. Crying. Real. Her responsibility.

She picked him up. "Shhh, sweet baby. Shhh."

A woman's form filled the doorway leading to the bedroom. "Here," said Carmela, the Rossi daughter. *"Dammi il bambino."*

Lottie brought her the child—as she'd done two other times during the long night. Carmela sat in a chair near the stove, and Lottie soon heard the sound of Fitz suckling. Carmela had been a godsend, nursing her own baby as well as Fitz, letting Lottie save the canned milk for later.

Yet this stranger's care emphasized Lottie's helplessness. She returned to her chair, leaned her head against the wall, and closed her eyes. If only she could transport herself back to her lovely bedroom in Wiltshire, where she was surrounded by pillows and soft linens, where the only sound to interrupt her sleep was that of the housemaid stoking the embers of the fireplace into a flame so Lottie would awaken to a warm room.

How nice it would be to wake up and request some hot chocolate and scones for breakfast. With orange marmalade.

Her stomach rumbled, reminding her it had been many hours since she'd eaten—and then, she'd eaten little, not wanting to impose upon the Rossis' hospitality by eating her fill during last evening's meal.

Lottie wrapped a borrowed shawl more closely around her shoulders.

Hungry, cold, and exhausted. Was this what the future held?

How long had she been in this country? She tried to remember the days, but found them a blur of one crisis heaped upon another. The snippets of light amid the darkness had faces: Lea, Sofia, Lucia, Sven . . .

And Fitz. Fitzwilliam, her baby.

Her baby?

What was I thinking?

She'd been virtually helpless seeing to his needs for one night, much less the rest of his life. Common sense was demanding and nonnegotiable.

Yet Fitz knew her now. When he was fed and dry he lay upon her lap, kicked his feet, cooed, and smiled. He seemed quite willing to accept her as his mother.

And she?

She too was willing and longed to keep him as her own with an intensity that frightened her. She, who'd never been around children, now found her heart softened by this baby, and by a little girl who lay sick in an apartment upstairs.

Lottie must have dozed off, for Carmela awakened her by placing Fitz in her arms. He was quiet now, content. "*Grazie*, Carmela." Lottie rocked him gently and traced a finger along his perfect cheek. "How can I keep you? How?"

She couldn't risk bringing Fitz to the Scarpellis', not with Sofia sick, and she couldn't intrude on the Rossis another night. She had no home, no time, and no money to care for her child.

I have the dollar.

The dollar she'd found and had intended to use to buy back her ruby necklace. The notion seemed silly now, and impossible—especially when a dollar would pay the Scarpellis some rent and buy Fitz food. The dollar *and* the dime from the pastor *and* the forty cents she'd earned by working for Sven would help them live another day.

But what of the next day? And the next week and month?

A sudden understanding flooded over her. The parents who'd left Fitz on the street must have suffered then as she did now with a hopelessness, frustration, and sorrow that ripped her in two.

Lottie lifted the boy to her lips and kissed his head. If she loved him, she knew what she must do.

Her prayers to keep the child changed to a plaintive plea. *Watch over him, Lord. And help me let him go.*

When Sven spotted her, his eyes immediately lowered to the bundle in her arms. "You're here."

"I'm here to work."

He shook his head. "But Fitz . . ."

She swallowed and found her throat tight. "I need to take him to the foundling home. Then I can work." She stared at Sven, challenging him. Despite her best efforts, a tear escaped. She swiped it away. She explained about Sofia. "Please. Tell me where it is."

"Would you rather not work?" he asked. "You need to be with Fitz and—"

"I need a job."

"But maybe you could find one you could do at home. Didn't you tell me Mrs. Scarpelli made flowers for hats?"

"I can't invade their flower business." Yet his query made her realize something else. "I want to work for you. I want to help you."

He looked confused. "But you're disgusted by what you see."

"But I admire what you're doing."

His face softened. "Really?"

"You're a good man who's trying to change the world."

He laughed. "A few blocks. I'm trying to change the conditions within a few blocks in one city in a very big world."

She didn't want him to think about it that way. "You're doing all you can. No one can be asked to do more."

He looked to the ground. "You're very kind."

"I'm very honest." Fitz began to squirm. She needed to complete her task. "I have to go. Tell me how to get to the foundling home, and I'll meet you later."

"I'll take you."

"No. I have to do this alone. Tell me a time later in the day to meet you, and I'll be there. Alone."

Sven pointed to the northeast. "Go to Bayard and Mott. Turn right. Third house on the left. We'll meet at ten, then?"

"Ten it will be."

"You're doing a good thing, Miss Hathaway. You saved that boy."

Saved him only to leave him.

Lottie walked away. Each step toward the home was a lost moment with Fitz and a further fissure in her heart.

※

The Merciful Child Foundling Home was a ramshackle house next to a church. The sign on the door told her to enter but also said:

Suffer little children to come unto me, and forbid them not: for of such is the kingdom of God.

She knocked and entered and was nearly bowled over by some boys racing down the stairs into the empty foyer. Only it wasn't empty, for a crib stood nearby. The boys ran past her into a parlor and took their seats among a dozen children. The room was filled with rows of mismatched chairs, all facing a woman. She held a hand-drawn poster of the alphabet.

She stopped her lesson and looked at Lottie. "May I help you, miss?"

"I . . ." She looked down at the baby. "This baby . . ." She took out the dollar coin and the other baby supplies. "I can give you this for his keeping. And I have a job. I'll bring more money when I—"

The woman nodded and left the children. "We'll be happy to take him in, no questions asked. But we'd really prefer if you could stay around and nurse your baby—and perhaps another."

"No, no," Lottie said. "You have it all wrong."

The woman's eyes were kind. "We know the hardships you're facing. We don't judge. We're here for you *and* your baby." She pulled the blanket aside to see Fitz's face. "He's a very handsome boy. You can put him right here in the crib if you'd like. We used to have the crib outside, but it filled up too quickly, so we brought it in. It's safe and warm in here, I assure you."

The children in the other room started yelling at each other, causing a ruckus. The woman called after them. "Behave yourselves—I'll be right back." She moved a blanket in the crib to make room for Fitz. "Just set him here, and I'll get to him—"

"No!" Lottie said, stepping away. "I'm not going to just leave him in a hallway."

The woman's kindness was replaced with exhaustion, and she looked perturbed. "Perhaps you should talk to the headmistress."

"Perhaps I should."

"Go straight back. You'll find her in the kitchen."

The hallway that ran parallel to the stairway was covered with faded wallpaper that had portions peeled away as though the original wall wished to be released from the paper's current ugliness. But the floor looked clean, and unlike the tenement, there was no garbage lying about.

At the back of the house was a kitchen. A woman stood at a cast-iron stove, stirring in a large pot.

"Excuse me? Are you the—?"

The woman turned around.

Lottie gasped.

"Nanny?"

The stirring was forgotten. "Lottie? Is that my Lottie?"

The two women met in the middle of the room, their embrace encasing little Fitz. Lottie never wanted to let go. "Oh, Nanny, Nanny . . ." It was all she could say. These tears she gladly let flow.

Nanny stood back to get a look at her and pulled a handkerchief from her sleeve. She dabbed at Lottie's tears and then her own. "Praise God! Out of all the places in the world . . . what are you doing here in New York? Here at Merciful? Here, standing before me?"

It was indeed a miracle. Lottie hadn't seen Nanny since she was a young woman, too old for a nanny to oversee her care. Instead of getting a new charge, Nanny had left England for America. Lottie regretted losing touch with her.

In spite of her neglect, had God brought them together? The one woman in the world who could help her? "Oh, Nanny, everything has gone so wrong, so awfully wrong."

Nanny pulled out a chair for Lottie and sat in one herself. "Tell me all about it. Everything. First off, tell me the name of your baby."

"He's not my baby, not really, and his name is Fitzwilliam. But he isn't the beginning of my story. That begins back home."

Lottie heard the front door open, a male voice, then heavy footsteps coming back to the kitchen. A man with curly red hair and a handlebar mustache appeared in the doorway.

"Oh. Mr. Dooley."

"Ma'am."

She stood. "I'd like you to meet a dear girl from my past, Miss Charlotte Gleason. She's just come here from England and—"

"Actually, I don't go by that name anymore, I call myself . . ." She smiled. "Lottie Hathaway."

Nanny put a hand to her chest. "That's my last name."

"I know . . ." She glanced at Mr. Dooley. Was he Nanny's husband? Or business partner? "It's a long story, but I needed a name and I could think of none better than yours."

"Well then," Nanny said. "I'll take that as a compliment." She turned to Mr. Dooley. "You're wanting the rent, then?"

He was Nanny's landlord? Lottie wished she hadn't said so much.

The man looked at Lottie far too long. "Yes, ma'am. Me boss didn't like it being late last month and won't tolerate it agin."

"No need." She went to a shelf and reached into a jar. "A benefactor gave us enough. For this month at least." She handed him the money. "God bless you, and may Jesus keep you safe till the next time."

He rolled his eyes as if he didn't believe God blessed anything, nor knew the name of Jesus other than hearing people swear by it. He tipped his hat to the both of them, readying to leave, yet once again his eyes lingered on Lottie in a most uncomfortable fashion. "Miss Hathaway, and Miss . . . Hathaway."

Once he left, Nanny returned to her chair. "Here, let me have Mr. Fitzwilliam while you tell me your story. All of it, Lottie-girl. I won't be having less."

Lottie set her thoughts of Mr. Dooley aside and began. The story was long in the telling, but Lottie found great release in letting Nanny know it. As she spoke, she studied Nanny's face, longing for her approval, or if not that, her acceptance. She finished by saying, "I can't have anything I want here, Nanny. In fact, I seem to have nothing."

"But do you have what you need?"

Lottie was taken aback. "Hardly."

"Think again, Lottie-girl. You have a roof over your head, food in your stomach, clothes on your back, and a job."

"I need more than that."

"Do you? Whether you want to see it or not, God's provided exactly what you need."

A sarcastic laugh escaped. "After He took everything away—my money and all my jewelry."

"Did He do that?"

"He sent someone to steal them right out of my arms."

"What about you putting your money in the jewelry box, or getting coins out for apples, right there in public where anyone could see?"

Oh.

"It's time you take responsibility for your own actions, Lottie-girl. If I were you, I'd be thanking God for taking care of you in spite of your own stupidity."

"I wasn't—" Lottie stopped her disclaimer. She *had* been stupid and naïve. And actually, things could have been worse. What if Lea hadn't come along? Or Sven? "You're right," she said. "I see you're right."

Nanny nodded once with emphasis. "I often am."

But Lottie had another concern. "It wasn't wrong of me to do this, was it, Nanny? By letting Dora take my place, I gave her a new start and a chance to live a rich life."

"A rich life has little to do with material riches. I hope you know that."

She did. Deep down. "But wasn't it good that I gave up my chance at a good match—for her?"

"So your first thoughts were to better Dora's life, were they?"

The gentle firmness was the Nanny she remembered—the Nanny who wouldn't let her get away with anything. "Not my first thoughts . . ."

"Nor second or third, I'd be guessing. You wanted to get away from home, you wanted adventure, and you wanted to find a mate— your way."

"Ralph rejected me, and if I'd stayed in Wiltshire, there would've been far more of that because of my family's situation. Besides, there were no beaus there who suited me."

"With an attitude like that, I think it's you who didn't suit them."

Lottie's defenses rose and her face grew hot. "You don't know how it felt, Nanny. No one came to my party. They shunned me. All because of something Father did. That's not fair."

"Welcome to life, Lottie-girl." She rocked Fitz in her arms. "You think it's fair this wee one was left in the gutter?"

Nothing seemed fair anymore, and Lottie abandoned her argument. "It's hard to let him go."

"Yes indeedy, doing the right thing is often hard. If it were easy, everyone would do it." She offered Lottie a wink.

"I think I love him."

"I'm not a-doubting it. But sometimes love means sacrifice for the good of the other."

Speaking of . . . Lottie retrieved the baby supplies and the dollar coin and put it on the table. "For his care. I'll bring you more when I get it." Then she held out her arms, needing Fitz to fill them. Once there, he immediately molded himself to her and returned to peaceful sleep. "I'll visit him, but . . . may I keep him—someday?"

"Perhaps. Someday. Until then, know that I love all twenty-eight of the children we keep here as if they were my own. And they are my own. God gave them into my care, and I won't be letting any of them go until I'm assured they leave for a better place, into better arms than mine."

"There are no arms better than yours."

Nanny reached over and ran a finger along Fitz's chin. "I won't argue with you there. Since I never had any of my own, I take His charge seriously. This is what I was born to do, and by His grace I'll do it well."

Which rendered a question. "What am *I* born to do?"

Nanny sat back. "There's the adventure you seek. Search for your purpose and there you'll find happiness."

"How do I do that?"

"Ask the one who created you *for* a unique purpose, then open your eyes. He'll show you the way in the proper time."

Time. Lottie looked around for a clock. "What time is it?"

Nanny looked at a watch pinned upon her bodice. "Quarter to ten."

Lottie rose. "I have to meet Mr. Svensson. I have to work."

"As do we all, Lottie-girl. As do we all."

⚜

Lottie hurried in a daze to meet Sven. To have found Nanny, to have let Fitz go . . . If only she could put herself into Nanny's charge and be cared for and nurtured as she had been as a child.

"Miss Hathaway!"

She saw Sven standing across the street, waited for a horse and cart to pass, then crossed to meet him.

"I see Fitz is not with you."

"Leaving him was the hardest thing I've ever done."

His face softened. "I'm very sorry for it."

"But not as awful as it might have been. My old nanny runs the foundling home—can you believe it? It's a miracle."

"I've heard of many such miracles in this new world. At least you can rest knowing Fitz is well looked after."

A sudden thought came to her. "Could you and your wife take him in? To know he was being cared for by a loving couple, to have a father and a mother . . ."

Sven gave her an odd look, then said, "No."

"That quickly? Perhaps you should ask your wife?"

"No. Just no."

Lottie didn't have the stamina to argue with him, and she couldn't think about it any longer. Fitz was safe. For now. She'd think about tomorrow tomorrow. "Where to, then? I need my mind kept busy."

"Busy, I can do," Sven said. "Come with me."

※

Charlotte had a decision to make: get out of bed and act well—and she truly did feel well this morning—or pretend to still be indisposed so she had more reason to see Dr. Greenfield when he came to call.

She reluctantly chose the latter. Just one more morning. It's not as though she was shirking any work. She sent Mary downstairs with the message to the family, then set about to get dressed—with a bit more care than usual.

"Should I wear these earrings, or these?" she asked Mary upon her return.

"I like the pearl ones."

It was silly, really, this pleasant anticipation of the doctor's visit. She barely knew the man, and but for a handful of meetings, knew him nearly as little as she knew . . .

Conrad.

She looked at herself in the mirror. What was she doing? Dr. Greenfield wasn't a suitor coming to court her. Perhaps he could have been, but as she'd told him on the ship, she was nearly betrothed.

Nearly, but not quite.

Maybe she didn't feel well after all.

※

Mary rushed into the bedroom, breathless. "He's here!"

The maid's excitement was disconcerting. Was she simply intuitive, pulling her clues from Charlotte's fastidious toilette this morning? Or . . . had she been listening at the door yesterday? Did she know the full truth of Charlotte's identity?

Charlotte didn't have time to consider more, for within moments the butler showed Dr. Greenfield into the room.

Charlotte waited for his eyes to meet hers. There was such life there, such vibrancy, such passion for . . .

"Can I get you anything, Doctor?" Mary asked.

"No, I—"

Charlotte broke in. "We would like some tea, Mary."

She made a face. "Again?" She clearly did not want to leave.

"Yes, again. Please."

Mary left them alone. Charlotte wanted to pretend she and the doctor were still on the *Etruria*, waltzing across the floor, strolling the decks, standing at the railing together as the city loomed. "Please sit, Doctor. And thank you for coming. Have you any news?"

He sat upon a brocade chair near hers. "First, I must return something of yours." He removed a lace-edged handkerchief from his pocket.

Charlotte saw the monogram, *DC*. Her eyes sought his. He nodded slightly. It was the handkerchief she'd given him at dinner. On the ship. For his shoes.

"Thank you," she said, pulling it close. "But you needn't—"

"It isn't mine to keep. Under the circumstances."

Without warning Charlotte wanted to take his hands and tell him, *But it is yours! I'm yours! Leaving you on the ship, telling you I was nearly engaged . . . it was the hardest thing I've ever done. You're the one I want. You! Edmund.*

He got down to business. "After our talk yesterday I stopped at the Collegiate Church to speak with Pastor Weston."

The world moved on. She'd lost him. She'd had her chance with this wonderful man, and now it was too late.

He continued. "I was discreet, I didn't tell him your name, and I gave the impression it was my own inquiry."

"I appreciate that," Charlotte said.

"But . . . the girl Pastor Weston spoke about, the one he mentioned in his sermon, it *was* your Lottie Hathaway."

Her sadness about Dr. Greenfield was pushed aside by the news. "Did he know her whereabouts?"

"Partially. He remembered her telling him that an Italian family took her in when she lost all her money and—"

"She lost all her money?"

"Apparently it was stolen."

Charlotte thought back to Castle Garden. The last she'd seen of Lottie, she'd been holding her jewel box to her chest and—

And she'd just placed all her money inside!

"She has nothing? No means of any sort?"

"The pastor didn't know the details but for the fact that an Italian family had taken her in to their home."

"And their name?"

He looked at the floor, then up again. "It starts with an *S*. He thinks."

Charlotte let out a huff of air. "That's no help at all."

"He did remember they lived in Five Points. On Mulberry Street."

"Where is that?"

"I'm new here too, so I asked my cousin." He shook his head. "It's not good. Five Points is a notorious place, overcrowded with immigrants and rife with crime and misery."

"Lottie's not used to any of those things."

"Few are."

She realized her statement was foolish, yet in Lottie's case it was far too true. "Lottie led a sheltered life. She wanted for nothing, was protected from the harshness of the world, and . . . and liked it that way."

"She must not have liked it too much," he said. "She left it all behind to come here and start anew."

Charlotte walked herself through Lottie's plan. "She was supposed to go to my cousin's house. We'd sent a letter and then a telegram announcing . . ." She stopped herself. "What if Lottie went there and was turned away?"

"It would be no wonder she came here if she'd lost everything."

The image of Lottie standing on the sidewalk outside the Tremaines', drenched to the skin, made Charlotte shiver. "Then why didn't she come to the door?"

Dr. Greenfield let his gaze wander the room. "You said you've known each other for years."

"Yes."

"And your being here, in this house, was her idea."

It all became clear. "She wouldn't want to ruin it for me." Charlotte thought of another reason that held equal ground. "And she wouldn't want to admit defeat. She can be quite stubborn."

"A trait that should come in handy, considering her situation."

"But what *is* her situation? We know she's found shelter, and we assume by their hospitality the family is a good one. But how will she survive? She has no skills, no experience in the world. She must be very fright—"

Mary brought in the tea, and on the tray . . . "A letter came for you, miss."

A letter from Lottie?

But no. The handwriting was that of Mrs. Gleason, Lottie's mother. Surely the letter Charlotte had sent to them hadn't had time to cross the ocean, so . . .

She looked at the postmark. It was sent the day after they'd left on their voyage to America. Charlotte opened it and read.

Dearest Daughter,

I regret to inform you that your father has been injured in an accident. He fell from a horse and has broken his leg. It's a bad break, but the doctor assures us he will recover with time and care.

Charlotte gasped.

"Bad news?"

"Mr.—" She looked at Mary and reminded herself to watch her words. "My father fell from a horse. He broke his leg very badly."

"Broken bones are extremely painful, and recovery can be tedious and slow."

"I don't need to hear that, Doctor."

"Forgive me." He pointed at the letter. "When did this occur?"

She looked at the date again. "The day after we left England."

"You should return home immediately," the doctor said.

Lottie should return.

He paused and she watched him embrace the predicament before saying, "Did your mother give any more information?"

Charlotte returned to the letter.

> I implore you, dear, do not come home. There is nothing you can do here, and what would ease your father's mind the most is knowing you are cared for and your future is assured. Aunt Agatha and I are managing his care as best we can.
>
> Please pray for your father and for us all.
>
> With warmest regards,
> Mother

"She tells me to stay here, with the Tremaines."

"Well then," the doctor said—with a glance at Mary. "But your friend. You must tell your friend."

She must tell Lottie. But how?

Suddenly she knew what must be done. "Will you take me there, Doctor? To . . ." *If only Mary would leave, if only I could think of a reason for her to leave.* "To that street we spoke about."

"You don't want to go there."

"But I must. Surely someone would have seen . . . seen Miss Hathaway." She thought of a way to cover up the excursion. "Miss Hathaway was my nanny for years and years. She must be told. And besides, I need her comfort in this stressful time." Charlotte was proud of herself for thinking on her feet so quickly. She was only half lying, because there was a real Miss Hathaway, Lottie's nanny.

Dr. Greenfield fidgeted in the chair. "The Tremaines will never allow you to—"

"They will if you make the petition for me. And if you say you will accompany me. And if you're not specific about the destination."

When he stood, there was reluctance in his stance. "I'll see what I can do. For the good of my patient."

But she didn't want to be his *patient*.

Chapter Sixteen

Mrs. Tremaine was skeptical about Dr. Greenfield's plan to take Charlotte to see her old nanny, but with both men of the family at work and Beatrice visiting friends, the lady of the house gave in. Charlotte wondered if she did so to be relieved of the chore of entertaining Charlotte for an afternoon.

Once they reached the area near Five Points, the open hack drove slowly out of necessity. The swell of people on the streets forbade easy travel. The crush forced Charlotte to cling to Dr. Greenfield's arm—or so she would say if pressed. She loved being so close to him. If only they were riding through Central Park, where they could marvel at the beauty.

There was little beauty here.

"The number of people astounds me," he said.

Her fantasy fully evaporated. "It's as though Castle Garden in its entirety has moved here."

"This *is* the destination of most immigrants," the doctor said. "My cousin told me sixty thousand come every month. There are a million people in this small space."

A *million?* "We'll never find Lottie."

He did not contradict her.

The driver spoke to them over his shoulder. "You're the second group I've taken down here this month—slumming it, seeing how the other half lives."

Charlotte hated his term. "We are not 'slumming it'; we are search-ing for a dear friend."

He shrugged.

Charlotte noticed men in black coats, black beards, and flat hats. Along either side of their faces were long tendrils of hair.

"Who are those men?" she asked Dr. Greenfield.

"They are Jewish, I believe." He pointed to some signs on the shops. "That's Hebrew. Or is it Russian?"

Charlotte didn't know.

"This here's Jewtown," the driver said. "A strange lot they are, but I've heard they're great tailors. The I-ties are straight ahead. Yessiree, we've got yer Jews here, Greeks, Irishmen, Chinamen, black men, and even some red ones. Toss a pebble and you'll hit somebody who speaks babble. And here," he pointed ahead. "Here's Mulberry Street."

The carriage turned south off Bayard Street, and within a block the population changed from Jewish to Italian.

Both sides of the street were lined with vendors of every sort. "Does everyone have something to sell?" she asked.

"They'd sell your mother if you let them," the driver said.

"Enough, if you please," Dr. Greenfield said.

"Suit yerself. Where do you want me to stop?"

Charlotte found her head shaking back and forth. It was all too daunting. How would they ever find Lottie? Yet she had to try. Lottie had to know about her father. And for her own sake, Charlotte needed to know Lottie was all right.

Dr. Greenfield pointed to a relatively clear space in the street ahead. "Let us off there." He looked to Charlotte. "Yes?"

"It's as good a place as any."

The hack stopped and Dr. Greenfield asked the driver to wait. Then he helped Charlotte from the carriage. Within two steps she found herself stepping over a heap of spilled ash—and worse. An old woman was sweeping the sidewalk with a handmade broom, but surely her task was eternal with this many people living in such close proximity.

As they walked toward the pushcarts, Charlotte spotted an old man sitting on a chair beside a brick wall with a baby lying on a coat on the ground beside him. He was tending his pipe with more interest than he gave the fussy child. Why didn't he pick—?

Just steps away from the hack, Charlotte and Dr. Greenfield were surrounded by a passel of children, their faces dirty, their clothes torn.

"Per favore, signora. Soldi."

"Dammi soldi."

"Signore, per favore mi aiuti."

Some offered a bit of coal or a wilted flower, but most accosted them with open hands.

"I have nothing to give them." Charlotte realized how odd it was to live in a palatial mansion yet not have a penny to her name.

Dr. Greenfield reached into his pocket and offered a few coins, then shooed the rest of the children away. He put an arm around her waist and led her toward the nearest pushcart.

"Ma'am?" he said to the woman there. "We're looking for a friend of this lady."

The woman offered them an apple. Then a potato. *"Mela, signore? O una bella patata?"*

"No, no," he said, waving away her wares. "We're looking for a woman. My name is Dr. Greenfield and this is Miss Gleason and—"

The woman's eyes grew wide. *"Dottore? Andare. Vada al piano superior. Le persone sono malate!"*

She took hold of his hand and did not let it go, even as she spoke to a boy nearby. He came forward, eyed the doctor and Charlotte, then nodded to the woman.

"Come," he said. "Follow."

"No, no," Dr. Greenfield said. "We're looking for a woman, an Englishwoman and—"

The boy gestured to the building beside them. "Upstairs. Sick. Come."

Dr. Greenfield looked at Charlotte. "Apparently I'm needed." He hesitated. "I don't feel right leaving you here."

She didn't feel right about that either. At home, or even in London, she might have felt at ease in crowds on the street, but this was America, or rather, it was like being in Italy. Either way she was a stranger in a strange land. There was no alternative but to go with him. "I'm coming too."

The building was dark upon entering, and Charlotte was immediately assailed with a feeling of suffocation. Gone was the brisk autumn air and the sounds of the multitude on the street. Inside, the air was fallow, and though it still held a chill, there was no invigoration in it, only a sense of desolation, the difference between cold that refreshed and cold that caused discomfort.

They started up the stairs with Charlotte holding Dr. Greenfield's arm with one hand and her skirts with the other. The sounds of the building took her back to her childhood, when she'd lived with her family in a third-story flat in London. There had been no privacy there, not even when they'd been in their two-room apartment, for the walls had only blocked the view of the neighbors. All sounds had been communal.

Even the smells that assailed her were familiar. Sweat, ash, damp, and rotting food. But as they turned the first landing, the pile of garbage announced the difference. Although their flat had been meager, it had owned a level of sanitation lacking here.

Or maybe as a child she simply hadn't noticed.

Dr. Greenfield glanced at her, his face pulled with concern. "Are you all right?"

Clearly, as Charlotte Gleason, a young woman of society, she was supposed to be appalled by such a place. Perhaps she should scrunch up her face in disgust or squeal in squeamish horror.

But Dr. Greenfield knew her true identity, and she felt neither the energy nor the inclination to put on such a show. "I'm fine."

His eyebrows lifted in surprise, and Charlotte reveled in it. She'd surprised him—in a good way. His reaction spurred a decision to bravely endure whatever was to come.

She lost count as to the number of floors they ascended and was relieved when the boy veered down a hall and stopped at a door. He knocked loudly.

A woman answered and the two exchanged words. Charlotte heard a word that sounded like *doctor*, and the woman's face changed from overwrought to hopeful. She looked up, saw them, and immediately motioned them inside.

She tucked some stray hairs behind her ears. "Doctor, yes?"

"My name is Dr. Greenfield. This is Miss Gleason. Are you in need of my services?"

Charlotte could see in the woman's eyes that she didn't understand every word, but she nodded and motioned them into an adjoining room, where a little girl lay on a bed, her hair matted to her head.

The doctor took one look and turned to Charlotte. "She's feverish. You must go into the other room."

The little girl looked so sweet, so weak. "No," Charlotte said. "I can help. What do you need? What can I do?"

He looked impressed by her willingness, but she hadn't offered in order to impress but to help. She'd been around sick people before.

"Not this time, Charlotte. Not when I don't know what's causing the fever. Please."

She reluctantly retreated. The mother stayed with the doctor, leaving her alone.

"*Buon giorno.*"

She started, a hand to her chest. A woman was sitting near the window at a table. She blended into the chaos of the room, which had household items piled halfway up the wall.

"Good day," Charlotte said.

She noticed the woman was making flowers of some sort and moved closer to see them. They were made of paper and looked like violets. They were very well done.

"These are lovely," Charlotte said, nodding and smiling, hoping she would be understood.

"*Per un cappello,*" the woman said.

"I'm sorry, I . . ."

The woman put a flower on top of her head.

"Oh, cap, hat. They go on a hat."

"Hat. *Sì.*"

They both turned toward the bedroom when they heard the girl whimper.

"*Sofia è malata. Prego che il medico la possa curare.*" Then the woman touched her forehead, her chest, and both shoulders.

Charlotte didn't understand the words or the gesture, but she understood their intent. She hoped Dr. Greenfield could help the girl.

Once again memories assailed her. Another little girl, a baby girl just born. Charlotte's baby sister had only lived a few days.

A prayer escaped. *Please make the girl well.*

Dr. Greenfield came out of the room, his face dour. "More cold cloths," he told the mother, motioning with his hands. "On her head. Over her body. The fever needs to break." He looked to Charlotte. "I wish I'd brought my bag. I need my stethoscope and tools." He turned back to the mother. "What is the address here? I'll send a messenger over with some tonic, some medicine. Medicino?" He made a drinking motion.

The mother pointed to a bottle on a table.

"No, no, I don't need a drink. I want to get Sofia some medicine." He pointed toward the girl, then himself, then made a drinking motion.

The mother nodded. *"Sì. Medicina."*

"Yes! *Medicina.* Now . . . what is your address?" He pointed downward, to the floor. "Here." He shrugged his shoulders. "Where are we?" He made a motion for her to write it down.

Her eyes lit up. *"Indirizzo stradale."* She found a pencil and wrote on a scrap of paper.

"Grazie," he said with a sigh.

Charlotte shared his frustration, and yet . . . there was one more thing she had to ask this woman.

"Pardon me, ma'am, but we're looking for my friend, Lottie Hathaway. She's British like me, and . . ." Charlotte knew she was using far too many words but couldn't think of a way to shorten her question.

The woman stared at her. Oddly. And then she said, "No, no. No Lottie Hathaway. *Non è qui. Non è qui."* She pressed a loaf of bread into the doctor's hands.

"My payment? No, no. No charge." He gave it back.

The woman shrugged, then ushered them to the door. *"Grazie, dottore, buon giorno.* Good day."

But on the way out Charlotte spotted something on top of a pile of suitcases. It was a green hat with a bow on top and a feather on the back of the crown.

"That's Lottie's hat!" she said. "Why do you have Lottie's hat?"

The woman became more adamant about saying her good-byes. She physically pressed Charlotte toward the door. "Good day, good-bye."

"But I can't leave. You know where Lottie is! You have her hat!"

When the woman opened the door, Charlotte and Dr. Greenfield were accosted by a crowd. The people pressed toward the doctor, all talking at once.

"Dottore, mia madre . . ."

"Mio padre è malato."

"Mi fa male lo stomaco."

"Venga a vedere mio bambino."

Dr. Greenfield shook his head. "I'm sorry, I don't have my medical bag with me. I can't help you. I wish I could but . . ." He reached for Charlotte's hand. "We need to get out of here."

"But Lottie's hat? That woman knows where she is. I have to—"

"Charlotte, we have to leave. Now."

With his arm protectively around her shoulder, they quickly descended the stairs and went out to the street. Some of the residents from the building followed, still talking, still wanting his help.

Dr. Greenfield looked to the left. "There. The hack. He actually waited."

They hurried through the throng and got inside.

"You've gained a following, I see," the driver said.

"Get us out of here," Dr. Greenfield said. "Now, man. Take us back to the Tremaines'."

Charlotte looked over her shoulder. "But I can't leave. That hat *was* Lottie's. She was wearing it the day we arrived here. That woman knows her. I saw it in her face."

"And I saw something in the faces of all those desperate people. I'm not prepared to help them. Even if I had my bag, I'm not sure I could help or that I would ever find an end to the need. I wish I could, but . . ."

She felt him shiver and shared his frustration.

"Caring for the royal family did *not* prepare me for this. I want to help each and every one, yet how can I?"

He was noticeably shaken. Charlotte set aside her own needs and patted his arm. "You helped the little girl. You did as much as you could."

"I offered a crumb to a girl in need of a feast." He closed his eyes and pressed a gloved hand to his forehead. "How can people live like that? What hope is there of good health when they're packed like sardines in a can, with no fresh air, no sanitation, no hope?"

Charlotte was a bit surprised at his distress—and his naïveté. She too was upset, but her past had dulled her reaction to the conditions. She'd lived in such a place. She knew hunger and poverty and even death.

As they turned away from Mulberry Street, the doctor gained his composure. "I'm so sorry. To have taken you into a place like that and subjected you to—"

"I don't mind such a place, for remember who I am, Doctor. I'm a maid in lady's clothing. I came from simple surroundings not so different from these."

He blinked as if he'd forgotten her true identity. "You lived like that?"

"For a time. Until I went into service at the Gleasons' when I was thirteen. Working as a maid took me away from such conditions."

"But you were forced to work when you were only a child."

"There was no other option. My father was killed in an accident and my mother was in service herself. She couldn't care for me, so I had to care for myself."

"You poor child."

She shook her head vehemently. "Not a poor child. A blessed child. I was hired by the Gleasons—good people. I lived with them for the best years of my life, a servant for certain, but with my needs met. And when Lottie grew too old for a nanny, I was allowed to become her personal maid. We became the best of friends and . . ." The reason for their visit to Mulberry Street returned. "She needs to know her father is hurt. I need to go back there and insist that woman tell me where she is."

"You will do no such thing." He reached into his vest pocket. "And luckily there's no need. See here? I have their address. You can send her a note."

I can send her a note!

A burden was lifted. Although Charlotte still wanted to see Lottie and speak to her, a note was better than nothing.

It was a start.

"Finally," Mrs. Tremaine said. "Where have you been? Your party is tomorrow and there are still preparations to be made."

Charlotte removed her hat and handed it to the butler. "Forgive me. The good doctor was kind enough to take me . . . to help me find my nanny, to tell her the news about my father."

She looked at Dr. Greenfield for the first time. "So? Were you successful?"

"Partially," he said. "I—"

Charlotte broke in. "We didn't find her in person, but we did find someone who knows her. If you'll excuse me, I must write her a note. Dr. Greenfield has been gracious enough to see to its delivery."

"A note," Mrs. Tremaine said. "That's what you should have done in the first place instead of traipsing around this city." She shuddered. "Well then, on with it."

Charlotte bobbed a curtsy. "As you wish, ma'am."

Mrs. Tremaine flashed her a look, and only then did Charlotte realize she'd responded in word and deed like a maid to her mistress. She considered saying something different, but decided saying anything more might only draw attention to her mistake. She addressed the doctor. "If you'll wait right here . . ."

"As you wish," he said.

She hurried up the stairs to her room.

Sven had promised to keep Lottie busy, and he was true to his word. At the end of the day, when she returned to the Scarpellis', the other workers were already home and the family was finishing their meal.

"Lottie," Lea said. "You are not at Rossis'? Where is baby?"

She felt too drained to give details but knew an explanation was necessary. She sank upon a chair and told them. Lucia and Lea translated for those who could not understand.

Francesca put a kind hand upon her back. *"Mi dispiace, ma è per lo meglio."*

Her concern didn't need translation. These people were like family. A swell of appreciation came over her, and she suddenly remembered . . .

She reached into a pocket and removed the coins Sven had given her for her work the day before, and the twenty cents for her work today. She kept back her original dime and extended sixty cents to Dante, a week's rent and then some. "For the rent."

He took the coins and looked confused.

Lottie pointed to herself, then to the floor. "For my boarding, for the expense of living here. I'll get you more next week."

"Per l'affitto, padre," Lucia said.

With a look to Lottie, Dante closed his hand upon the coins and nodded to her. *"Grazie."*

Then Lea handed her a plate of pasta and gave her a hunk of bread. The white sauce had congealed. *Yes, yes, I suppose I have to eat. Is Fitz eating? Is he well? I hope the dollar I gave Nanny is enough to last a while.*

Lea spoke to her family, shooing them away. They looked curious but did as they were told. Then Lea pulled a chair close. The look on her face was serious.

"What?" Lottie asked. She glanced toward the bedroom. "Is Sofia worse?"

"No, no, Sofia . . ." Lea sighed heavily. "Doctor come. He send medicine."

"A doctor came here?" Lottie couldn't imagine any doctor having the courage to venture into the squalor and chaos of Five Points. If they helped one, a thousand would quickly form a queue.

"God sent him," Lea said. She looked heavenward as though offering a prayer of gratitude.

A doctor *was* a godsend, an answer to Lottie's prayers. Sofia couldn't die, not when Lottie loved . . . She started to rise. "Please let me see—"

Lea put a hand upon her arm, making her stay. "There was woman with doctor. She ask you."

She ask me? "She asked about me?"

"*Sì*. About you."

Lottie was confused. There was no one in the entire city who knew she was there except Nanny and . . .

"Was her name Charlotte Gleason?"

"Miss Gleason. *Sì*."

The food was forgotten, as was her fatigue. "Charlotte was here? She found me? Where is she? Where did she go?"

Lea let off a long string of words, her hands gesturing. Her face was apologetic, and the way she occasionally touched Lottie's arm or back seemed conciliatory. Was she apologizing for not telling Charlotte that Lottie was there?

Finally a few words of English came forth. "She went with doctor."

Charlotte was with the doctor? How did she know Sofia was sick?

It made no sense. Yet the details didn't matter. Charlotte had been there. "Did she seem happy?" When Lea looked confused, Lottie smiled and pointed at her own face. "Happy?"

Lea's brow furrowed. "She . . ." She searched for the word, then slipped her arm through Lottie's. "*Scivolò la mano sotto il braccio.*"

"She took his arm?"

Lea nodded. "*Dottore* Greenfield. Good friend."

Greenfield? Lottie gasped. "Doctor Greenfield? Edmund Greenfield? Dora met him on the ship! They danced. He wanted to see her while she was in New York, but she told him no, she was engaged—"

Lea looked confused.

Had Charlotte given up on the prospect of becoming engaged to Conrad Tremaine? Had she made her choice of beau, and that beau was Edmund Greenfield?

Then Conrad isn't spoken for . . .

Lottie shook her head against the shocking thought.

And yet . . . why not? If Charlotte was happy with Edmund, then what would keep Lottie from going to the Tremaines' and telling them who owned the true identity of Charlotte Gleason? They wouldn't want to hear it, but she would insist. It was a matter of life and death—Fitz's life. She'd do it for him.

Lea pulled an envelope from her pocket. "Friend send. For you." A note! Lottie broke open the seal and Lea left her alone.

Dearest Lottie,

I hope this note finds its way to you. I asked the woman in the flat about you, but she said she didn't know you. Yet upon leaving I saw your hat. Are you well? Please contact me at the Tremaines'.

I hesitate to tell you, but I must. . . . Your father fell from a horse and broke his leg. Your mother and aunt are caring for him. This happened just after we left. I've received no other word.

Please contact me. I miss you desperately.

All my love and prayers,
Dora

"My father?"

Lea was at the stove and glanced over her shoulder. *"Scusi?"*

"My . . . *padre.*" Lottie pressed a hand to her brow, finding it hard to comprehend. Her father had broken a leg? A familiar image appeared, of him riding wildly, his face flushed with the joy of it. He still rode as if he were a young man. And if not a wild ride for joy . . . she'd also seen him ride as a release from distress. There'd certainly been enough of that lately.

Lea interrupted her memory. "Is father hurt?"

Lottie pointed to her leg, then made a breaking motion. "Broken leg."

"Oh! You go! See."

If only . . . Her thoughts swam. "I can't go to him. He's in England. I can't afford to go back. But I must . . . I must write to my mother."

She looked around the flat and saw a small piece of paper. She held it up and mimicked writing upon it. "Can I have this?"

"*Sì, sì.*" Lea got her a pencil.

Lottie sat at the table and wrote to her family. But after voicing her sympathy and offering her prayers, she stopped short of telling them about all she'd done, where she was, the name she was living under . . .

Let them contact Dora with an answer. At the Tremaines'. Or perhaps very soon she herself would be at the Tremaines' in Dora's stead and there would be no need to ever tell her parents of their failed masquerade.

She used the envelope from Dora's note and wrote her parents' address on it. "Mail? Post?"

Lea pointed to another letter ready to be sent. It contained a penny stamp. Lottie fumbled for the dime in her pocket.

Lea shook her head, murmuring to herself, and got a stamp out of a cup. "Here."

Add it to her bill. "*Grazie.*"

Lea nodded. Then she pointed to Lottie's cold dinner. "Eat."

She had no appetite but consumed the food anyway. She'd need the energy. Tomorrow would be a long day. Tomorrow she would go to the Tremaines' and put an end to this fiasco.

Tomorrow she would claim her rightful place.

❦

As Charlotte and the Tremaines were leaving the dining room after dinner, Conrad touched her arm. "May I speak with you a moment, Miss Gleason?"

A sense of unease coursed up her spine. "Of course." The Tremaines had been especially quiet at dinner, and the air had been tight, as though the room were filled to the breaking point and one wrong word would make it pop. Mr. Tremaine had offered his sympathies for her father's injuries, but that being said had been all. Charlotte was quite certain

Mrs. Tremaine had let her husband—and Conrad—know about her outing with the doctor, and they probably had a rousing private discussion about what she was really up to. But when nothing was said in her presence, Charlotte was relieved.

Until Conrad touched her arm.

With few words he led her to an area of the house she'd never seen. "I thought it was time you saw the gallery." He opened double doors and with a sweep of his arm said, "Voilà!"

The room was twice the size of the drawing room, with ceilings and columns adorned with the now familiar filigree. But the walls of this room were covered edge to edge, ceiling to wainscot, with huge paintings. Charlotte walked toward the center of the room and turned in a circle. "I've never seen anything like this."

"No one has," Conrad said, strolling into the room, one arm behind his back. "This is Mother's project. She has the largest collection of art in the city. The Metropolitan Art Museum salivates at the mention of her name—which is the point, I believe."

Charlotte strolled through the room, her neck craned to see the looming landscapes, portraits, and paintings depicting ancient stories. In a corner behind a settee was an easel. A copy of a pastoral landscape was in progress. Is this what Conrad wanted to show her?

"Do you have hidden talents?" she asked.

He came around the furniture and looked at the painting. "I didn't know anyone used this space . . ." He studied the canvas. "It's quite good, actually."

Then she remembered . . . "This must belong to Beatrice."

He looked aghast. "Surely not."

"Why not?"

Conrad lowered his chin and eyed the painting a second time. "As I said, it's quite good."

"So are your sister's paintings. Surely you've seen some of her work?"

"I knew she dabbled with paints when she was a child, but—"

"It's far more than dabbling. You should ask to see what she's created."

He shook his head and walked away from the easel.

"You should also open this gallery to the public," Charlotte added.

Conrad laughed. "That *isn't* Mother's intent. The right people know of it, and that's enough for her."

It was such a waste. "You mentioned a museum. Wouldn't these paintings be better—?"

He turned to face her. "I didn't bring you in here for the art, Miss Gleason. I brought you to the gallery *because* no one comes here. I wanted to tell you some exciting news."

His face was aglow in a way she'd never seen, and her worries about being chastised for going out in the city alone with the doctor evaporated. "It's obviously good news."

He nodded. "Remember when I took you to the store and showed you the displays in the windows?"

"Of course." How could she forget the lackluster displays.

"I saw them with new eyes that day, and your advice . . ." He took a new breath. "I took your advice and I've had them changed. I'd like to show them to you tomorrow."

"I—"

He put up a hand, stopping her words. "I know tomorrow night is your party, and Mother can keep you busy all day preparing for it, but all I need is an hour or two. Will you come with me and see them?"

She was moved by his need. "I'd love to see the windows."

His pleasure was evident. He was a man without artifice, and with little effort Charlotte could imagine such an expression on a baker or milliner who wanted to show off his handiwork. Conrad seemed so separate from his family, who—with the exception of Beatrice's sarcastic ways—seemed intent on never letting down their guard to show true emotion. He was a good man. She was blessed to know him.

She would be blessed to marry him.

Edmund.

"Charlotte?" He was offering her his arm.

She took it. The second arm she'd taken that day.

The second good man.

*

When it was time to retire, Charlotte passed the closed door of Beatrice's bedroom.

On impulse she backtracked and knocked.

She heard rustling inside. Then Beatrice opened the door a crack—which seemed odd. She wasn't in her nightgown yet, for Charlotte spotted the green of the dress she'd worn to dinner.

"Is something wrong?" Beatrice asked.

"Not at all, I was just . . . I saw your easel in the gallery, and I wanted to tell you that I think you're very talented."

Beatrice stared at her for a brief moment, then dodged her head into the hall, looking both ways. "Come in," she whispered.

Why all the secrecy? Charlotte entered and Beatrice quickly closed the door behind her.

Charlotte expected to find a bedroom similar to her own, if not more grand. She did not expect to find a room lined with paintings. They were leaned against the walls and sat upon countless chairs. Most were reminiscent of the colorful painting Beatrice had tried to show her mother and her friends at tea, but Charlotte recognized others as copies of paintings with the more realistic style of those in the gallery.

"These are magnificent, Beatrice," she said. "I'm no expert, but even I can see true talent here." She began to pick up a smaller one, then pulled her hands away. "May I?"

"As you wish."

The painting was of Central Park, but unlike the paintings in the gallery that could be photographs, the lines were less distinct and the colors applied in layers, giving the figures texture as well as shape. "The Mall, yes?"

Beatrice smiled, and with her smile, Charlotte realized how few times she'd witnessed that expression. "I would love to take an easel there and paint on site as I've seen some do, but Mother would have a fit. You heard her at tea. She and her friends cannot fathom the idea of a woman artist. And so . . ." She swept her arms to encompass the room. "I created my own gallery."

Charlotte set the painting down and moved to another. "But surely your mother has seen—"

"She doesn't come to my room, and I don't invite her."

How sad. Yet Charlotte couldn't remember Mrs. Gleason ever visiting Lottie's room either. Parents and children met in the public areas of the house like acquaintances attending to their duty.

"You should ask to have your work displayed in your mother's gallery," Charlotte said.

Beatrice laughed. "But don't you see? I don't qualify, for I'm neither male nor deceased."

It was unfathomable. To have such a talent and be unable to share it. "It's like . . ." Charlotte hesitated, then said it anyway. "God tells us not to put our light under a basket. We're told to let it shine for all the world to see."

"Ah, but only if one's light fits within the limits of society. Or one is male."

Beatrice's pain was Charlotte's own. "I'm so sorry, Beatrice. Surely there's some way you can show your work."

She raised her chin as though assuming a familiar mental stance. "I don't need others to give my work worth. I paint for myself, an audience of one."

"Two," Charlotte said. When Beatrice raised an eyebrow, Charlotte pointed heavenward. "The Giver of the gift sees and appreciates."

Beatrice looked at a painting as if studying it, but Charlotte could see her thoughts were elsewhere.

"I should be going," Charlotte said.

Beatrice nodded and moved toward the door with her. Then she said, "I'm sorry to hear about your father. Are you close?"

Charlotte's thoughts bypassed Mr. Gleason and moved to her own father. She'd never known him as an adult. "When I was small we were."

Beatrice put her hand on the doorknob. "I used to be Daddy's little princess."

"Maybe you still are?"

Beatrice shook her head. "My father doesn't even see me anymore. I'm a disappointment."

"Don't say that."

"Why not? It's the truth." She opened the door. "Sleep well, Charlotte. Come back anytime."

"Thank you, I will."

If not for herself, for Beatrice.

Chapter Seventeen

I might not be back.

It was an awkward morning at the Scarpellis'. Unbeknownst to them, today Lottie was going to the Tremaines'. If all went well . . .

Eating a piece of bread, she looked around their apartment. It was hard to imagine that this had ever been home to her. She remembered her first night, crammed into the bedroom, lying on the floor, afraid of the dark.

Although conditions hadn't changed, she'd changed. What had seemed appalling was now appreciated. That these strangers had cared for her, had saved her . . .

She looked at Sofia, sitting on Lea's lap, weak but on the mend. Their eyes met, and Lottie made a funny face to make her smile. Then she watched as Dante and Aldo talked about the upcoming day over their coffee. Francesca scolded Vittorio for something as she started to get out the supplies to make paper flowers. Lucia made lunches for all of them. Everyone had a purpose, a place.

Except Lottie. She helped as much as she could, but unlike the others who were bound by blood and history, she stood alone.

What will be different at the Tremaines'?

They were her people.

Or were they? She had never witnessed New York society. Would she feel at home there? Or would they gather in their own little groups, once more leaving her set apart?

Movement in the room increased, indicating it was time for all to go to work. Lottie lingered, pretending to have an issue with her shoe. She wanted to be the last one out; she wanted to have a moment with Sofia and Lea.

Lucia paused at the door, waiting for her.

"*Solo un minuto,*" Lottie said. "*Ciao.* See you later."

Lucia nodded and left the apartment without her. Lottie despaired at seeing her go. How she wished she could have told Lucia her plans and offered a full good-bye. But to do so would be to admit her deception. Lottie didn't want Lucia to think badly of her. After everything was settled—if it was settled—Lottie would come back and explain.

She finished tying her shoe with true difficulty. She was wearing her corset today, and the suit she'd worn the first day Lea had seen her at Castle Garden. She needed to look her best for the Tremaines but feared her suit would raise questions with Lea.

"Well, I'm going," she said, dropping her skirt over her shoes.

Francesca gave her a glance, and Lea said, "You pretty."

"Thank you. I thought it was time I wear my own clothes." She didn't know how much Lea understood. She didn't want to share her plans, or that she might not be back, because the truth was, she *might* be back this very evening. Her stomach tightened at the uncertainty of her day. Yet this had to work. It was the only way for her to move forward and create a life with her baby.

When Lottie stood, Sofia slipped out of her mother's arms and ran to her. Lottie scooped her up, and as usual, Sofia wrapped her legs around her hips. But instead of looking at each other eye to eye, sharing smiles and words, Sofia wrapped her arms around Lottie, leaning her head upon her shoulder.

It's as if she knows.

Lottie battled tears. They were unacceptable until she was alone. She put a hand on the back of Sofia's head and whispered in her ear, "I love you, little girl. You were a light in this very dark place. God bless you and keep you safe and well."

She kissed her forehead and let her go. Lea looked at her quizzically. Lottie longed to fully express her gratitude, but now wasn't the time. When she was established at the Tremaines', she'd find a way. Perhaps she could convince Conrad to find the Scarpellis a proper home—at his expense. Then she could see them anytime she wished. After all, they were her family.

As Lottie opened the door, Sofia brought Lottie her hat. Lottie held it a moment and was tempted to take it, for it would make her look like a lady. But as she moved the hat toward her head, her hands detoured and put it on Sofia's head instead of her own.

"This is yours, sweet girl. Forever and always. To remember me by." Then she left.

Tears accompanied her down the stairs to the street.

"I can't work today," Lottie declared to Sven.

He paused and adjusted the equipment on his shoulder. "Is something wrong?"

She hesitated to say anything. "I have something I must attend to."

"Is Fitz all right?" He looked genuinely concerned.

"Fitz is fine. It has to do with . . . well . . . with the Tremaines."

His eyebrow lifted and he cleared his throat. "Your work ethic is sorely lacking, Miss Hathaway."

She hated to hear the disappointment in his voice. "I can work as well as the best of them."

"But you choose not to." He reached out and grabbed the arm of a young boy walking past. "Need a job, boy?"

The boy nodded.

"Good, then come with me and—"

Lottie ran in front of Sven, blocking his path. "You discard me so quickly?"

He cocked his head. "Who discarded who here?"

"I didn't quit. I only said I can't work today." And yet that was a lie. If events occurred at the Tremaines' as she hoped they would occur . . .

Sven reached into his pocket and handed the boy a coin. "Sorry, son. No work today." He turned his attention to Lottie. "So. Will you explain exactly what's keeping me from your companionship today?"

She smiled. "Companionship?" So he *had* succumbed to her charms, just a little?

He reddened. "Association. Presence here. With me. As I work."

"How is your wife today, Mr. Svensson?"

His brow furrowed. "*Uff da*, woman."

She gave him a smile, enjoying that she'd rattled him, even as she felt wistful at leaving him.

Sven shook his head and sighed. "Go on with you, then. I'll do fine without you. But be back here tomorrow or I'll hire another."

"As you say. Good-bye, Sven."

But as Lottie strode away from him, she faltered. She might not be there tomorrow. Or the next day. Or ever again.

She looked over her shoulder at him, needing one last glance.

He was looking after her. Their eyes met.

He raised a hand to wave. Then he said, "Come back again, Lottie. I need you."

She turned away and walked faster.

She missed him already.

One more thing to do before Lottie went to the Tremaines'.

As soon as Nanny placed Fitz in Lottie's arms, his body melted to hers. She cupped his face with a hand. *How can I leave you behind?*

"Ah, there," Nanny said, tracing a curlicue in the air between them. "Just as I thought. What's going on in that head of yours?"

"You always could read me."

"Someone had to." She handed Lottie a cloth and pointed to the drool on the baby's chin. "Out with it."

Lottie had not planned on telling Nanny her plan.

Or had she?

Had she come to see Fitz and Nanny knowing Nanny would see the conflict teeming inside her?

There was no need for a definitive answer. She gave Fitz her finger to gnaw upon and began. "I discovered that Dora isn't interested in Conrad Tremaine, but in another man we met on the ship."

"That's her prerogative," Nanny said. "Just because she took your place doesn't mean love for Conrad would follow. Unless you wish for her to marry without love?"

"No, of course . . ." Or was that exactly what she'd hoped would happen? With Dora and Conrad married, the deception would be complete. Nonreversible. Was their marriage a guarantee against Lottie changing her mind?

"You're not talking, Lottie. And my ears are waiting."

She avoided Nanny's eyes and gazed at Fitz, who didn't care what her name was as long as she held him. "Things haven't worked out as I hoped they would."

Nanny harrumphed. "If you want to make God laugh, tell Him your plans."

"But things usually work out for me, Nanny. I've never had things go wrong—so terribly wrong."

" 'He that trusteth in his own heart is a fool: but whoso walketh wisely, he shall be delivered.' "

Was Nanny calling Lottie a fool? Was the title deserved?

She made her defense. "Since there might be a chance to marry Conrad myself, I have to try."

When Nanny lowered her chin and raised an eyebrow, Lottie knew she was in for a scolding. "You think Conrad Tremaine will marry you just because you walk through the door and smile at him?"

"It will take more than a smile. I know that."

"Do you?"

Lottie held Fitz under his arms so he could sit upon her lap. "You act as though I'm shallow, as though I have no feeling—"

"You're planning to march in and marry a man you've never met—a man you deceived—as though a husband were a bonnet on a rack to be perused and purchased."

It did sound cold. Calculating. Fitz squirmed and Lottie settled him upon her shoulder in the way Sven had shown her. The baby's need made her think of a way to justify her plan. "I'm not thinking of myself. If I married Conrad, we could adopt Fitz. Fitzwilliam Tremaine. That's a name steeped in power and authority, don't you think?"

" 'Remove far from me vanity and lies: give me neither poverty nor riches.' "

"I'm not vain! I'm trying to do the right thing."

Nanny crossed her arms in front of her ample chest and glared at her. Lottie felt six again, uncertain and scared. "Do you actually believe the Tremaines will take you in after your deception, *and* accept your abandoned foundling as their own?"

Until now, Lottie had not allowed logic to enter into her plan. She didn't like hearing it now. She needed things to work out in spite of her own actions. "I . . . I'm just tired of being alone, Nanny. I came to America hoping to find adventure and maybe romance, and all I've found is crisis and pain. I just want—"

Nanny sat forward, pointing a finger at her. "What I'm about to tell you may sound odd, especially considering my admonition, but here I'll say it: you've always thought too little of yourself, Lottie-girl. I tried to make you recognize your potential, but obviously I failed. We all want love. I too wanted the love of a man in my time. But that can't be the end-all of your journey. You don't need a man for your very being. You're a grown woman now, a strong, intelligent, vibrant woman. Let love find you and it will be a strong love. But first be strong in yourself, in your faith, and in your God."

Lottie felt the sting of tears. "But I'm not strong or smart. Someone's always been there to tell me what to do. I came to think it was a bad thing, a prison of sorts, but now, left on my own . . ." She sighed. "I'd love for someone to tell me exactly what to do and take care of me again. I'm tired of trying to do it myself."

"Then stop trying."

"What?"

"Stop trying to do it yourself. None of us are meant to go the way alone. God got you this far; He'll get you the rest of the way."

When was the last time she'd prayed? There'd been a few prayers scattered through the days, but when things continued to worsen and get more complicated, she'd taken hold of the reins of her life without looking to the right or the left. Or within. To Him. And yet . . . and yet . . .

Nanny was watching her and, with a shake of her head, moved her chair forward and put a hand on Lottie's knee. "Father, guide this child toward your will. Keep her safe and help her do the right thing. Amen."

That was all very nice, but . . . "What's the right thing?"

Nanny sighed with exasperation. "Patience is a virtue, Lottie. Be on the lookout. He'll be showing it to you."

"Promise?"

She crossed her heart. "Promise."

Lottie gazed at Fitz a long moment. So . . . what *should* she do? She closed her eyes, hoping God would place an image in her thoughts, some direction she could follow.

She found nothing but confusion.

"I have to go now," she said, getting up.

"That quickly? You know where you're supposed to go?"

"No. But until I do, I'm going to the Tremaines'."

"Lottie, that's not the way it works. You shouldn't rush ahead like a dog pulling on a leash. Remember who's the Master. Walk beside Him and let Him do the leading."

Lottie shook her head. "I can't wait. Time is against me. I have to get to the Tremaines' and make my claim before something else goes wrong. I have to try."

"Try and die . . ."

"What do you mean by that?" she asked.

"Those who barrel ahead run into the fire."

"I can't just stand here."

"You could. Until *He* moves you on."

She could, if only it were in her nature. Which it wasn't.

Lottie kissed Fitz and placed him in Nanny's arms. "I'll see you soon."

"Is that a promise?"

Was it?

It had to be.

Lottie crossed her heart. "I promise."

With her one and only dime, Lottie hired a hack to take her to the Tremaines' home. It was too far to walk, especially in her corset and suit. She needed to arrive in a presentable fashion.

But as she rehearsed what she would say to them, the hack stopped. "This is it."

She looked out the window. "No it's not." She spotted a street sign. "This is Twentieth. I need Thirty-fourth."

"Then I need more money."

"I told you where I was going before we left. You agreed."

He shrugged. "I agreed to take you there. And I will. It's your choice. Here, or there. For more money."

She smiled at him, tipping her head just so. "Please, sir? I don't wish to arrive disheveled, and the wind today is brisk and—"

He held out his hand for more coins.

This was ridiculous. As she got out, her skirt caught on the door handle, and she heard a ripping sound as her feet met the ground.

"You tore my skirt!"

"*You* tore your skirt. Have a good day." He drove on without her.

Lottie yelled after him, "Your ploy for more money didn't work, did it, mister?"

But as he drove out of earshot, and as Lottie found people looking at her, she realized the driver's ploy had worked fine. For he'd let her off on a street full of fancy stores. He would have no trouble getting another fare.

She, on the other hand . . .

She examined the tear in her skirt. An entire panel of vertical pleats had pulled away from her waist and was drooping forlornly. She tried tucking it in, but it refused to stay in place. The damage was impossible to conceal. The entire world would see.

A couple strolled by, staring at her. She fiddled with the sagging panel, offering an explanation. "I'll never hire a hack from that company again."

The man nodded and the couple walked on.

As did Lottie. What choice did she have?

But as she looked around, her attention was drawn to the shops. Hats, flowers, gloves, dresses, jewelry, parasols . . . *Oooh, isn't that brown hat divine?*

Then she realized that the shop windows she'd been looking at actually belonged to one store. It was a huge department store taking up the entire block. Looking up, she saw that it was Tremaine's Dry Goods.

Her heart flipped. Tremaine's! This was their store. This would be *her* store when she married Conrad.

She had to go inside.

The foyer opened to multiple stories with a sweeping staircase luring shoppers deeper into the store.

I'm home.

Lottie belonged in a store such as this. In London she'd shopped at Harrods with her mother and Aunt Agatha. The clerks had catered to their every need and desire.

A clerk approached from the department to her immediate left. "Good morning, miss. Can I interest you in a bonnet?"

Lottie put a hand to her head. She was bareheaded. No woman of standing went into public without a hat.

"Yes, I believe you can," she said. After the hack ride she had no money, but the millinery department wasn't terribly busy. She wanted— no, she needed—to try on a few bonnets, just to remember what it was like. It would be a reawakening, a transition from the working girl Lottie Hathaway to the socialite Charlotte Gleason.

The woman showed her a display of a dozen bonnets, and Lottie felt her heart beat faster. "They are all so beautiful," she said.

"Indeed." The clerk put a finger to her lips, assessing Lottie's attire. "There is a certain bonnet in the window that would be perfect. . . . Just a moment and I'll get it." She moved to a display that stood in front of the large street windows and returned with a hat. "The violets on the crown would accentuate the green cast of your suit."

She was right. It was a wonderful bonnet. And the violets looked exactly like the ones Francesca and Lea made every day. But Lottie took it off, needing more. "May I try on that one, please? And perhaps that one?"

The clerk was solicitous, and Lottie experienced a surge of joy. She felt like herself again.

Until . . .

"May I box these up for you, miss? And we have a team of seamstresses on duty who could mend that nasty tear in your skirt."

The hats had made Lottie forget the tear. As for the bonnets? "I . . ."

"I would be happy to put them on your family's . . . perhaps your husband's account?"

With intense regret, Lottie removed the bonnet and handed it to the clerk. "Not today."

The clerk gave her a knowing look, and there was a hint of annoyance in her eyes. "As you wish."

The old Lottie would have charged them to her father's account— all of them. The new Lottie . . .

First things first. First she had to get to the Tremaines'.

She took one last lingering look at the store, exited to the street, and turned north. With difficulty she kept her eyes averted from the temptations of the stores.

※

"Let us off here."

The Tremaine carriage stopped at the far corner of the store, and Conrad helped Charlotte to the sidewalk. "I want you to see the windows as the shopper does, at eye level."

His excitement was catching. And fetching. Charlotte had never known a man who truly enjoyed his profession. Mr. Gleason hadn't, the servants she'd worked with in the Gleason home hadn't, and certainly neither had her Barney.

Her Barney?

Just Barney now.

Conrad placed himself on the street side, and Charlotte took his arm for their stroll. As they approached the first window he patted her hand. "And here . . . here it begins."

The window—which had previously contained a single item on a pedestal—now offered a grouping of hats on different levels, showcased in different ways. Some were on mannequin heads; one was on a chair along with a scarf and gloves as if cast off after an outing. While they were looking at the display, a clerk appeared and propped a lavender bonnet with violets against a pair of lavender evening shoes, with a fan half opened nearby.

The clerk looked out the window at Conrad and Charlotte, recognized Mr. Tremaine, and smiled. Conrad pointed at the bonnet and indicated she should tilt it a bit to the left. Which she did.

"The items in this window seem so genuine," Charlotte said. "As if they're items to be used—bought and used. They aren't stagnant as they were before. They make me want to go inside and try them on."

"Exactly!" Conrad led her toward the next window. "I'm especially proud of this one."

There were four mannequins in the window: a woman, a man, a little boy, and a young girl. They were dressed for a Sunday walk in the park. The girl carried a doll.

"I can imagine them in Central Park," Charlotte said. "They're even facing the right direction."

"I'm so glad you noticed. The clerk who was helping me thought such a detail was silly."

"Not at all. Those shoppers who notice will feel like they've discovered a secret."

The glow on his face made Charlotte wish she could find a hundred nice things to say.

They moved to the third window. "I tried to create a still-life scene as in one of the paintings in Mother's gallery."

The composition was excellent: a table draped with a fringe-edged cloth of damask, set with china, crystal, a fruit compote, and candelabrum. An urn painted with a pastoral scene stood on a pedestal nearby.

It was beautiful, but something seemed to be miss—

Charlotte gasped.

"What is it?"

"I know what will make all the windows complete."

"They aren't complete?"

She squeezed his arm. "Yes, but I know how to make them extraordinary."

"Then tell me."

She looked down the street. Where was their carriage? "We have to get home first."

"Home? But I don't understand."

"You will."

※

The front door of the Tremaine residence opened before Conrad could do it himself. A man with curly red hair and a long mustache was exiting. He paused on the stoop a moment and tipped his hat. "Mr. Tremaine."

"Mr. Dooley."

The way he eyed Charlotte made her take a step back, using Conrad as a shield.

"I brought the rent for yer father."

"Thank you."

"The place is jumping," the man said. "Your mother said there's a party here tonight?"

Conrad gently pulled Charlotte forward. "Yes indeed. A welcome party for Miss Gleason, a friend from England."

"So your mother said." His eyes seemed to hint at a knowledge that made Charlotte even more uncomfortable. He tipped his hat to her. "Miss Gleason." The way he stroked her name . . .

"Good day, Mr. Dooley," Conrad said as he led Charlotte inside.

Once Childs had closed the door, Charlotte asked, "Who was that man?"

"Father has rental properties in the southeast portion of the city, and Mr. Dooley collects the rent."

Southeast? Five Points and the apartment where Lottie was staying was in that part of the city. Charlotte couldn't imagine the Tremaines being the landlord to any of the awful tenements she'd experienced with Edmund.

She didn't want to ruin the moment, and yet . . . "I've heard that part of the city is filled with the most terrible tenements. Surely you don't own—"

"I don't have anything to do with the rentals," Conrad said. "I have enough on my plate with the store."

That Conrad wasn't involved offered her a little relief. Hopefully his father's properties were of better quality than the buildings she'd seen.

When they entered the foyer, Mrs. Tremaine came out of her morning room. "Where have you two been? There are preparations for the party to attend to. You can't go gallivanting around—"

"Where's Beatrice?" Conrad asked.

"I'm not sure. I suppose she's in her—"

Conrad took the stairs two at a time. Charlotte rushed after him, excitement propelling her upward.

Mrs. Tremaine called after them, "What's going on? Conrad?"

When Conrad ignored her, Charlotte stopped her climb and looked over the railing. "We'll be down in a few minutes, Mrs. Tremaine. I promise." She hated leaving her in ignorance, but this was Conrad's moment.

By the time Charlotte reached the second floor, Conrad was already knocking on the door to Beatrice's bedroom. "Bea? Come to the door. It's important."

The door opened. "What's all the racket? Is something wrong?"

Charlotte reached the door, a hand upon her corset, out of breath. "Not at all," she said. "Listen to your brother. Show him your room."

Beatrice hesitated, her eyes flitting from Conrad to Charlotte and back again. "Come in, then," she said.

They entered and Conrad's gaze devoured the bedroom. "Bea . . . these paintings . . . they're beautiful." He turned full circle, then looked at her. "You painted all these?"

"Of course I did."

"When?"

"While you and Father are at work and Mother is busy climbing the social ladder, I have to do something with my time."

"A good use, I'd say." He seemed to remember why they were there and looked toward Charlotte. "I see what you mean, and I believe you're right."

"What are you talking about?" Beatrice asked.

Conrad gestured to Charlotte to do the honors. But she shook her head. It would mean more to Beatrice coming from him.

"Miss Gleason and I were just at the store, where I've taken her advice in regard to the window displays. And though the displays are much improved, she still thought something was missing, and—"

"Not missing," Charlotte said. "But I realized the displays could be further enhanced if they had some—"

Beatrice waved her words away. "One of you get to the point."

Conrad pressed a hand against his chest, finding a fresh breath. "I—we—would like to display your paintings in the windows of the store."

Beatrice blinked once, then shook her head. "I don't think so. I don't want people gawking at my paintings."

"They would gawk in awe, sister." He walked to a landscape sitting on the floor beside the fireplace. "This was inspired by Central Park, yes?"

"Anyone can see it's the Mall."

Charlotte knew what Conrad was thinking. "It would look perfect in the window with the family taking a Sunday outing," she said.

"That's what I was thinking." Conrad scanned the room. "We could put this one, and perhaps that one, and that . . . on easels behind the family, creating a backdrop to their stroll."

Charlotte's mind raced. "Or instead of easels, perhaps the paintings could be hung from the ceiling on wires. The wires would be nearly invisible, so it would look like the paintings were floating and—"

"Stop!"

They looked at Beatrice. "Who says I wish to have my paintings on display to the world? I'm quite content having them here, for my own enjoyment."

"But that's not right," Charlotte said.

The subsequent silence indicated she'd spoken too harshly. She tried again. "You have great talent. But as I told you before, God gave it to you—to share. It's not to be locked in a room."

"What if Michelangelo had only painted the ceiling of his bedroom," Conrad said, "or Botticelli's Venus was displayed in a bath?"

"I have seen neither, brother. Only you were afforded the grand tour of Europe."

Conrad blushed but wasn't deterred. "My point is that art is meant to be seen."

"I am not Michelangelo or Botticelli, or even Monet."

"Who?"

Beatrice shook her head. "My point stands. I'm not . . . them."

"No, you're not," Conrad said. "But that doesn't mean your paintings aren't worth seeing." He picked a still life off a chair and held it toward Charlotte. "The china window?"

"Perfect."

Beatrice snatched the painting out of his hands. "As I stated, I don't wish for my work to be gawked at and judged and—"

"I judge it to be very excellent, my dear."

They all turned toward the doorway. Mrs. Tremaine entered the room, her reaction similar to her son's. "I knew you painted, daughter, but I had no idea it was to this extent, nor that you had grown so accomplished."

Beatrice's face . . . Charlotte had never seen such an expression. Gone were the tightness and the sarcastic wall. Beatrice was a child again, longing for her mother's approval. "Do you . . . I mean, can you see some good in them?" she asked quietly.

"Much good." Mrs. Tremaine strode to her daughter, cupped her head with a hand, and kissed her forehead. Then she removed the still life from her grasp. "The way you've captured the light and shadow is masterful." She looked at her son. "You wish to use this in a window display at the store?"

As mother and son discussed the idea, Charlotte moved closer to Beatrice. "I hope you don't mind that I told Conrad about your work."

Charlotte received a quick shake of the head. The space between Beatrice's eyes dipped, and Charlotte could tell she was fighting emotion.

Finally, Charlotte heard a soft whisper. "Thank you."

Charlotte whispered back, "You're welcome."

At least it wasn't raining.

Standing in front of the Tremaines' mansion, Lottie remembered the last time she'd been there—soaked to the skin, looking like a drowned puppy.

Although she was exhausted from the walk, today she could approach the front door with some semblance of confidence. She was wearing the same traveling suit—still sans a proper bonnet—but with a few last-minute corrections to tidy her hair, she was ready.

Please, God, let this be over.

She straightened her back, took a fresh breath, and ascended the stairs leading to the front door. Her hand trembled as she reached for the bell.

A butler answered—the same man who had shooed her away the last time. Would he recognize her?

He looked her over, head to toe, in one quick moment. "The servants' entrance is around back."

She reached down to the torn skirt. "I'm not a servant, sir. I simply tore my skirt when my hack driver—"

He closed the door on her.

Hack driver. The Tremaine set didn't hire hacks. They hired carriages. Or owned their own.

Lottie wanted to yell at the door: *I'm the real Charlotte Gleason! Let me in!* but she predicted such aggression would be seen as hysteria or insanity, negating her ever getting inside.

"The servants' entrance is around back."

She looked in the direction the butler pointed. The back entrance wasn't her entry of choice, but at least it would get her in the house.

She retreated to the sidewalk and walked around the side of the house, finding a narrow walkway leading to the back. There were no stairs to climb here, but rather a few stairs down to an entrance below ground level.

Lottie looked at the hanging trim of her dress and got an idea. With a few yanks, she pulled the length off the skirt. Then she knocked.

A very young girl wearing a mobcap came to the door. "May I help you?"

"I was wondering if I could borrow a needle and thread to mend my—"

"Are you here to help with the party?"

"What party?"

"The party to welcome Miss Gleason."

"Miss . . . ?"

The girl gripped the doorframe to lean closer in confidence. Her hands were red and chapped. "She's goin' to be the wife of Mr. Conrad. But none of the Four Hundred knows her, so tonight they's introducing her and . . . You want a job? They can use the help."

Wife?

The girl glanced behind her, as if nervous someone would snap at her for lingering at the door. Then she looked back at Lottie. "Well, do ya want the job?"

"I do."

Lottie had never—ever—worked so hard.

The Tremaines' cook, Mrs. Dyson, had accepted her presence with nary a glance. Help was help—at least in the kitchen. Lottie was told to go in a storeroom and find something to wear. She'd heard Mrs. Dyson add under her breath, "Who does she think she is? Coming for a job wearing a fancy suit."

A suit too fancy for downstairs and not fancy enough for above-stairs.

After she'd changed into a faded skirt and blouse that still smelled of the previous wearer, Lottie was told to peel potatoes.

There were two baskets stacked high. "All of them?" slipped out.

"No. Just one or two." Mrs. Dyson pointed to a knife. "Don't you start complainin' befores you even get started."

Lottie made a few slices of the potato skin, but it was awkward. The girl who'd met her at the door came to her rescue. "Like this," the girl whispered. She held the potato in the palm of her hand and ably ran the knife down its side. "Don't push too hard or you'll waste the potato and have to peel more."

"Thank you," Lottie said.

"And don't cut yerself. Cook don't like blood in the potatoes."

Very funny.

As Lottie worked so did a dozen others, not counting the steady stream of deliverymen bringing in bushels of fruit and vegetables. The top of the cast-iron stove was covered with pots boiling and pans simmering. The large table that sat as an island in the middle of the room was used by four servants, cutting, dicing, kneading, and mixing.

The scene brought Lottie back to her childhood, when she'd often visited the servants belowstairs. Mrs. Movery the cook, Mr. Davies the butler, and Mrs. Reynolds the housekeeper . . . they'd often seemed more her family than her mother and father. They told her stories and she learned about their lives. They let her lick the cake bowl and . . .

Another memory demanded attention. It was her tenth birthday and her parents had forgotten. Feeling low, Lottie had gone downstairs to discover that Mrs. Movery had made an apple cake just for her. And the other servants had gone together to buy her a copy of *Mansfield Park*. It had been her best—and worst—birthday.

She rinsed a peeled potato in the sink and looked around the room. The smell of baking bread was heavenly, and the murmur of voices mingled with the sounds of utensils at work was somehow comforting.

Yet to think all of this was for Dora.

It could have been for me.

The thought brought her back to the reason she was at the Tremaines'. It wasn't to help with the party, but to . . .

To what?

Crash the party?

Could she really do that? How would she do that? She didn't want to embarrass Dora in front of New York society. That wouldn't serve her own purposes well. For her to wait for the party to begin, clang a spoon against a serving tray to get their attention, and then declare, "I'm the real Charlotte Gleason" would lead to her own ostracism instead of acceptance.

And the maid had said Charlotte and Conrad were going to be engaged. What of Dr. Greenfield? Lea had implied he and Charlotte were a pair.

She needed to talk to Dora. Alone.

But how could she accomplish that if she was stuck in the kitchen?

Why couldn't things be easy?

Lottie was so enrapt with her thoughts that she didn't notice Mrs. Dyson coming up behind her. "Come on, girl. We need those potatoes in the pot. Now."

"I'm sorry. I'm just not very good—"

Mrs. Dyson plucked the knife out of her hands. "Over here." She nodded to another girl. "Potatoes, Millie."

Millie glared at Lottie but left her place in the corner where she was . . .

No, no . . . don't make me do that!

"Here you go," Mrs. Dyson said. "There's no talent to plucking feathers. Get to it."

Lottie chided herself for not catching on to potato peeling. To touch a dead chicken. To pull its feathers out . . .

"Don't give me that look, girl. Ain't you ever seen a chicken before?"

"Not in its . . . entirety."

Mrs. Dyson rolled her eyes. "Well, introduce yerself. I need girls who can help, not hinder."

Lottie sat on the stool. "Actually, my experience is with serving dinner, not making it."

Mrs. Dyson put her hands on her hips. "Well, aren't you lardy-dardy."

The other servants offered their own looks of contempt. Lottie hated their reaction, yet she wasn't there to make friends.

All eyes turned toward the door leading to the house as the butler came in—the same man who'd met her at the front door.

He seemed to sense something was amiss and looked at Mrs. Dyson. "Is there a problem here?"

"No, Mr. Childs. No problem. Just a little mutiny by one of the girls. She says she's only used to serving the food, not making it."

Lottie's first inclination was to avert her head. She didn't want Mr. Childs to recognize—

Or did she?

"If you'll excuse me, sir," Lottie said. "My experience is upstairs, not in the kitchen."

The butler looked her over. "We *could* use another maid to serve. What are your references?"

I've eaten a lot of food served by maids. . . . "I just got in from Wilt-shire, where I'm familiar with the homes of Sir Charles Sonomish, Mr. Thomas Standish, and the Reginald Byrons." She added the *pièce de résistance*. "I've also been in attendance at the Prince Regent's on more than one occasion." She did not add "as a guest."

The butler's eyebrows rose. "Mrs. Dyson, you'll have to deal with two fewer hands. Come with me . . . ?"

"Lottie," she said. "Lottie Hathaway."

Chapter Eighteen

The interior of the Tremaine mansion was grander than any English home Lottie had ever seen. It rivaled even the royal palaces. *To think this could be mine.*

Mr. Childs led Lottie into the dining room and introduced her to the housekeeper, Mrs. Sinclair. He looked pointedly at Lottie before leaving her. "You do whatever Mrs. Sinclair tells you to, understand?"

Lottie bobbed a curtsy as she'd seen her own servants do a thousand times. "Yes, Mr. Childs."

Mrs. Sinclair eyed her skeptically. "He says you have experience serving?"

Lottie felt a knot in her stomach. Being served and serving were far different things. "Yes, ma'am."

"Your attire . . . you can wear those clothes now because we have work to do setting the table and such, but you'll have to change into blacks for tonight."

"Understood, Mrs. Sinclair."

The older woman stepped to the side, revealing a long credenza piled high with china and glassware. "All this has to go there," she said, pointing to the enormous dining table that had been covered with a lace tablecloth.

Lottie felt panic rise. She'd attended dozens of formal affairs and knew which fork to use for what, but setting a table to the Tremaines' specifications was daunting. And how would the Tremaines accept her as the real Charlotte Gleason if they remembered her serving them as a maid?

First things first. She felt her plan—such as it was—was better served abovestairs rather than below, so she had to do a good job.

"I don't wish to do it wrong, Mrs. Sinclair. Would you mind setting up one place as you'd like it and I'll do the rest?"

Mrs. Sinclair's look was indecipherable. Had Lottie given herself away? Did all maids know how to set such a table?

But then the housekeeper nodded once and said, "That's the smartest thing I've ever heard said to me, girl. There's no shame in not knowing, only in not asking. Here, let me show you how it's to be done."

Lottie watched intently, feeling quite triumphant.

※

Out of the corner of her eye, Lottie spotted Mrs. Sinclair bob a curtsy. She looked to the door of the dining room and saw a regal-looking woman enter. Was this—?

"Mrs. Tremaine," Mrs. Sinclair said, halting the placement of candles in the four sterling candelabra.

The lady of the house walked toward the dining room table, her eyes seeing everything.

Lottie stopped her work and had to retrieve her heart from her shoes. This was the woman. This was her future mother-in-law.

Step up! Tell her who you are!

But instead of stepping forward, Lottie found herself taking two steps back, away from the table, giving Mrs. Tremaine room to walk around unhindered.

The woman adjusted a fork here, a glass there—a quarter of an inch at the most. After she'd moved to the other side of the table, she looked up and saw Lottie. Her eyes lingered a moment.

Does she recognize me from the photograph we sent them? In the split second that followed, Lottie tried to remember her expression in that photograph. If she matched it just so . . .

She offered a slight smile.

But too late. Mrs. Tremaine had moved on, her eyes on the table. "Who is responsible for the setting?" she asked Mrs. Sinclair.

"That girl, over there. A new girl brought in for the party."

Once again, Mrs. Tremaine stopped and looked at Lottie. "The job is done well, girl."

"Thank you, Mrs. Tremaine." Her impulses warred with common sense. *I'm not a maid! I'm Charlotte Gleason! You see, it was all an idiotic idea of mine to let my maid take my place and—*

"What's your name, girl?"

Oh. My. Goodness. Now was her chance.

Lottie tried to suppress the frantic beating of her heart. "My name is Lottie, Lottie—"

Crash!

Mrs. Tremaine hurried into the foyer, followed by Mrs. Sinclair. There was commotion and Lottie heard reference to a vase and flowers.

She stood alone in the dining room, transfixed, unable to move. Her head began to shake in small bursts. Because she'd hesitated, her chance had been lost. Gone.

Was the lost chance a blessing or a blunder?

Mrs. Sinclair returned. "Stupid boy. Can't even carry a vase from one room to the other without tripping over his own feet." She glanced at Lottie. "You did good, girl, but back to work with you."

"But Mrs. Tremaine? Is she coming back?"

"What? You want further praise? Be thankful for what you got. Mrs. Tremaine has more to do than gush over you. And so do I. When you get done with the table, I'm going to have you help me set up a beverage buffet in the drawing room."

Now that Lottie had seen one of the Tremaines, now that she'd spoken to one, she didn't want to be relegated to busywork. She had to see Dora, and see her now.

"If Miss Gleason needs extra help getting ready, I would be happy to oblige."

Mrs. Sinclair turned toward her, candle in hand. "What are you? A jack-of-all-trades?"

"I used to be a lady's maid too."

"Well, aren't you special? Did you also work as a stableboy and a butler?"

"No, I just—"

"You just do as you're told. One compliment from the mistress doesn't earn you the right to choose your work. Now finish up."

Lottie's mind swam. *How can I get to Dora? How can I talk to—?*

Mrs. Sinclair stood with her arms crossed. "I'm waiting."

For what?

"Say, 'Yes, Mrs. Sinclair.' You'd better show some respect, girl, or I'll have Mr. Childs toss your bum on the street."

He wouldn't dare. But even though her anger had been ignited, she said the words that were required. "Yes, Mrs. Sinclair."

Servitude was clearly not her forte.

※

"The dress is so heavy."

Mary was right. The pink and green gown that Mrs. Tremaine had made for Charlotte felt like a hundred stones had been tied around her body, weighing her down, pulling her down . . .

Drowning her.

If only she could have worn the garnet dress Conrad purchased for her at the store. That dress made her feel pretty and elegant, while this one made her feel as though she were strapped to a garden arbor.

From handling Lottie's dresses, Charlotte had long ago realized that the wealthy somehow equated layers, bulk, and ornament with status. The heavier the fabric, and the more drapery, bustle, fringe, and bead, the better. With this as a measurement, this evening's dress earned her the title of countess. Or princess. An American princess who was bringing her own flowers.

There was a knock on the door. Mary answered it, letting Beatrice in.

"Mother said she forgot to order you gloves, so I'm to loan you some of mine." She handed Charlotte some long butter-colored gloves, then gave the dress a look. She didn't smile. "So. Do you like the dress?"

Once again, now wasn't the time for the truth. "As you said, it's perfection."

"Humph. I may have said that, but I never meant it."

"You didn't?"

Beatrice shook her head. "Mother's trying too hard with that dress, which means—"

"I look like I'm trying too hard."

She shrugged. "At least Mother believes you *can* be accepted by the Four Hundred. She's given up on me."

"I'm sure that's not true."

Beatrice adjusted a yellow flower on Lottie's hip. "Do you think it's easy being plain?"

"I . . ."

"My brother, who's no looker himself, gets to marry you, a beauty. But because I'm not beautiful, I'm sought after by no one. Even my father's money can't make me desirable." She picked a ribbon from the dressing table and wrapped it around a finger. "Even that scallywag Ward McAllister doesn't pay attention to me."

Charlotte remembered Mr. McAllister from their walk in Central Park. The man's innuendo toward Charlotte had been discomfiting. "I expect there are many women who yearn to be ignored by Mr. McAllister."

Beatrice let the ribbon spiral from finger to table. "It doesn't matter. I've accepted my state." She looked up. "As of today."

"Today?"

Beatrice moved to Charlotte's side, adjusting the trim on a sleeve. "Since you found a way for my paintings to be displayed, I've found my true purpose."

Charlotte smiled. "I was happy to do it. And you'll be doing Conrad a favor, your family's store a favor."

"You did me a favor."

Their eyes met for only a moment, but it was enough. This was Beatrice's way of making amends. When the older girl looked away, Charlotte said, "Do you really think this dress is too much?"

"Absolutely. But Mother, Mrs. Astor, and Mrs. Vanderbilt will love it, and that's what counts."

There was another knock on the door, but this time Beatrice answered it. It was Mr. Childs, with a box. Beatrice brought it to Charlotte. "Childs says this is for you. From Conrad."

"Why didn't he bring it himself?" she asked, taking the blue velvet box.

"If you haven't noticed, my brother isn't the most courageous of beings."

Yet. In the short time Charlotte had known him, Conrad had made many positive strides in the right direction.

"Well?" Beatrice said. "Aren't you going to open it?"

Charlotte undid the clasp and opened—

She gasped.

"Emeralds," Beatrice said. "If I'm not mistaken, they were my grandmother's."

Charlotte carefully lifted the necklace, marveling at the sparkle of the green jewels and the diamonds that surrounded them. "It's magnificent. I've never seen anything like it."

Beatrice took it from her, working to open the clasp. "Of course you haven't." She put the necklace on Charlotte and hooked the clasp. "There. Take a look."

Charlotte moved to the full-length mirror. The green in the emeralds perfectly enhanced the green velvet ribbons on her dress. Her fingers flitted from stone to stone as if testing to see if they were truly hers.

"Quite lovely, if I do say so." Beatrice sighed. "It appears my brother is set on marrying you. He wouldn't give these to you otherwise."

"Really?"

"That *is* why you're here, isn't it?"

"Yes, of course, but . . ." Charlotte let it go. She couldn't think about that right now. She had to get through the evening.

"I'll leave you, then, for I have some primping of my own to do—as if it will matter. I'll see you soon."

"Of course," Charlotte said. "Thank you for stopping—"

But as Beatrice left, Mrs. Tremaine entered. She scanned Charlotte from head to toe and back again, finally resting her gaze upon the necklace.

"Conrad just gave it to me."

Her left eyebrow rose. She turned to Mary. "Leave us."

Mary looked as surprised as Charlotte felt. Was something wrong?

"Please sit." Mrs. Tremaine indicated a specific chair. She, however, remained standing. "Firstly, I wanted to tell you that I appreciate what you have done for my children."

"I haven't—"

She raised a hand, stopping Charlotte's words. "I am not ignorant to the travails of growing up in a wealthy home, expecting the world, yet having the world expect little in return."

Charlotte was genuinely interested. She would never have imagined such a statement from Mrs. Tremaine.

The woman strolled as she talked, the train of her dress following obediently behind her. "I know my children's weaknesses: Conrad gives in too easily, and Beatrice has erected a wall of sarcasm. Yet you, in your brief time here, have given them purpose. I've never seen Conrad so enthusiastic about the store, nor seen Beatrice drop her guard enough to let me witness a glimmer of the innocent, hopeful girl she once was."

Charlotte was going to denounce her involvement, yet decided just to say, "I'm glad you approve."

"I do more than approve, I'm grateful." She paused in front of the empty jewel box and shut it with a snap. "When you first arrived I was skeptical, and honestly, you didn't seem to be the girl we thought you were. There were times—" she found Charlotte's eyes—"times when I didn't know *who* you were."

Charlotte felt sick to her stomach. What had started as a conversation of gratitude had veered toward one of exposure.

I know who you are, Miss Gleason—or should I say, Miss Connors?

"I'm sorry if I've disappointed you in any way," Charlotte said. "And I apologize for the mistakes I've made. It's been a bit unnerving coming here, across the world. I've done my best to—"

"I received some information earlier today, from a man who works for my husband."

The man with the red curly hair and the droopy mustache? Charlotte tried to recall if she'd ever seen the man before and thought not. So what could he have against her?

Mrs. Tremaine moved the jewelry box to Charlotte's vanity table. "Honestly, I don't know what to think of his allegations."

"Allegations? I . . ." The defense *I've done nothing wrong* was halted before the lie could fall into the space between them.

Mrs. Tremaine looked upon Charlotte long enough for the girl to feel a twitch in her jaw and a clenching of her innards.

I have to tell her. She deserves to know. She already knows. It was wonderful while it lasted, but Lottie and I were stupid to think we could ever get away with—

Mrs. Tremaine broke her stance and walked to the mantel. "Did you know my maiden name was Gertie Gooseman?"

Surely she was joking.

Her lack of a smile revealed otherwise. "I didn't know that," Charlotte said.

"I came to America with my parents in 1850. We escaped the horrible potato famine in Ireland. My two siblings died on the trip over, and my mother died the next year in childbirth. My father . . . amid his sorrow he took to drink."

"I'm so sorry," Charlotte said. "I've lost family too and—" She realized she'd said too much.

But Mrs. Tremaine seemed not to notice as she traced her fingers over the porcelain figurines and silver candlesticks above the fireplace. "I was fortunate enough to become a governess." She looked right at Charlotte. "To the Tremaine family."

"Oh my."

Mrs. Tremaine nodded and continued her tactile journey. "Martin—Mr. Tremaine—was two years my senior. As I taught his younger siblings he became enamored with me. And I with him. He was so dashing, so full of life."

Charlotte wanted to ask how Gertie Gooseman had ever been allowed to marry Martin Tremaine, when the answer was given.

"The Tremaines were not wealthy back then, but Martin had dreams of opening a department store. He was working with his father, selling lace in a small shop when he asked me to be his wife. And now, thirty years later . . ." She spread her hands.

"It's the sort of story one often hears about in America," Charlotte said.

Mrs. Tremaine nodded. "It's a story I understand. It's a story I must condone or call myself a hypocrite."

What was she saying?

"Do you love my son?"

Charlotte jerked at the question. "I . . . I believe I could."

Mrs. Tremaine nodded. "In spite of the dictates of society—dictates that have become my own for lack of something better—I believe love must be present in a marriage. If either party is marrying for reasons other than love, the marriage should not take place." She cocked her head ever so slightly. "Do you agree?"

Charlotte found her throat dry. "I do."

"Good." She walked briskly to the door. "Be ready by seven sharp. I'll send Mary back in to help you."

Charlotte was glad she was seated, for she had no strength left. The only reason she could imagine Mrs. Tremaine sharing that story was if she wanted to draw a parallel between her own humble beginnings and—

Mary slipped into the room, her face full of questions. "Mrs. Tremaine looked a bit sad. Did something happen?"

"No, nothing," Charlotte said. "She merely wanted to wish me well."

She stood and let Mary help her with the finishing touches of her costume.

Costume.

For carrying out a masquerade.

Be polite, prompt, pretty, and proper."

Lottie's instructions about being a lady came back to Charlotte as she stood at the door of her bedroom ready to proceed downstairs for her welcome party. Her heart beat like a clock gone wild, and she could find no breath deep enough to sustain her. Her legs were weak, as if her bones had decided to leave the support to her muscles alone.

Mary held her elbow. "Do you want me to call Dr. Greenfield?"

Like a comet, Charlotte's thoughts raced to Edmund. If only he could be at the party, supporting her with a glance, encouraging her with a smile.

But even if he could, why would he? The party was one more step toward marrying Conrad. She knew Edmund had feelings for her, and she had feelings for him. To witness the gap between them growing before his eyes and be helpless to change it . . .

Then stop all this now. Walk down those stairs and keep walking out the door and away. You don't have to do this. Edmund doesn't care if you're high society; all he wants is you.

"And all I want is . . . ?"

"Pardon, miss?"

Her bravado left her. Whether she wished to admit it or not, Charlotte was excited about her party. What woman wouldn't be? Tonight was her chance to be the toast of New York City, an American princess.

"Open the door, Mary. It's time."

⁂

Conrad's mouth dropped as Charlotte walked down the staircase, reinforcing her decision to move on with the evening. The sparkle in his eye and the depth of his smile filled her up, causing her back to straighten and her neck to lengthen.

He walked to the bottom of the stairway and took her hand. "You're ravishing."

"Thank you."

As she took his arm, he leaned close. "You like the necklace?"

She put a gloved hand to the gems. "How could I not? It's beautiful."

"The first of many gifts."

Was she dreaming? Was this real?

"Let me show you around before people arrive." Conrad led her to the dining room, where the table was set for thirty. At the Gleasons' she'd witnessed many fancy dinners, but none compared to the opulence of this table. The china was set on silver chargers and the glasses were rimmed in the same silver. The middle of the table contained five floral displays of red roses, yellow lilies, and orange zinnias. As filler in the arrangements were cuttings of trees, with their leaves the colors of a vivid autumn. Four silver candelabra were ready to light. And compotes of fresh fruit were arranged to entice—but not to touch—as stands of molded butter promised fresh bread.

"It's all for you," Conrad said.

Charlotte put a hand to her mouth as tears threatened. "But I don't deserve this. I'm not . . . it's too much."

"It's just enough. Just the beginning." He turned her toward the foyer again. "Come see the drawing room. There's a floral arrangement inside that has to be five feet in height."

Five feet—at least. It stood on a mahogany pedestal next to the entrance, refusing to be missed.

"Here she is," Conrad said. His parents and Beatrice were already present.

Mr. Tremaine came to greet her first, his face florid with pleasure. "My, my, look at you. If Caroline Astor doesn't drool over that dress, then I'll move us to Albany." He kissed Charlotte's hand, then glanced at his wife. "Well done, my dear. Well done."

Mrs. Tremaine accepted his praise. "The dress often makes the woman, but sometimes I do believe the woman makes the dress."

Was that a compliment?

Beatrice hung back, her blue gown its own lovely masterpiece. And yet . . . her grim countenance lessened its beauty. Perhaps Mrs. Tremaine's statement was correct. There was something about attitude that made a gown extraordinary.

Charlotte started when the doorbell chimed. "They're here."

Mrs. Tremaine placed herself next to her husband. "Indeed they are."

❦

The black fabric of the maid's uniform was starched, stiff, and uncomfortable. Lottie was used to lush fabrics like silk and velvet, not this scratchy cotton. She put the white ruffled apron over her head and tied the bow in back. She attempted to see her rear view, but the small mirror on the wall of the storage room offered scant reflection.

Next, the cap. It was a silly thing with a tiny row of lace along its edge and a fluttering of fabric down the back. Two hairpins had been provided to secure it to her hair—which Mrs. Sinclair had told her must be upswept and contained, with not a single strand loose.

Lovely.

Finally ready, Lottie took one last look at herself. When she'd come up with the idea of having Dora take her place, she'd assumed she would find a new life in America, but had never imagined herself in Dora's position as the hired help. Once again God must be having a good laugh at her expense.

She looked heavenward and gave Him her opinion. "You laugh now, but just wait. The night is young."

In a few hours everything would once again be as it should be.

Or would it? Logically, the Tremaines would not celebrate the details of the truth that would play out this night. It would take time for Lottie to earn their trust and a place in their lives and home.

Lottie hated logic. And waiting.

⁂

Mrs. Astor didn't look very happy for being the head of the Four Hundred, the queen of New York society. Her mouth was slightly pulled as if she'd smelled something unseemly, and her eyebrows were raised above eyes that missed nothing and judged everything.

When it was time for Charlotte to be presented, she nearly took the woman's hand and kissed it, offering a full curtsy as she'd heard was proper when meeting Queen Victoria. But Mrs. Tremaine had warned her that all that was required—or sought—was a deferential nod.

And then it was done. Mrs. Astor moved away without saying a word.

"Not even a hello," Charlotte murmured.

Beatrice took her elbow and led her aside. "She has no need to talk to others. The fact she is even here is a victory for Mother."

"Is she unmarried? I see no Mr. Astor."

"William B. is the second son and, as such, has little to do. Rumor has it he spends most of his time at his upstate New York estate or on his yacht—which admittedly is the largest in the world."

"She doesn't go with him?"

"Heavens no. Her kingdom is here. Her brother-in-law JJ—John Jacob—is the heir and lived next door to William and Caroline until he died, and now *his* son causes a score of trouble for 'Aunt Lina,' as he calls her. He's furious she calls herself '*the* Mrs. Astor,' as if she's the only one. It's even written that way on her calling card. The nephew's wife takes offense, which is probably why Mrs. Astor does it."

Charlotte looked around the room. The other woman Mrs. Tremaine had urged her to impress was Mrs. Vanderbilt. Yet looking at her and Mrs. Astor, holding court on opposite sides of the room . . . "Mrs. Astor and Mrs. Vanderbilt don't seem to care much for each other."

"Mrs. Astor has family roots that go back to colonial times and has made a point of not associating with tradesmen. The Vanderbilts are *nouveau riche*—newly rich. A grandfather made his money in railroads, I believe. But the fact remains they *are* rich. Two years ago, after their grand house was finished, Mrs. Vanderbilt planned a great masquerade ball and didn't invite Mrs. Astor because Mrs. Astor hadn't called and left her card. But Mrs. Astor's daughter wanted to go so badly that Mrs. Astor gave in and had her driver bring her card by. Since then, they've accepted each other, but they are certainly not friends. Even our family has been slow to be accepted. I know that's one reason Father built this mansion right across from Mrs. Astor's. It makes their brownstone look like a tenement. It forces our position."

"It's all so complicated," Charlotte said. *And too much an eye for an eye*.

"Such is friendship when money and power are involved."

Beatrice motioned a maid to bring a tray of champagne flutes close. She took a glass for herself, but Charlotte shook her head. Her stomach was still in knots.

"Are you sure, Miss Gleason?" the maid asked.

For the first time, Charlotte looked at the servant's face.

And nearly fainted.

It was Lottie!

Charlotte gasped and stepped back. Alarmed, Beatrice took her arm. "What's wrong?"

Lottie slipped away into the crowd. "I'm . . . I just need to sit down."

"Over here." Beatrice indicated a chair close by.

It was too close. "If you don't mind, I think I'll step into the foyer for a few moments. All these people . . ."

"I'll go with—"

"No. I'll be all right. I just need a few moments."

A few thousand.

⁂

Lottie saw Dora exit the room. She still had four glasses on her tray, so she made a sweep through the crowd, quickly emptying it.

She followed Dora into the grand foyer, finding it hard not to run.

Lottie didn't see her at first, but then, to the left, behind a statue . . .

"*Psst!*"

Dora extended her hands to Lottie. "You're here! I can't believe you're here. I've missed you so much."

For a moment, Lottie was shocked by the greeting. She'd been so focused on seeing Dora for the express purpose of calling off the charade that she'd ignored the reunion aspect of their meeting. But once in Dora's presence, she took pleasure in the comfort and familiarity of the contact.

Except that Dora was dressed in satin and lace and she . . .

Dora stepped back to look at her and smiled. "My, my. I never thought I'd see you in a shirtwaist and bib. It's not your best look."

Lottie was embarrassed to have their roles so utterly reversed, but it led nicely toward her mission. She looked around the foyer. It was too risky to remain. They might be found, and it would be hard to come up with an explanation. Although she wanted to expose the farce, the situation must be handled with aplomb.

"Is there a place we could talk?" she asked.

Dora hesitated for only a moment. "The gallery. Follow me."

The room took her by surprise. "It's like a museum."

"I know," Dora said. "Yet no one ever comes here."

Lottie pointed to a painting of some Flemish peasants at an open market. "Is that a Bruegel?"

Dora looked up. "I have no idea."

"This is astounding," Lottie said.

"We don't have time for this, I must get back." Dora took Lottie's hand. "I went to Five Points. I saw your hat in that apartment. Did you go to my cousin's? Where are you staying now? How are you?"

The events that had occurred since arriving in America raced through Lottie's mind—and were quickly discarded. None of that mattered now. For *now* was about to change everything.

"I want to call it off."

"Off?"

"I want to be myself again."

Dora stared at her, her mouth agape. "But you can't do that. I . . . this is my welcome party. I've just been presented to the elite of New York society. You can't just pop in and say *you* are the real Charlotte Gleason."

"Actually, I can. I could."

Dora's expression crumpled. "But I've made a life here."

"Are you engaged yet?"

"Not yet, but—"

"What about Dr. Greenfield?"

Dora's eyes widened. "How do you know about him?"

"He was at the Scarpellis', yes? Lea told me you two looked as though you had feelings for each other."

Dora found a chair. "I do. We do. It's a miracle he found me. When he walked into my bedroom here, it was as though God had brought him to me."

"Do you love him?"

"I . . ." She faltered. "Conrad is a good man too, and we care for each other, and—"

Lottie pounced. "So you have two men on your hook?"

"No, yes, I mean . . ."

"Isn't that being a bit greedy?"

The look on Dora's face softened Lottie's heart. She'd been unnecessarily cruel. This was her best friend. The two of them were in this predicament because of *her* idea.

She knelt beside Dora's chair. "I'm sorry to spring this on you. But ever since you left me at Castle Garden, things have gone from bad to worse. I thought being alone in America would afford me adventure and fresh chances, but instead I've endured poverty and hopelessness." The thought of Sven and Fitz flashed by, but she didn't let their images land. Sven was married. As much as she admired him, he had no feelings for her. And Fitz . . . she was doing this for Fitz. If she could get established in a prosperous home, if things went as planned, Fitz could have all the advantages money could buy.

Perhaps the mention of Fitz would help her cause. "I have a child," she said.

Dora's eyes widened. "What? You have a—?"

"I found a baby abandoned on the street and took him in. I love him, Dora. I never thought I could love someone like I love that boy. But he needs a good home."

"Where is he now?"

"With Nanny. I found Nanny running a foundling home. That is *my* miracle."

Dora shook her head, and Lottie could tell it was too much for her to comprehend. "I have to go," Dora said. "I have to get back." She stood and moved to the door, then stopped. "You're not going to do anything tonight, are you?"

Although Lottie had thought about it . . . "No. I promise you that. Not tonight. But come to me tomorrow at the foundling home and we'll talk some more." She pulled an address from her pocket. "Tomorrow."

Dora took the note, nodded, and left the room.

There. It was done.

Left alone in the gallery, Lottie turned a full circle, taking it all in. She gave her own nod to the paintings. "I'll be back."

Chapter Nineteen

Charlotte was relieved the dinner in her honor wasn't as prone to silence as the usual Tremaine meals. This sampling of the elite of New York society were skilled at banter. Meaningless banter. There was no talk of politics, religion, or money, but plenty mention of opera, balls, and gossip. Ward McAllister provided much of that. Other than the occasional polite question, they ignored Charlotte. Which was fine with her.

Her main point of nervousness was caused by Lottie's presence. Every time she looked in her direction, Lottie looked back. It was as though they had already resumed their original roles. Charlotte might be wearing satin and emeralds and Lottie a maid's uniform, but Lottie was the one in control, and Charlotte felt the restraints of their old relationship falling into place, the dynamics of Lottie the mistress and Charlotte—Dora—the maid.

But it's not fair! She can't come back here and ruin everything!

This whole thing had been Lottie's idea. Dora hadn't asked to assume her identity. She would never have thought of such a notion. But now that things were nicely in place . . .

It was just like Lottie to change her mind and expect the world to stop turning so she could step back on.

"Miss Gleason?"

Lottie stood behind Charlotte's shoulder, waiting to serve the squab with cherry sauce.

"Yes. Please."

Lottie used silver tongs to put the bird on Charlotte's plate, then changed utensils to spoon the sauce over it. She brushed Charlotte's arm. Charlotte felt one of her gloves slip from her lap to the floor—where she left it.

"Pardon me, miss."

The brush had been on purpose. Charlotte knew it.

She wanted Lottie to leave. Charlotte's excitement about seeing her again had been replaced by a growing anger at her audacity. If Lottie *was* going to declare the farce to the world, why didn't she just do it? Why this torture?

Lottie served Conrad next, then moved on.

"Mrs. Astor?" Lottie said, ready to serve society's headmistress.

Charlotte glanced to her left and saw a look of consternation on Mrs. Astor's face, and also on Mrs. Tremaine's. And then she knew what was wrong. Servants didn't address the guests. They were invisible—hands to help and arms to aid. They had no personality, no names, no opinions, and certainly no voice.

Lottie had grown bold. Too bold.

Mrs. Tremaine flashed a look at the butler, who quickly assessed the problem. As soon as Mrs. Astor was served and before Lottie could continue her service, he stepped forward, touched her arm, and whispered something for her ears alone.

"But . . ."

He took the tray from her and continued the rounds himself. The housekeeper quickly showed Lottie the door.

Charlotte could only imagine what transpired next. Poor Lottie.

Yet her sympathy was far overshadowed by relief.

❧

"You must leave. At once," Mrs. Sinclair said.

Lottie shook her hand off her arm. "Why would I do that?"

"Your services are no longer required. Come with me."

Mrs. Sinclair took her arm and tried to lead her toward the back stairs to the kitchen.

Once again, Lottie pulled out of her grasp. "No! I won't go. I belong here."

"Apparently you don't. What were you thinking addressing the guests by name?"

So that was it? "I was polite. I used their proper names."

"Exactly," Mrs. Sinclair whispered. "You used their *names*. I don't know what kind of household you worked in before, but here at the Tremaines' that's completely unacceptable." She nodded to a footman to come to her assistance.

This wasn't the way it was supposed to transpire. Lottie wouldn't be manhandled by these servants and removed from the house like some criminal.

As soon as she felt the man's hands upon her, all reason fell away. "Get your hands off me!"

There was a scuffle, and even as Lottie was in the midst of it—kicking and hitting—she thought, *What am I doing? This isn't like me!*

"What's going on out here?"

All three of them froze.

"Mr. Tremaine," Mrs. Sinclair said. "I'm sorry, we're just trying to deal with this servant and she refuses to leave."

"What's the problem, girl?"

Lottie smoothed her uniform, her thoughts spinning. Now was her chance to proclaim the truth. And yet . . .

If she truly wanted to take her place in the Tremaine family and among New York society, she couldn't do it this way, making a scene, dressed as a maid on the verge of being thrown out. Besides, she'd promised Charlotte she wouldn't do anything tonight.

"No problem, sir. I'm sorry to have disturbed you. I'm leaving now."

He looked a little surprised at her agreeable exit but nodded once before returning to the dining room. Lottie could only imagine the table conversation that would follow.

It couldn't be helped. She'd accomplished what she'd come to do. She'd spoken with Charlotte—with Dora. Now she had to be patient.

Lottie walked toward the back stairs. When the footman and Mrs. Sinclair began to follow, she kept walking, raised a hand to them, and said, "No need. I'll see myself out."

So there.

※

Mr. Tremaine returned to his seat with all eyes upon him. "A small altercation with the help. Nothing more. Carry on. Enjoy your dinner."

Mrs. Astor shook her head. "Where *do* you get your help, Martin?"

He smiled and took a sip of his wine. "Off the streets, Caroline. Isn't that where you find yours?"

Soft laughter ensued and Charlotte let herself breathe. It sounded as though Lottie was gone, and she obviously hadn't revealed their secret. For the moment, all was well. She felt sorry for Lottie but was glad she was gone.

At her right Conrad spoke only to her. "Quite the eventful evening, eh, Miss Gleason?"

"Quite."

If he only knew.

※

"Drop me here," Lottie called over her shoulder to the driver.

The cart of firewood came to a stop, and Lottie hopped off the open back. "Thank you."

The man gave her a one-finger salute and moved along the dark street.

Lottie staggered toward the Merciful Child Foundling Home. She tried the door, but it was locked. She knocked. If no one answered, she vowed to sleep on the stoop, for she could go no farther.

She had no idea what time it was. After she'd left the Tremaines' she'd walked south until the upper-class streets had deteriorated into neighborhoods where few risked the darkness. Along the way she'd considered stopping at the church again, but the thought of seeing Fitz drew her onward.

When a cart had come by, Lottie flagged it down and begged a ride. The thought *A Gleason does not beg for anything* had come and gone before it even became a completed thought. Who was she to say what a Gleason did anymore? Her family's status was waning—if it wasn't already completely lost, her father was injured, and her mother and aunt were playing nursemaid. Nothing was as it had been. Nothing was as it should be.

Lifting her fist to knock one last time took enormous effort, but luckily the door opened before her feeble attempt could fail.

"Lottie!"

Nanny. Dear Nanny.

Lottie fell into her arms and let herself be led into the warm kitchen. "It all went wrong. I went to the Tremaines' and ended up being a servant and—"

"Shh," Nanny said as they entered the room. "Fitz is sleeping."

Lottie looked toward the fire and was shocked to see Sven there, holding the boy. "Miss Hathaway."

"Sven. What are you doing—?"

"Mr. Svensson came over after his work was finished for the day to check on little Fitzwilliam." Nanny led Lottie to a chair by the fire. "Fitz has a cold and was fussy, and no one was able to comfort him like Sven."

"He just wanted to be swaddled tight," Sven said. He adjusted the blanket under the boy's chin, then rose to give him to Lottie. *"Søde baby, søde dreng."*

Although Lottie was exhausted beyond measure, the feel of the baby in her arms tapped into a hidden source of strength. "Oh, sweet baby, I missed you so much."

Fitz opened his eyes for but a moment before falling back to sleep.

"Apparently you also have a knack with him, child," Nanny said.

Lottie looked at Sven. For him to spend his entire evening, helping out . . .

"I really appreciate your help, Sven. But you can go now. I'm sure your wife is worried about you."

Sven plucked a string from his pants and let it float to the floor. "I need to talk to you."

"Yes, he does," Nanny said. She abruptly turned on her heel and left the room.

"What's all this about?" Lottie asked.

Sven escaped the bondage of his chair and moved behind it, gripping its back. "I . . . I missed you, Miss Hathaway. More than I expected."

She felt a twinge of pleasure. "I was only gone a short time."

"But with the intention of being gone forever. You may not have said so, but I knew." He cocked his head. "So your plan to regain your rightful place as Charlotte Gleason didn't turn out?"

"No." Then she added, "Not yet."

"Oh."

She was surprised by his look of distress. Why would he care if she was successful at the Tremaines' or—?

Lottie looked down at the baby. "I see you've grown attached to Fitz."

His face softened as his gaze fell upon the boy. "I have. He's a fighter, that one is. A survivor. He smiles at me."

"Of course he does."

Sven opened his mouth to speak, closed it, then tried again. "But you think wrongly, Miss Hathaway, about my reasons for being interested in your success at the Tremaines'."

"Oh?"

"I . . ." He began to pace, running a hand through his hair. "I didn't mean to tell you a falsehood, but when you assumed . . . I should have righted the misconception at once, but your interest and abilities were a little unnerving and—"

He certainly had her interest. "What *are* you taking about?"

He returned to his place behind the chair. "I'm not married. I don't have a wife."

Lottie was glad she was sitting down. "But you—"

"I said I was good with children and you assumed I meant *my* children. And I . . . I let you continue the assumption."

She tried to remember the first conversation where his marital status had come up, but couldn't recall who'd said what. There begged a larger question. "But why didn't you set me straight?"

Even by the firelight she could see his blush. "This may sound conceited, but I could tell you were interested in me—as a man. I haven't had that much experience with women, Miss Hathaway, and your skill—"

She didn't like the way he was making it sound. "I haven't had that much experience with men, either, Mr. Svensson. I assure you—"

"No, no. I meant no offense against your character or reputation, I only meant to say that you were so at ease talking with me, teasing me, being charming."

"Flirtation is a talent finely honed in high society. I was only doing what I was brought up to do. I didn't mean to unnerve you."

"I know, and I should have reacted differently. But when you left me . . ." He came around the chair and sat upon it, leaning toward her with his arms resting upon his legs. "I have feelings for you, Miss Hathaway. And the thought of losing you forever . . . I haven't taken a single photo since you left." He sighed. "I need you."

Lottie laughed. "So you didn't replace me?"

"You have no replacement. And . . ." He paused. "My need goes far beyond my work. *I* need you. Me. Sven."

His eyes were so sincere, his face so open and hopeful.

Lottie was disconcerted. She looked to Fitz to hide her confusion.

Sven had feelings for her? And Fitz? Images of the three of them being a family elicited an overwhelming sense of warmth, security, constancy, and togetherness.

He suddenly sat back. "I'm sorry. I've spoken when I should have remained silent. You don't belong in this world, but to another. I have little to offer you." He began to rise.

She rose too and reached for his hand. "I'm glad you spoke as you did. It's just so new. . . . It changes everything."

"Does it?"

She hesitated. She wouldn't lead him on. "Perhaps."

He nodded. "But may I say one thing more before I leave you to think?"

"Of course."

"No one is the same person they started out to be. That's the way of life. We are supposed to change—for the better. You didn't plan to be here, but here you are, different from whom you sought to be. Yet . . . I don't care whether your name is Hathaway or Gleason. What I wish is for your name to be Svensson."

A laugh escaped. "Is that a proposal, sir?"

Sven gathered his coat and hat. "Which person will you become? It's your choice."

She'd always wanted the chance to choose for herself. Yet now, to be offered *this* choice was daunting.

He moved to the door. "I'll give you the time you need. For I too have changed because of you and Fitz." He returned to them and put a hand upon Fitz's head. "I am sincere, Miss Hathaway. I speak what's on my heart."

He kissed the baby's head, and then . . . Lottie's cheek.

She heard his footsteps recede down the hall and the door tap shut. Within moments Nanny returned.

"So?" she asked.

"What should I do?"

Nanny put her hands on her hips and shook her head. "The right thing." She took Fitz from her arms. "I'll put the babe to bed and be up on the roof if you need me."

"The roof?"

Nanny nodded toward the stairs. "If you need me."

❦

The last guest left.

Mr. Tremaine turned to his family and sighed. "Quite successful, I think." He looked to his wife. "Don't you agree?"

Mrs. Tremaine shrugged. "I did grow tired of Mrs. Vanderbilt going on and on about wanting to marry Consuelo off to some titled European. How gauche."

The two of them moved toward the staircase as if the three young people left behind didn't exist.

Beatrice turned to follow. "Good night. You did fine, Charlotte. Really."

Charlotte was surprised by Beatrice's . . . civility. Were they finally friends? "Thank you, Beatrice," she said. Then she called after the elder Tremaines, who were ascending the stairs. "And thank *you* for the lovely party."

Mr. Tremaine didn't turn around but acknowledged her gratitude with a raised hand. All in a day's work.

Charlotte touched Conrad's arm. "I wish to thank you too. You helped me through every snare."

"I should have warned you that this set tends to sneer rather than smile, at least until they get to know you."

"And accept me."

He scanned the foyer, then took her hand. "Come with me."

Charlotte was far too tired for the evening to be extended even shortly, but she had no choice. When Conrad led her into the gallery, her thoughts immediately returned to Lottie and the conversation that had transpired just hours before.

I want to call the whole thing off. I want to be myself again.

Once in the room, Conrad swung her away, then toward him under his arm, as if they were dancing. His face was positively giddy. Had the evening pleased him that much?

He ended the figure by drawing her toward himself. When he stopped, his giddiness faded. In its place was an earnestness that drew her gaze to his.

Then suddenly he dropped to one knee.

A proposal? A proposal!

Before she had time to think further, he began. "Miss Gleason, Charlotte. In the short time we've known each other I've grown to respect you and care for you very much. I appreciate your unique ability of seeing the truth and telling me your opinions in a way that brings out the best in me. Better than the best, for you have awakened in me ideas and enthusiasm I never knew I owned. In short, dear Charlotte, I'm a better man for knowing you."

Charlotte only half heard his compliments as she tried to figure out what to do. She cared for him too, but if Lottie was going to go through with her plan to halt the scheme . . .

Conrad changed from one knee to the next, trying to find comfort on the marble floor. "I didn't plan on doing this tonight, so I have no ring, but please know this proposal isn't extended on a whim but is something I've intended to do ever since our walk in Central Park. Did you enjoy that walk as much as I did?"

This question she could answer. "I did enjoy it. Immensely." It had also been a turning point for her, as it had been the first time she'd seen Conrad as a true friend—with the possibility of being more than a friend.

Conrad bit his lip, then said the words, "Will you marry me, Charlotte Gleason?"

But I'm not Charlotte Gleason and—

"Will you?"

A tiny voice in her head niggled at her like a fly demanding attention. *Say yes and you will fully claim the position of Charlotte Gleason. If you don't do it, Lottie will.*

So she said it.

"Yes. Yes, I'll marry you."

With a moan and groan, and with her assistance, Conrad rose from his knees. Once upright, he awkwardly put a hand on her arm and leaned forward to kiss her.

She kissed him back. Just one short kiss. A seal to their pact.

And it was done. She was engaged. Charlotte Gleason was engaged.

But what of Dora Connors?

The right thing. Nanny told me to do the right thing.

Which was?

Lottie sat in the chair by the fireplace. The fire was just embers now, and despite the time elapsed, she had no answer.

When a log gave way to a weaker one beneath, she started . . . and remembered Nanny's offer. *"I'll be up on the roof if you need me."*

Lottie sat upright, gripping the arms of the chair. Certainly too much time had passed for Nanny to still be there, yet she had to try. Nanny was the wisest person she knew. She'd been stupid to try to figure out this predicament on her own.

Lottie lit a lamp and climbed the stairs of the foundling home to a landing that led to many bedrooms. Around again, up another flight to more rooms with more closed doors. Yet in the dim light of the lamp she noticed one small door ajar.

She opened it and saw a steep narrow stair. This must be the way.

Lottie held her skirts high to negotiate the steps and at the top found another door ajar. All she had to do was push it open.

And there was the roof, a flat space nearly as large as the footprint of the house, dotted with chimneys and stacks. Lottie walked carefully to the edge and peered down at the street four stories below. It made her dizzy, so she took a step back and looked out upon the city. The moon was the only brightness in this dark place. Rooftops lay before

363

her like stepping-stones above an abyss. In the moonlight she could see laundry strung from chimney to chimney, furniture scattered about, the occasional glow of a lamp. Did people sleep on their roofs?

The night was chilly and she wished she'd brought a shawl.

"Here," came a voice from behind her. "Put this on or you'll catch your death." Nanny came out of the shadows, a shawl covering her own head and shoulders. "I thought you'd never come."

Lottie gratefully took the extra shawl and wrapped it close. "I'm sorry. I tried to figure it out on my own, but then I realized I needed to turn to you."

Nanny shook her head. "Not me, dear girl." Then she pointed skyward.

Ah. Yes. God.

Lottie lowered her head, ashamed. "Why do I forget?"

"People with everything given to them often do. Only when it's taken away do you realize He's all you've got. All you need."

Nanny led her to the other side of the roof, where two chairs had been placed. They sat and both turned their eyes to the moon.

Lottie remembered her time on the *Etruria* when she'd found comfort in the moon that shone over home, and sea, and now here. "The inconstant moon," she murmured.

Nanny shook her head. "Not inconstant at all. It's always there, a faithful witness in the sky."

"Witness to my confusion?"

"What confuses you?"

Lottie was taken aback. "What *doesn't* confuse me? I come to America and end up in this awful place."

"This awful place gave you Fitzwilliam and brought you to me."

Oh. Yes. But. "But I should never have given up my position."

"Why not?"

"It's my birthright."

Nanny shrugged. "This is America, Lottie. Anyone can achieve anything with hard work. The people who own the positions of high society in New York scraped and earned their way there. It's up to their children to earn *their* way, to find their own way. Just as it's up to you to earn and find your own way."

"But I don't know the way."

"Of course you do."

Lottie sat forward, shaking her head. "But I don't. A part of me wants to go back to the Tremaines' and tell the truth. Wouldn't God approve of that?"

"You don't want to go there for truth's sake but for your own."

She sat back. "I know the life there. I understand it. I belong there."

"What about Fitz?"

"I'll take him with me. That's why I want to marry Conrad now, to provide a good home for my baby."

Nanny shook her head. "We've been through this before. I think you're dreaming if you think they'll welcome you and a strange baby into their household."

"They will if I explain everything."

"Explain that you lied to them, deceived them?"

Lottie hated hearing Nanny's words.

Nanny continued. "Even if, miracle of miracles, they'd take you in, do you know the Tremaines? Do you know that Conrad would be a good father?"

"I read his letters. He seems nice enough."

Nanny snickered. "Nice enough to marry and bring up your child."

"Well . . . yes."

"Or is he merely rich enough?"

"Money is important, Nanny."

"Money is necessary. But how much do you need? Does Fitz need satin britches and gilded rooms?"

Lottie knew Nanny was merely making a point, but she was amazed at how accurate she was. The Tremaines' home was a palace.

"Of course he doesn't need those things, but . . ."

"Then what does he need?"

Lottie felt herself being expertly drawn toward a conclusion she wanted to reach, yet feared reaching.

"He needs love. And he has it. With me."

"And with who else?"

"With you."

"And . . . ?"

And there it was. The essence of the entire dilemma.

"Sven. With Sven. That's what you want me to say, isn't it?"

"I don't want you to *say* anything, Lottie. I want you to know, to believe, to do."

Lottie rubbed her face roughly. Nanny made it sound easy, but it wasn't.

She felt Nanny's hand upon her knee. "What do you know, Lottie-girl?"

"I know I love Fitz and want to be his mother. A good mother."

"Agreed. What do you believe?"

"About what?"

"About life."

No one had ever asked her that. To Lottie life just *was*. She'd always let the days play out according to the scenario of others. She'd been a player in someone else's production. Until America. Until now. "I believe I can be a good mother. I believe I can be a good wife. I believe I can have a good life and be happy and even . . . even help change things for the better."

"By doing what?"

The faces of two men flashed before her eyes. Conrad's image didn't stay long, for she'd only seen him in passing. It was the face of Sven that lingered and journeyed through a myriad of memories, replete with words said, emotions expressed, and deeds accomplished. She had spent time with Sven. She knew him and wanted to know even more; she respected the man and his work. He'd said he needed her. And she . . . she loved the idea of being needed.

Her thoughts flashed back to her home in Wiltshire in the weeks before her birthday. She'd been restless, thinking about being of *use*, of doing something worthwhile.

A final image usurped her past as she remembered Sven holding Fitz in his arms, loving the baby as if he were his—

"Sven."

"Sven what?"

"I care for Sven." She angled her body toward Nanny. "I care for him, he cares for me, and we both care for Fitz."

Nanny threw her hands into the air and let them fall upon her lap. "Well then."

It suddenly became as clear as the night sky. "Was I brought here for this, Nanny? Was everything taken from me so I'd end up with the Scarpellis? Was I assaulted on my job so Sven would take me under his wing? Did I find Fitz and find you so . . . all this could happen?"

Nanny laughed. "So you're not mad at the Almighty anymore?"

I'll watch over you.

Lottie must have gasped, because Nanny said, "What's wrong?"

"I just remembered a feeling I had on the deck of the ship coming over here. I was looking at the moon and . . . I get the same feeling now."

"What feeling is that?"

"It's as if God is saying He'll watch over me. And actually, I asked Him to do just that."

Nanny spread her hands. "And He answered. You are where you're supposed to be."

Could it be as simple as that? Could her purpose be here?

Through a tightened throat Lottie nodded, accepting it all.

⁂

"I'm engaged! What am I going to do?" Charlotte asked herself. There were no other ears to hear. Or care. She had absolutely no one to talk to.

She'd never felt so alone.

Charlotte sat on the window seat in her bedroom, in her nightgown, unable to sleep. Most girls who were newly betrothed would be restless due to excitement and joy. But Charlotte . . .

She pulled the lace curtain aside and sought the moon. There it was. It was comforting—and rather awe-inspiring—to know that everyone the whole world over saw this same moon. Had her mother looked at the moon tonight? Or Barney?

Her past relationship with Barney had grown hazy. He appeared in her memory in snippets, nearly static, like a mental photograph without life or movement. It was hard to imagine marrying him, and yet that was the path she'd been following.

Besides her mother and Barney, who else did she have in her life?

Her best friend was Lottie. But at the moment, could Lottie truly be considered a friend? Did friends threaten to spoil and upset another friend's life?

Conrad had proposed. This was exactly what they'd wanted to happen. Their plan had succeeded.

For the moment. Until Lottie came back and ruined everything.

Maybe she'll have a change of heart.

Charlotte remembered the commotion Lottie caused outside the dining room during dinner. It was classic Lottie, wanting her own way and fighting to get it. Apparently, in spite of the hardships she'd endured since coming to America, she hadn't mellowed. If anything, she seemed poised to fight harder to regain what she'd lost.

Who else was there?

Edmund.

The name fell into her thoughts like a droplet of rain, cool and gentle, with the promise of refreshment and restoration.

Unlike her thoughts of Barney, her images of Edmund were vibrant and full of life, sound, and light. She closed her eyes and easily saw them dancing on the ship, saw his face when they first spoke, and felt the proximity of his body against hers in the carriage as they ventured to Five Points.

But it was more than the physical spark that fueled her thoughts. Charlotte remembered his kindness, his joy, his humor, and his tender nature.

To think it had all started with a spilled glass and a handkerchief. She still had that handkerchief. He'd returned it to her.

She needed it now.

Charlotte went to the dressing table, where she kept it close and—

It was gone.

She turned on the gas lamp and scoured the tabletop, the drawers, the porcelain boxes. She got on her hands and knees and searched the floor.

"Where is it?"

Charlotte reached for the bell pull that would call Mary, then stopped. If the Tremaine house was anything like the Gleasons', any pull of a bell would sound in the basement, causing the housekeeper or butler to trudge up to the third story to summon Mary, who would have to get dressed and—

She couldn't do that. She wouldn't. The handkerchief hadn't been thrown away. It was *somewhere*. And in spite of her frenzy, it wasn't a holy artifact.

Holy. God. Holy God.

Charlotte sank upon the bench of the dressing table. All her worries about having no one to talk to . . .

She clasped her hands to her chin and looked heavenward. "I'm sorry for forgetting about you. Please help. It's all too complicated for me." She paused a moment, trying to determine exactly what to pray for. What did she really want? What was best? What *should* happen? Her confusion led to the only prayer that made any sense. "Do what you think is best."

That said, Charlotte returned to her bed.

God was the only one who could handle the situation.

Charlotte only hoped she'd like what He had in mind.

Chapter Twenty

Lottie felt herself rise to the surface of her dreams. She heard whispers. Sensed movement.

She opened her eyes. Three faces stood inches away.

She blinked, trying to focus, and as she did so, she saw that her entire bed was surrounded with children—ragged, ragtag children with enormous eyes and hair rumpled from sleep.

"Who are you?" asked a boy with a German pull to his voice.

"I'm Lottie."

"Are you Fitz's mamma?" asked another.

She didn't hesitate. "Yes, I am."

"Can you be my mamma too?"

The other children chimed in, each making their case. They touched her, pulled her to sitting, and climbed upon the cot with her, crowding in.

At first it was disconcerting. Yet as they snuggled close, she found herself letting them in, wanting them upon her lap and under her arm, relishing the feel of their hands in her own.

"I be son," said an Italian boy. "Fitz's *fratello*."

"No, I be Fitz's *Bruder*," the first boy said. "I here first."

A near scuffle ensued, causing Lottie to stand and let the little bodies fall upon each other in her absence.

She faced the bed and clapped her hands, getting their attention. Once she had it, she wasn't sure what to do. Spotting a kerchief on a girl's head, she took it off and wrapped it around her hand, pulling up two ears and pulling down a makeshift nose. Then she made the hand-animal talk. "Hello! How are you today?"

The children giggled and laughed, and a cap was added by the German boy, making the animal very funny indeed.

Lottie saw Nanny enter the room with Fitz. "My, my, we have quite a show going on here."

A little girl was trying to make her own kerchief animal, and Lottie had to stop in order to help wrap the scarf properly. Once finished Lottie took Fitz into her arms. The children clamored to see the baby, so she sat on the bed and let them fill the space around her.

"Gentle, now," she told their eager hands.

Fitz responded to the attention with smiles and coos, which elicited more smiles from the children. Lottie looked at Nanny and saw approval in her eyes. "They want me to be their mother."

"And why wouldn't they? They know a good heart when they see it."

Me? Have a good heart?

Lottie's consternation must have shown upon her face, for Nanny gave her a surely-you-know-this look.

"I didn't know I could feel this way about others, about children I don't even know," Lottie said.

" 'If we love one another, God dwelleth in us, and his love is perfected in us.' " Nanny shook her head. "What I'm seeing before me is pretty perfect."

"It feels perfect."

"Well then. There you have it."

"Just like that?"

Nanny scooted a child over so she could sit next to Lottie. "Not just like that. You've always had the potential to love, Lottie-girl. It's just been asleep, waiting." She put a finger in Fitz's hand. "This little boy did the waking, God bless him."

God bless him indeed.

※

Charlotte awakened, surprised she'd slept. She sensed movement in the room and sat up. Mary was putting away a stack of newly pressed clothing.

"Morning, miss. Did you sleep—?"

"Did you take the handkerchief I had on my dressing table?"

Mary was taken aback. "Why yes, miss. I put it in the laundry. It looked rumpled and used." She set the stack on a bureau. "Let's see if it's in here."

Charlotte leapt out of bed to witness the looking. Although she would have rather had the handkerchief in the same condition that Edmund had given it to her, just having it at all would be enough.

Mary reached the bottom of the pile. "It's not here."

"Look again."

Mary repeated the process to no avail.

"Let me." Charlotte took each piece of clothing, each camisole, each stocking, each petticoat and bloomer, and shook it, willing the handkerchief to float to the floor.

"Perhaps it got in with someone else's clothing," Mary said. "I could go check—"

Check for a woman's handkerchief that was monogrammed with *DC*? "You needn't bother."

It was lost. Her one token from Edmund was gone forever.

Charlotte retrieved a petticoat and began to fold it, but Mary took it out of her arms. "I'll do that, miss."

Of course she would.

"Would you like me to draw you a bath?"

Why not? She could sit and soak and prune.

And wonder about what could have been—and what would be.

✤

Charlotte passed the butter to Conrad, trying to meet his eyes. When she'd come down to breakfast she'd expected to be greeted with congratulations from his family. But the meal had commenced without fanfare. Either Conrad hadn't told them of their engagement or . . . perhaps they disapproved?

Yet certainly they would have been vociferous about the latter.

Was Conrad having second thoughts? Or had the old Conrad slunk back, the Conrad who would never think of risking his parents' ire?

Finally, just after the sausages were served, Conrad put down his fork, pushed back his chair, and stood. "I have an announcement to make."

"Just a minute, brother." Beatrice pulled something from her sleeve. "Before you make any announcement, I have a question for Charlotte." She unfurled the item, revealing Charlotte's handkerchief.

"Where did you get that?" Charlotte asked.

"So you admit it's yours?"

"Of course . . ." She stopped, unsure what to say.

Beatrice rearranged the handkerchief, smoothing the lace edge to showcase the monogram. "Hmm. If this is Charlotte's handkerchief, one would think the monogram would read *CG*."

"*DC*?" Mr. Tremaine asked. "Who is *DC*?"

Beatrice glared at Charlotte. "Perhaps you'd like to answer that?"

A lie came to her, a story she could make up. But the effort was too much.

And so it was over. Just like that.

Conrad's head shook back and forth. "Beatrice, enough."

"Not enough, I say. Let her answer. Or are you afraid of what she'll say?"

Conrad looked to his mother for support, but even Mrs. Tremaine looked away. Mrs. Tremaine knew the truth, but did Conrad?

Mr. Tremaine slammed his napkin upon the table. "Will someone please tell me what's going on here?"

Beatrice tossed the handkerchief across the table toward Charlotte. It missed its mark, landing near her goblet.

Charlotte wasn't sure if she should retrieve it, but she finally did, drawing it into safekeeping in her lap.

"It *is* my handkerchief. And . . ." The next words would change her world forever, yet how could she not say them? *The truth shall make you free.*

"My name is not Charlotte Gleason. My name is Dora Connors."

Conrad sat down, clearly stunned. He hadn't known? Only Mrs. Tremaine seemed unsurprised.

"Who is Dora Connors?" Mr. Tremaine asked.

"I am—I was—the maid of Charlotte Gleason."

"A maid?" he asked.

Beatrice nodded, her face showing great satisfaction. "I suspected it from the beginning. She's an imposter, trying to marry Conrad for our family's riches."

"I was not after the riches," Charlotte said. She couldn't have Conrad think that. She looked at him, but he was staring at the table. "I care for you. I really do. But . . ." And then, as if a veil had been lifted, she knew the full truth of it. "But I can't marry you."

"You proposed?" Mr. Tremaine asked. "When was this?"

"Last night after the party," he said quietly. "And Charlotte accepted." His eyes found hers. "You accepted."

Beatrice slapped the table. "What are you talking about? She's a maid pretending to be a lady! You can't marry her, no matter how nice she seems."

"Actually he could." It was the first time Mrs. Tremaine had spoken. She looked to her husband. "Remember, I was but a governess."

Beatrice was clearly beside herself. Her face was florid, her eyes darting. "Then why not just pull someone off the street?"

Charlotte remembered the discussion at dinner the night before regarding servants, about getting their servants off the street. "Actually, the real Charlotte Gleason was here last night."

That stunned the listeners to silence.

For a moment.

"Where?" Mrs. Tremaine asked.

"The maid who got into trouble, the one you had to dismiss? That was Charlotte Gleason."

Mrs. Tremaine nodded as if connecting the dots.

"So you traded places? She's now a maid?" Beatrice asked.

"Not exactly." How could she explain it in the simplest of terms? Once she began, Dora avoided looking at Conrad. "Lottie was on her way here to marry Conrad, and I was her companion. But on the ship she changed her mind. She has an adventurous streak. It was nothing against any of you."

"Sounds like a slight to me," Mr. Tremaine said.

"Lottie is actually very caring. Instead of just saying no and letting that be that, she thought of her parents and how much they were depending—" That wasn't the right word. "How excited they were at the idea of her marriage."

Beatrice slapped the table again. "Excited about their daughter marrying Conrad for his money."

Dora shook her head. "Not at all. Lottie gave up the chance to live this wonderful life. But she didn't want to disappoint her parents. That's why she asked me to take her place—which I was very willing to do."

"Of course you were," Beatrice said, linking her arms across her chest. "You had a chance to marry one of the richest men in New York."

Charlotte could have denied it, but chose not to. "Of course that intrigued me. I've been in service since I was thirteen. It's all I've ever known. To have the chance to live a different life, a better life? What girl wouldn't take that chance if offered?"

"Indeed," Mrs. Tremaine said.

"Then how did the real Charlotte end up a maid?" Mr. Tremaine asked.

"She's not really a maid. She came here to see me, to ask me to end our charade. She decided impersonating a maid would get her in the door."

"There is far too much deception going on here," he said.

"I know," Charlotte agreed. "And I apologize for all of it. We truly meant no harm. It was a way to get to America. To start over." She thought of the stories she'd heard. "Isn't that how America came to be? Through people wanting to start fresh?"

"At whose expense?" Beatrice asked. "You duped us."

Charlotte remembered the softer Beatrice who'd showed Charlotte her paintings and who'd come alive with the thought of displaying them at her family's store. "No matter what name I came under, I've lived here as myself. All I've said and shared and felt has been genuine." She looked at each Tremaine. "I care for all of you. I have lied by assuming another identity, but I've been totally honest with you in all my other actions."

The silence was palpable, and Charlotte lowered her head, avoiding their eyes.

Finally Conrad spoke. "So? Will you still marry me?"

She looked up. "Marry—?"

"I don't know about that, son."

Mrs. Tremaine shushed them. "Let her answer."

Conrad found Charlotte's hand and took it in his. "Will you marry me, Char . . . Dora?"

Charlotte was stunned. All this time she'd feared exposure and its consequences, yet now she was going to be allowed . . .

She clutched the handkerchief in her lap and raised it enough to see it and remember all it represented.

Edmund. I love Edmund.

With tears in her eyes, she looked upon Conrad. He was so trusting, so generous to ignore her deception. "Thank you, Conrad, but . . . but I can't marry you."

"What?" Mr. Tremaine threw his hands in the air. "Are you crazy, girl?"

"Perhaps," she said. And she meant it. She had no guarantee that Edmund would want to marry her. By giving up Conrad she might lose both men in her life. But the truth had come this far; she couldn't backtrack into a lie.

Conrad leaned close as if trying to achieve a measure of intimacy amid his family's presence. "Why, Dora? Why change your mind? I forgive you. I love you no matter what your name is."

Oh, how she hated to hurt him. She put a hand upon his cheek. "You're an amazing man, Conrad Tremaine. You're creative and strong and wise and kind, and your family is privileged to have you take over the business. But you deserve someone who loves you as a wife should love a husband. I'll always love you as the dearest friend. But I can't marry you."

He studied her a long moment, then touched the hand upon his cheek, kissed it, and let her go.

Charlotte rose. She couldn't stay among them a moment longer. "I must go now. I'll pack and—"

"You're not taking all those dresses we got for you," Beatrice said.

Mrs. Tremaine raised a hand. "She can take whatever she wishes." She extended her hand toward Charlotte.

Her generosity and forgiving nature were surprising. Charlotte went to her, gripped her hand, and gave her a kiss upon the cheek.

"Be well, dear girl. And remember that Gertie is here if you need her."

Charlotte ran from the room.

Dora burst into her bedroom and shut the door. Then she fell to her knees, letting her hands cushion her forehead upon the carpet. "Oh, God, thank you. I never ever imagined it could happen like this."

She stayed in that position before the heavenly throne a good while, her heart overflowing with gratitude and awe. Her exposure had ended in a manner beyond her imaginings. Not only had she not been kicked out, not only were the police not called, but Dora Connors was leaving with the family's blessings.

Only a knock on the door pulled her from her prayers.

"Yes?"

Mary popped her head inside and showed surprise at seeing her mistress on the floor. "Are you all right?"

Dora held out her hand and Mary helped her to standing. "I'm fine."

Mary faltered. "I thought maybe you was feeling poorly, because Dr. Greenfield is here to see you."

Dora laughed aloud at God's amazing provision. "Send him up."

With Mary gone to fetch him, Dora looked at the handkerchief that had started and consummated her amazing journey from Dora to Charlotte and back again.

There was a soft rap on the door. Dora's heart leapt as she said, "Come in."

Dr. Greenfield entered—Edmund entered, his countenance clearly confused. "Your maid said I should come up? Are you feeling poorly?"

She grinned. "Not at all."

He was still confused. "You seem very happy."

"Oh yes."

A nod. "I came here to see . . . I passed Conrad on his way out. He said he'd proposed and . . . I was to ask you about it?" He straightened his back, putting on a mask of formality. "I wish to congratulate you on your engagement."

She was nearly bursting, wanting to proclaim her love. Yet she couldn't, not without knowing how he felt.

"I'm not engaged to Conrad," she said. "He asked, but I told him I couldn't marry him."

Edmund blinked, then blinked again. "Couldn't?"

"No, I couldn't. Because I didn't love . . . *him.*"

She watched as comprehension washed over his face. His eyes began to sparkle. "I'm sorry," he said.

"I'm not." She reached out a hand. If he took it . . .

Edmund stared at it for but a second before taking hold, then found her other hand and pulled her close. "It appears I am not sorry either."

"Because . . . ?" She smiled up at him.

"Because if he were to marry you, then . . . then I could not."

She stepped back and spread their arms wide, lifting her face to the heavens, fully and completely happy.

Edmund took a step closer and pulled their hands to the center until they were all that kept them apart. "I love you, Charlotte Gleason."

"The name is Dora."

An eyebrow rose. "So you're fully back again?"

"I am back where I belong."

"And your answer, Dora?"

"My answer is yes. Very much yes."

He brought her hands to his lips and kissed them. "Then my prayers have indeed been answered. God has finished our story."

Dora remembered their parting on the ship and something else Edmund had said. "Until fate allows," she murmured.

He nodded, also remembering. "Until fate allows. Until now."

"Until now."

"May I kiss you, Dora?"

She was giddy. "Oh yes. Please."

The kiss that sealed their promise made her . . . swoon.

Dora held the emerald necklace in her hands. Of all the beautiful things she'd been given since coming to the Tremaines', this was the hardest to relinquish. Not for its monetary worth—which was beyond her grasp—but because it was a family heirloom given to her by Conrad.

She took it out of the box and held it around her neck once more. She'd never felt as glamorous as she had last night when she'd donned the extravagant dress that had been custom-made for her. Never so glamorous, yet . . .

She closed her eyes and remembered a more recent memory, when she and Edmund had looked into each other's eyes and declared their love. That moment won the prize for making her feel more beautiful than any other moment in her life.

Her fingers touched the stones one more time before she carefully put the necklace back in the box and reread the note she'd written to Conrad: *Give these to a woman who deserves your love, for she is out there, Conrad. You are a man worthy of the world, and I'll always remember you with the fondest regard. Many blessings, Dora.*

She closed the jewel case, setting the note on top. Then she scanned her bedroom one last time. It was truly a palace within itself. She let her eyes move upward to the enormous golden chandelier that loomed over her bed and smiled as she remembered what Beatrice had first told her: *"If you have trouble sleeping with that chandelier looming above you, put a pillow over your face."*

Perhaps such lavishness was not meant for human consumption.

Perhaps none of the life of high society was. The extravagant dresses, the sumptuous meals, the decadent jewels. She didn't begrudge the Tremaines their riches, for she knew they had earned them. Riches in themselves were not evil, it was the love of money that gained God's ire. And she didn't think the Tremaines loved it as much as many. Mrs. Tremaine—Gertie—still remembered her roots, and both Beatrice and

Conrad longed for meaningful work and purpose. Perhaps with the encouragement she'd given them, they might find it.

She hoped so. For she would leave the mansion better for having known them. Wasn't that the true test of an experience?

It was time to go. Edmund had told her he knew of a woman's boardinghouse that could take her in until they married and found a place of their own.

A place of their own. The concept was unfathomable and beyond exciting. When she'd considered marrying Conrad, a "place of their own" had been involved, yet a sense of restrictive attachment and dependence had been tightly wound around the notion. But with Edmund there would be no ties to bind them except to each other. *They* were the roots from which a new tree would grow.

Her trunks were packed with the clothing she'd brought with her, and she wore her original traveling ensemble. She now realized it was a bit out of fashion, but knew Edmund wouldn't mind.

She put on her bonnet and looked in the mirror to adjust the bow. Then she checked the dressing table one more time. Yes, she had the handkerchief . . . she'd made very sure of that.

There appeared to be nothing else of hers to take, so—

Dora did a double take, letting her gaze fall upon a lone bloom in a vase. It was the flower Conrad had plucked for her in Central Park. Although it had lost its vibrancy, its petals were still intact.

She removed it and stuck in into the brim of her bonnet.

Now she was ready to leave. To move on. To start again.

With dearest Edmund.

<hr>

"Can't we go any faster?"

Edmund put a hand upon Dora's, calming her. "The driver is going as fast as he's able."

She knew that to be true. But once she'd decided to tell Lottie the coast was clear and she could be herself again, a minute was too long.

The carriage slowed, but Dora didn't get excited. The stop-and-go traffic in New York had fooled her too many times already.

But this time the carriage stopped completely.

Edmund looked out the window. "This is it."

With great difficulty, Dora waited until Edmund exited. If only she could burst into the house like a child with great news to share. *Lottie! Lottie! You'll never believe what happened! The coast is clear!*

Instead she took Edmund's hand and stepped onto the pavement and up to the door. A sign said they could enter, but they rang the bell.

A young boy answered. "You're pretty," he said.

"Why, thank you. Is Lottie Hathaway here?"

He nodded, then turned and ran inside, leaving the door open for them.

"Miss Lottie! Someone's to see you."

"Don't shout, Otto. I'm coming."

Dora watched Lottie descend the front stairway holding a baby.

She stopped. And stared.

"Dora. You came. And Dr. Greenfield?"

Edmund tipped his hat, then removed it to enter the house. "Nice to see you again, Miss . . ."

Ah. The issue at hand fell between them. Was Lottie a Hathaway or a Gleason?

Dora's eyes as well as her hand sought the baby. "Is this the boy you found?"

"His name is Fitzwilliam. He's my son."

Dora pulled her hand away from the blanket. "You've truly adopted him?"

"In all but paperwork." Lottie nodded at the bevy of children running through the house. "With such a need, the process can be expedited."

"He looks quite healthy," Edmund said. "But for a cold?"

"A small one." Lottie led them into the parlor. "Do come and sit down." She shooed a few children away and sat with the baby in her lap. "So," she said. "I suppose my outburst at the Tremaines' was the talk of the party."

"Not at all," Dora said.

Lottie seemed disappointed. "Mr. Tremaine made no mention of it?"

"Not too much."

"Just as well." Fitzwilliam struggled against the blanket and she set him loose, letting him stand upon her legs. "You're getting so strong, aren't you, sweetheart?"

Dora marveled at the sight before her. "I've never seen you like this," she said. "I didn't know you liked children."

"I didn't either. It's almost disconcerting the way they melt my heart." She set the boy in the crook of her arm and let him play with her fingers. "So. I asked you to come and you did."

"You wanted to have your place back. Your name."

"Yes, well . . ."

Dora looked to Edmund for support. He nodded. *Just tell it.*

"Conrad proposed and I accepted, but—"

Lottie's eyebrows rose. "That was quick work of him."

Dora raised her hands, stopping Lottie's presumption. "But I'm not marrying him. I'm marrying Edmund." Dora took his hand, feeling fortified by its strength. "Beyond that, the way is clear. The Tremaines know everything, know all about the masquerade. So you see, you can go to them now and claim your rightful place as Charlotte Gleason. It will be awkward, and they will demand some hard answers, but I've seen you charm harder folk than they."

Dora expected Lottie to jump in, to make some Lottie-ish comment like *it's about time*, or *finally*, or . . .

"That won't be necessary."

Dora wasn't sure she understood. "What won't be necessary?"

"I don't want to claim my place. I don't want to go to the Tremaines' at all. I want to stay here. With Fitz."

Dora was confused. "But you said you wanted to bring Fitz with you to the Tremaines'. You wanted to marry Conrad so Fitz would have a father." In spite of her declaration, Dora felt odd casting Conrad as Lottie's fiancé so quickly after breaking her own engagement to him. There was no guarantee he would find Lottie agreeable. And in all honesty, Dora wasn't sure the two of them were at all suited to each other.

Lottie broke into Dora's thoughts. "Fitz *will* have a father."

A man came into the room from the hallway. He was strong in build with Nordic features. "Hello. I'm Anders Svensson, Lottie's fiancé."

Dora felt her head give a bow but could hardly summon a single word of response. Lottie was engaged?

Mr. Svensson moved to Edmund and the two shook hands. Then he took a seat on the settee next to Lottie, kissed her on the cheek, and drew Fitz into his arms, making the funny faces adults make when a baby is near.

Lottie let out a laugh. "I see I've managed to surprise you. Even shock you?"

Dora tried to grasp what she'd heard. "But . . . you came to the Tremaines' expressly to talk to me, to tell me you wanted to end the charade. You wanted to marry Conrad. What happened between—?"

"Then and now?" Lottie slipped her hand through her fiancé's arm. "Sven happened, and God and the moon and Nanny and wisdom and—"

A portly woman joined the group with a two-year-old on her hip. Dora recognized her immediately. "Miss Hathaway!"

"In the flesh. Nice to see you, Dora. My, my, I see you've grown into a lovely young lady." She kissed Dora on the cheek, then turned her attention to Edmund. "So this is the doctor who met my girls on the ship?"

"Edmund Greenfield, at your service."

"Actually, with all these wee ones around, I may take you up on that." Once she was settled in a rocking chair, she set the child on the floor. "So now, I take it Lottie has told you about her choice?"

"A little."

Nanny shook her head. "That's our Lottie. She always gets what she wants."

Lottie leaned her head against Sven's shoulder. "Only this time, it took a little doing for me to know what that was."

Dora marveled at the new Lottie, the soft, loving, giving Lottie who sat before her. It was as if she'd grown up in spite of all the hardships she'd endured.

Or because of all the hardships she'd endured?

And what about herself? Had Dora changed in such a dramatic manner? For the good, not the bad?

Nanny rocked up and back, murmuring to herself, "Yes indeedy. 'A man's heart deviseth his way: but the Lord directeth his steps.' That's the way of it. The good way of it."

Yes indeedy.

"There's so much to tell you," Lottie said.

"There's so much to tell *you*."

Lottie started first. "I really want you to meet the Scarpellis. They saved me when my money and jewels were stolen, when I had nothing and no place to go."

Dora slipped her hand through Edmund's arm. "I met the mother and saw the little girl when Edmund and I were looking for you. How is the girl?"

"Fully recovered." Lottie glanced at Dr. Greenfield. "Thanks to you." She continued. "You met Lea and Sofia. But there's a daughter a bit younger than us named Lucia. You'd like her. And guess what? I even learned a little Italian." Lottie cleared her throat and spoke with a wonderful attempt at an accent, *"Grazie. Prego. Ciao."*

Dora laughed and offered some applause. "And I want to show you the Tremaines' department store. It has five stories and there's a Frenchwoman named Madame Foulard who helped me and—"

"I was there!"

"When?"

"I was trying to get to the Tremaines', but the hack driver dropped me off on Broadway and—"

"Did you see the window displays? Conrad did those and—"

"I liked the one of the family taking a walk."

"Did you notice they're facing Central Park?"

"What's Central Park?"

"Oh, Lottie, it's a glorious place that reminds me of home. We'll have to go."

"And take Fitz."

"There's a lake and boats and lots of grass where he could run." Dora took a breath, enjoying the banter back and forth across the cozy room.

Lottie's mind had moved on. "And we simply must discuss that hideous dress you were wearing last night. It looked like you had two funeral wreaths on your hips. I thought you had better taste."

"*I* didn't pick it out. Mrs. Tremaine had it made for me and . . . What are you going to tell your parents about all this?"

Lottie gave a determined nod, as if the issue was clearly settled. "The truth. It will be a shock, but they'll accept it—eventually. Mother will know why I did it . . . she'll understand I wanted to marry for love. She'll be happy that I'm happy and cared for."

"And your father?"

"I hope he'll learn to be happy for me."

"Will they be happy to know they have a grandson?"

Lottie's attention turned to her son, sitting in Sven's lap, playing with his pocket watch. "The presence of Fitz will take some explaining, but in the end I predict Mother will want to dress him in a fancy suit."

"A suit with a sailor collar and—"

Nanny interrupted the conversation by standing. "Well then. Coffee anyone? I know these two. It's going to be awhile."

A long while. There was so much to tell Lottie, so much to hear from her. Yet before they continued, there was one thing Dora had to do.

She relinquished Edmund's arm, crossed the room, and took Lottie's hands, urging her to stand. "I have missed you so much."

Dora looked into Lottie's eyes and saw the girl she'd played with, the young woman she'd served, and the wiser woman Lottie had become in her absence. She saw a person who was on the threshold of finding her own strength, her own purpose, and her own place in the world.

And Dora felt different too. She wasn't Lottie's maid anymore. Out on her own she'd become a lady, and with the help of all in the room—and God—she would continue to grow in that respect as Edmund's wife.

"Yes?" Lottie said.

Dora smiled at Lottie's impatience. Maybe she hadn't changed *that* much.

Without another word, Dora pulled Lottie into a full embrace. She relished the contact and within moments felt Lottie submit and hug her back. It was a contact Dora would never have initiated before.

But now, such affection was acceptable. Now it was essential. Now it was a blessing.

For no longer were they maid and mistress.

A world away from where they had started, they were finally what God had intended all along.

True sisters for all time.

Dear Reader

I have never had so much fun writing a book as I did writing *Masquerade*. The girls' switch, the unimaginable wealth of the Gilded Age, the amazing fashion, and the inspiring tenacity of the immigrants coming to America for a new beginning . . . It was like combining *The Prince and the Pauper, Titanic, The Age of Innocence,* and *Far and Away* all in one. In fact, I openly admit that the dance scene on Mulberry Street was in honor of my favorite scene in *Titanic* when Rose goes belowdecks and has some real fun dancing to the immigrants' music.

This story also touched me because of my own immigrant roots. I stand in awe of the first English immigrant on my father's side, who entered America in 1638 at what became Newport, Rhode Island, and the Swedish immigrants on my mother's side who homesteaded in Minnesota in the late 1800s. Talk about taking a chance, moving forward in faith. I would not have the life I live now without their courage.

Masquerade begs the question of who we are and who we are expected to be. It's all about roles. A society girl and her maid. The rich and the poor. The good and the bad. Sometimes God takes us out of our comfort zones in order to make us see there is more to us than we imagine. The station in life that we happen to be born into does not form the boundaries of our purpose; it's just a jumping-off point. The finish line can be reached via a myriad of roads. Life is not the process of discovering who we are but of discovering who we are supposed to be.

Some thank-yous . . . I must thank Dr. MaryAnn Diorio for going through all my pitiful Italian and making it real. By the way, I purposely left a lot of Italian untranslated because I wanted you, the reader, to feel as befuddled as Lottie did. I hope you didn't mind too much. I also want to thank my editor, Helen Motter, and readers Stephanie Whitson, Julie Klassen, and Crys Mach for helping me see the better book hidden within the chaos.

Another reason this book was such a joy to write was that the characters completely took over. Fitz came out of nowhere, as did the handkerchief. And Dr. Greenfield? On the ship he wasn't a doctor. But one day, as I was writing the scene where Charlotte is at the Tremaines' with a headache, and a doctor comes into her room . . . the door opened and suddenly I thought, *The doctor can be the man on the ship! They could truly fall in love!* Honestly, until that point I had her marrying Conrad.

And I never planned on having Lottie pose as a maid at the Tremaines'. She just ended up at the servants' entrance of their house, the door opened, and suddenly a servant asked her if she wanted a job. Uh . . . sure. Again, up until that point I had not planned for her to truly trade places with Dora. I should have planned for such a thing, but didn't. These characters can be troublemakers. But they can also be oh so wise. Two opened doors, two plot changes. I think I'll keep that in mind in future books. If I'm ever stuck, I'll just arrange to have someone be at the door.

That's what I love about writing novels. The unpredictability of it all. With one word, one glance, one knock on the door, everything can change.

Sounds a bit like life, doesn't it?

So here's to you, dear reader. Knock on some doors, risk new roles, and step out in faith to find your true purpose.

Nancy Moser

Fact or Fiction in *Masquerade*

✦ Lottie and Dora lived near Lacock, in Wiltshire, England. Lacock has been preserved by the National Trust and was used to film the miniseries *Cranford*. The Abbey there, where William Fox Talbot lived (the inventor of the photographic negative), was used as a set for some of the Harry Potter movies.

✦ In Chapter 5, Lottie and Dora board the steamship *Etruria*. This was a real ship that traveled between Liverpool and New York. One of its passengers during my characters' voyage was Bram Stoker, the author of *Dracula*. Nine years after *Masquerade* takes place, twenty-year-old Winston Churchill took this ship to New York City, his first visit to the birthplace of his mother. He did not enjoy himself. "There are no nice people on board to speak of, certainly none to write of . . . There is to be a concert on board tonight at which all the stupid people among the passengers intend to perform and the stupider ones applaud."

✦ The Statue of Liberty was unveiled and dedicated on October 28, 1886, by President Grover Cleveland, soon after Lottie and Dora sail past.

✦ Castle Garden: In the early 1800s, Castle Clinton, as it is now known, was created as a fortification to protect the city. In peacetime, during the 1820s, it assumed a resortlike purpose with a theater and restaurant. People would stroll around the walls of Battery Park, take warm seawater baths, read newspapers from around the world, and drink mint juleps. Many inventions were first demonstrated there: the submarine, the telegraph, and the steam-fired engine. In the mid-1800s, a huge domed roof was erected over the fort, and the Swedish opera star Jenny Lind gave her first U.S. concert there. In the 1840s, because of the Irish potato famine, hundreds of thousands of immigrants came to America. Castle Garden was appropriated to deal with the influx. Once Ellis Island opened to handle the immigrants in 1892, Castle Garden was turned into the New York Aquarium.

* The apple woman at Castle Garden in Chapter 8 was Jane Noonan. For decades she sold her apples, first at Castle Garden, and later at Ellis Island.

* The Tremaine home in Chapter 9 is based on the home of A. T. Stewart and his wife, Cornelia. It sat on the northwest corner of Fifth Avenue and West Thirty-fourth Street. It took five hundred workers five years to build, and cost $1.5 million (about $37.5 million today). It had 55 rooms, yet only two people lived in the house, and the Stewarts shunned society. They did have an extensive art collection in their home gallery. Across the street lived the Astors, in a far simpler brownstone. The house was demolished in 1901. The Empire State Building was built across the street on the site of the Astor home. Like the Tremaines, A. T. Stewart had a department store and got his start selling lace. His store was eventually bought by Wanamaker's.

* Five Points, the area where the Scarpellis live, at one time was a neighborhood for the middle class. But when they had water problems because of an underground spring, the area was abandoned to the poor. It was the first American slum. In 1880 there were 37,000 tenements that housed nearly 1.1 million people. More than 100,000 lived in rear apartments unfit for human habitation. "In a

room not thirteen feet either way slept twelve men and women, two or three in bunks set in a sort of alcove, the rest on the floor." (*How the Other Half Lives: Studies Among the Tenements of New York*, by Jacob August Riis). Most people worked more than twelve hours a day, and there were thousands of homeless children on the streets. In the summer months three to four babies would suffocate in the airless tenements every night. Mulberry Bend was one of the worst stretches in the slums, and in 1896 it was demolished to be turned into Columbus Park. Chinatown and Little Italy encroached, as did federal buildings to the south.

❧ The character of Anders Svensson is inspired by Jacob Riis, a photojournalist who used his talents to elicit social change in the slums. In his book mentioned in the previous paragraph, he said, "One half of the world has no idea how the other half lives." In this book you can see his photographs of the dead horse and the children, the grandfather baby-sitting a child on the ground, and the back tenements as I describe in *Masquerade*.

❧ In Chapter 10, Lottie is upset when she gets horse dung on her shoes. She was used to having crossing sweepers in England, who kept the manure off the streets so women wouldn't soil their gowns. Sounds like a good idea.

❧ In Chapter 10, Mrs. Tremaine mentions Thorley's House of Flowers. This was a real store that catered to the rich. They were the first to use the long white box full of long-stemmed flowers packed in tissue. The exterior of their building was also an attraction, as it was decorated top to bottom with plants and flowers.

❧ The New York social season was divided into two main seasons: winter and summer. The winter season began November 15 with the opera season and included debutante coming-out receptions in December, and then balls and other society parties after Christmas. During Lent there were quieter get-togethers and charity functions. In spring there were a flurry of weddings before people went to their summer residences in Newport and the Adirondacks, which each had their own distinct social calendar of events.

❧ In Chapter 12, Lottie and the Scarpellis attend mass at St. Patrick's Cathedral at 263 Mulberry Street. This is *not* the massive St. Patrick's (built in 1879) most people know about in New York City. The older church was called "St. Patrick's Old Cathedral" or "Old St. Patrick's." Old St. Patrick's was used in two *Godfather* movies. It was the setting for the baptism scene in *The Godfather*, and also a scene where Michael Corleone receives an honor in *The Godfather, Part III*.

❧ Marble Collegiate Church, where Lottie takes refuge in Chapter 11, still stands on the corner of Fifth Avenue at Twenty-ninth. The church bell has tolled at the death of every president since Martin Van Buren in 1862. Norman Vincent Peale was their pastor for fifty-two years.

❧ Appearing in Chapter 12, Ward McAllister was a social advisor to the elite of New York City during the Gilded Age. He created the phrase "the Four Hundred." He declared this to be the number of people in NYC that mattered. He is quoted as saying, "If you go outside that number you strike people who are either not at ease in a ballroom or else make other people not at ease." His patroness was Mrs. William Astor, and he helped her become queen of New York society. He was largely responsible for making Newport, Rhode Island, a vacation mecca for the rich. His downfall came when he published his memoirs: *Society as I Have Found It*. The old rich didn't like their privacy invaded, and he died in disgrace while dining alone at the Union Club in 1895.

❧ The Ladies' Mile stretched from Ninth to Twenty-third on Broadway and was *the* place to window-shop, and see and be seen. Men were not used to buying their clothes in a department store, so to entice them and allow them a quick job of shopping, many stores placed the men's departments on the first floor. Stores also catered to women by offering customization of clothing and accessories, changing colors and trim to please the customer. The clothing Conrad purchased for Charlotte is outfits from an actual 1886 Bloomingdale's catalog.

Mentioned during Charlotte's shopping spree, "Congo" and "Palestine" are colors that came into being in 1883 and have since been declared obsolete and even replaced by "a rich burnished coppery gold" and "a pink mauve" in the *Dictionary of Colours* issued by the British Colour Council. Who knew there was such a thing!

Foundling Homes. The Children's Society, started in the 1850s, took care of more than 300,000 homeless children in its lodging houses, and found homes for 70,000 children in the West. The scene where Lottie brings Fitz into the foundling home and is told about a crib in the foyer that used to be outside—until it would fill up too quickly—is true.

The Fashion of *Masquerade*[1]

Harper's Bazar February 17, 1883

Chapter 5: *(left)* "By her own right, Lottie looked stunning in her gown of sage green, and their chokers made of rhinestones still managed to glisten under the gaslights."

Chapter 5: *(right)* "Dora's was made of sky-blue satin and brocade, with an overlay of ecru lace ruffled at the bodice and floor. She had no idea how many yards of fabric were used to make the bustle, train, and drapery, or how many different beads or measures of trim decorated her dress, but the result was stunning. And heavy. Dora felt as if she were dragging several sacks of flour or grain behind her, or perhaps a good-sized child had become a stowaway on board her train, taking a ride."

---

[1] Illustrations from: *Victorian Fashions & Costumes from Harper's Bazar 1867–1898*. Dover Publications 1974, AND *Bloomingdale's Illustrated 1886 Catalog* by Bloomingdale Brothers. Dover Publications 1988.

Bloomingdale's 1886 Catalog

Chapter 8: *(right)* "Dora felt both tailored and feminine in her navy blue walking suit with its zouave-style cape and wood buttons. She appreciated Lottie's taste in adding a red feather to her bonnet."

Chapter 9: *(left)* "Although Lottie's clothing was a simple traveling suit, the jaunty bow and feather on her hat, the striped green fabric of her bodice, and the drape of the bustle in the back singled her out as a stranger."

Harper's Bazar Cover, October 28, 1882

Chapter 12: *(left)* "Before coming to the park, Charlotte had liked her own costume, but now she found its layers of black chantilly lace too mournful, the glimpses of burgundy decoration too few. She much preferred Beatrice's ensemble *[right]*, which combined a gray-blue cashmere with Turkey-red borders and bows. Even Beatrice's parasol was adorned with a red bow. Charlotte's was solid black."

Harper's Bazar Cover, December 1, 1883

Chapter 13: *(left)* "Before the excursion was over Conrad had purchased . . . a forest green and ivory walking costume . . ."

Chapter 14: *(right)* "The gown Mrs. Tremaine had ordered made for Charlotte's party was a complicated affair in rose and green. Its lower skirt was layered with odd pointed flounces that hung like pink petals. Covering the hips and creating a bustle was silk drapery that was pleated in scarves and held in place with bows and loops of green velvet ribbon to which two huge bouquets of multicolored flowers were added—one for each hip. The dress had short puffed sleeves and a center bodice panel made from rows of lace and edged with a wide band of the velvet ribbon. It looked as though the seamstress had utilized every style, every trick in her book."

Discussion Questions for *Masquerade*

1. At the beginning of the story both Lottie and Dora long for a "true sister," a bosom friend. Their place in society keeps them from seeing that this bond is in progress with each other. Who is your true sister? Was it an instant connection or did it take some time for the bond to develop?

2. On the ship, the girls discover new things about themselves. Dora comes to life and discovers an unknown talent for being charming, which results in being the belle of the ball. And Lottie had no idea she possessed such a heart for children. What unexpected talent or gift has revealed itself in your life? What were the circumstances?

3. When Lottie first gets to America, her money and jewels are stolen and she is mad at God and declares she'll handle things without Him. Have you ever felt this way? What were the circumstances? How did you rid yourself of these feelings? Or have you?

4. In Chapter 10, Lottie sees a necklace in a pawnshop—the ruby necklace her mother gave her for her birthday, the one she disdained. Then. But now it's suddenly important to her. What else is suddenly important to Lottie that she took for granted before?

5. In Chapter 12, both girls go to church, and Charlotte notes, "The organ played a song to remind everyone that God had arrived."

Although we know God is everywhere, church is called "God's house." Why do you think this is so?

6. Does the dynamic between Mrs. Astor and Mrs. Vanderbilt, and the thin line that separated being a part of society or not, still exist today? What kind of line is present today between those in high society and those who are trying to climb higher? Can you think of TV shows or movies that showcase this social juggling?

7. In Chapter 15, while talking with Nanny, Lottie realizes she has to take responsibility for what's happened to her, and God *has* provided for her in amazing ways—in spite of her blunders. How has God provided for you in spite of your mistakes? How long did it take you to realize what He'd done?

8. In Chapter 19, Lottie finally sees how God turned bad into good: "Was I brought here for this, Nanny? Was everything taken from me so I'd end up with the Scarpellis? Was I assaulted on my job so Sven would take me under his wing? Did I find Fitz and find you so . . . all this could happen?" Dora could name a similar sequence of circumstances that brought her together with Dr. Greenfield. Name a time in your life when you can see a string of events that had God's hands all over them.

9. Everyone has a need to find their purpose, to answer the question "Why am I here? Now?" As Lottie asked Nanny, "What am I born to do?" Have you discovered your purpose yet? Do you see glimpses of it? What have you done to seek it? What could you do?

10. Many times throughout the book the moon inspired Lottie to think deeply about her life and purpose. What element of nature inspires you when you need to think? What special place?

11. In the end, Lottie and Dora realize by being apart they grew into the women God intended them to be. Do you think they could have accomplished that same growth if they'd remained maid and mistress in Dornby Manor?